THE BLOOD & ROSES SERIES

PART THREE

CALLIE HART

Formatted by Max Effect
    www.formaxeffect.com

TWISTED

Zeth

THE SOUND OF THE SEA.

That's one of my earliest memories: the sound of the sea and eating an ice cream. A boardwalk by the ocean—not sure which beach—and the feel of the sun, baking hot, warming the crown of my head.

I dream about the beach. Unlike most people, I don't have the luxury of a variety of different dreams. I only have two. When I do dream, it's either that sunny day on the Californian coast when I was four years old, or...it's not. It's the other dream.

Tonight, thankfully, I'm visited by the lesser of two evils.

"Come here, baby. You've got it all over you." Gentle laughter. The scent of fresh flowers and soap, my mother's long fingers folding tissue to wipe me clean. The bright glare of the sun has stolen my mother's face. She's been a sweet-smelling ghost wrapped in a floral dress for the past twenty-five years, and in all that time I never see her face. Or at least I don't see it until later, anyway.

"Where's Daddy? Shall we go find him? It's almost time for me to go to work, baby." My mother takes my hand and guides me down the boardwalk—the sounds of the amusement rides, the arcade machines, coins rattling and the smell of candy. These combined sights and sounds have created a physical place that exists within me.

I squint into the sun. I lick my ice cream. I hold my mother's hand, and I walk with her down the pier. A man is waiting for us at the end of the pier; my father. He's dressed in faded blue jeans and a sleeveless T-shirt; his dark hair is being lifted in the breeze. He turns and waves, but for some reason he's not smiling.

"There he is, baby. You wanna go hang out with Daddy for an hour while I do my work real quick?" My mother lets go of my hand and bends down to straighten my Danger Mouse T-shirt. "I won't be long, sweetheart, I promise." The sunlight glints off the loose blonde curls that flow around her face. I should be able to see her properly now, but I can't.

Then I'm with my father. He smells of the ocean—that's where he was; he went down to the water for a swim. He lets me walk without having to hold onto his hand. He doesn't complain that I'm sticky with melted ice cream. We visit the rides and the arcade games, and my father lifts me onto his shoulders, carrying me up high so I can see everything over the tops of the crowds.

He needs to leave me for a moment, he says. I wait by the mechanical fortune-teller, tying knots into the drawstring of my fluoro pink shorts (this was the eighties), watching the groups of people who pass by become smaller and smaller.

It gets dark.

I get scared.

A man comes and asks me where my parents are, but then I see my mother over his shoulder and tell him that I'm fine. I go to meet my mother. Her back is to me, and a tall man I don't recognize is holding her by the arm. She's making soft crying sounds, and it looks like the man is pinching her skin. Her legs collapse from underneath her and one of her shoes comes half off her foot, but the stranger has a tight hold on her. He pulls her up again.

"That's the last time. The last fucking time you're ever gonna say no to me, bitch!" he snaps.

My mom cries and cries and cries. She sees me—her hand reaches out, open, gesturing me to stay back, and her palm is covered in blood. "My son. My son. Please, not in front of—"

The stranger hits my mother across the face, and her crying cuts off abruptly. By this time *I've* started crying anyway. I cry for the both of us. Why is the man hurting her? Where is my dad? I look for him, but there's no one around now. Everyone has gone home from their day at the beach.

"You shouldn't have brought him with you," the stranger says, towering over my mom. "If you didn't want him to see your true colors, you should never have brought him along. Now stand up properly and fucking kiss me."

Even at four I know a bad word when I hear one. Fuck is a very bad word, and my mother isn't supposed to kiss men who aren't my dad. That's not how it works. My mother shakes her head. She reaches into the pocket of her flowery dress—torn at the hip now—and holds out a bundle of crumpled bills to the stranger.

"We don't do that. Here, take it. Have it back. I just want to go."

The man grabs hold of my mom with both hands now, and he shakes her. He shakes her hard. "I want what I paid for. And I want a fucking kiss. Now."

"No. I'm sorry, I—" He hits her hard once more, this time with the back of his hand. My mom stumbles backwards, holding a hand to her cheek. Her shoe has come off all the way now; I pick it up and hug it to my chest, watching as she gets dragged toward the man again.

3

"You want more?" the angry man asks. My mom shakes her head, crying silently. "Good. Then do as your fucking told." He grabs her again, but this time he palms her breast and squeezes it. He places his other hand around the back of my mother's neck and pulls her forward. Their lips smash together, and then the stranger is kissing my mother. It's not how my dad kisses her, though. This man is rough and cruel; he bites my mother's lip, and then shoves his tongue into her mouth. I can see she's trying to stop him. I can see she doesn't want him to do it, but the man keeps on forcing her mouth open and biting at her lips.

"She doesn't like it," I say, but the man pays no attention. I say it louder. "She doesn't like it!"

The man stops kissing my mother, and slaps her so hard across the face that she falls to the ground. I hurry to her side, still clutching onto her shoe, and I bend down, not knowing what to do. I am four years old, and it's dark, and I don't know what to do.

My mother looks up at me and now is when her face pulls into focus. Now, with desperation shaping her features into a mask of fear. There are small globes of water clinging to the tips of her eyelashes, and her cheek is split open. She looks like she's in pain, but she tries to smile for me anyway. "It's okay, baby. It's okay. Momma's okay." Her already bruised lips part and she flashes me a broader smile, but all I see is blood. The blood seeping from her split upper lip. The bright crimson of the blood that stains her teeth from white to red.

The stranger steps forward, hands clenched by his sides, and I do the first thing that comes to mind; I turn and I put myself in between my mother and the man. I think he will hit me; he looks angrier than before, but then he hawks and spits on my mother's bare legs.

"You're a fucking whore. I tell you what I want, I pay you, and you fucking do it. That's how this goes. You'd better know that for next time. Now get out of here before I fuck you raw in front of your little bastard."

My mother scrambles to her feet, her breath coming out in short, sharp little pants; she grabs hold of me and lifts me into her arms, and then she's running away from the man, crying into my hair. "I'm sorry, baby. I'm sorry, baby. I'm so, so sorry." She says this over and over again, in between her ragged gulps for air. I hang onto my mother's shoe, listening to the uneven slap of her one bare foot hitting the boardwalk as she runs, and I watch the angry man glaring after us as we go.

My mother carries me to the parking lot, where my dad is waiting in our car. My mother puts me down and takes her shoe from me. She tucks her hair behind her ears and wipes her tears from her cheeks, although she doesn't stop crying.

"There. We're okay now, Zeth," she tells me. Her hands shake as she opens the rear door of the car and lifts me onto the back seat. She clips me in, closes the door, and then stands for a moment, fingers bridged against her forehead, her eyes closed. Then she gets in the car and I hear my father's breath catch in his throat. He doesn't say anything, and neither does my mother. But she's still crying. And so is he.

Like most nights, the dream starts over again. The sun beating down on my head. The ice cream. Me and my father playing skeeball. The darkness. My mother being beaten. The sun beating down on my head. The ice cream. Me and my father playing skeeball. The darkness; my mother being beaten. The sun beating down on my head. The ice cream. Me and my father playing skeeball. The dark. My mother being beaten.

My mother being beaten.

The blood in her teeth.

The violent words that come out of the angry man's mouth: *You're a fucking whore. I tell you what I want, I pay you and you fucking do it.*

And my own words.

She doesn't like it.

I WAKE WITH my heart in my mouth.

I wake with my hands clenched into fists and the bed sheets wrapped around my body, tangled up in my legs. As usual, I feel like I can't fucking breathe. After all these years, after experiencing it over and over, you'd think it would get a little better, but it doesn't. It's the same. Always the same.

"Fuck." I lean forward, resting my elbows on my knees, dragging my hands back through my hair. She's gone. Both of them are— have been for years—and yet every time I have the beach dream, I wake up feeling like I need to save her. Like I might be able to go back and stop that asshole's hand before it connects with her cheek. To pile drive my fucking fist into his face before he gets a chance to maul her mouth the way he did. The very thought of it makes me feel sick.

The clock on the bedside table reads five forty-three, which is about right. I never sleep past six, and what would be the point in trying now anyway? Knowing my luck, I'll be hit with the *other* dream instead, just to top off my wonderful fucking start to the day. I climb out of bed and hit the shower instead, washing the sweat from my body.

I'm thinking one thing as I get clean: Sloane. I'm thinking her name over and over. The knowledge that she's here, in the warehouse, one room over sleeping in my spare bed, is enough to temper the discomfort of the dream, if not to eradicate it altogether. I close my eyes and let the water wash over me, and I let the knowledge of her wash over me, too. She's never going to be the first thing I think of when I open my eyes—my nightmares will take care of that—but she's a close fucking second. And...and I like it. I fucking like it a lot.

I need her skin against mine. Right now.

I leave the water running as I pace, completely naked, out of my en suite, out of my room, into the hallway and then through the door and into her room. I'm leaving wet footprints everywhere but I don't care. Sloane's laid out on her back, one arm thrown up over her head, her fingers twitching in her sleep. Her eyelashes look like smudges of charcoal against the pale porcelain of her cheeks.

She's perfect.

I rip the covers off her body, smirking to myself when she nearly rockets out of the bed, eyes snapping open in a fright. "Oh my god. Zeth, what is it? What's the matter? Is it your stomach?"

My stomach is healing just fine. I shake my head, staring down at her, the cover still clenched in my hand.

Her eyes grow even wider when she finally wakes up enough to take me in properly. "Oh," she says. "I see."

I'll bet she does. My cock is pretty much at her eye level, and it's doing a pretty good job of waving good morning. I don't say anything. I just lean down and pick her up, right out of the bed.

She wraps her arms around my neck, frowning at me as I carry her out of the room. "Zeth? Zeth, what are you doing?"

Down the hall, back into my room, back into the bathroom. I carry her straight into the shower, ignoring her protests as the water hits us. I need her. I need her right now.

"Zeth! I'm still wearing—"

"Elephant pajamas. I can see that." The water blasts us both; her

7

hair is instantly soaked, her clothes drenched no less than two seconds later. She looks incredible. I slam her up against the wall, lifting her so that her thighs are wrapped around my hips. I bury my face in her neck, holding her tight, and I lick and suck and graze my teeth across her skin. Her breath comes out in a jagged stutter, and I know she's on board.

She wraps her arms around my neck and digs her hands into my hair, pulling me closer. Sloane's strong for a woman. She's fit and has just the right ratio of muscle tone to curves, but compared to me she's physically weak. She's a clear foot shorter than me, and I'm three times her body weight. Yet right now, with her arms around my shoulders, holding me to her, she has me trapped. I wouldn't...couldn't move from here even if I wanted to.

"Oh my god, Zeth. What...what the hell?" she pants.

I use my weight to pin her up against the side of the shower. My hands find their way up her T-shirt—her fucking tits are amazing. I can't get enough as I pinch and roll her nipples, kneading my hands over the swell of her skin. She squeezes her thighs against my hips and I know what I'm doing is affecting her in other areas. I just fucking love how connected the female body is. I especially love how connected Sloane's body is; she comes alive under my hands. And for someone who's been asleep for so long, journeying through each day in a haze, hardly *living* at all, it gives me great pleasure to inspire this sort of reaction in her.

My dick is so fucking hard right now. I push myself up against her, grinding my hips against her pussy through her soaking wet, ridiculous elephant pajama pants, and her breath catches in her throat again. I look up and her eyes are closed against the downpour of water running over her face, and I can barely hold back. She. Is. Fucking. Amazing.

Her chin is tilted upward, exposing her neck to me, and the look of sheer ecstasy on her face takes my own breath away. I love putting that look on her face. I love the effect I can have on her. It feels like a fucking privilege I sure as shit don't deserve.

"Are you awake yet, Sloane?" I murmur against her skin.

"Maybe. Maybe not. Given what's happening right now, I could still be asleep," she moans.

A half smile pulls my mouth up to one side. Well, this is interesting. Really fucking interesting. "Oh, Sloane...have you been dreaming about me?"

Her eyes crack open, and she gazes at me, a small smile forming on her own lips. "Maybe."

Oh, this is fucking *perfect*. I bite at her collarbone, pressing my dick up against her some more. I want to strip her naked and fuck her, but I want to hear about this first. "What have you been dreaming, angry girl?"

She drags her teeth over her bottom lip, shaking her head slightly. I think I'm gonna have to employ some corporal punishment to make her talk—she must see my thoughts on my face, because she swallows and then says, "Bad things."

I ease back just enough that I can slide my hand in between our bodies, and then I slip my hand down the front of her PJs. "What kind of bad things?"

She inhales sharply when my fingers find what they're looking for. She's wet, yes, and not from the shower. There's a distinct difference between the feel of the water battering our bodies and the silky, glossy texture of the wetness between her legs. It drives me fucking crazy. I find her clit, and I gently stroke the tips of my fingers against the small, swollen bud of nerve endings. I won't give her more until she gives *me* what *I* want.

Sloane knows this.

"We were in your car," she pants. "You pulled over to the side of the road and told me you were going to fuck me. I thought you were joking, but then you unzipped your pants and you were...you..." Her eyes travel down to my cock. It's trapped between us, rigid, and just the power of her eyes on my hard skin makes me want to push her to her knees so she can take me into her mouth.

"I was what, Sloane?"

"You were hard. And big." She swallows. "You took hold of my hand and closed my fist around you, and then you told me to make you come."

"And did you?"

She nods slowly, her eyes still fixed on my dick. "Yes. I jerked you off while you sat in the driver's seat, and when you came, I licked it off your skin and my hands. I licked you clean."

This girl is seriously pushing my buttons now. I was the one who was supposed to be shocking her with my surprise sex, but it would seem she's turning the tables on me now. Even the words—her describing that action—are making it harder for me to hold back.

"Did you like it, Sloane? Did you like licking me clean?"

Her eyes lift to mine; with the water running down our faces, she does remarkably well not to blink as she looks at me. "Yes. Yes, I liked it very much."

I haven't come in Sloane's mouth before, but I definitely want to now. From the look on her face, it's clear she wants me to. But not this time around. Right now I need more than that. I need to be inside her. I need to feel her pussy tighten around me as she comes. I need to feel her mouth on my skin, and her nails digging into my back.

"And then what? Did I fuck you?" I push my fingers forward, almost to the entrance of her pussy, and Sloane shudders.

"Y—Yes. You lowered my seat and you climbed on t—top of me and you fucked me so hard," she stammers. Her eyes close again, and this time it's just too much. I have to have her. I can't be gentle about it. I have to own her. I have to consume her.

With nothing more than the pressure of my hips against her to pin her against the wall, I rip her T-shirt off her body, smiling to myself as it makes a wet slap against the tiles. Her hair, absolutely drenched, gets caught up in the rivers of water running down her body, and dark strands fall across her heavy breasts. I swipe them out of the way, arching my back so I can take her into my mouth. She digs her hands into my hair again, fastening a firm hold on me, and a fire starts up in my veins. She wants me. She wants me as much as I want her. I trail my tongue upward, licking the water from her skin, and Sloane makes a frustrated groaning sound at the back of her throat; it's the sexiest thing I've ever fucking heard. The sound grows louder when she turns her head to mine and places her lips against my temple.

Years. Years of conditioning make me go still. I can't fucking help it, but I'm also surprised. I don't automatically shove her away. I don't flinch back from the contact of her mouth on my face. I close my eyes and I dig my hands into her skin, waiting. Waiting to see what she does next. Sloane must notice my change in pace because she stops breathing. Her lips move away from me. My temple burns as though they're still there, though.

Sloane leans into me, and then she's speaking into my ear, her voice firm and controlled. "Zeth, you don't need to—I'm never going to do more than that. I know—"

I don't want to lose the moment. I don't want to give power to my fucked-up issues. I pull back so she can see my face, and I put my hand over her mouth. Her eyes grow wide, staring back at me like I'm the only thing in the world that exists. "Don't. It's not a problem." It *is* a problem, but not one I'm willing to let affect what's happening between us right now. I remove my palm from her mouth, and then I take her face in both hands. Her breath is hot and sweet against me as I place my forehead against hers. "I'm going to fuck you now. I'm going to slide my dick inside you, and I'm going to make you scream my name. Are you ready?"

I don't know where the scream my name thing came from—maybe from the last time she did it, back at her house—but I realize that I want it. I want to hear my fucking name being ripped from her vocal chords like a goddamn plea for help. Sloane's hands slide over my shoulders, skating across my skin. She laces them behind my neck and she nods. "I'm ready," she says. I barely hear her, but I can see it's what she wants. Her voice might be quiet under the rush of the shower, but her eyes are yelling out her answer to me.

I growl in the base of my throat, growing hungrier and hungrier by the second. "Good. Hold on tight." There's no controlling this now. I reach behind her and grab hold of her pajama bottoms, and then I rip them down as far as they'll go—just over her butt. From there I have to put her down to tear them from her body. I'm not careful. I'm not gentle. I can't be. Sloane gasps; the way she digs her fingernails into my skin doesn't exactly tell me she's hating the rough treatment.

She stands naked before me, eyes glazed over with lust, and I know I've met my match with this woman. Usually now's around about the time I would spin the woman I was fucking around so I didn't have to look into her face while I was coming, but not now. Not with her. I want to see her break apart. I want to study the look on her fucking face as I make her come; I want to commit every last second of the moment to memory as her body shakes and writhes against me.

I grab her up, hooking her legs around me again, but this time there's no clothing between us. Only our scorching hot skin, slick and pressing together everywhere it possibly can. There's no foreplay. We're way past that. I reach down and I guide my cock to where it needs to be, forcefully making my way inside her. She clings to me, her eyes wide, and no sound coming out of her open mouth as I sink myself as deep as I possibly can. She's tight and warm—no pussy has ever felt like this. I've never felt...I've never felt like I'm snapping a piece of a puzzle together when I've screwed people in the past. They've been quick fuck experiences, not like I'm becoming *whole*. I sound like a woman. I know I fucking sound like a woman, and yet I can't help it.

"Fuck," Sloane mouths, but her voice is still MIA.

Yeah, my sentiments exactly. Fuck. I am in deep fucking trouble. I know I am, but I don't want to focus on that right now. I want to focus on how deep I can sink myself inside the beautiful woman currently sitting on my cock. I reach behind her, and I wind her wet hair around my fist, pulling her head back.

And then I fuck her. I feel like I have the force of a fucking freight train behind me as I pound myself into her over and over again. A part of me tries to hold back, to prevent myself from hurting her, but when Sloane buries her nails in my back again, scratching me, then holding onto me so tight I think she's trying to choke me out, I give up entirely. She loves what I'm giving to her. She's loving every second of it.

"Oh, fuck. Fuck, Zeth. I need you," she gasps, her legs tightening even further around me. "*I need you.*"

That's what pushes me over the edge. Those words. *I need you.* They carry such an imposing weight I'm practically crushed under them as my body pours its release into her. I roar, slamming a hand out against the shower wall, struggling to make sure my legs don't completely quit and fucking dump us onto the wet tiles. Sloane's trembling in my arms. I'm still granite hard; I don't stop thrusting into her. I keep going, hammering myself home as hard as I can. It's only a minute longer before I can feel her tightening around me, the walls of her pussy squeezing me inside her as her eyelids fall closed and her body locks up.

This is it, the reason why I didn't spin her around. Her lips are slightly parted, and her cheeks have blossomed into a bright crimson color. Those eyelashes of hers are dark against her fine cheekbones, and her eyebrows are drawn together into a tensed frown as a string of expletives fall from her mouth.

"Fuck, Zeth. Oh—shit, goddamn, motherfucker. Fuck me, Zeth. Fuck. Ahh, shit. Ah, *ZETH!*"

It's like music to my perverted ears.

Her body falls limp against me, and I know I don't have a chance of putting her down. She won't be able to stand after that. Not for half an hour or so, anyway. I hold her to me, and I turn off the shower. Sloane's head lolls against me; she ends up resting her cheek on my shoulder, which pretty much knocks the fucking wind out of me. She just rests it there against me, like this is the safest she's ever been.

I'm not ready for her to be covered up yet, so I carry her, legs still wrapped around me, through to my bedroom, where I climb up onto the bed on my knees. I bend forward and I place her down in the middle of the mussed-up sheets.

When I lean back, she's gazing up at me with a sleepy look on her face. Fuck. *Fuck, fuck, fuck!* What would I normally do right now, if this were any other girl? I was never enough of an asshole to make my conquests get dressed and get the fuck out of my sight straight away, but I sure as fuck didn't wanna hang out with them, that's for sure. I would leave. I would vanish like motherfucking Houdini. But with her...

I sink down onto my stomach and I trail my hand down her body, pushing her legs apart.

"What are you doing?" she asks.

"Signing my masterpiece." I can feel the evidence of my presence inside her body. With my fingers coated in my own come, I trace them up through the folds of her pussy, making her shiver, and then up higher. Over her thighs. Her hips. Her stomach. Her breasts. The sexy fucking hollow at the base of her throat. Sloane just lies there, letting me mark her, watching with an intense look on her face. When I'm done, she catches hold of my hand and brings it to her mouth; she slowly licks her tongue at my fingertips, and then shudders as she takes my index and middle finger into her mouth.

No woman has ever done that before. No woman has ever made me want to claim her. And no woman has ever claimed *me* in such a way in return.

A part of me wants to run like fuck away from the primal urge I'm experiencing to *keep* this woman...but then again, another very large part of me wants me to say fuck it. Because I know I will kill any other man who tries to touch her. I will kill any other man who dares to fucking look at her. I will destroy anyone and anything that threatens to ruin this. There's very little point in trying to fight that.

2

Sloane

THE SOUND OF THE TELEVISION TELLS ME LACEY IS AWAKE.
I'm beginning to get used to this rhythm of life here in the
warehouse, although Zeth's early morning wake-up call isn't
something that's happened before. Not that I couldn't get used to it
if it does become a regular occurrence. Zeth's hands have traveled
all over me in the last half an hour—I haven't questioned it. That
feels like a dangerous thing to do, and I don't want to risk him
stopping because it feels really, insanely good, but as soon as he
hears the television it's like an electric shock runs through his
body. He stands up, scrubbing his hands over his face.

"I better get out there."

I prop myself up on my elbows, watching him as he pads
completely naked and barefoot into his en-suite bathroom. Back to
the scene of the crime. I'm treated with a glorious view of his
behind as he vanishes through the door. "Come get clean, Sloane,"
he says.

He's right; I am dirty, and not just externally. Because a sick part of me doesn't want to go shower. It wants to just get dressed and go through the day, knowing that he's all over me. Knowing that his come is still marking my skin. It's absolutely, socially, unequivocally wrong to go around covered in another person's bodily fluids, though, so I follow him into the bathroom. He's waiting for me there, one hand leaning against the wall. He points into the shower, where my saturated PJ bottoms are still wadded up in a wet heap on the tiles.

"In," he commands.

"Are you coming with me?" My body probably isn't ready to receive any more of his attention, and yet at this point I'd be willing to try. Zeth shakes his head, though.

"Not this time."

I climb into the shower and turn the taps on, wondering what the hell he's going to do in here while I shower; we are so not at a stage where I'd be comfortable with him conducting the grosser of the triple-S preparations boys usually complete in the morning. Shower and a shave I can cope with, but nothing that requires him sitting down on that toilet. I soap myself up, using his extremely manly looking black bottled shower gel, and then I begin to massage it into my hair.

Zeth leans back against the wall, watching me. There's a flat look on his face; I've learned when he looks like that there's usually a lot going on inside that head of his. I know there's no point asking him what he's doing, so I just wash my hair and body, and I let him watch. When I'm done and rinsed off, I step out of the shower into the massive towel he's holding out for me.

He wraps it around me, scratches his jaw, and then he walks out of the bathroom and closes the door behind him.

I stand for a moment, staring at the closed door in front of me, wondering what the hell that was all about. Seriously. This man is so utterly confusing. At any one time I rarely have a clue what's going on inside his head. That's half good, half bad, I think. A part of me wants to know what he's thinking, but then another part of me would be too scared to catch an inside glimpse into the machinations of Zeth Mayfair's head. Who knows what's lurking in the dark corners of his mind? I'm already scared witless by the monsters that have begun taking up residence in my own.

I hear Zeth's bedroom close and I know he's thrown some clothes on and gone to check on Lacey. I pin the towel tightly around my body and head back to my room—when did it become *my* room?—just in time to catch my cell phone ringing.

I've had the thing switched off for days but I plugged it in to charge last night, wanting to face the music. I'd been a little surprised when it hadn't blown up on the spot due to the influx of missed calls and texts. Worried even. No contact from work? No contact from the police? What did that mean? I did, admittedly, have a million text messages from my parents asking if I was okay. Plenty of shots of them on the beach, enjoying the vacation I've bankrolled—flights, hotel, bar tab, room service, the works—to get them the hell out of dodge. My mother spent pretty much every last cent of their life savings trying to find Alexis, so they would never have been able to afford it themselves. I suspect my dad wouldn't have spent everything they had if it hadn't seemed to keep my mother content. I'm beginning to suspect a lot of things about my dad. His reaction to my story about where Alexis has been the last two years was off-the-charts weird. As soon as they get back and Charlie Holsan's out of the picture, I'm making the trip to L.A. to have a little word with him. But in the meantime—

I pick my cell phone up off the bedside table, frowning at the name on the screen: Olly.

Oliver Massey: my ever-increasingly concerned colleague and sort-of best friend at the hospital. Should I answer it? I remember his words when I saw him last, after the crash that ruined my car—

Just...the moment you realize that you're in way over your head, come see me, okay? Don't leave it too late—and I instantly feel terrible. Oliver and I used to catch drinks after work once or twice a week. He'd bring in leftovers for lunch for us when he knew it was bolognese day at the canteen, because he knew how much I hated bolognese. We used to be a whole lot closer than we are right now; I've basically ignored him ever since Zeth came onto the scene. If our roles were reversed, I'd definitely be concerned about him. And mad at him, too. I've left him to imagine whether I'm dead or alive for days. I answer the call.

"Hey."

I'm met with silence. I begin to think I actually didn't pick up in time, but just as I'm about to check the screen to see if it's connected, there's a loud, exasperated sigh on the other end of the line. "Hey? *Hey?*"

Oh, boy. He sounds pissed. Seriously pissed. "I take it you've been trying to get hold of me, then?"

I can practically feel the tension radiating off Oliver down the connection. It makes my skin prickle. "Trying to get hold of you? Sloane, what the fuck is wrong with you? I've been tearing this city apart looking for you!"

"You—you *have?*"

"Yes! Of course I fucking—" He stops short, and I can imagine the frustration on his face. I've seen him too angry to speak before; it's pretty frightening. "Sloane, you are the most thoughtless, careless person I've ever met, you know that?"

"I'm sorry, okay? I know I should have called you, but—"

"No! Fuck." He breathes in, taking a moment. "It doesn't matter you didn't call me. Well, it does, but that's not what I mean. How long were you in med school? How hard did you fight to get a residency at St Peter's? Huh?"

The impact of his words hit home with the force of a bullet. Shit.

"Sloane? How long? Because I know this has cost me years and years of no fucking sleep and gallons of my blood, sweat, and tears, and I've been slacking off compared to how hard you've been working. So were you *thinking* about that when you ran away from a fucking DEA agent, Sloane? Were you *caring* about everything you were throwing away? Because I'm seriously at a loss over here."

He's right. He's absolutely right, and yet I couldn't have made another choice. Not with Charlie Holsan stalking the hallways of the hospital. Not after he'd tried to force me off the road in his pretentious Aston Martin in an attempt to get Zeth's attention. Not after he'd poisoned Nannette Richards, a completely innocent person, and killed her in an attempt to capture *my* attention.

"I know you're mad right now," I say. "But I made the only choice I could at the time. I wasn't safe there. And that agent shot my sister, Olly. I was kind of spun out. I sure as hell didn't want to go anywhere with her."

"Your *sister*? I thought your sister was dead?"

It feels like the contents of my stomach are boiling now. I feel sick. I feel so, so sick and on the verge of crying. Of course Oliver thinks Alexis is dead. That's what I told him and everyone else in a vain attempt at getting myself some closure, back when I thought I was never going to see her again. Back when things were simpler and the only problem in my life was suffering the loss of a kidnapped sibling. The thought flashes through me—maybe it would have been better if I'd never found Alexis. I'm shocked by the pain I feel. Living with the uncertainty of whether she actually was or wasn't alive was brutal, but her betrayal is almost twice as painful.

"Well, it turns out she's alive after all. And she's involved in some pretty scary stuff. That...that agent told me in the Chief's office that she was responsible for nearly killing her. I couldn't exactly think straight after that, Ol."

"Bullshit. You haven't been thinking straight for weeks now. You went way off the reservation long before that civilian turned up with your name Sharpie'd onto her body. I mean *what the fuck*, Sloane? When did you become the sort of person to get caught up in this shit?"

I know the answer to that question. I can pinpoint the moment exactly. It wasn't when I made the decision to compromise myself in order to find out information about my sister. It wasn't when I first met Zeth in that hotel room. Those moments changed me, sure, but I could have continued being the old me even through the trauma of that experience. No, I became the sort of person to lie, steal, protect criminals, and flee law enforcement when Zeth pinned me up against a wall in a corridor in St. Peter's and demanded I protect Lacey. To make sure she wasn't sectioned. I became that person when he told me he was coming for me again in two days' time...and I wanted him to.

"You don't understand," I whisper.

"No. You're right. I don't understand. I would if you actually talked to me."

Talking to Oliver about this can only mean one thing for him; it would only drag him into this mess, and that's the last thing I want for him. My career is ruined now. There's no way I'm going to ruin his, too. "I'm sorry, Oliver. I just—I can't. It wouldn't be fair."

"Fair to who?" he snaps. "Fair to you? Or fair to me? Because I'm the one watching cops cordon off your locker at work. I'm the one watching cops crawl all over your house, tearing it apart. I'm the one wondering where the hell you are right now, when I offered to protect you and you threw it back in my face."

My cheeks are burning hot, stinging as though he's just slapped me. "Oliver, I never threw it back in your face. I—"

"It doesn't matter. None of it matters. We both know why you're wherever you are right now instead of here at work. It's because of

21

that guy."

"It's far more complicated than that. It's not about him. Not all of it."

"Then tell me you're not with him right now. Tell me you're as far away from him as you can get."

I don't say anything. Oliver makes a sound of pure frustration on the other end of the phone. "Tell me you're at least smart enough not to have developed serious feelings for this guy, Sloane. Please tell me that."

My heart is hammering against my ribcage, and strangely, I feel I'm on the verge of tears. Again. He sounds so, so disappointed in me, and that hurts like hell, but I won't lie to him about this. I won't. "I can't say that. I—I'm in love with him."

A deathly silence forms. Maybe that's why I hear the sound behind me. The soft, sharp inhalation of breath that lets me know someone's standing in the doorway to my room.

A rush of horror ricochets around my body. Oh, fuck. Oh, no fucking way! I turn and there he is, silhouetted in the rectangle of light shining into the darkened room from the hallway beyond. He's looked like this before, when he left me the first time, except he was facing the other way. He was leaving me behind; I thought I was never going to see him again, and I didn't know his name. I hadn't even seen his face. Now I can see his face, though, and he looks...he looks like he's about to go on a killing spree.

"Then I guess there's nothing more to say," Oliver tells me quietly, but I'm barely paying attention anymore. I'm staring at the man in the doorway, who's staring right back at me, with eyes so intense that I feel like I might catch fire.

"No," I whisper. "There's nothing more to say."

3

Zeth

LACEY'S SITTING ON THE COUCH, KNEES TUCKED UP UNDER-
neath her chin. Jimmy Kimmel's on the TV. She sits through hours
of comedy show reruns when she's especially low, which
immediately puts me on edge when I see what she's watching. She
smiles brightly at me, though, which lessens the unease a little.

"Where's Sloane?" she asks.

"She's coming. Or at least she was," I reply, not even bothering to
hide my smirk. Lacey knows what I mean by that. She screws up
her face, scowling at me.

"You're disgusting."

I pad over to the refrigerator and open it, looking inside. "Yes.
Yes I am. But just so you know…so is Sloane."

"Gross!" I duck behind the fridge door just in time to narrowly
avoid a balled-up pair of socks that Lacey hurls at me. "You owe me
a new phone, remember. You said you were going to get me one."

Ahh, yeah, right. A new phone. I smashed her last one after I
called Sloane's mom and found out Charlie had been there. Men like

me have a stash of cell phones dotted around the place, just in case. A burner for this. An emergency contact for that. I open a drawer in the kitchen and pull out the spare I've kept there for years. It's old but it works. I toss it to her, and she catches it out of the air. "There. Don't fucking turn it on, though. I need to replace the SIM first. I'll get you another one today."

Lacey pulls a face at the ancient piece of tech I've just given her. "This thing's older than me. I could bludgeon someone to death with it, Zee."

"You won't need to bludgeon anyone to death with it, because you're not gonna be out of my sight. Until further notice, you're on house arrest."

If anything, Lacey looks relieved by this news. Does she give a fuck about being told what to do? Nope. Does she mind that I'm restricting her to the insides of these four walls? That's a negative, Ghost Rider. She only cares that I'll be around for her to lean on if she needs me.

Sloane on the other hand...Sloane's gonna be fucking pissed when I tell her she's on lockdown, too. The DEA doesn't know where the warehouse is. It's better if she stays here and keeps her head down until I can figure out this whole shitty, messy situation.

I need to buy more fucking food. I slam the fridge door shut—where the hell is Michael? He usually sorts out things like that. He doesn't go do grocery shopping for me; that would be a complete waste of his unique talents. No, but he normally *does* arrange for someone else to stock up, though. I shoot him a text—*Supplies*—and get an instant ping back.

On it.

Lacey seems content enough munching on her bowl of cereal. I leave her and head back toward my room, wondering if Sloane's still going to be in there, half naked, getting ready. My dick stirs at the thought. I've always liked sex, but this? This is different. There's no naked woman standing in front of me, offering herself up to me on a platter. There's just the memory of the way Sloane feels and tastes and smells, and it's enough to make me fully hard.

"—Wouldn't be fair."

The sound of her voice stops me in my tracks. She's not in my room at all; she's in hers, and the door is wide open. Her back is to me, beaded with water from the shower. She's talking to someone on the phone. I can hear the buzz of an angry voice coming from her handset. Sloane's shoulders are tense, drawn up an inch around her ears as she listens.

"Oliver, I never threw it back in your face. I—" She pauses. And then, "It's far more complicated than that. It's not about him. Not all of it."

There's more intense buzzing coming from her phone—I can't make out specific words—and Sloane's breath catches in her throat. There's silence, and then she finally speaks. Her words are the kind made to stop a man's heart. They're the kind of words that have started wars and burned the world to the ground.

"I can't say that. I—I'm in love with him."

I pull in a sharp breath; I can't even fucking help it. It feels as though I've just been belted in the stomach with a battering ram. Sloane must hear—she spins around, and every last drop of color drains from her face. We stare at each other for a moment, and then she whispers into her phone. "No. There's nothing more to say."

She slowly lowers the phone from her ear and cancels the call, looking down at the screen and biting her lip. I just stand there like a fucking moron, waiting for my body to catch up with the screaming inside my head. What. The. Fuck? What the fucking fuck? She loves me? I'm assuming she was talking about me. She hasn't been hanging around with any other guys since we began playing this game.

"You weren't supposed to hear that," she says softly under hear breath.

"I can imagine."

She looks up at me, and for the very first time ever I think there are tears in her eyes. She's strong. When she was dealing with me in the beginning, when she slept with me, when I promised to help her get Alexis back, heading out to Julio's—through none of that did I ever see her cry. But fuck me if she isn't on the brink of breaking down right now. I curl my hand into a fist, desperate to smash it into something.

"Don't you want to say anything?" she asks quietly, her voice shaking slightly. "I'd have thought you would have had plenty of practice at berating silly women who let themselves get too close to you."

Pain. I need pain. Right now. I need to feel something strong and constant that will wipe away this rushing, roaring inside my head. "No. They were smart, Sloane. None of them were ever stupid or unfortunate enough to fall in love with me." I turn and hurry back the way I came down the hallway. I have to get out. I have to get the fuck out of here. I can't...I need to smash something into tiny pieces, or it's *me* who will be in bits. Seriously, I feel like I can't even fucking breathe right now. She *loves* me. She loves me, and I will break her. I will ruin this. I will lose this. I will hurt her and I can't be trusted, and I am too fucked up to cope with the thought of what will happen if she realizes all of this and leaves. These are the things that push me away from her. I can't...I wish I hadn't fucking heard that. I shake my head, trying to empty the thoughts out, but all I hear are those words: *I'm in love with him.* They won't stop repeating themselves, and the sick fucking thing is the reason I can't shake them is because I won't let them go. I'm running scared, but the confession...it makes my heart feel like it's on fire. *Fuck!*

"Zeth?"

I don't turn around.

"*Zeth!*"

I don't stop walking.

I can't.

I grab up my leather jacket from the back of the couch; I shove my arms into the sleeves, nearly tearing it apart at the seams when I can't wrestle it on right away. Lacey says something I don't hear, and then I'm leaving the apartment and slamming the door behind me.

4

Zeth

I STORM OUT OF THE WAREHOUSE, GROWLING UNDER MY breath and feeling strangely sick to my stomach. It's not a sensation I'm used to. Not one I've experienced before, so I don't really know how to fucking deal with it. The first thing that comes to mind is alcohol, but that sounds like a bad plan. I enjoy a glass of whiskey every once in a while, but the fact I feel like I *need* one right now makes me veer off it. It would end badly. Probably with a trip to the hospital.

Despite how extraordinarily fucked up I am right now, I'm still never off my game. I'm barely out of the door when I find a solution to my problems. A man, lurking in the shadows outside the warehouse, steps out in front of me and it's like a gift from up on high; my reactions are pretty much what you might expect from a guy like me, times a thousand. I'm pissed. It's more than that, though. I'm freaking the fuck out, which makes me want to pile drive my fist into things. In this case, a stranger's face.

I realize mid-way through my first swing that this guy isn't a stranger, though. It's Andreas Medina. And there's a narrow, vicious-looking blade in his hand, which is coming right for me.

Not. Fucking. Happening. I've been stabbed enough to last a lifetime. I don't ever intend on letting another person sink steel into my body again. I let out a roar as I grab hold of Andreas' wrist. There's a look of surprise on the motherfucker's face—he must have thought he was going to get the jump on me—and then a flash of pain in his eyes as he drops hold of his weapon. I barely have to apply any pressure; the reason for this is simple. I already broke Andreas' arm back at the compound nearly three weeks ago, and despite the fact he's not wearing a sling, his arm can't be anywhere near healed. I pull back my left hand and I smash it into the side of his head, sending him sprawling sideways into a pile of crushed cardboard boxes.

"Fuck!" he hisses. He's all arms and legs for a moment as he makes a pretty abysmal attempt at getting up. He's not getting up, though; I'm not going to allow it. I place the sole of my boot on Andreas' back and I flatten the guy. Nose crushed into the concrete.

"Yeah. Fuck is right, asshole. You just made a very big mistake."

"You're making the mistake, *ese*. I'm going to fucking kill you!"

The turmoil I found myself in a few moments ago has vanished now; it's like a Christmas fucking miracle. Poof—just gone. I'm used to this. The flat, cold nothing that takes hold of me, stripping away my emotion. I'm so grateful I could almost shake the man's hand. "Really? 'Cause the way I see it, you're scrambling in the dirt, pinned under one of my size elevens, motherfucker, and I'm in the mood to crush some cockroaches."

Andreas laughs a shaky laugh, still trying and failing to push himself up. "You're not gonna kill me," he says. "Not when you hear what I have to say."

I hate when they do this. *Hate* it. Because now, according to the sensible part of my brain, I need to find out what the hell is so important he thinks it's going to save his life. The rest of me wants to pick the bastard up, toss his ass in a dumpster, chain it shut, and push the damn thing into the Puget Sound.

Fuck it. The sensible side of my brain is unreliable anyway; so far it's led me directly into the clusterfuck I have going on back in the warehouse; how much worse can things get if I ignore it?

I pull out the Desert Eagle from the back of my waistband and plant the muzzle against the base of Andreas' neck. "Sorry. No dice, my friend." I flick the safety. "You can save your bullshit. I'm done listening. To anyone. Period."

"Wait, wait, wait. *Wait*! Julio's in town and he's got your friend. He's gonna kill him, man."

A volt of energy slams through me. Shit. This is what I'm talking about. How the hell am I supposed to kill him now? I exhale, clenching my jaw. "You're lying. I just spoke to my friend."

Andreas is shaking his head, a wide smile of relief marking his face now he knows he has my attention. "Not the black guy. Your *other* friend. The one who blew up half of Julio's villa once you and that *puta* burned off."

"Cade? The Widow Maker?" When was the last time I spoke to him? I've been so distracted the past few days worrying about Sloane and finding Charlie, I haven't seen anyone. Both Cade and Carnie have been staying with Michael, though. Michael would have said something straight away if one of them were gone. I lean closer to Andreas, crouching low over him, pressing the gun a little harder into his neck. "Still lying," I growl.

Andreas' laugh is high-pitched and seriously fucking irritating. "Okay, *ese*. I'm lying. But what if I'm not? What if your friend dies because I don't get back to Julio before dark, huh?"

Man, this motherfucker really is ruining a perfectly good beat down. I need to call Michael. I need to hear from him whether everyone is present and accounted for at the other apartment. In the meantime, just in case…. "I don't suppose you feel like telling me where he is?"

Medina's eyeball swivels in his head, looking up at me. There's madness and a decent helping of hatred there, staring right back at me. "No fucking way, *pendejo*. I tell you, you kill me. That's how it goes. And besides, I wouldn't tell you shit anyway." He spits, his saliva barely missing my jeans. Dirty bastard. I lift the gun and tap it on the back of his head. For all his big words, Andreas' eyes widen in fear. "Whoa. Whoa, what are you gonna do?"

"Well, you seem to have caught me at a very opportune moment. I'm in the mood to kill a few hours. I'm also in the mood to kill *you* for what you did to my friend back in Anaheim. Not to mention I'm one to hold a grudge. You shouldn't have manhandled Sloane like that back at the compound, either, asshole." It suddenly dawns on me that this whole interaction is taking place outside the warehouse, the location of which I've always been very careful to keep on the down low. "How d'you find out about this place?" I snap, driving a well-placed knuckle into the guy's spine.

Medina gasps in pain "Fuck you." This time I pull back and jab into his back with as much force as I can muster. The asshole quickly changes his mind about being a smartass. "I followed that guy yesterday, Rebel's cousin. I saw him coming out of an oyster bar downtown. It was a complete fluke."

Hmmm. Michael's usually more on the ball when it comes to noticing a tail. "So Julio knows where this place is now?"

"No. I came alone."

"Why?"

"Because I wanted to fucking kill you, *ese*," he spits, and for once I believe him. "What are you gonna do now?" Medina groans.

"Well, first things first, I think you and I are going for a little drive." I raise the gun; this time I bring it smashing down over the back of Andreas' head. The fucker goes limp as soon as the butt of the weapon hits his skull, and I get out my phone and dial Michael's number. I'm tossing a hundred and fifty pounds of Mexican into the trunk of the Camaro when my man picks up.

"Michael. Where the hell are you? And where the hell is Cade?"

"He went out last night. I haven't seen him yet this morning."

"Fuck! What the hell, Michael? I've just found Medina outside my place, and he's saying Julio's picked Cade up. They weren't supposed to go anywhere."

Michael swears softly. "He said he was getting some pussy, man. What am I supposed to do, tell him he isn't allowed to go get his dick wet?"

I grit my teeth, trying to rein in the urge to scream. "You're right. Fuck."

"We'll find him. Julio's not gonna kill a Widow Maker, Zee. It would be suicide. Rebel would come after him with everything he's got."

This is probably true, but I just can't see it anymore. "No offense, Michael, but your cousin doesn't exactly seem to be the hardass everyone makes him out to be, y'know?"

Michael makes a derisive, faintly entertained sound. "In this instance, appearances are most *definitely* deceiving. Trust me. Julio would *not* want to alienate Rebel."

"Alright, well I'm counting on that. Because Andreas Medina is not making it back to *El Jeffe* before nightfall. Not until he's physically or metaphorically spilled his guts for me." Right on cue, a series of loud bangs rattle through the car, coming from the trunk. Looks like my little friend has woken up and he sounds suitably pissed off. His bad mood is gonna get a whole lot worse when he realizes what I have in store for him.

"Head over to the warehouse. Watch the girls for me. Make sure they're safe. Call some people. Find out anything you can about Julio coming to town. Any weird rentals on the outskirts of the city.

You know the drill."

"You sure you don't want me to handle Medina? I owe that motherfucker a few loose teeth after the welcome he gave me back at the compound. That way you can make sure Lacey and Sloane are safe yourself."

There's a tone in his voice I don't like. He's far too perceptive for his own good. I've never breathed a word to him about what those girls mean to me, but he knows it all the same. That makes me incredibly uncomfortable. "Just get your ass to the warehouse, Michael."

There's a pause on the other end of the line; I can tell he wants to say something, but he has to know I'm not in a mood to be fucked with. "Okay, Zee. You're the boss."

I *am* the boss. I am the motherfucking boss, and yet I'm too messed up to go back to my own house. I'd rather be out putting the hurt on an asshole like Medina than facing a stubborn brunette who weighs a hundred and twenty pounds soaking wet.

5

Sloane

I FEEL LIKE I'M GOING TO THROW UP.

When I was a teenager, I used to get the worst panic attacks. My mom couldn't understand what that really meant. I'd be sitting happily enough, getting my work done in class, watching TV at home, eating a meal out with my folks, and then the next second I was overcome with this absolute, bone-deep sense of dread that was impossible to overcome. It would feel like there was a huge weight pressing down on my chest, which would lead me to feeling like I couldn't breathe. Like I just couldn't quite get a deep enough draw of oxygen into my lungs, which in turn meant that my heart would start racing. This wasn't just a racing heart, though. Not something you would experience if you'd been running track or doing anything to exhaust yourself physically. This was the kind of accelerated heartbeat made by an imbalance within the brain. An imbalance of hormones and adrenaline. An imbalance that felt like it would never be righted again, no matter how many times my mother told me to just relax. She couldn't understand the problem, that my attacks were irrational. I didn't have to be in direct harm or in an overwhelming place to succumb to them. I didn't have to be doing anything out of the ordinary at all. It would just happen, and I had absolutely no control over it. That was part of it, too—feeling like I had no control.

My dad used a more medical approach to explain it to my mom, but she never really got it. She only saw her teenage daughter freaking out and causing a scene, and she wanted it to stop. In the end, she quit trying to reason with me after I explained panic attacks *weren't reasonable*, and she just let me get on with it.

That was better for the both of us back then, but right now the only thing I can think of is my mother telling me to take some deep breaths and stop being so silly. I almost want to hear that. To believe it. To be able to snatch back some control. Because at this exact moment in time, I feel like I'm right back there. I feel like I'm fifteen again and my heart is about to explode, only this time there *is* a reason for my panic attack. That reason is six foot three, dark-haired, covered in tattoos, and apparently horrified by the thought that I might love him.

Fuck.

I get dressed with shaking hands and head out to find Lacey; she's sitting on the sofa scrolling through a cell phone that looks like it was made in the early nineties. She rolls her eyes when she sees me. "Zeth left. He says you're disgusting. Please tell me you didn't do anything too weird with my brother this morning."

Oh, good god. Seriously? He made a comment like that to Lacey? I've never been this girl. I've never been the girl to let anything a boy says affect her, and yet right now I feel like my heart's breaking. Is there some technique to holding yourself together when this happens?

"Are you okay? You don't look very well." Lacey tucks the phone into the pocket of her jeans. I can see the square of light from the display lighting up through the material of her pants. I just stare at it until it goes dark, and then I snap out of my daze.

"I need to see Pippa. You wanna come?"

Lacey's brows draw together. "I don't think Zee would like that. He told me he wanted us to stay here. Admittedly he said he was staying here, too, but…"

"Well, screw him, Lacey. If he can't be bothered to stick around, then why the hell should we?" This sounds perfectly logical to me right now. I'm not a complete idiot; I know the police are looking for me, but I also know Charlie knows where Zeth lives. Without Zeth around to unscrupulously shoot people, I doubt we're actually safe.

Lacey looks me up and down, her forehead crinkled. The crinkles disappear when she makes up her mind. "Okay. But just so you know, Pippa said some nasty things about Zee's…about *my* mom last time we saw her. She was really mean."

About Zeth's mother? How the hell would Pippa know anything about Zeth's mom? I sincerely doubt he's been forthcoming with any information, and Lacey never even got to meet her. "What did she say?" I ask.

Lacey shakes her head. "I don't wanna talk about it."

When Lacey says she doesn't want to talk about something, it's generally not a good idea to push. "Okay. Never mind. You don't have to worry, though. I'll make sure she's nice, okay?"

We leave the warehouse, and it's only when I'm outside that I remember I don't have a fucking car. The insurance must have come through by now, but I haven't really been concerned with administrative things like checking my bank balance. I call a cab, and Lacey and I wait outside the warehouse, huddled together for warmth. We could go back inside, but I don't think either of us want that right now. The phone in Lacey's pocket rings three times before our ride shows up.

"Who *is* that?"

Lacey kicks her worn, once-red Converse at the ground, shrugging her shoulders. "I don't know. It's just some guy. He keeps calling." She takes the phone out and switches it off. Our cab arrives; we're about to get inside when Michael's sedan appears farther up the street.

"Oh dear," Lacey says.

"Yeah. Oh, dear." I think we're in trouble now. Michael's usually placid face is livid as he pulls up behind the taxi. He slams the car into park and jumps out, rushing around to meet us.

"What the hell is wrong with you?" he hisses. "You trying to make Zeth kill me or something?"

"We're not your responsibility, Michael," I throw back.

Lacey sniffs, covering a mild chuckle. "Actually, I'll bet we are. Zee's sent you on babysitting duty, right?"

Michael doesn't grace us with an answer. He leans into the cab and hands over a twenty, telling the driver to get gone and fast. The driver does as he's told, and then Lace and I are standing outside the warehouse with one mighty pissed-off Michael. "You're going back inside," he informs us.

"No, we're *not*." I am so sick of feeling trapped. There's no way I'm going back inside that building. Not until Zeth's traumatized, furious expression is a distant memory. "I'm going to see Pippa," I tell him.

"The shrink? What the hell for? Lacey's just had an appointment."

"This isn't for her. This is for me. Your boss is a grade-A asshole and I need to talk to my friend."

My immovability on this subject must be clear as day, because Michael huffs out a frustrated sigh and then throws his hands up. "Okay. Fine. But I'm driving, and I'll be coming up to the apartment with you, too." He mutters under his breath as he storms back around to the driver's side of the car. All I hear are the words *irresponsible*, *walking bait*, and *death wish*.

I don't mean to frustrate Michael; he's a good guy, but I'm just too worried right now. Worried over everything. I thought Zeth and I were turning a corner, but after his reaction to my confession just now, I don't know if we're even on the same street anymore. There will come a day when all this uncertainty and panic is over, and right now that day just can't come quick enough.

Zeth

"MOTHERFUCKER, YOU BETTER *LET. ME. OUT!* WE'RE GONNA kill you and that old English bastard, too!"

Old English bastard? Why the hell would they think I'd care if they killed Charlie? Frankly, they'd be doing me a favor, although there would be something very sweet about doing the job myself. I frown, swerving like a maniac through the streets of downtown Seattle. Not far to go now. I'll worry about Charlie and Julio, and every other malevolent force out for my balls, when I don't have a guy locked in the trunk of my car. It occurs to me that there's only one real way to deal with Andreas. It also occurs to me I can't just kill the man. Not anymore.

Not now I'm involved with a woman who swore a highly fucking inconvenient oath. Hippocrates obviously never came across any of the people I deal with on a daily basis. If he had, he would have amended that oath to say, *I will prescribe regimens for the good of my patients according to my ability and my judgment and never do harm to anyone. (Unless they're rolling up on me. In which case, it's game on, motherfucker.)*

I'm still puzzling over how the hell to make this whole kidnapping situation work by the time I pull into the underground garage of the apartment building on West Ave. Maybe not the smartest move, bringing Medina here, but I have an arrangement with the owner of the place. In return for a small and rather violent favor I did him, he gave me access to the basement storage areas underneath the building. No one else has a key—not even him. I've used the place a couple of times to put the hurt on a few people, and at the end of the day it's central. I need to be around in case Michael calls.

I park and make sure no one else is around before I open the trunk. Just in case he's stupid enough to try anything, the Desert Eagle is already trained on Andreas. His eyes shift quickly, adjusting to the light—yeah, the asshole was gonna make a move. His legs are drawn to his chest, as though he's about to lash out with his feet. I'm beyond his reach, though. "Get out," I growl.

Medina looks at me. Looks at the underground parking lot we're in, and then says, "No."

"No?"

"No way, *ese*. I get out of this car, it's the last thing I ever do."

I should have hit the asshole harder. This would be going a whole lot easier if he were still unconscious right now; I could have just lifted his scrawny ass out of there and slung him over my shoulder. As it stands, I'm gonna have to get persuasive. I shove his feet out of the way, leaning into the trunk, pressing the muzzle of the gun directly against his forehead. "You have two choices right now, *ese*. You can either die in the trunk of a car, or you can have a conversation with me about my friend and maybe come through the other side of this alive, depending on how badly you piss me off. Up to you."

Medina's jaw works, eyes sharp and assessing. "Fine." He heaves himself out of the trunk with as much dignity as a man with a recently broken arm can, staring me down the whole time. I'm used to this look. A lot of people have used it on me. A lot of people have hated me, wished me dead. Imagined how they would kill me—played it over so forcefully in their heads that I can almost see the moment where they imagine my death register on their faces. It doesn't bother me. Everyone can dream, after all. Shame for him that's all it is, though—nothing more than a dream.

I shove him with the gun right in the solar plexus. "Move." Medina narrows his eyes at me, but gets moving. I guide him to the service entrance at the far end of the parking garage, making sure no one sees me forcing a man to unlock the door at gunpoint. There are some seriously shady characters living in this building but even they get innocent houseguests who might witness this scene and think it a little fucking suspicious.

I take the key back from Medina and push him into the corridor. Lit by emergency strip lighting, the place pretty much looks like a set of a horror film. Medina isn't exactly thrilled at following my directions as I point him where I want him to go, but he knows the alternative is for me to shoot him right here and now. We head through a maze of passageways before we reach the room I'm looking for.

Inside the empty concrete box is nothing but a single chair and a naked light hanging from the ceiling. Medina balks right away—this is the same thing Michael was faced with when Andreas took him down into Julio's basement. It's only right Andreas gets a taste. I dig the gun into his back, growling low under my breath.

"You'd better move your ass or I'll knock you the fuck out and drag you over to that chair myself."

Andreas must know I'm not the type of guy to exaggerate. He swears in Spanish under his breath and mans up, stalking over to the chair and sitting down on it, fixing a hateful gaze on me. "If you kill me, you'll never be able to set foot in California again, my friend."

I smile at that, scratching my temple with the butt of the Desert Eagle. "California's overrated in my book. I've had my fill for a lifetime."

Andreas' eyes narrow, a thin, nasty smile spreading on his face. "Oh yeah, that's right. You grew up in Cali, didn't you? Heard all about that. Your mama, she got herself all banged up in a car accident, no? Was *she* a pretty one? I bet I would have liked to fuck her, if—"

I shoot him. The Desert Eagle feels like it's vibrating in my hands as I aim it at Medina's right shin and I pull the trigger. The sound of the shot resonates off the walls, echoing around the small concrete box so loud that my ears ring. Medina's blood curdling scream rides over the top of it, making the hairs on the back of my neck stand to attention. There's a good deal of blood splattered all over the floor. The wound on Medina's leg looks pretty neat and small. He's still screaming when I pace behind him—there's an exit hole. I find the round crushed and spent, half buried into the bare concrete floor.

"You fucker! You crazy motherfucker! You shot me!" Medina wails. He's trying to get up, but his leg won't hold his weight. I place my hands on his shoulders, forcing him back down onto the chair.

"Put your hands behind your back," I tell him calmly.

For a moment I don't think he's going to do it—maybe I will get to put him down after all—but then the guy does as he's told, still hissing and spitting and swearing under his breath. I cuff him one hand at a time. The chain links between the cuff loops feeds through the back of the chair so that he can't stand up without taking the whole seat with him.

Medina's hyperventilating now, deep, gasping breaths, as he undoubtedly tries to fight through the pain. I take off my belt, stoop down, and I tie the band of leather around his thigh, creating a tourniquet; the wound's a through-and-through, but he could still bleed to death. I can't let that happen; I have other plans for him. "You got no idea what you're involving yourself in here, *ese*," Medina grunts out. "Charlie's got big fucking balls, but he's gotta be seriously insane to go up against Julio. The two of you are risking everything for a game you have to know you can't win. Fuck, man. You guys aren't even contenders."

There he goes with that Charlie shit again. It makes no sense. They know I broke ties with my old boss, so what the hell does he think to gain from telling me the old man's in the shit? "Hate to break it to you, buddy, but Charlie and me, we aren't exactly best friends right now. If you're trying to make my heart bleed, the only way you're going to make that happen is if you take this gun from me and put a bullet through it. And I think I'm out of ammo now."

Medina pants, a vain attempt at laughter, wincing. "Yeah, Julio may have believed that fucking line, but not me. I knew better than that. I saw through your lies. I saw through the bullshit you spun about that whore you brought along with you, too."

Did he seriously just say what I think he said? He has *got* to be fucking kidding. "You disrespect my mother and I shoot you in the leg. You call my girl a whore, what do you think I'm gonna do to you now, asshole?" I smash my fist into the side of Andreas' face, feeling a grim sense of satisfaction overcome me as my knuckles connect with his cheekbone. His head rocks to the side, his neck cracking in a sickeningly loud crunch. If there's one thing Andreas Medina should not be doing right now, it's talking shit about Sloane. If he had absolutely any fucking sense whatsoever, he wouldn't be talking at all. Period. He rolls his head so that his chin is resting on his chest, a thin strand of bloody saliva hanging down from his open mouth.

"He did say you are crazy about that bitch," he wheezes, laughing. I crouch down in front of him, lifting his head up by grabbing a fistful of his close-cropped hair.

"Didn't our last meeting give you an indication that perhaps you shouldn't insult my girl? As I recall, you couldn't walk for a week after you dared to fucking touch her." I shake my head. Stand up. Swing back. Hit home. "Now you're calling her a whore?" I'm filled with a black rage I doubt I'm going to be able to quench by beating my fists against this disgusting piece of shit's face, but I'm willing to give it a shot. Once, twice, three more times, I lay my hands on him, transferring my rage through my body into my fists and directly into his face. Medina takes the first few hits well, laughing like a maniac. Blood sprays everywhere as I rain down my wrath upon him, but by the end, he's gasping for air and his eye sockets are already starting to swell and bruise.

"That woman's worth a thousand times more than the disgusting bitch who pushed you out of her body," I snarl.

Medina's a complete mess. There's blood everywhere, his face swollen beyond recognition, but he still tries to smile. "It makes no difference what she's worth, *ese*. When Julio gets his hands on her, he ain't gonna sell her ass. He's gonna chain her to a bed and let every single one of us take a turn on her. He swore it. Should never have stepped up to him, man. Your old lady is gonna find out the hard way what it means to lie to a man like Julio. And when I say hard, I mean really fucking hard." Medina sucks his bottom lip into his mouth, biting down in a mocked expression of lust.

That's it. That is seriously fucking it. He's just trying to rile me, to goad me into losing it, probably with some half-assed hope of escaping somehow. I know all of this and yet I can't help myself—I react. I jam the tips of my index finger and middle finger into the base of his throat, cutting off his oxygen supply. With my other hand, I press down firmly on the dip below his right ear, just underneath his jaw. I can see he's fighting it, but it's pointless. You can fight human nature. You can fight against the will of others, but when it comes to fighting off your own nerve endings...yeah, good

43

luck with that. His jaw drops, *Open fucking Sesame.*

I scoot down again, and make a show of inspecting the inside of his mouth. I frown, nodding at what I find inside—a selection of decaying teeth and a particularly bad case of halitosis. "Yeah. That's what I thought. Just the right size." I let him go, and Medina draws in a gasp of air that sounds like a car engine trying to start. I start for the door, and I can tell by the scrape of the chair legs against the concrete and Andreas' coughing that he regrets pushing my buttons.

"Wait. Wait, man. Where are you going?"

I look back over my shoulder, just enough so that he can see the intent in my eyes. "Oh, don't worry. I won't be long. I'm just going to get my bag."

MY PHONE STARTS blowing up as soon as I hit the parking lot. I check it only to see I have seven missed calls all from Michael. What the fuck? I try calling him back but I have no reception. Fucking underground parking lot. I'm about to take the elevator up a floor just so I can get a bar when a text comes through.

Michael:
Girls insisted on going to the shrink's. I've gone with them.

As soon as I see the word *girls,* my whole body feels like it's been electrocuted. In the split second it takes me to read through the clipped message, I imagine it says three different things instead: *Girls are dead. Girls are gone. Girls have fled the state—said they were sick of your bullshit.* But no. They've just gone to see Newan. What the fuck? They were safe in the warehouse, and now they're out traipsing all over Seattle, where they could be found by any number of people. Charlie. Julio. That DEA bitch.

They need to be somewhere safe. Somewhere none of the dangerous elements in my life can find them. Somewhere none of them know to look. I have an idea where that might be, but first things first I need to get to them and drag their asses back to the warehouse.

I jump in the Camaro, gunning the engine. Medina just got a reprieve. He doesn't know it yet, but my pressing responsibilities have just prevented something very unpleasant from taking place. It's seriously gonna fuck with his head when I don't come back. The thought almost makes me laugh.

I slam the Camaro into gear, pausing to message Michael back before I burn out of the lot.

Me:
Okay. Don't let them out of your sight. I'm coming.

6

Sloane

"YOU CAN WAIT HERE, Y'KNOW. WE'RE ONLY GOING TO BE half an hour." Michael doesn't look too impressed by my attempts to ditch him. I knew there was no way he was going to wait in the foyer of Pippa's building, but still...it was worth a shot. He raises an eyebrow at me, pursing his lips.

"What floor?"

Lacey huffs and weaves her way around him, stabbing at the button marked with an eight. Michael gives me a polite smile, though I can read the amusement in his eyes. "It's okay. I'm not going to listen in on you complaining about my employer if that's what you're worried about." The elevator doors roll shut, and my mind whips me back to another elevator. To the very beginning of this whole nightmare when I was riding up to a hotel room and feeling sick at the prospect of what I was about to do. There had been three guys in the elevator with me that day. One of them was concerned about me—said I didn't look well.

And now I'm riding in an elevator car with people I never would have met if it hadn't have been for that day. For the man I met in that hotel room two years ago. If I could have looked into the future and seen what my life was going to be like now because of that one decision—to press the button and go up—I wonder how I would have felt. Because yes, it was fucked up, and yes *my life* is royally fucked up now, but I care about these people. Michael would die to protect Lacey and me—I know without a shadow of a doubt—and Lacey is now like family. It may sound harsh, but I care about her right now more than I do my own sister, given Alexis was the one who got me into this whole mess in the first place.

As if she can read my thoughts, Lacey slips her hand into the pocket of my jacket and threads her fingers through mine. Honestly, I'm a little shocked by the action. I look down at her and she beams back up at me, wrinkling her nose.

"It's going to be fine," she whispers, and the way she says it makes me believe she's not simply talking about me showing up on Pippa's doorstep with an imposing, though rather beautiful, tattooed black guy who clearly works for a man she detests. In fact, it sounds more like Lacey, who is often so withdrawn from the world, has come into some knowledge that Zeth and I, and everyone else in this life are not privy to. Perhaps the fact she's so withdrawn gives her a unique insight—you can see so much more of the world when you stand back to take a proper look at it.

I squeeze her hand. "Thanks, Lace."

The elevator dings and the doors roll back, and there's Pippa, briefcase and jacket in hand, looking more than a little startled. "Sloane! What—" She lays eyes on Michael and stops talking. Her reaction is almost laughable. She may not have been expecting me, but she *definitely* wasn't expecting anyone Michael sized, or Michael *shaped*.

"Are you leaving?" Lacey asks, stepping out into the hallway. Pip blinks at Michael one last time, masters her facial expression, and then refocuses on us.

"Uh, yes. I was headed to the office. Is everything okay? Did we have a session booked?"

A session? I try to remember to breathe deeply, but my efforts feel wasted; my chest still feels tight and constricted. It's felt that way since I turned around and saw Zeth standing in my bedroom doorway. "No, we—I just wanted to talk to you." I didn't make the decision to come here lightly. I'm still mad at her for interfering and misjudging me, but at the end of the day she's still one of my oldest friends. And I need a friend right now. Not a psychiatrist. I need the woman who's been known to feed me ice cream and let me vent; she used to be that person, and I think she still can be. My eyes are pricking even just thinking about that comfort. Pippa's cautious expression fades, softening her face.

"Oh, okay. Well, sure. Uh..." She glances back at Michael, raising her eyes. She clearly doesn't know what to make of him. Not even a little bit. I'm about to introduce him to her when Michael holds his hand out, ever the gentleman.

"Good morning. I'm Michael. I'm an acquaintance of Zeth's."

"An acquaintance?" She eyes his hand like it's actually a coiled snake, but she slowly reaches out and shakes it. "And when you say acquaintance, do you mean an associate who kills people for a living?"

Michael doesn't flinch at Pippa's direct line of questioning. He's charm personified when he leans forward and places a kiss on the back of her hand. "You could say that," he tells her. "But don't worry. It's an infrequent arrangement."

Lacey breaks the tension by holding out her hand to Pip, looking up at her expectantly. Pippa seems a little flummoxed by Michael's candor. She's obviously very distracted as she roots in the pocket of her pant suit and then deposits her apartment keys into Lacey's outstretched palm. "Okay, then," she says. "Yes, well I suppose we had better go inside."

"ONE PERCENT. SWEET." Lacey immediately starts helping herself to Pip's cereal, while Michael walks through the apartment, moving gracefully from room to room. I'm the last one to enter the apartment, right behind a very confused Pippa. "What the hell is he doing?" she hisses. "And how the hell does he move like that? He looks like a trained ballerina that went overboard on the steroids."

He really does. "Checking the place over," I inform her.

She spins around, fixing me with a hostile glare. "For people he wants to kill? I thought he said that part of his work was infrequent?"

"Yeah, usually it is. Look, Pip, can we—"

"I'm sorry."

I stop short. "*What?*" In all the time I've known Pippa, I've never heard her say those two words so plainly. Yes, we've both been shitty to each other sometimes, and yes, we've both had to apologize, but Pippa's proud. She normally takes the long way around. *I regret that what I said made you feel...I realize that it probably wasn't great of me to...I see where you're coming from, and I understand that I could have...*

There has never been an *I'm sorry* moment with Pippa. Hearing her saying it now takes me back a little. She reaches out and takes my hands, the same way she did the last time I sat in her kitchen when she basically told me she didn't trust me to know what the hell I was doing.

Now that I look at everything that's happened, perhaps she was right, but—

"I'm really, really sorry," she says. Her face is stoic and devoid of all expression. I think it has to be in order for her to get those words out. "I know I'm a major bitch sometimes. Captain Bitch of Bitchtopia. I suck, I really do. It was cold and cruel of me to tear into you like that the other day. And it was really unprofessional of me to go searching through Zeth's history. I'm sorry. Please—say you'll forgive me? I swear to you I won't ever do it again. You can date Charles Manson for all I care, so long as you're still my best friend."

I open my mouth, not quite knowing what to say. Pip announced her speech loud enough for Lacey and Michael to hear, but doesn't seem to care. That's even more out of character. It's one thing to be sorry, but it's another thing entirely to undergo a public apology. Not that it matters; Zeth's sister and personal right-hand man weren't listening by the looks of them—Lacey's offering Michael a spoon full of food and Michael, surprisingly, is accepting it, both talking in hushed tones. I know him, of course. I know there's a very strong probability he heard, processed and stored every single word.

"Can we just go back to how everything was six weeks ago?" Pippa continues. "No, screw that. Let's go back to how things were two and a half years ago, when the only things we had to worry about were exams and which doctor's service we wanted to get on."

"Okaaay. Sure. I guess?" This is weird. Really freaking weird.

Pippa's shoulders slump, as though a weight has just been lifted from them. "Thank you," she says, smiling. "Come on. Come and sit down. I'll make us some tea."

I sit down on the sofa, and Pip does as she says, making us some tea. It seems to be a habitual act for her whenever she has company. Lacey declines, though Michael very graciously accepts—

unlike Zeth at my parents' house, somehow Michael holding a cup of English Breakfast just seems *right*. Pip brings me mine, offering me out the same cup she always gives me when I visit. "Here. I'll just run to the bathroom and then we can talk, okay?"

"Okay."

She's not gone long. Michael and Lacey sit in the window seat across the other side of the vast room, overlooking the city, talking together, and me and Pippa sit in silence watching them for a moment. Eventually she speaks. "He cares about her," she observes.

"Everyone cares about her. It's hard not to."

"Hmmm. Yes, I suppose you're right. Has she told Zeth yet?"

I shake my head. Drink my tea. We sit in silence some more. And then, "I'm glad you're here, Sloane. I really am. I thought it was going to be months before I got to see you again."

"Yes, well, things have been pretty crazy. I wanted a sane shoulder to cry on."

She pivots in her seat, frowning at me. "Why? What happened? Are you okay?"

"Yeah, I'm fine. Well, not fine, but...I'm okay. I just—Zeth overheard me arguing with Oliver. He heard me telling him that...he heard me telling Oliver that I'm in love with him." God, I even feel terrible just saying it. What an idiot. From the very beginning I've known this whole thing with him isn't conventional. It never will be conventional, but it appears as though my stupid heart didn't get the memo on that one. It's somehow managed to convince itself that a very conventional let's-all-fall-in-love-with-Zeth-Mayfair fest is totally on the cards, and it won't take no for an answer.

I'm so absorbed in berating myself for my own stupidity that it takes me a moment to notice Pippa's face has gone sheet-white. She looks...she looks horrified. "Oh. Yeah, I can imagine how that would have been embarrassing," she says, lifting her teacup to her mouth.

She takes a sip, though the liquid is still way, way, way too hot to drink. "What did he say?"

Puzzled, I look down at my hands, not sure what to tell her. Admit that he fled the scene while looking murderous? Hmmm. Maybe not a good idea. "He was pretty silent on the matter."

"Did he definitely hear you?"

The image of his stricken face is not one I'll be forgetting any time soon. "Oh, yeah. He heard me alright."

"So what are you going to do?"

I tap my nail against the side of my cup, thinking on that one. "I don't know. Things are complicated." I let my head rock back so it's propped against the back of the couch. "Everything is *so* fucking complicated."

Pippa clears her throat. I let my head roll to the side so I can look at her. Her eyebrows are halfway up her forehead. "What? What is it?" She's probably going to tell me it's only complicated because I let it be complicated—that I can walk away any time I see fit. That I most definitely should walk away. That's not what she says, though.

"It's nothing. I've just never heard you swear like that before."

My swearing? I did say fuck just now, but I'm sure I've said in front of her before. Haven't I? I can't even remember. "Sorry, Pip. I don't even know where that came from."

"I do. You've been spending more time with people who might use that kind of vocabulary."

My hackles rise at that—a not-so-subtle dig at Zeth, who punctuates his sentences with the word. It just sounds so perfect tripping off his tongue, though. He's made it into an institution for me. My skin prickles every time I hear him say it, because it reminds me of when he's whispering it into my ear, telling me what he wants to do to me. Pippa's going to have trouble making me feel bad about that.

"He's changing you. You realize that, don't you?" she asks

quietly, not looking at me. "You're not the same person you were at the beginning of the year."

I just look at her. She's seriously going to pull that card? The whole *you've changed* bullcrap? My mouth feels suddenly very dry. "Pippa, I thought my sister was being raped repeatedly against her will for the past two years. I thought some disgusting pimp had put the hook in her and she was addicted to heroin or something. I've thought she was *dead*. I've *hoped* she was dead, just so that she wouldn't be going through everything I've been imagining. I moved heaven and earth to find her, only to discover she's been absolutely fine this whole time. So yeah, if I've changed since discovering that information..." I exhale, trying to keep my cool. It won't help either of us if I start screaming right now. "If I've picked up a few curse words along the way throughout this hellish journey, I think I might be entitled to use them, don't you?"

Pippa looks stung. Her cheeks are a little red, though I have no idea why. We've had much bigger disagreements before and she's been as cool and collected as they come. But right now—

"Look, Sloane, I—"

A knock at the door cuts her off. Pippa swallows whatever she was about to say, blowing out a quick breath. I know just by looking at her that something awful is about to happen.

"What have you done, Pip?"

Michael is on his feet in a split second, pacing quickly toward the door, casting a sharp eye over Pippa. She shrinks away from his glance, turning to face me. "I'm sorry, sweetheart, I really am. You just...you just left me no other choice."

7

Zeth

I KNOW SOMETHING'S UP AS SOON AS I DRIVE BY NEWAN'S apartment block; there are two black SUVs parked down the side street that runs parallel to the building. One of them sitting there would have been easy to explain away—some suburbanite soccer mom taking her kids to play in the park across the street. But two of them? Parked one after the other? The same make and model?

Seriously, guys. Get a fucking clue.

I pull out my phone. Dial Michael. He picks up on the first ring. "We got trouble," he tells me.

"I can see that. DEA?"

"Sounds like that bitch from back at the hospital. She wants us to open the door."

"Fucking pitbull," I snap. "Got a way out?"

Michael makes an affirmative sound. "Side window. Leads out onto an emergency escape. We're leaving now." I can hear muffled voices in the back—one of them belongs to Sloane. It sounds as if she's freaking out.

"Put her on the line, Michael." I park the Camaro, find a dark blue ball cap in the glove compartment, put it on, and then climb out. Make my way across the road toward the SUVs. If I had time, I would so be slashing some of those fucking tires.

Sloane's voice grows louder. "I can't believe she's done this. I can not fucking believe it."

"Sloane, you there?"

"Yes. Oh my god. Lacey's freaking out. You have to make sure they don't arrest her. She keeps on saying something about a guy named Mallory."

My blood ices over—Mallory. I know who that is. I think I know why Lacey's losing her shit, besides the obvious, of course. "Mallory was her last foster parent. Just try and keep her calm. Go with Michael, okay? Now."

I hang up. No time for screwing around. There are no agents waiting back with the vehicles. Two SUVs? That's eight people at least, so where are the motherfuckers? There'll be at least four knocking politely on Newan's door right now, but the other four? They must be covering the other exits. There's a rear entrance to the apartment building that can be used by the residents; they'll definitely have people there. Maybe they haven't thought about the fire escape, though.

We're not that lucky. When I run to the corner of the building, pressing myself flat against the wall and peering around, I get a visual on two agents. They're talking into their radios, but neither of them are looking up...at Michael, Sloane, Lacey and Newan as they move rapidly down the fire escape. I have to move. As soon as those bastards see them, they'll raise the alarm on their radios and the guys around the back will be right on top of us.

Michael's at least had the forethought to grab the Newan bitch as a hostage. I see she's not coming willingly; his arm is locked tightly around her body, and he's leaning over the emergency fire exit, directing his gun at the two cops below—a precautionary measure in case they start doing their jobs and bother looking up.

A multitude of different scenarios play out inside my head. If I kill these cops, I'm suddenly America's most wanted. If I shoot to injure, I'm still pretty fucking high on the DEA's shit list. No, I have to be smart about this.

I pull out the Desert Eagle and I do fire it...at their shiny black SUVs. The bullet impacts the door of the front driver's side of the closest car, and the vehicle's lights instantly start to flash. The alarm follows right after.

"What the fuck?" Agent One yells. I can barely hear him over the wail of the alarm. I scoot back around the side of the building so I won't be seen. I wait. One, two, thr—the guy comes running. I grab hold of him before he can even look to cross the street. He smells like stale coffee and laundry detergent as I drag him to the side and lock my arms around his throat. He claws at me as I choke him out, desperately trying to wrestle free. That's not happening, though. Not a chance. He loses consciousness in a mere six seconds—way for holding out there, buddy—but that's still six seconds too long. When I glance back around the corner, the other DEA agent is holding his gun up in typical police fashion, both hands on the weapon, and he's screaming at Michael and the others.

"Let the woman go!"

On the very last flight of stairs before hitting the ground now, Michael doesn't look like he's going to be letting Newan go any time soon. "Take off the radio, asshole." This is why I keep Michael around; he's fucking smart. He knows the deal as well as I do. If that guy so much as twitches in the wrong direction, if he so much as looks like he's *thinking* about raising the alarm, my boy will blow his head off.

Right now that's not the kind of attention we want to be drawing, though. I don't have a hope in hell of sneaking up on the agent, so I lock my gun on him and clear my throat. "Might wanna put down the weapon there, friend."

The guy, *the kid*—when he spins at the sound of my voice, he looks no older than twenty-two, twenty-three—nearly shits his pants. "Fuck. *Fuck, fuck, fuck*," he hisses. "You both need to put down your weapons," he tells us, head swiveling from Michael to me and back again. "Do it now, and you won't get hurt."

It's like they give these kids a script or something. When they're so fresh on the job they don't know any better than to use it. Do it now and you won't get hurt? I'm almost fucking laughing over here. Not quite, because I catch sight of Sloane and suddenly this isn't even mildly entertaining. Her face is bleached of all color, and her hands are trembling like crazy as she holds Lacey to her.

Fuck.

"There's no way either of us are backing down," I say. "Drop the gun and I won't shoot you in the fucking head."

The agent's arms quiver, his body twitching as his resolve falters. He looks from me to Michael again, and Michael tips his head to one side. "Two seconds. Better do as he says."

There's shouting from above us. Loud calls and squawks from cop radios. The radio on the young agent's chest emits a blast of white noise, and then a voice I recognize immediately: fucking Denise Lowell. *"We're in. Search the place. Every room. Agents at all exits, on your toes."*

"Fuck," the kid repeats. "They're gonna kick my ass off the unit."

"Wanna be dead or unemployed?" I growl.

The kid drops the gun to his side. "Okay, okay. Shit."

I charge forward and grab his weapon from him. I grab his handcuffs from him next. Michael, Sloane and the others hurry down the alleyway toward me while I cuff the agent to a rusted downpipe on the opposite building. He looks like he's about to burst into tears. Michael launches at him, swinging back and leveling the fucker out with one single, well-aimed left hook. The kid's eyes roll back into his head, and he sags to the floor.

"What the hell did you do that for?" Newan screams.

"So it doesn't look like he cooperated," I snarl, emptying the kid's clip and tossing his gun back at his feet—the agency really does fire operatives who lose their weapons.

"Hold it! Stop! Get down on the ground!" Behind Michael, three more agents are racing toward us, and there are more climbing out of Newan's window and down the fire escape.

"Fuck! Move!" I don't need to tell Michael twice. He's rushing forward, shoving the three girls in front of him. Sloane and Newan are moving like they're taking this really fucking seriously. Lacey on the other hand is frozen still—she's been like this before, so gripped by fear she can't move. I grab her and toss her over my shoulder, and then we're running.

Shots begin to rain down on us.

Crack. Crack, crack! Three loud bangs, and none of them hit home.

Sloane's clearly acting on instinct. She throws herself into the back seat of the Camaro. Michael has to bodily force Newan inside; he follows after her. That leaves the front seat for Lacey. I bundle her inside, race around the car, start the engine, and tear off up the street in less than two seconds flat.

Five people in one fucking Camaro? Yeah, even with the engine modifications I made, our zero to sixty is epically fucking slow.

"Hail Mary full of Grace, the Lord is with thee. Blessed art thou among women—" Lacey's eyes are screwed tightly shut, and she's already started to rock. Her words of prayer are barely audible in between her ragged gulps for air. We don't have long before she reaches the pinnacle of her breakdown. She can't fucking handle the front of the car. She's gonna explode any second now. Fuck.

"Take a left. Left," Michael commands. I swing the car through the corner, not even daring to see if we're being followed. We *are* being followed; I just don't wanna see how close they are. "Pull over," Michael shouts.

We're around the other side of the park, so I swerve in and hop out of the car. No agents, but that won't last long. We're working with seconds here. Michael jumps out of the car and gets in the driver's seat, while I run around and grab Lacey from the front. She's shaking like a leaf in my arms.

"I'll get them back to the West Ave apartment," Michael tells me. "Be safe, brother."

I lock eyes with Sloane in the back—she's pale. There's a degree of horror on her face, but her jaw is clenched tight. She's fighting to keep calm. Pride surges through me—she's so fucking resilient. Our eyes remain fixed on each other, until Michael burns off in the Camaro and then she's gone. I immediately regret not telling Sloane to come with me. Fuck. Fuck! She's out of my reach now. I can't protect her. I can't do anything. Fuck. I suddenly feel helpless. I'm not, though; I have to take care of the girl I'm carrying in my arms. I slip into the park just in time to avoid being seen by the single SUV that roars past. God knows where the other car is. I have no idea what took them so long to get around the corner, but I'm sure as hell not complaining. It's likely the shots I fired on the vehicles actually did some damage. We shouldn't have gotten away from there. We should have all been arrested in that alleyway and been well on our way to a field office for questioning.

"Why won't you just...why won't you just fucking *die?*" Lacey sobs, burying her face into my chest. "Die! Just—*just fucking die!*" It's not me she's talking to. She's lost inside her head right now. This is some god-awful memory she apparently endures on a playback loop whenever her brain shuts down like this—I've seen it happen before. I've heard her crying out the same words, over and over. It'll be a while before she starts making any sense again, which is a problem. I now need to find a car to steal, and her crying at the top of her lungs over a man who I'm nearly a hundred percent sure she killed is going to prove problematic.

I know there's no point in trying to talk her down from this. Been there, tried that—it doesn't work. There's only one thing for me to do: I clamp my hand over her mouth and prepare to be bitten.

I can tolerate it. I can deal with it long enough to find a vehicle, and then I'm taking this girl and I'm getting her the hell out of here.

8

Sloane

OF ALL THE THINGS I HAD PLANNED FOR TODAY, BEING thrown around the back of Zeth's Camaro, pouring blood all over the upholstery while being chased by the Drug Enforcement Administration wasn't on the list. Michael drives like he plays too much *Need For Speed:* cutting, drifting, and screeching around corners no matter how dangerous it might seem. On-coming traffic howls at us as we dodge and weave through the vehicles, and Michael remains quiet, his eyes stoically fixed on the road ahead of him as he pumps the gas. Not once does he look behind him; not once does he look to see where the unmarked DEA cars are. Pippa does, though.

"They're not there anymore! You can pull over and let me out."

"There's probably a helicopter on us," Michael says mildly.

My arm is on fire. It feels like I have liquid napalm in my veins instead of blood. I'm pressing my forehead against the window, trying to breathe through the pain, when Pip notices me holding onto my shoulder.

"I can't hear a heli—whoa, Sloane, are you *bleeding?*"

My hand is itching to reach out and slap her so hard she sees stars—this is all her fault—but I need to keep pressure on the bullet wound in the top of my left arm, which is currently pumping copious amounts of blood out of my body. Instead I turn on her, my fury no longer a containable force. "When did she speak to you?" I demand. "When did you decide you should turn me in to the freaking *cops*, Pip?"

"You mean, when did I decide enough was enough?" she snipes back. "Oh, I don't know. When you were being questioned by a member of a national crime unit and you ran out on her? Or maybe it was when Oliver contacted me earlier, so worked up he could barely speak. But maybe, just maybe, it was when some awful woman was blackmailing me, telling me that you would be exonerated of any involvement in this mess so long as she gets the information she needs about your sister. That's all she wants, Sloane. That bastard has been feeding you lies, no doubt, telling you they're going to send you to jail or something. All you have to do is cooperate and you'll be in the clear. I don't want to watch this happen to you, okay? I don't want to see you flush your life down the drain for a criminal who's not worth—"

"SHUT UP!" Michael hollers, throwing the car around another bend. Both Pip and I slam to the left, and my injured arm explodes with pain as I'm shoved up against the door. I haven't had a chance to recover from the injury I sustained when Charlie wrote my car off, but it was getting slightly better each day. Now I've been shot, I'm back at square one. Worse than square one—this hurts so bad it makes my whole body burn. "Ahhh! Damnit!"

Pippa leans across me, drawing aside the torn, blood-soaked fabric of my shirt to reveal the deep gash at the top of my arm. "Oh, good lord, Sloane. Seriously? We need to take you to St. Peter's."

"We're not going to St. Peter's. We're not going to any hospital, so you can just close your damn mouth." She recoils like I've just turned on her unexpectedly. Like I'm a pet dog that's been a beloved member of her family for years, always as soft as they come, and all of a sudden I'm baring my teeth. Well I am baring my teeth. And maybe I've been relatively easy going and easily controlled since she's known me, but not any more. "Don't say another word, Pippa, or I swear I'll duct tape your mouth closed. *I* will deal with my injury. We're not going to pull over and let you out, and I'm sure as hell not going to be telling Detective Lowell anything about my sister anytime soon. Are we clear?"

Pippa's eyes are like reinforced steel. She's not used to being spoken to like that, and the shock of it has turned to anger before I'm even done. She exhales out of her nose, flaring her nostrils.

"Perfectly. Perfectly, crystal clear."

I recognize where we're going as soon as we hit Seattle west. Michael pulls the car underneath the Spokane Street Swing Bridge and gets out of the car. Pippa looks like she's weighing her options, deciding whether or not she wants to jump out of the car and make a bolt for it.

"I wouldn't bother. He's very polite most of the time, but Michael will have absolutely no qualms about tackling your ass to the ground."

"And you'd let him do that?" she says, her voice cold and hard.

I just look at her. She called the cops on me, informed them where I was, wanted to hand me over, got me shot in the process... yeah, she can clearly see from my expression what I would let Michael do to her, I'm sure.

Michael hails a taxi, and then opens the car door for us. Cars rip by, the drivers leaning on their horns at the inconveniently abandoned Camaro on the side of the road, and Michael ushers us into the cab. We're lucky it's peak hour traffic, commuters headed to work, otherwise we wouldn't have a chance of getting a ride.

We leave the Camaro behind.

By the time we're out from underneath the cover of the swing bridge, we're safely stowed in a sea of vehicles, a high percentage of which are taxis exactly like the one we are in. Michael wraps his suit jacket around me—three thousand dollars worth of Valentino, ruined—and glares formal but very serious daggers at Pippa. His message is clear: breathe one word inside this cab and you're done for. Pip understands him just fine. She sits in stony silence. We all do, apart from the driver who hums along with the radio, oblivious to the fact that we're all literally on the edge of our seats back here.

It takes twenty minutes in slow traffic to reach Kilpatrick, an oyster restaurant three blocks from Zeth's other apartment. We get out, Michael pays the driver, slipping him an extra fifty, perhaps so he won't mention the odd fare he just had, and then we're walking through the blustery streets of Seattle.

"You can't keep me with you forever, you realize," Pip announces, walking close against Michael's side. So close, the people we pass in the street can't see he's actually holding onto her arm, guiding her.

"We won't need to keep you forever," Michael replies. "Just long enough for Lowell to forget all about Sloane and her sister."

Pippa snorts. "You haven't heard this woman talk. She's never going to forget about Sloane or her sister."

Now it's Michael's turn to laugh under his breath. "Then perhaps you'd better get comfortable, after all."

TWISTED   CALLIE HART

I'M SHIVERING BY the time we get inside; my body is going into mild shock, and it doesn't help matters that the apartment is freezing cold. Michael immediately starts loading split logs into a real fireplace. I haven't seen an apartment with a real fireplace in so long that the scene Michael creates banking the wood, shoving balled-up newspaper into the gaps and lighting it, is surreal. Pippa sits herself down on a white chaise longue—the last time I was here, a slim Asian woman was giving a handsome guy in a black leather mask a blowjob while some other guy screwed her from behind. Maybe I should warn Pip, but then again, maybe I shouldn't. There's no way Zeth would have kept ruined furniture, but even so...it serves her right if she sits in something unsavory.

Michael leads me to a hard-backed chair by the huge, polished wood table in the center of the room that looks like it's new. He sits me down. "What do you need?" he asks.

"Boiling water." I wince, the prospect already turning my stomach. "A knife. A sewing kit. Alcohol wipes if you have them. A bottle of vodka if you don't."

Thank crap for Michael. He nods then moves quickly through to the rear of the apartment, making very little noise as he locates what I need. When he comes back, he has a large first aid kit with him. Upon inspection, I find there's a proper suture kit inside, along with a small ten blade, tweezers, and an anti-bacterial wash kit. After performing such a hack-job surgery on Alexis in Julio's compound, this kit is very much a luxury.

"Do you need help?" Michael asks, sitting at the table with me.

"Maybe." I have a reasonably high pain threshold, especially when I'm in control of the pain and I can stop at any time—that's not the problem. The problem is coping through the pain and being able to see what I'm doing properly at the same time. Common sense would suggest that Pippa help me out right now—she's a psychiatrist, yes, but she went through general training just like I

65

did in the beginning. It's how we met. She knows how to cut and stitch, and she would undoubtedly know how to check and see if there are any bullet fragments in my arm. But I don't ask Pippa. I don't want to be anywhere near her right now. Thankfully she's not stupid enough to even offer to help. I can't believe I even thought about sharing Ben and Jerry's with that woman not an hour ago.

I hand Michael the scalpel and the cleaning wash and give him directions. He listens intently and then sets to work. About what I said a moment ago—the whole *I have a high pain threshold* comment? Yeah, I may have massively overestimated myself there. The room starts spinning as soon as he puts pressure on the laceration.

"You okay? You look like you're going to throw up."

I might throw up. I might pass out, but I grit my teeth and let him continue; we need to get this done. Once the wound is clean, Michael holds up a small mirror—the kind you get in a make up compact—and a flashlight, while I dig around inside the cut with the tweezers. It feels like there are a thousand shards of glass in there, piercing me, burrowing their way deeper with every light nudge of the blade. It's agony. It's pure, burning fire racing up and down my whole body. I manage to pull out two tiny slivers of metal, but it still feels like there are more in there. After twenty minutes of trying and failing to find anything else, I'm covered in sweat and I feel like I can't breathe.

"Sloane, let me do it," Pippa says. My back is to her, so she doesn't see me clench my jaw, staring down at the tabletop at my blood that's pooled and splattered everywhere.

"I can try," Michael says. "If you want me to. But she's the better option."

I close my eyes and put down the tweezers. I'm so mad; I can't even do this one thing without her riding in to the rescue, fixing things. Fixing the mess I'm in. "Fine. Come get it over with," I snap.

Pippa's face is entirely blank as she takes Michael's seat and picks up the blade. "Do you want a drink? Some alcohol?" she asks.

I shake my head.

"Okay, get ready." She slides the flat edge of the scalpel into the wound and begins to dig. The pain lances through me, white hot and so intense that it short-circuits my brain. I can hardly see. Definitely can't think anything other than, fuck.

Fuck.

Fuck!

My vision's so blurred I can barely focus on the twisted curl of burnished silver metal Pippa extracts from deep inside my arm.

My heartbeat is a living, breathing, thumping pressure all over my body. And then everything is black.

9

Zeth

"I'M REALLY SORRY," LACEY MUMBLES. THESE ARE THE FIRST words she's said that aren't Mallory related since I had to throw her over my shoulder. She's lying on the backseat of the boring as fuck Chevy I've 'borrowed'—I actually *will* send Michael back with it later. She's been quiet for the past twenty minutes while I've driven around, assessing the lay of the land, looking out for any suspect DEA cars that might have followed Michael back to the apartment. Lacey's small hand slips up into the front between the passenger and the driver's seat, and it rests there on top of the console. I take it and give her a squeeze—*it's alright. It's okay. It's not your fault.*

This is the language we speak in sometimes: a gentle shoulder bump, a quick and tight squeeze of a hand. Our actions communicate more than either of us could effectively convey with words. I've never questioned this. It's how things are between people like Lacey and me.

"Are we nearly home?" she asks softly.

"Yes. Just arrived," I tell her. I get a weird sense of déjà vu as I pull into the underground parking lot, and the reason for the distinct memory replay suddenly hits me. I haven't been to this apartment building for at least a month, but I was here today. Andreas Medina. Andreas fucking Medina cuffed to a chair, shot in the leg, and locked in one of the utility rooms, and my friend Cade out there somewhere, being held by one seriously pissed off Mexican gang lord. Fuck. I haven't forgotten about Medina or Cade, but time did kind of slip away from me. Medina said nightfall. If he wasn't back by dark, then Cade is pretty much as good as dead.

I park, collect Lace from the backseat, ride up in the elevator to the apartment with her, but I don't go in when we get there. "I just have to take care of something," I tell Lace. "I'll only be fifteen minutes. Michael and Sloane will already be inside." In all honesty, if I walk through that door right now and lay eyes on Sloane, I'm going to be screwed. I'll want to stay put with her for the rest of the night, not let her out of my sight, and Medina will have starved to death and pissed everywhere by morning. No, better to go let him go to the bathroom, feed him, make sure he doesn't dehydrate and die from the network of slightly leaky, vastly outdated heating pipes down there. It's sweltering even during the coldest of days, and he's been sweating it out for hours now. Perhaps the rise in temperature will have given him added incentive to talk.

Lacey looks less than happy with me for abandoning her, but she nods. She enters the apartment without a fuss—a minor miracle— and I'm free to go check on my captive.

He's exactly where I left him, except now he's very washed out and a considerable pool of blood has turned the concrete sticky and black. His eyes are wild and furious when they lock on me. "You said you were coming right back, *pendejo*. Your time is nearly up."

With the bullshit I've already been through today, this guy's dirty mood isn't going to make my own improve any. I send him a sideways glance that would probably have made someone like Rick Lamfetti shit his chinos. It's then I recall the reason I left Andreas in the first place; why I went back to the car earlier. My bag. My tools. My original duffel is still in the back of the Camaro. I have another just like it upstairs in the bottom of the wardrobe in my bedroom, but right now I have nothing down here. I'm at a loss once more. I have no means of forcing Andreas to talk other than with my fists, and Andreas strikes me as the sort of person who can take a beating. Someone who would suffer through it in silence, spitting out their teeth one by one, taking hit after hit and still stubbornly refusing to part with a word. No, I'll need more than my fists to get Cade's location out of this motherfucker.

I give him a chance to prove me wrong. To save us both a lot of time and energy and blood. "Where's the Widow Maker, Andreas?"

Andreas sucks on his teeth, leans forward as far as he can on his chair, and spits onto the floor. "I'm not telling you shit, *ese*. Not a fucking chance on this earth."

I stand and stare at him for a long, tension-packed moment. Three months ago, fuck, *one* month ago there's a very specific way I would have handled this situation. I would have let loose the anger boiling inside me on this person; I would have allowed a very dark and dangerous side of myself free rein in order to get what I wanted. There would have been a considerable amount of blood, sweat, and probably some tears thrown into the mix—none of it mine—and I would either have gotten the information I needed, or Andreas Medina would be dead.

A part of me is considering that option even now, wanting to get the ball rolling, but then again another part of me, a side of me that's been having his way more and more often lately, won't allow it.

I'd like, in some small way, to say that I can't torture Andreas Medina to breaking point because I am a reformed man, and I don't want to hurt people anymore. There is an element of truth in that—I've never relished or enjoyed causing harm to others. I don't do it for fun, and I *am* steering clear of that course of action as often as I can now—but the truth is I'm stopping myself because of Sloane. She's never told me to quit my line of work, but I know her well enough to realize going on a killing spree is gonna drive a pretty large wedge between us. Highly inconvenient. There's nothing else for it; I shrug my shoulders. "Okay." I turn and make to leave.

"What, you're just gonna let your buddy die, punk? Julio's gonna tear your boy into tiny pieces and you're just gonna walk away from me?"

The panic in Andreas' voice all but confirms what I suspect—Medina is playing a delicate bluffing game with me. Julio won't kill Cade. Or at least he won't kill him tonight. Rebel will know one of his guys is missing by now, either because Cade hasn't checked in or because Michael's had a chance to call or message him. He'll have already been on to Julio, making it perfectly clear what will happen if a single hair on the head of the Widow Maker's VP is harmed. Julio won't do anything to damage the relationship he shares with Rebel unless it's a desperate situation, and having one of his men vanish for less than twenty-four hours hardly qualifies just yet. Or at least that's what I'm hoping. Cade's life depends on it.

I look Medina in the eye, letting a sharp smile spread across my face. "Yes. I'm just gonna walk away." And so I go. I walk out of the room, lock the door, walk down the corridor, and out into the underground parking lot once more. My heart's working double time when I reach the "borrowed" Chevy; I hope I made the right fucking decision. If my friend dies horrifically because I'm going soft, then I will never forgive myself. I won't be able to. My phone starts buzzing as I'm waiting for the elevator. I pull it out, inhaling sharply when I see that it's Michael. Why the hell would he be calling if he knows I'm just down in the basement?

"What's up?" The elevator doors open, but I don't go in. I hold them open with the toe of my boot, waiting to hear what Michael has to say.

"Forget whatever business you're conducting right now and get back up here, man," he says.

"Why? What is it? What?"

"Sloane," he says, exhaling her name in a stressed sigh. "Sloane got *shot.*"

I go still. "What did you just say?"

"Sloane got shot," he repeats. "Don't lose your shit, though. She's fine. She was hit in the arm, but she lost a lot of blood. I just think it would be better if you were up here instead of down there right now."

Sloane. Got. Shot.

"What the fuck?" It doesn't matter that Michael says she's fine. I won't believe it until I see her with my own eyes. "I'm coming. Give us some space," I say, and end the call. For the whole journey in the elevator, my body doesn't feel like it's my own. It feels foreign and numb, unwilling to cooperate with me. For the first time since I was a kid, for the first time since my uncle dared to raise his fist to me, I feel panic. A pure, bottomless panic that hollows me out and robs me of any fucking sense. *Sloane. Got. Shot.* I'm already planning what I'm going to do to the person responsible by the time I reach the apartment door.

Sloane got shot.

Fucking rude awakening indeed.

10

Zeth

I JAM THE KEY INTO THE LOCK, OPEN THE DOOR, AND THERE
she is, sitting on the sofa—a sofa that was once white but is now
mottled with splotches of bright, ruby red. She's been bleeding.
She's been bleeding all over that fucking couch, and I was off
running around Seattle, trying to get Lacey to calm the fuck down. I
should have been here. I should have *known* she was hurt. Her face
in the back of the car when Michael drove her away was totally
washed out, her expression terrified, but I'd put that down to the
ordeal she'd just been through. Not even considered for a second
that one of those shots had gotten lucky. I silently enter the
apartment, feeling my pulse throbbing oddly in every single part of
my body. I'm measured and careful as I walk toward the table in
the middle of the room. I can't go straight to her. I can't even look at
her. I'm struggling to keep my fucking cool; there's a desperation
inside me demanding to be answered, though no good can come of
that. Sloane won't be better if I smash up my apartment. She won't
be magically healed if I break every last stick of furniture, smash

every single plate, punch holes in every single wall I can reach before my knuckles turn raw and bloody.

"Are you okay?" I ask, allowing myself a quick glance at her.

She nods, looking like a small child bundled in the blanket she has tucked around her body. "It was just a graze." She gingerly lifts her left arm, indicating where she was hurt and wincing at the effort. "Still stings like a bitch, though."

Fucking hell. I can't believe she was actually shot. Graze or no graze it should never have happened. I suddenly regret not doing more damage to that DEA agent; that would have been a small consolation for what they did to Sloane. I brace myself against the table and close my eyes, trying to somehow maneuver past the urge to go on a rampage. Trying to breathe through it all. If only Dr. Walcott, the psych guy from Chino, could see me now. *Well done, Zeth. Gold fucking star, Zeth. Keep it up, Zeth.*

"The Camaro's gone," Sloane whispers.

I let out a blast of bitter laughter. "Fuck the Camaro."

I couldn't care less about a car right now. Maybe in a few days I'll be pissed about it—I will *definitely* be pissed about it—but right now I'm wading my way through waist-high shit, and a vehicle doesn't factor very high on my list of concerns.

"I'm sorry, okay?"

My head snaps up. Sloane's eyes look huge in her face—she's staring right at me, unblinking, and she looks exhausted. Heartbroken. And a hundred other things I can't even put a name to, though none of them good. "What are you sorry for?" I whisper.

She swallows. Her head tips back to rest against the sofa, and I can see the fine strands of hair plastered against her forehead. She's been through hell today. I can see she's in pain just from looking at her. "I'm sorry for leaving the warehouse. We took Michael, though. I thought…" She trails off, like the effort of even speaking is just too much for her.

I am a wretched, wretched man. I wasn't here to help her, and she thinks I'm mad at her. Fuck. "You have nothing to apologize for, Sloane. Never apologize to me again."

She makes a surprised sound at the back of her throat, a combination of choking and pained laughter. "I'm sure you'll be taking that back in a couple of days."

I shake my head. Pull in a deep breath. I'm not really ready for this, but I'll be waiting forever to reach a point where I'm ready to feel the way I do. To not be absolutely fucking stunned by how weak caring about her makes me feel. I want...I want to reach out to her, but I can't. "You're never going to apologize to me again, Sloane. If you fuck up and make a mistake, that's on *me*. If you get hurt, that's on *me*. For as long as you're willing to tolerate being in this situation, everything that happens to you *is on me*. I'm the one who's sorry." I straighten up, scrubbing my hands through my hair. I can hear sounds in the apartment: Michael taking care of Lacey, making sure she's okay, hiding that bitch doctor out of my sight, giving Sloane and me the space I asked for. He's been here this whole time, watching over my girls for me while I couldn't. I feel sick.

"Zeth, come here." Sloane's holding up a hand—the right one, her uninjured arm—and the image, the very sight of her reaching out toward me makes my stomach feel like it's filled with battery acid. She shouldn't still be doing this; she shouldn't still be reaching out. She should be pushing me away by now, but she's not. I'm the worst kind of monster, because I'm relieved. So relieved my body feels like it's going into shock. I walk toward her, not quite sure what to do when I get there. I don't think I've ever been unsure of anything in my life. Ever.

Sloane doesn't seem to be having the same problem. She takes ahold of my wrist and tugs at me gently, pulling me down to sit beside her on the sofa. She places my hand palm up in her lap, and carefully traces her index finger across the lines, creases and callouses that I've collected over a lifetime. They're not the focus of her interest, though. It's the multitude of scars, deep and ugly, her fingertips linger over.

"You might be responsible for the fact I'm not sitting at home, watching a rerun of Seinfeld on my own right now, Zeth. You might be responsible for the fact that I'm not voluntarily working an extra shift at the hospital. I had a safe life, I did, I know that, and it really does suck that being shot at is now a part of my everyday routine. But..." She takes a deep breath. "You heard what I said to Oliver. What I told him...how I feel about you. I did mean that. So while you're responsible for a lot of crappy things right now, you're also responsible for that. You've woken me up. You've made me stronger. You've made me feel something I thought I'd never feel."

My head is spinning. I want to curl my fingers closed and withdraw my hand from her touch, but that seems the coward's way out of this conversation. I leave it where it is, forcing myself to hear it. To hear her say the words. To feel it, too.

"I know you probably never wanted this, Zeth. I can understand why. But I do...I do—"

"I know," I say, cutting her off. I may have heard the words once today already, but she wasn't actually giving them to me. Handing them over to me like a fragile, delicate gift. A gift so overwhelming, and confusing, and undeserved that I feel like packing up my shit and leaving the fucking state. She was telling someone else, and I'm not prepared for her to be telling *me* just yet.

"What are you afraid of, Zeth?" she whispers. "Why am I scaring you so badly right now? It's not like I'm expecting you to say it back."

I laugh, unable to fight it anymore. I just can't help it. I close my hand into a fist. "I'm not scared of you, Sloane."

She gives me a sad look. It's the kind of look that can make a man feel two inches tall. "Yes, you are," she says. "Of course you are. You're *terrified*."

11

Sloane

I WAKE UP IN A BED I RECOGNIZE ALL TOO WELL—ZETH'S bed, from the night he hosted his party and I came to collect my phone. He carried me into this room, away from hungry, interested eyes, so he could have me all to himself. He's not here right now, though. I'm alone, I'm cold and I'm seriously freaking sore. I've always wondered what it felt like to get shot, mildly curious, but now it's happened to me my curiosity has evaporated, and I can't wait for the throbbing, pounding pain to subside. If anything it seems worse today.

A gentle knock at the door pulls me out from under the comforting blanket of sleep I am hiding beneath, then a voice. "Sloane? You awake?"

It's a soft, female voice. Can only be Lacey. "Uh-huh. You can come in."

The door cracks open and Lacey shuffles in, dressed in a huge T-shirt that comes down to her knees. I doubt this one is Zeth's; it would even be too big for him. She closes the door and hurries across the room, hovering at the edge of the bed.

"What time is it, Lace?" I ask, rubbing at my face. There are heavy, dark curtains at the windows—the kind of curtains people like me buy, who work nights and need to sleep during the day—so I can't tell whether it's morning or not. Certainly doesn't feel like morning.

"It's ten minutes past five," she whispers. Her bottom lip disappears into her mouth. "Um..." She shifts from one foot to the other, gathering the great swathes of t-shirt into her fist. In the half-light, she looks pale. Dark shadows underneath her eyes make her face look puffy and distorted. I suddenly realize what she wants. What she's finding hard to say.

"You wanna hop in?" I ask, lifting the covers.

Lacey looks like she's going to cry. She nods and I shift over so she can climb underneath the covers. I'm not sure whether I'm supposed to say anything or not, but I feel like I have to. She was so anxious at Pippa's apartment, so absolutely crippled by fear. Her chanting, *"Mallory. They're here because of* him. *They're going to take me away. They've found out about Mallory,"* tells a story all of its own. "Do you want to talk about it?" I whisper.

Lacey stares straight at the ceiling, her eyes open wide, unblinking. She's still bunching and un-bunching her T-shirt under the covers. I let her lie there for a moment, not willing to push too hard. If she wants to talk, she now knows she can. I'm hardly a good substitute for Pippa when it comes to accurately treating mental healthcare patients, but I can be a good listener. I'm hoping she knows *that,* too, when she opens her mouth and a strangled sound comes out, like she was about to say something and cut herself off before she could form the first syllable. I root around underneath the cover until my hand meets skin—Lacey's hand. I take hold of it and squeeze—*it's okay. Take your time.*

"I didn't—" she chokes out. "I didn't mean to do it." Her voice sounds thick, as though her throat is closing up. "It was just—it was one of those things. I don't normally get angry, I've never been that angry before, but that day I did, and I—I—I'd just had enough, y'know?"

This is something important, I can tell. I rethink my line of questioning. Perhaps Zeth should be the person Lacey is talking to like this. Perhaps I should go and get him, wherever he is, and let them do this together. I'm on my way to suggesting this when Lacey lets go of my hand and turns onto her side, away from me, curling up into a ball. The sounds of her unmistakable crying are faint but heartbreaking. She's crying like a child who has found herself lost and alone and in the dark, but too afraid to call out to anyone for help.

I decide then and there I won't be leaving her to get Zeth. I won't be leaving her until I know she's okay. Whatever it is she didn't mean to do, I can be the person she confides in. "It's okay, Lace." I place my palm flat against her back, giving her that small sense of human contact. "Just tell me."

She sniffles. Carries on crying. "M—Mallory," she whispers. The skin across her back breaks out into gooseflesh; I can feel it even through the T-shirt, as though the very name of this person is enough to grip her in an unbearable fear. "Mallory used to like...me to give him what he wanted, when he...wanted," she stutters. "He would come into my room when I was in bed, and I would pretend to be as...asleep, but that never worked. I don't know why I tried it every time. It used to make him so mad. If I didn't get up quickly enough when he told me to, he would h—hit me with a leather strap. He carried it—carried it everywhere he went, just in case I misbehaved, he said."

My stomach is rolling. This person, this Mallory, he is the person Lacey spoke about the first time I took her to Pippa for treatment. He's the sick son of a bitch who raped her over and over. The day

80

she'd told Pip and me about that, her voice had been totally flat, lifeless, completely controlled. Now she's the opposite; she's distraught, her breath coming out in labored gasps. My heart is breaking for her. I rub my hand up and down her back, knowing what a small and inconsequential gesture it is, but doing it all the same.

"Every Sunday he would take me to church. He said I was dirty. He said—" Her words catch in her throat.

"It's okay. Take your time," I whisper, closing my eyes. This is so harrowing for her, but it's also crushing me. I've never heard her like this before. Never. I've witnessed the way she can be—mood swings, depression, withdrawn into her own world—but this is different. This is so painful for her the both of us are shaking.

"He said," she continues, "that I was a whore. He said that I seduced him. That I was wrong to lead him on all the time. I was a bad girl for getting him so excited and I had to go to church to repent and clean myself of my sins. He would wait outside the confessional every week. Every Sunday for a—" She gasps. Breathes in deeply. Exhales. Her sobbing quiets a little, though by no means stops. And then in whispers, she tells me the rest. "He would wait outside the confessional every Sunday for an entire year. I wanted to tell the priest I didn't want to do it, that he made me do it every single time, but I knew *he* was sitting outside, listening. It—it made him excited to hear me say it all. He would get really hard while he was waiting for me, and then in the car he would cry and say I was evil and torturing him. He wouldn't touch me, though. When we got home, he would touch himself and he would make me watch. It would be Tuesday by the time he came to me again. Wednesday if I was lucky.

"But this one week after church, Mallory didn't touch himself when we got home. He was mad. The priest...the priest said it wasn't my fault; he refused to give me any Hail Marys. Mallory made me tell the priest that his name was Curtis so he wouldn't get into any trouble. But this time, the priest asked me how old I was. How old Curtis was. And I didn't even think. I just—I just told the truth. I told him I was fourteen and that Curtis was forty-three."

Lacey falls silent—a good thing, because I need a moment to process what I'm hearing. Fourteen years old. Fourteen fucking years old. I wasn't allowed out of my mother's sight when I was fourteen. I resented the restrictions at the time, but now, with the hindsight of adulthood, I was so lucky. So, so lucky to have someone to watch out for me.

"The priest wanted me to go to the police," Lacey says. She sounds flat, and her shoulders have stopped shaking now. "But I said no. I knew Mallory would be mad I'd told the priest how old he was, but it was too late to take it back, so I did my best to keep my mouth shut. The priest said Mallory was sick in the head and needed help, and I needed to go away to a proper school or something.

"I didn't even finish confession. Mallory snatched back the curtain and grabbed hold of me. Dragged me out of there. He said we had to sit and wait in the car for a while, just in case the cops showed up. They didn't. Mallory kept asking me why I was trying to get him into trouble when it was me who'd been bad. I knew I was going to be in trouble when I got back to the house anyway, so I just clammed up. And when we got back, I couldn't—I couldn't get away," she sobs. "He beat me. He tied me to a chair in the kitchen and cut my clothes off me with scissors. He told me exactly what he was going to do to me. I was so afraid I...I wet myself. He got mad at me for that, too—untied me and made me clean it up, naked, while he watched, touching himself."

I can almost smell the urine and the cleaning products. I can hear fourteen-year-old Lacey's frightened crying as she scrubbed, on her hands and knees, at the mess she'd made. I'm suddenly filled with such an overwhelming rage that I want to go and find this man and kill him. I want to hurt him badly enough that he can never use his manhood to pee again, let alone use it to hurt another poor little girl. I shuffle forward so I'm spooning Lacey, and I tug her to me so I can put my arms around her. She trembles against me so violently I can hear her teeth chattering.

"And then he...then he *really* hurt me," Lacey says simply.

I want to know what she means, but I'm too revolted and hurt for the poor woman I'm holding in my arms to do it. I know enough. I know he hurt her so badly she's still suffering at the memory of his hands nearly twelve years later.

"Have you told anyone else about this, Lacey?" I ask, trying to keep my own tears at bay now.

She shakes her head. "He was still asleep when I woke up the next morning. I had to make his breakfast. Every day, I had to make him eggs and grits and take them to him in bed. I was sore and I could barely walk, though. Everything was hurting me, and I just...I just *snapped.* I cooked his eggs and grits, and I put orange juice in his glass, but I didn't fill it all the way to the top. I only filled it halfway." She pauses as though she's reliving the actions—sliding the eggs onto the plate, spooning out the grits, spilling some juice onto the countertop.

"The bleach was still out," she tells me. "From the night before. From when he'd made me clean up. I saw the bottle and I just—*did it.* I didn't even hesitate. I filled up the rest of his glass from *that* bottle, and then I took it into him. He was already awake. He was in a good mood. He called me his sweet thing and stroked my cheek over the bruises he'd put on my face, and told me to sit with him while he ate. I didn't want to. There were these pictures all over his walls of Jesus and Mary and all these angels flying around in Heaven, and I remember I didn't want to sit there while they watched down on what I'd done. Mallory wouldn't let me go,

83

though."

She doesn't hold back now; Lacey just lies here and sobs. I hold her to me, fighting back the urge to rush to the bathroom and throw up. She fed him bleach. She fed him bleach, and I can't make myself believe it. My horror deepens when I remember the look on Lacey's face when I took her to my parents' house for the first time: the panic in her eyes when she saw the religious icons and paintings on my parents' living room walls. *Fuck*. I left her there for days.

"What happened, Lacey?" I murmur into her hair. I don't really want to hear to be honest, but now that we've gotten to this point she needs to tell me. She needs to tell me every last detail; it's vitally important she does. If she doesn't, she'll never face what happened. She starts tapping her fingers against the arm I have wrapped around her—pinkie, ring finger, middle finger, index finger. Index, middle, ring, pinkie. Back and forth, back and forth, clearly a nervous tic, a coping mechanism.

"He...drank it. I checked first. It didn't smell so bad. He didn't notice there was anything wrong with it until he put down the glass. And then...and then he dropped the tray from the bed and the eggs went everywhere. He started shaking. There was...there was blood. I ran to the door, but I couldn't go. I turned and pressed my back against the wall, and I watched. He was spitting blood everywhere and clawing at his throat. It went on for ages. I waited and I waited, but he just kept on clawing at his throat. So I knew what I had to do. I climbed back up on the bed. Mallory..." Lacey chokes. Breathes. "Mallory thought I'd come to help him. He looked so *relieved*. I took one of his pillows, and I held it over his face. I pressed down as hard as I could, and I screamed. I begged him to die. I told him he had to, and then he did. As soon as he went still, I threw up onto his bed and then ran out of the room. I had scrambled eggs all over my feet. I grabbed a bag, gathered some clothes, took the money Mallory hid in his Bible and I ran. I ran and I ran and I ran and I—"

She continues talking, saying the same thing over and over again. *I ran and I ran.* This girl has *never* stopped running. I hold her to me as tight as I can and I let her cry. She's hysterical for at least thirty minutes before exhaustion seems to catch up with her. That's when I feel like I can talk to her and she will actually hear me.

"Lacey?" She's not going to like this. "You should *not* be feeling guilty. That priest was right—Mallory *was* a sick man. You need to talk to Zeth, okay? You need to tell him all of this. And you need to tell him he's your brother."

She goes still, her crying slowing even further. "I can't," she says quietly.

"Sweetheart, you have to. He can help you. He has a right to know you share the same blood."

The back of her head nudges my chin as she nods. "I know," she whispers. "But I can't tell him."

"Why not?"

"Because he'll know I'm dirty." She shakes even more violently, sniffing. "He won't...he won't want me to be his sister. He won't love me anymore."

A pain way worse than my gunshot wound lances through me, right down to the core. I've never experienced anything like it before. I'm crying before I can even pull myself together to speak. "That's not true, Lacey. That can never be true. Nothing will ever stop Zeth from loving you, no matter what, okay? But more importantly, you are *not* dirty. You never needed to confess what he did to you. You were a child. He abused the power he held over you when he should have cared for you."

A shudder rolls through Lacey. It's as though even imagining it— this Mallory guy being kind and caring for her the way he should have—disturbs her. "I know you think that, but it's not the way I feel. I just can't tell him, okay? I wouldn't be able to find the words."

I hold my breath, trying to think of something, anything to make her change her mind. I come up blank. "Okay, sweetheart. It's okay. Try and get some sleep."

SHE DOES EVENTUALLY go to sleep, although I don't. I lie in bed, running over and over everything that she's told me. It's late by the time she startles awake next to me. There's no brief moment where she doesn't remember what took place when she came to find me last night. No, the pain and shame are already there, lurking in her eyes when she opens them and looks at me.

"I'm sorry," is all she says.

I feel like hugging her again, although I can tell by the way she draws her hands into her chest that she's not ready for that now. I just shake my head at her, letting her know she shouldn't ever, *ever* be sorry. "I've been thinking," I say carefully. "You can't tell Zeth what happened. How would you feel if *I* told him?"

She draws in a tight breath, and so do I. Neither of us exhale. We just look at each other, and I watch the internal debate going on in Lacey's head manifest itself on her face—indecision, fear, panic. Maybe a little hope. She blinks first, then, carefully, slowly gives me a single nod of her head.

"And...how would you feel about me telling him you're his—that you're his sister?"

Lacey remains immobile; no blinking or nodding now. It takes her longer to come to a decision this time. Eventually, in a very small, tired voice, she says, "I think that would be okay."

"Okay." I climb out of bed, and I'm hit with a wall of vertigo and nausea that make me regret the sudden movement. I feel like shit, there's no denying that, but I can *not* stay in bed all day recovering. I just can't even tolerate the thought of it. Every single part of me throbs, but I'd much rather be walking about and in pain than lying there doing nothing. Lacey grabs hold of my wrist.

"You're going to tell him *right now*?" The anxiety in her voice is sharp and obvious.

"No, Lace. I'm going to take a shower. I'll tell him when he and I are alone, okay?"

She nods, looking relieved.

The apartment is quiet, no boys around. I find Pippa still asleep on the floor of the main bathroom—Michael handcuffed her to the waste drainpipe last night and she's been there ever since. Her eyes flicker open while I'm standing there, as though the pressure of my gaze alone is powerful enough to make her start from sleep. I give her a dry, "Good morning."

"Is it?" she replies. From where she's lying, I don't suppose the morning is looking all that great. The tiny key to the police-issue handcuffs sits on top of the window sill. I collect it and undo her restraints while she watches me with shocked eyes.

"You're letting me go?" she asks.

"I'm un-cuffing you," I clarify. "I wouldn't try leaving this apartment if I were you. After the stunt you pulled yesterday, god knows what Zeth will do if you cause any more trouble."

"You'll see I was only trying to help," she tells me, sitting up. She rubs at her wrists, giving me a prideful, dignified glare.

"I doubt that. You can go and get some food if you like, but I'd keep a low profile when Zeth shows up." I turn and head for the door.

"I'm not going to eat anything," Pippa snaps angrily. "I'm not going to leave this bathroom until you see sense."

I don't need this. Not right now. I roll my eyes, not even bothering to look back at her as I walk away. "Then you should make yourself comfortable, shouldn't you?"

I shower in the ensuite of one of the other bedrooms, doing my best to keep the dressing on my arm dry. My mind flies through a million different ways to impart Lacey's information to Zeth and doesn't find a single satisfactory way that won't be like a ton of bricks coming down on him. Maybe I'll just have to assess the situation when the time comes and make a judgment from there. I'm dashing back to my room, chilled from the cold air of the apartment, when I hear Lacey's voice. She's no longer in my room; she's back in one of the rooms off the main corridor—her own room, I assume.

"I know. Thank you. I'm...I'm glad, too." I push gently against the door—is that *Zeth* she's talking to?—to find her huddled into a ball on top of her messy bed, pressing that huge, chunky cell phone to her ear. She looks up and sees me, and her eyes go wide. "I have to go. Yes. Me, too. Bye."

"Was that Michael?" I ask, even though something tells me deep down it wasn't Michael or Zeth. For some reason, from the horrified look on her face, it feels as though she's talking to someone she shouldn't be. Like she's talking to Mallory from beyond the grave and she's feeling guilty about it. That obviously can't be the case, but still...

Her eyes grow even wider. "No, not Michael," she says. "Just a friend."

"Did I hear my name?" a voice asks behind me. Michael, wearing a tight-fitting T-shirt and loose cotton pants hanging off his hips. He scratches at the stubble marking his jaw, raising an eyebrow and wincing at the violent purple bruise on my upper arm that seems intent on spreading well past my fresh bandages. "Zeth's just run out for a second. I saw you've un-cuffed your friend. She won't come out of the bathroom."

"I know."

Michael shrugs, as though he's used to dealing with difficult hostages. "You guys want breakfast?" he asks. "I'm making huevos rancheros?"

I give him a brief smile, pulling my towel tighter. "Friend locked in the bathroom? World crumbling around our ears? Zeth already up and out the door? Sure, huevos rancheros sound great, thanks."

He gives me a dry look, winks, and then peers at the tiny woman bundled up on her bed in the room beyond me. "Lace? Lucky charms?"

She gives him a watery smile and nods, and I'm hit with the realization that even though he might not know *why*, Michael obviously knows not to offer Lacey food that might involve either eggs or grits.

12

Sloane

LACE AND MICHAEL HAVE BOTH EATEN AND DISAPPEARED BY the time Zeth returns to the apartment, looking more than a little frustrated. He sheds his leather jacket, tosses it onto the sofa, and then vanishes into the same en suite bathroom I used. There are few things in this life that render me speechless, but when Zeth Mayfair later walks into the kitchen of his apartment, dripping wet from a shower with nothing but a towel around his waist, I suddenly forget I have a tongue. Or rather, I don't exactly forget. I'm all too aware of it, and what I would like to be doing with it. He looks horrified by my tragic attempts to eat my breakfast. Yes, I may be right-handed and yes, it may be my left arm that is completely out of commission, but cutting and stabbing and scooping one-handed is still pretty difficult.

"Need some assistance?" he rumbles, opening the fridge and taking out a bottle of water. He pops the cap and drinks from the bottle long and deep, the muscles in his throat working, all the while staring right at me. I swallow the small amount of food I've managed to spear onto my fork.

"I'm fine, thank you very much. Where did you go this morning?"

He lifts one eyebrow. Stops drinking. Puts the cap back on the bottle. Not looking at me, he says, "Feeding a pet project I have in the basement."

I can tell from the way he mumbles he doesn't want to tell me this information. That makes me mighty suspicious. "What pet project?"

He leans back against the countertop and folds his arms across his chest. I'm not distracted by his biceps. Nope, not at all. That would be incredibly shallow of me. He gives me an appraising look, frowning slightly, and then says something that makes my heart leap into my throat. "Andreas Medina. Julio's in town. He's taken Cade."

"You have *Andreas* in the basement of this building? And what do you mean, *he's taken Cade?*"

Zeth prowls around the counter where I'm sitting, removing the fork from my hand. He slides some of the food from my plate onto it, raises it, and lifts both eyebrows. "Open, Sloane."

I can't believe him. He's just told me that he has someone held captive and that a very dangerous man has kidnapped his friend, and he wants me to eat. "I will not fucking *open*," I snap. "Tell me what the hell is going on."

A small smile tics at the corner of his mouth. Those full lips of his pout a little as he puts down the fork. "It's not as bad as it sounds."

"How? *How* is it not as bad as it sounds?"

"Because Julio won't fuck with Rebel. Julio's an insect compared to the Widow Makers. There's no way he would kill one of their members, let alone the V.P. of the club. Not if he didn't want his whole crew murdered brutally in their sleep."

"And what about Andreas? Why have you got him locked away in the basement?"

Zeth shrugs. He swipes his index finger slowly through the maple syrup that I've put all over my breakfast—I'm sick, I know—and then lifts his finger up to my mouth. I'm kind of stunned. I'm not sure what he wants me to do—suck it? He smirks when I give him a questioning look, but then traces the pad of his finger across my lower lip. I'm a little dazed when he puts his finger into his own mouth and sucks off the excess maple syrup. I draw my lip into my mouth and run my tongue over the burning skin where he just touched me, my mouth watering at the explosion of sugar. Zeth leans forward, clenching his jaw, lowering himself so he's at my level.

"Medina's tied up in the basement for three reasons, Sloane. Firstly, he came at me with a fucking knife—a pretty big fucking mistake on his part. Secondly, he knows where Cade is and I aim to make him tell me. Thirdly—" He's staring at my mouth, watching me still sucking on my lip. "Thirdly, he acted in a very ungentle-manly way with you back at Julio's. He also said some rather ill-thought-out shit when I dragged him back here. So I'm not exactly feeling like a gracious host, if you get what I'm saying."

I do get what he's saying. He's telling me that he has plans for Andreas Medina, and non-too-pleasant ones. "You're not going to kill him," I say.

Something like amusement mixed with a little anger flashes in those deep brown eyes. "I'm aware of what I *am* and am *not* gonna do, Sloane. And no, I'm not gonna kill him, despite the fact the motherfucker deserves it. He and I had a little *chat* this morning. He gave me some information in return for my guarantee I'll offer Julio a trade: my guy for his."

A chat? I have the worst images inside my head right now. They all involve blood. And very sharp objects. And a half-dead Mexican gang member. "What do you mean, you had a 'little chat'? What kind of little chat?"

Zeth gives me a blank look, tipping his head to one side. He walks over to the sofa where he tossed his jacket when he came in, rifles inside the pocket, apparently finds whatever he's looking for, and comes back to the open-plan kitchen. He hands me a small black box.

I look at the box, look back up at him. "I get the distinct impression there's going to be a severed thumb inside. Is there a severed thumb in this box? Because if there is, I have seen enough of those in the ER to last me a lifetime, thanks all the same."

"Open it," he growls. He doesn't look impressed by my lack of faith in him. I open the box and inside there are a handful of...of *paperclips?*

"What does this mean?"

"Something the guys used to do in prison," Zeth says, his voice utterly controlled. "Chino is..." He pauses, apparently intent on choosing his words carefully. "Chino's a hard place. People construct weapons out of anything." He selects a paperclip from the box and begins unbending it with those huge hands of his. The paperclip is then no longer a paperclip but a four-inch length of wire; Zeth holds it up for me to see properly. "The inmates had quite a few uses for something like this."

I can imagine all too well what the inmates might have done with something like that. The thought sends a jolt of horror sizzling through my body. Zeth was there. Zeth was inside while that kind of thing was happening all around him. I'm hit by a wave of worry that makes my mouth drier than the Sahara. "Did you hurt him?" I ask.

Zeth places the wire down on the counter, picks up my fork again, still loaded with the food he put on it a moment ago, and looks at me. He looks me right in the eye with such an intensity that my skin feels like it's humming with electricity. "Do you think I hurt him, Sloane?"

This isn't one of those off-the-cuff questions people ask and don't really expect an answer to. This is a question about who I think he is, and he's waiting intently for the answer. What I've thought has never been important before, but I can tell that now it very much is.

I think on it so I know I'm going to be telling him the fully considered, fully weighed-out truth. I come to an answer pretty quickly. "No. No, I don't think you did. I don't think you would harm someone who couldn't defend themselves."

That makes him smirk again. "You have a very high opinion of me, Sloane. Now, please, open your mouth."

I oblige him. He slides the fork into my mouth, and I take the food, enjoying the way he pulls the tines so slowly away from my lips. He watches my mouth closely, his expression carefully constructed into a blank mask. "I didn't even touch him. This time," Zeth whispers. "He gave me Julio's cell number, and now I have to go see if I can get Cade back."

I'm not even going to ask about the subtle *this time* that he just slipped in there. That would only lead us to a dark place I'm positive I don't want to go. "Are you taking Michael?"

He nods. "You're going to stay here with Lacey and your friend. Do not let either of them out of your sight."

I'm suddenly gripped by panic. I don't want him to go; every time he leaves, something freaking terrible happens and I end up being pursued by the cops. Or shot at. Or both. "We need to stick together right now, don't you think?"

"No. I don't. You're injured, Newan's an unwilling participant in all of this, and Lacey isn't right at the moment. It would be a very bad idea to take one of you, let alone all three."

I'd argue this point, irrespective of the fact I can see where he's coming from, but then Michael enters, wearing a T-shirt drenched with sweat. He left to go running straight after he ate. A bad idea in

94

my book—running on a full stomach—but he seems to have made it work.

"You ready?" he asks. It's like a wall shutters over Zeth's face; the dark, brooding anger in his eyes is almost breathtaking.

"Yeah, I'm ready. Time to teach that asshole he can't get away with taking one of ours."

I feel like pointing out Cade isn't actually "one of ours", he's one of Rebel's, but then the ingratitude of the thought hits home. Of course Cade is one of ours. He spent time in prison with Zeth, and he risked his own safety and freedom to come and help me when Charlie was at St Peter's. It's only right that the boys try and free him, but at what cost? That's what everything boils down to these days—the cost of our actions. There can be no more carefree or reckless decisions made within our group. *Our* group. I am a part of this now, and that knowledge makes me very uncomfortable.

Zeth stands, finishes the bottle of water, crushes it and tosses it in the bin. He looks to me, two distinct lines marring the skin between his brows. "I mean it, Sloane. Do *not* leave this apartment."

I nod my head, trying not to look quite as concerned as I'm feeling right now. "I know, I know. There'll be hell to pay."

Zeth smirks. "Oh no, angry girl. You'll be paying *me*. And trust me—that is far, *far* worse."

He does something then that makes my fingers and toes tingle; he leans down and plants a whisper-soft kiss on the top of my head. "We'll be back soon," he tells me. "And we'll have Cade with us."

The look on Michael's face is classic—complete surprise. I think he's as stunned as I am by his employer's show of affection. Zeth dresses quickly and the two of them leave, and the spot where Zeth kissed me on the top of my crown still burns like crazy.

PIPPA IS *STILL* refusing to come out of the bathroom. I don't want her to come out, so it's no great loss to me, but a small part of me does want her to be comfortable. And sitting on cold tiles all day and night definitely can *not* be comfortable. I'm too angry to go and talk to her, though, so I figure the next best thing is to rope Lacey into the task.

I'm about to knock on Lacey's door when it flies open to reveal the girl's pale face, eyes huge in her head as usual. She looks stricken. "Where's Zee?" she asks breathlessly.

"He's just gone to handle a few things. He won't be gone long. A couple of hours, max."

This news does not seem to please Lacey. Zeth didn't say goodbye to her, and for very good reason. She's never been good about him leaving her, but after yesterday's meltdown she probably would have flipped, not let him walk out the door. That's undoubtedly why he ran out without saying a word to her.

"I need to talk to him," she says. "It's important."

"Sorry, Lace. Honestly, though, he will be back soon."

Lacey blows out a frustrated breath, shaking her head. "You don't understand. Here, look." She holds out something to me—her chunky cellphone—and on the screen a web page is loaded. I'm surprised the thing even has data. I squint at the tiny writing, trying to read the blocks of narrow, black text, but Lacey is twitching so much it's damn near impossible.

"Give it to me." I take the phone off her and read quickly, my head spinning at the content of what turns out to be a newspaper article. The spinning grows much, much worse when I see the name *Oliver Massey*, and the emblem of St Peter's Hospital a little farther down the page.

The woman, brought into St Peter's Hospital close to two weeks ago, has still not been identified. Her condition continues to worsen. Her doctors indicate the female patient, currently on life support, is unlikely to survive another twenty-four hours. Dr. Oliver Massey, of St Peter's, believes someone must be able to identify this woman. 'It would be devastating if this woman's family members missed out on the opportunity to say goodbye because they were unaware their mother or aunt or sister was in hospital. We would ask Seattle Tribune readers to look closely at the picture of our patient and search their memory. Do they know this woman, and if so, could they assist us in reaching her next of kin?'"

Underneath the block of text there's an image of a woman, pale, long blonde hair fanned around her head like spun silk, eyes closed, clearly in a coma. I recognize the woman straightaway. During the one incredibly hectic and stressful day I spent back at work, the nurses had filled me in on the Jane Doe in room 136. She'd been brought into the hospital by an anonymous member of the public, unceremoniously abandoned, and left to die. She'd already been in a coma then; I'm almost surprised she's lasted as long as this.

"What is it, Lace? Do you know this woman?"

Lacey nods, head bobbing up and down. "She's the one who stabbed Zeth. She's Charlie's woman."

"And you think Zeth would want to see her?" That seems very backwards to me. Very backwards indeed. Lacey doesn't bother to answer me, though.

"If she's dying, then we have to see her. We *have* to. We have to go now. She might die before we get there."

I have no idea where this is coming from, but the frantic glint in Lacey's eye, coupled with the anxious tone of her voice, tells me the next words out of my mouth are going to cause some serious problems. "I'm sorry, sweetie. None of us are going anywhere until Zeth gets back."

I can practically see the thundercloud form over the tiny woman's nimbus of golden curls. She angles her head down, her chin almost touching her breastbone, and looks up at me with the most sinister look in her eyes. For a moment I don't even recognize her. "I'm going, Sloane. You can't stop me."

"The front door's locked, Lace. We are on the eighth floor. There are no fire escapes for you to bolt down. I don't need to stop you; I just won't give you the key."

"You will," she tells me. "You will or I'll take it from you."

Alarm bells, no, a freaking klaxon begins to sound inside my head. I've never seen her like this before. I've seen her sad and upset, downcast and withdrawn, but I have never seen her angry and determined. I get the feeling an angry and determined Lacey might actually be a force to be reckoned with, even though she's almost less than half my size.

"Why do *you* need to see her, Lacey? Explain it to me and maybe we can work something out."

"I just do, okay?" She snatches her cell phone away from me, holding her hands to her temples. "It's none of your damn business, Sloane. You think just 'cause my brother is fucking you that you're gonna be around long enough to witness the next big fucking disaster that sweeps through our lives, but you're *not*. You're gonna be sick of us by the end of next fucking week. You're gonna go back to live with your churchy parents. You're gonna go back to wearing twin sets and playing golf with your doctor buddies, and your little slumming session with Zeth and his fucked-up sister is gonna be over. It's gonna be me and him left to deal with all this shit. *Me and him!*" Those last words come out of her mouth as a choked sob. There's so much rage and doubt in her. The quiet, reserved Lacey I know, who climbed into my bed this morning, has vanished altogether.

"Don't you think it's time you admit that?" she asks. Her eyes are filled to brimming over with tears. "Don't you think it would be better to just walk away now before you're dragged into this any further and you feel like you have to stay because you have no other option? Because things have gotten so bad and so irreparable that you *can't* leave?"

With each word it feels like she's slapping me around the face. When I first met her I was unsure of her, unsure of her connection to Zeth and therefore cautious, but recently I've cared for her. Looked out for her. Hell, she confessed she'd murdered someone to me only a few hours ago in my bed and I did nothing but hold her and tell her everything was going to be all right. So yes, it hurts incredibly that she's speaking to me like this. It's breaking my heart.

"Where's this coming from, Lace?"

"It's coming from a land called *reality*, where we have been living while you've been up on your little hill above the city, looking down on the rest of us."

"Lacey, I'm not—I've—"

"She's never worn a twinset," comes a voice from my right. Pippa, leaning against the doorframe, arms folded across her chest. Finally she's come out of the bathroom, probably just to watch this tiny woman kick my ass. That's where things look like they're headed right now. Lacey screws up her face, scowling at Pippa.

"You're just as bad," she snaps. "You were mean about my mother, and you had no right. No right to say anything about her whatsoever."

Pippa retains that cool, calm, and collected exterior that she wears whenever she's working with someone in her office. "You're right. That was out of line. I'm sorry, Lacey. But you're attacking the wrong person here right now. Sloane's not a judgmental person, and she's not one to commit herself to something and then bail. And that's what she's done here—she's committed herself to you and Zeth. That's why I've been so worried. Because I know there's no way she'll ever walk out on you now. She won't even be dragged kicking and screaming. I should think yesterday's events with the police were proof enough of that."

Lacey doesn't back down. Not for a second. She's bordering on hysteria; I can see it staring back at me out of her troubled eyes. "You're not my family. You're *not* my family. We need to be together again. Only family can protect family. Blood is thicker than water, Sloane. You have to let me go. You have to let me."

It's pathetic but I'm beginning to take this personally now. I thought Lacey liked me. I thought she *did* think of me as family in some weird, warped way. "I'm sorry," I whisper. "I'm sure Zeth will take you to see her as soon as he can."

Lacey covers her face with her hands, sucking in deep, erratic breaths, sobbing harder now. "Not good enough. Not. Good. Enough!" Her hands fly down, and Pippa sees what's happening long before I do. Or maybe I do see it, but I just don't believe it— Lacey coming at me, her mouth pulled down in grim determination. Pippa's taller than I am, and stronger too, no doubt. I would have been able to hold my own, but Pippa practically takes Lace off her feet as she tackles her into the wall of the corridor.

"Get off me! Get the fuck off me, bitch! I'm gonna kill you!" Lacey roars. I stand there, watching them struggle, completely confounded.

"Sloane, a hand?" Pippa calls through gritted teeth. She's managed to pin both of Lacey's wrists behind her back, but the girl's putting up a valiant fight. I step into the breach, grabbing hold of Lacey's ankles. I get a kick to my injured arm and a shock wave of pain blasts through me, so sharp and potent, I gag. Pippa and I manage to carry Lacey's screaming butt into a room at the back of the apartment. It's the room I found Zeth sitting alone in the dark when I first came here. There are no windows, no other ways out of the room bar the entrance we just came through. It's sparsely furnished, too—only a bed and a small side table, along with a wardrobe and a soft sheepskin rug on the floor. Pippa and I half carry, half drag Lacey to the bed where we put her down, and then Pippa has hold of me and she's dragging *me* out of the room before Lacey can even get to her feet. The door slams closed, and Pippa is holding the handle shut.

"Do you have keys for this thing?" she grinds out.

"Uh, yeah. Yes, hang on." I run back through the apartment, snatch the keys from the countertop where Zeth left them, and hurry back. It takes me a solid minute to find the right key, during which time Lacey kicks and screams and pummels her fists against the other side of the door, demanding to be let the fuck out.

"Do you have any sedatives here?" Pippa asks.

"Do you think I'd have let you stitch me up without any proper pain relief if I had my medical bag with me?" I snap. Now that the door's locked, Pippa backs away, holding up her hands.

"Just asking. My incarceration in this ridiculously over-the-top apartment would be a whole lot more bearable without that noise going on."

She's right. It's going to be a nightmare sitting here listening to Lacey lose her mind. I stalk through the apartment, wondering if I should call Zeth back. He told me she has these breakdowns but I wasn't prepared for this. Not to this scale. Not being so abusive, and apparently out of nowhere.

"I hate to be saying this yet again, Sloane," Pippa says, following behind me. "But are you sure your new friends are the type of people you want to be associating with? I mean, with the police—"

I turn around and stab my finger into her chest, trying to breathe through my spike of anger. "Don't you even mention the police. *You* were the one who called the police."

Pippa looks like she's about to defend her actions—god help her if she does—but the sound of a ringing alarm prevents it from happening. No, not the sound of a ringing alarm. It's a ringing cell phone. Both Pip and I see it at the same time—the blocky cell phone Lacey was holding in her hand. It's on the floor, lit up, flashing and playing that infamous old school ringtone that used to drive people mad all over the world. Lacey must have dropped the phone in the struggle.

I pace over and pick it up, and Lacey goes silent—she must be able to hear the phone. On the screen, three words are blinking up at me:

The Old Man.

My stomach drops through the floor. I know who that is. I've heard Zeth call him that before.

"Sloane? Sloane, let me answer the phone!" Lacey screams from behind the door. "I need to answer that. It's for me!"

It literally feels like the insides of my head are exploding. Seriously? Seriously, *this* is who Lacey has been talking to? Part of me just can't accept or believe it. Won't. I hit the answer button and hold the handset to my ear. My blood runs cold as soon as I hear the voice.

"Knock, knock, sweetheart. You be a good girl and come and let me in, why don't you?"

13

Zeth

I HAVE TO ADMIT, I WAS AS SURPRISED AS SLOANE I DIDN'T get my hands bloody this morning. Andreas *did* give up Julio's cell number without a fight; a brief conversation about loyalty—he still insists they know Charlie and I are working together—and one look at those fucking paperclips and Andreas Medina was an open book. He told me Julio and his boys were out somewhere near Mount Rainier, but he couldn't give me a specific address because they're moving around. Fucker better not have been lying.

Michael and I are almost at Mount Rainier, when I finally get through on the cell number Medina gave me. The line rings three times before someone picks up. *"¿Hola?"*

Definitely the right number.

"Hola," I reply. *"Quiero hablar con el jefe, por favor."* Hi, I wanna *speak to the boss, please.* I put just enough pep into my voice to sound like a cheerful Mexican telesales operative. I don't normally do pep; my teeth feel itchy.

"Who is this?" the person on the other end of the line asks in a thick accent.

"It's Zeth motherfucking Mayfair, bitch. Now put Julio on the phone." There we go; that's more my speed. The person on the other end of the line responds by swearing in Spanish. There's muted chatter in the background and he's there, the man himself, talking live and direct right into my right ear.

"Zeth, my friend. So good to hear from you. I trust you are well?"

"Never better," I clip out. It's started to rain. The windshield wipers in Michael's sedan automatically begin to sweep across the windshield, blurring the lights of the other cars into long streaks of white and red as they pass us by. "I believe we have a small matter to discuss," I say.

"Oh? And what might that be?" There's a layer of cordiality to Julio's voice, but I can hear the violence beneath it. Men like him smile and say polite things while plotting all the ways in which they plan on fucking killing you. I know this all too well.

"The fact you've taken a friend of mine. The fact I've taken a friend of yours."

Julio gives me a half-amused laugh. "I'm afraid I have no idea what you're talking about, Zeth. I have a missing member of a motorcycle club staying with me at the moment. His boss is on his way over here to retrieve him. As far as people on my end..." He sniffs, pauses for effect. "It seems as though everyone is accounted for over here."

Andreas is missing and he knows it; he's just trying to be a smart motherfucker, make me believe he doesn't care about his guy when I know all too well that he does. Andreas is a fucking liability. He's hot-headed and reckless. Most people in Julio's position would have killed him a long time ago, which means the gang lord must have a soft spot for him. I wouldn't be surprised if Medina is related to him in some way. So how to play this? How to play this the right way? And why would Julio pick Cade up if he were planning on handing him straight over to Rebel? It makes no sense.

"Fine," I say. "So Rebel comes for Cade, and I dispose of my house guest. *Permanently.* You're happy that this is how shit is gonna go down?"

There's another pause on the other end of the line—I can imagine the expression on Julio's face, mouth pulled down in a pout of nonchalance, shoulders shrugged up around his ears. I can almost *hear* the fucking bravado. "Whatever, man. You do what you gotta do."

I grunt, nodding my head. I'm thinking. Thinking hard about what the hell our next move should be when Julio speaks again. "You should know you've made me very unhappy, *ese*. No, I'm not very happy with you at all."

"I can see why you might feel that way," I concede. "If it's any consolation, it was nothing personal. It was a favor for a friend."

There's a rhythmic snapping sound down the phone—Julio tutting. "I don't give a shit about the girl, *ese*," he says. "I give a shit about you deceiving me in my own house. About you spying for Charlie."

It's one thing to hear it coming from Andreas—the guy is paranoid as fuck—but now Julio thinks I came to the compound to do Charlie's bidding? "I said I was there for the girl. I wasn't there for Charlie, asshole. The motherfucker's been trying to kill me for the past few weeks."

"Ha!" Julio's loud blast of laughter almost deafens me. "So why the fuck did he come burning up here as soon as my guys told him you were here, huh? Why did he show up at my door only six hours after you left, when my home was in ruins, and pay me an obscene amount of money to not come after you? Why did he sign over his drugs business to me to settle the debt you owed, when your friends blew up my villa?"

"*What?*"

"He may have bought your life for you, Zee, but let me tell you this. If you come creepin' up on me again, no amount of money in the world will save you."

Still focusing on the road ahead of us as he drives, Micheal's eyes widen; he must be able to hear Julio. I try to comprehend what the guy is saying to me, but yet again it makes no fucking sense. I can't remember the last time anything did make sense, but this? This is just off the charts fucking bizarre. Charlie paid Julio to keep him off my back?

"Why would he do that?" I ask. I feel stupid. I feel like the guy who's missing some vital, crucial piece of information everyone else is in fucking possession of but I am not.

Julio gives me that laugh again—that arrogant, *fuck you* laugh. "It's the same deal world over, my friend. It's all well and good wanting to kill your family members when they've done something to piss you off. But if someone else comes along and fucks with them...that's a whole different story."

Man, this guy just doesn't seem to fucking listen. "I told you then and I'll tell you now, asshole, I'm not part of Charlie's family anymore. I left. I quit. I fucking walked away."

The quiet that stretches out seems to last a lifetime. This isn't getting us anywhere. I need to get off the phone so I can call Rebel and find out what the hell's going on. I need to—

"Oh, come now, Zee. Even you should know this. You can never walk away from a man like Charlie Holsan," Julio chides. "You might try and walk away from his organization. You probably wouldn't live to tell the tale, but still you could try. You, on the other hand...he'll never let *you* walk away from *him*."

"And why's that?" I snap.

"Because with a man like Charlie Holsan, you can never turn your back on blood."

14

Sloane

I HANG UP THE PHONE, MY HEART IN MY MOUTH. IT immediately starts ringing again. "You're sure it's him?" Pippa asks. She's asked me this three times already, and I'm starting to get pissed off.

"Yes! Yes, it's him. What the hell am I supposed to do?"

Pippa just gives me a pitying look—she doesn't understand my panic. Doesn't feel the full weight of it pressing down on her like it's currently pressing down on me.

"Here," she says, holding out her hand. "Give it to me."

She wants the cell phone, and frankly I'm very keen to get rid of it. I slap the thing into her hand and cover my mouth with my fingertips, watching her to see what she'll do next. The very *last* thing I expect her to do is to answer the damn call.

"Dr. Pippa Newan," she says calmly. Pippa's face remains controlled, although her eyebrows twitch ever so slightly. I don't know what that means, whether it means anything at all. I just wait, holding my breath.

"I don't think that would be a good idea," she says calmly. She frowns some more. My heart clatters in my chest like a pair of castanets. She looks at me, eyes filled with sudden surprise. "There really is no need for that kind of language," she says. "We are well within our rights to deny you access —"

There's a sharp thud at the door, not from the top, as though someone has knocked, but from the bottom as though they've kicked instead. Through the three-inch thick solid wood door, a very bemused voice calls out. "I think you're getting confused, sweetheart. This ain't a fucking traveling door-to-door salesman. This ain't *optional*. Now open the fucking door."

Pippa drops the phone from her ear, turning the thing to look at the screen. She blinks at it. "He hung up on me." She turns her back to me then, a look of mild panic forming on her face—the gravity of the situation finally appears to be hitting her. "I don't think he's going to leave."

"No kidding." I hurry over to the counter where my bag is sitting—even through the panic back at Pippa's, Michael had the foresight to shove the thing at me so I didn't leave it behind—and I scramble through the items inside until I come across my own cell phone. I dial Zeth, my hands shaking as I hit the call button.

'The number you have called is currently busy. Please hang up and try again later.'

Currently busy? Zeth's on the phone. Typical. He's picked *now* to get a freaking social life? Who the hell could he be talking to? He's already with Michael, the only person who ever seems to call him. I hang up and then immediately dial Michael. His phone isn't busy, but it still doesn't get picked up. "Fuck!" A text message is the next best thing, though not ideal at all.

Me:
Get bk here! Now!

A series of heavy bangs rain down on the front door. "Might as well just let me in, Dr Pippa Newan. Me and my boys ain't goin' nowhere. It would save an awful lot of time and a rather well-made door if you just do what I fuckin' tell you to."

There's no way we are opening the door. No way in hell. I cast an eye over the apartment, searching for something appropriately heavy; the sofa that I bled all over last night's probably the most suitable option for what I have in mind. I hurry over and start pushing the thing, leaning my full weight against its considerable size. My shoulder is killing me; I feel sick, like I might pass out again. The wound I received yesterday was nowhere near as bad as it could have been, but it still ran fairly deep. The last thing I should be doing is trying to lift heavy furniture, but it doesn't look like I have much of a choice.

"Don't just stand there staring at me. Get over here!" I shout at Pippa. Her gawking isn't helping anybody. In fact, her stunned inaction is enough to make me want to slap her all over again. She flusters, but then hurries to the other end of the couch, lifting it with me. Between the two of us we can barely get the thing an inch off the ground—it's one of those seriously weighty pieces of furniture with scrolled wooden armrests—but it's enough to awkwardly shuffle it toward the door.

"He's not going to hurt you!" Lacey screams from the other end of the apartment. "He's come for me. Let me out and I'll go with him. He won't touch you, I swear!"

The ferocity of the next series of impacts on the door suggest otherwise; the violence behind them suggests the person on the other side is not a patient, calm or reasonable person. It suggests that when the person on the other side has finally beaten their way through, they're going to keep on hitting things. And, yeah, I really don't want to be one of those things.

I ignore Lacey and address the man on the other side of the

door; I address *Charlie*. "Zeth's on his way here, asshole. I wouldn't want to be here when he gets back!"

There's laughter through the door. "You mean the master of the house ain't at 'ome right now? Well ain't that just peachy. I wouldn't 'ave thought he'd leave his girls unprotected. That don't sound like 'im at all. And I so was 'oping to 'ave a little chat with 'im."

Crap. It's likely Charlie suspected Zeth wasn't here—admittedly, Zeth would have been at the door and shooting everyone in the head at the first sign of trouble—but I've just gone and confirmed it for him. Perfect.

"Just let him inside, Sloane. This is none of your business!" Lacey yells.

But it is my business. This is the guy who sent two men around to my house and tried to kidnap Lacey, who tried to run me off the road and nearly got me killed, who murdered an innocent girl, poisoned her, for no other purpose than to get Zeth's attention, with the lovely added bonus of ruining my fucking life. Even if I did have a guarantee he wouldn't hurt either Pip or me, which I'm pretty sure he will, I would never let Lacey go with him. Something's obviously happened here that I'm unaware of to make Lacey think it's safe to be with Charlie, but there's no doubt about it—she's not going anywhere. Not if I have anything to say about it. I head to the open plan kitchen, pull open a drawer and take out the largest knife I can find. I give it straight to Pip.

"If they come through, use this. Don't hesitate."

Pippa's eyes are as big as saucers. "You can't be serious. There's no way I'm stabbing anybody."

"How about if they're trying to kill you? How would you feel about stabbing them then?"

"Well, I suppose—"

"Then get ready." I walk away, hurrying through the apartment. I head straight for the room opposite Lacey's—the one I know belongs to Michael. Inside everything is immaculate, just as I would expect it to be with a man like him. I'd hoped to find some sort of weapons stash under the bed or something, but all I find are a pair of Armani slippers. No guns. No flamethrowers. No ninja stars. What kind of right-hand man is this guy?

I do spot a baseball bat on the wall, though. It's mounted on a stand and looks like a player has signed it. It probably isn't something Michael would appreciate being used to cave someone's head in but it's going to have to do. I snatch it off the stand and head back out into the hallway. I cross straight over to the room where Lacey is still going crazy, hammering on the door, demanding to be let out.

"I don't get it, Lace. You're gonna have to help me out here. Why do you suddenly want to go with Charlie? What's he told you?"

She goes quiet, although I can hear her stuttering breaths; she's crying. "He's told me the truth," she whispers. "All this time, all these years I thought Zeth was the only one I had. The only one who cared about me, even if he didn't know I was his sister. But I was wrong. I had Charlie. I had...I had *my dad*."

My dad.

There have been no words ever spoken in the English language that have shocked me more than these. I almost drop the baseball bat. "Lace, I don't think—I think you're mistaken. I don't think —"

"He *is*! He's my father. It's the truth, I know it is."

"When did he tell you this?"

"About an hour ago. The cell phone Zeth gave me...Charlie messaged it yesterday morning. He thought I was Zeth. He said he knew where I was. As soon as he found out who I was, he told me the truth. He told me that was why he tried to take me from your place. Those men, they weren't going to hurt me, Sloane. Charlie just wanted me to be safe. He wants me to be with him."

Lacey's been glued to that phone for the past two days. Two fucking days that Charlie Holsan has been filling Lacey's head with lies. He must have a good read on people, or at least he must have studied Lacey in some way to know how important family is to her. He's taken the one thing that can flip her switches and turn her crazy and he's used them against her.

"He's lying to you, babe. I promise you he is. He'd say anything to get to Zeth. He almost killed me, remember? He tried to drive me off the road."

There's silence at that. A thick silence, punctuated only by the sounds of one of the most dangerous criminals in Seattle trying to force his way inside the apartment. Lacey doesn't say a word. She knows I'm right; she knows it deep down, and yet I know she's not hearing me. I know *her*. She's lost in this wonderful idea that she has a father. A real, biological father, who can take care of her and make everything right in her world again.

"Lacey, your father was killed in a car accident. He's been dead for twenty-six years."

"That man *wasn't* my father. He was one of Charlie's men. He *stole* me."

Oh, boy. There's no way I can argue this out with her now. With a mind as sensitive to suggestion as Lacey's, I'll never be able to convince her she's been fooled. Especially since she *wants* to believe this fallacy.

"Sloane? Sloane! Get through here," Pippa shouts. Her voice is three octaves higher than usual and shaky. I'll have to deal with Lacey later. I run down the hallway, baseball bat gripped in two hands, only to find—

"Oh, *shit!*"

The door is off its hinges at the top left of the frame, and the paneled wood is splintering apart under the force of the kicks smashing into it. "You're gonna be sorry you didn't save my boys the time and energy, here," Charlie tells us, and this time his voice is worryingly clear. We have seconds before they're through.

My cell phone starts ringing.

My heart is hammering.

Pippa looks like she's about to throw up. I feel as though *I'm* about to throw up.

"Stand there. Stay there. Don't move," I whisper, pointing at the spot on the ground right in front of the door where she's already standing. She gives me a single, terrified nod of her head. I slip around the side of the door, twisting the bat over and over in my hands, waiting.

This is so clichéd; I almost want to laugh. I *would* laugh, except for the fact that I'm shitting myself. I'm hiding behind a door, getting ready to smash a baseball bat into an intruder's face. They're bound to see this coming, surely?

And then it happens. Except it's not like in the movies, where the door explodes from its hinges and the furniture flies out of the way. The door buckles and cracks open, creating a foot-wide gap, and then an arm, shoulder, and half the torso appear inside the gap and all I can think of is Jack Nicholson in The Shining, grinning at us and announcing, *here's Johnny.*

Well *here's Sloane, motherfucker.* I don't hesitate; I forget about the whole leaping out from behind the door bit and instead bring the bat swinging down onto the shoulder of the man who is trying to shove the sofa out of the way. The wood connects with a satisfying crack, and the doctor in me immediately begins making calculations. Dislocation? Shattered joint? From the agonized cry that comes from the other side of the door, the chances are reasonably high that I've done some serious damage.

"Ahhhh! Fucking bitch just hit me," a voice cries. I lash out and hit the guy again, this time in the arm. "Fuck!" The arm attached to the man on the other side falls limp and dangles loosely as he tries to pull himself back through to safety. I'm feeling a little proud of myself when the guy's body vanishes and suddenly I'm staring into the face of a grey-haired, attractive guy in his fifties, with a glint of insanity lurking in his irises. I know this face. The cops passed a photo of Charlie around the hospital—he looked normal. Unassuming—when Archie Monterello was shot, but seeing the man in the flesh is entirely different. Way more intimidating.

A labored silence follows where the man grins broadly at me, quick eyes giving me an amused once over. The sound of my continually ringing cell phone serves to make the moment even tenser. The man takes a step forward and places the muzzle of a large, heavy handgun through the gap in the wood. His grin expands even further, displaying a wall of perfectly straight, perfectly white teeth.

"Well hello, Princess. Don't you think you ought to get that?"

15

Zeth

JULIO DOESN'T EXPAND ON HIS BIZARRE COMMENT. HE hangs up and I make a quick phone call to Rebel, but the words are lingering throughout the conversation I have with the president of the Widow Makers MC.

Rebel answers quickly and efficiently, already well aware of who is calling him. "Well, isn't this a pleasant surprise?"

"I'm sure it's not fucking surprising at all," I reply. *He'll never let you walk away from him.*

"Okay, maybe not. But I *am* honored that you've deigned me worthy of contact now, given I've been trying to reach you and your lovely girlfriend for some time. What can I do for you?"

Because with a man like Charlie Holsan, you can never turn your back on blood. "Sloane's business with her sister is exactly that— hers. If she hasn't been very receptive in responding to you or your wife, then maybe Alexis shouldn't have cut her out of her life and left her to worry for two fucking years."

Rebel makes a grunting sound on the other end of the line. "Not our fight to have, brother. This one's on the girls, but you know things are never as simple as they seem. Take this situation with my boy for example. Our Mexican friend has taken Cade and is telling me he'll only let him go if I'm present to collect him. Now, why do you think that might be?"

So he does already know about Cade. As for his question, there's only one reason I can think of and that's a glaringly obvious one. "Because he's planning on killing you and he needs to know where you're going to be."

"Exactly what I figured. So here I am, on my way to pick up my boy, knowing Julio's planning on shooting me in the face. Now why do you think *that* is?"

"Because Cade's your boy. And you have something on Julio. You must have for him to be so careful around you. Fuck, I hear you have something on everyone."

Rebel laughs again, his breath crackling down the line. "You might just be right, brother. It's always advantageous to have a few interesting pieces of information up your sleeve at all times, especially when dealing with people like these. With people like *you*."

If that's Rebel's idea of a subtle way to let me know he has information on me, he needs to work on his delivery. "Whatever, man. You have this Julio thing fucking handled or what? 'Cause I have other places I can be. I just wanted to make sure Cade was safe."

"You can rest easy. Cade'll be fine, and so will I. Information isn't the only thing that I have on Julio Perez. I've had a gun trained on his back for the last three years. It's a good idea to plant a guy every once in awhile. An inside man, if you will."

This guy seems to have everything worked out. It's almost a relief; Rebel will take care of his VP, and I can go back to the apartment and have a conversation with Sloane. She needs to leave town for a while. She's not gonna like it, not one bit, but it's the only solution I can think of where she'll be safe while I deal with the Charlie situation.

The fucking Charlie situation. *You can never walk away from a man like Charlie Holsan. You can never turn your back on blood.*

I inhale sharply, trying to push that thought out of my head. There's no way Charlie is blood to me. No fucking way in hell. I would know. After all the years of working for him, living with him, doing exactly what he asks, I would fucking know if he was related to me. It's just not possible. "When everything is squared away with the Mexicans, come by my apartment. I trust you know where that is?"

"I may. Any chance you feel like telling me why?"

"I have something I need you to take back to New Mexico with you."

Rebel's a smart guy; he knows what I'm talking about straight away. "Right. And is this package going to be screaming and punching me in the back of the head across numerous state lines?"

My turn to laugh now. "Will that be a problem?"

"Not at all. Can't say I'm not used to it. As soon as I've spoken to Medina and dealt with Julio, I'll be there."

My breath freezes in my lungs. "Medina?"

"Yeah, Medina. He's my man inside. You've met the guy, right? Arrogant motherfucker. Owed me a debt. He'll let me know what Julio has planned before I even step foot into that meeting."

Oh. Holy. Shit.

Well, this is just fucking perfect. Seriously, absolutely, typically motherfucking perfect. What were the chances? What were the chances it would have to be Medina? I grind my teeth together, cursing my luck. "Actually, we may have a problem after all. Andreas Medina is currently tied up in my basement."

The line goes quiet. And then, "*Why* is he currently tied up in your basement?"

"The fucker tried to kill me. Good enough for you?"

More silence. Michael gives me a raised eyebrow—*what's going on?* I wait for Rebel to think on this for a moment, and then I say, "Maybe you'd better come to my apartment first instead."

There's a quiet, controlled way that Rebel speaks; it's the same way I speak when I'm trying my hardest not to lose my shit. "Seems as though you're right. I'll be there shortly."

I hit *end call* before he can say anything else. Michael spins the car around without me even asking; he probably heard most of that. "How the hell are all these people so interlinked?" he says on an exhale. I'd love to be able to give him an answer. I'd love to know why every one of these fuckers is so far up in each other's business, but I honestly have no clue. It's as though Lady Fate is in a serious mood to fuck with me.

"Let's just get back there, Michael. Quickly."

Michael hits the gas pedal—he seriously should have had a career in NASCAR—and we're speeding through the night, back toward the apartment. The corner of his mouth is twitching, and I know he's dying to say something. The fact he's holding it in tells me that it's probably something I won't want to hear.

"Spit it out, man. Things are about to get crazy here. If you have something to say, then say it."

"Okay, fine. Have you spoken to Sloane about sending her to New Mexico? She is *not* going to like that idea."

I give him The Look. "What do *you* think?"

"Yeah. Well, if my cousin's on his way here and you intend on sending her away with him, I would think a heads up would be in order. Don't just spring it on her, boss. It'll end very badly." Again with the taking liberties. No one else in the world would dare give me advice on anything, let alone how to handle a girl. A woman. *My* woman. Michael gets away with it most days, but he's walking a fine fucking line.

"I got it handled. You don't need to worry yourself over how Sloane's going to react to anything. If she's got any sense whatsoever, then she'll go without causing a fuss."

Michael pulls a cautious face. "No offense, Zee, but I think her feelings for you might outweigh any sense she may or may not have."

We are bordering on dangerous territory here. Michael and I never discuss anything so trivial as *feelings*. If we did, I might be inclined to tell him how fucked my head is right now. I'm trying to concentrate, trying to figure out how the shit with Julio, Cade and Rebel is gonna work out, how the hell I'm going to get Sloane to agree to leave Seattle without me, but I can't. All I'm thinking about is what Julio said. My brain is working overtime, so many cogs turning at once, and yet those words just keep on pushing their way to the forefront of my mind.

You can never turn your back on blood.

You can never turn your back on blood.

You can never turn your back on blood.

I know it's not possible, but there's this swelling knot of dread sitting like a lead weight in the pit of my stomach. Is there—is there any way it could be *true*? Fuck. I can't. I just can't do this right now. Michael's right—I need to speak to Sloane, and soon. Sounds like Rebel will be right with us, and she really *will* lose her head if I don't give her some notice.

I haven't stored any numbers in my current burner, though. There's a real risk I could lose it or it could fall into the wrong hands, and I don't want to give Charlie or the DEA direct access to anyone I care about. "Give me your phone," I growl at Michael. "I need Sloane's number."

He reaches into the inside pocket of his suit and slides it out, handing it over to me and doing a pretty damn good job of not looking smug. I know the bastard, though. He's definitely fucking smug. I looked down at the phone and—

What the fuck?

3 missed calls
- The Doc

I turn the phone on its side and sure enough the fucking button is flicked across, showing an orange indicator. It's on silent. Michael sees what I'm doing and swears under his breath. "What? What is it?"

I'm already calling her back, pressing the phone to my ear, my heart jack hammering away in my chest. "Your phone was on fucking silent, man. Sloane's been trying to reach us." He swears again, and I swear—she's not picking up the phone. I hang up and try again, clenching and unclenching my hand into a fist.

"Come on, come on, come on."

Nothing.

If it's at all possible, Michael drives even faster. "I'm sorry, Zee, I never put it on silent, I swear." I know he's telling the truth—he never would have, knowing the girls might need us—but right now I'm not feeling very gracious. I'm feeling like I'm being pushed toward the edge of a very steep cliff and I'm doing everything in my power to prevent myself from falling over the edge. I give him a tight glance out of the corner of my eye, waiting. Waiting for the sound of the *ring, ring*ing in my ear to turn into Sloane Romera's beautiful fucking voice.

It just keeps on ringing.

Part of me is being sensible, reminding me she could have wanted anything. There are a million reasons why she could have called Michael, but the rest of me knows better. That's not how things in my world work. It's always been the most dire outcome; the most serious result; the most dangerous consequence.

"Should we call Rebel back? He might get there before—"

"He'd better *not* get there before us. It had better not take us more than another few minutes to get back to that girl, otherwise I'm going to start breaking things," I tell him. I'm fighting hard right now. I'm battling not to get seriously fucking mad at him—accidents happen, the buttons on cell phones get knocked onto silent mode all the time—but it's proving very difficult. I suck in a deep breath, blow it back out again. "Look, it's fine. I'm sure she just wanted to tell—" The ringing suddenly stops; I hear the click of the line connecting.

"Zeth, where the hell are you?" Sloane's voice sounds stressed and angry, but it's still a relief to hear. "You need to get back here *right now.*"

"I'm coming. What's happened, Sloane?"

There's a pause, and then my worst fears are confirmed. "You have a visitor. Your former employer has broken down the door and is now demanding that Lacey goes with him."

This can't be fucking happening. "*What?* Why does he want to take Lace?"

"You do not want to know. He—" There's a scuffling sound, scraping, shouting, a high-pitched scream—not Sloane's—and the muffled sounds of a cell phone being fumbled.

"Hello, son. I 'ear you're having a bit of trouble getting hold of your Mrs. I have to say, seeing her close up like this, I can understand what all the fuss is about now."

My blood is boiling in my veins. "Stay the fuck away from her, Charlie. I mean it."

"Oh, come on now." He sounds almost offended. "What, don't ya think it's about time I met your beautiful girlfriend? Honestly, I'm nowhere near as bad as you've made me out to be in your 'ead, son."

That's fucking laughable. "Charlie, I used to kill people for a living and even I think you're evil incarnate, now *get the fuck away from her.*"

"Alright, alright. I can sense there's going to be drama here. I know 'ow sensitive you can be."

There's talking in the background. Women talking and someone raising their voice. It sounds like Lacey. "If I come back there and you've hurt a hair on either one of their heads, I will skin you alive. That's a promise. I'll skin you alive, and I'll fucking enjoy it, motherfucker."

Charlie tuts. "That's a very nasty name," he says. "Though I can't say it's totally undeserved. You don't have a thing to worry about, though, my boy, I promise you. The Duchess is coming off life support. She's gonna die today. I've sworn off all killing, maiming and actual bodily harm for the next twenty-four hours in 'er honor."

So the Duchess is finally on the outs. That's hardly a surprise. However, if that's the case, what the hell is Charlie playing at? He should be with her. "Why are you at that apartment, Charlie? Charlie? *Charlie!*"

The line is dead. Charlie's gone, and he's at the apartment with the only two people in the world who mean anything to me. I suddenly feel vicious, like I want to soak my hands in blood. The blood of absolutely anyone who thinks twice about coming between those girls and me. I throw the phone into the foot well between my feet and press my fingertips into my forehead. This is fucked. This is so, so fucked.

"Get me to that apartment right now, Michael. Run every red. Break every speed limit. Get me to that fucking apartment."

Sloane

CHARLIE HOLSAN IS A FUCKING PIG. I'VE NEVER THOUGHT ILL of anybody so badly that I've wanted to see them suffer. It's sick to admit this, but I don't even hate the guys who took my sister as much as I hate this man. I despise him all the more right now because he has let Lacey out of her room and is currently walking out of the front door with her.

I feel so pathetic; there's nothing I can do to stop them from leaving. My wrists are locked behind my back, tied together, burning like crazy. "Lacey, please don't do this." I've been trying to appeal to her common sense, but it seems to have fled her entirely. She's looking up to this guy like he's the freaking Dalai Lama, not the murderous, vile piece of scum that he is. Charlie's got his two asshole henchmen—the same ones who I dealt with back at my place what seems like forever ago—standing in between Lace and me, blocking my path. One of them is clutching his right arm with a look of violence in his eyes—directed at me, of course.

"You heard me, princess," Charlie says to me, his arm falling over Lacey's shoulders. "The woman who has stood by me for the past thirty years is about to die. I'm filled wiv very benevolent, sad feelings right now. But don't fuckin' push me, girl. Just because you're whoring yourself out to Zeth don't mean much to me."

Lacey's eyes are filled with tears. She's reverted to the calm, quiet girl I've gotten to know. I can't believe how she changed so drastically. "I'm sorry, Sloane. I didn't mean what I said," she whispers. "I'm just—I've never had parents before. Can you tell Zeth I'm sorry, too?"

I'm at a loss for words. I literally can't think of another thing to say to her that will make her change her mind. I've tried everything. It's Pippa, wrists tied behind her back on the floor in the corner of the room, who tries to talk her around.

"Lacey, remember how we talked about this in your last session? I told you I thought your relationship with your brother was a little unhealthy. We discussed how you had transformed him into a father figure because you so desperately needed that person in your life? This man is taking advantage of your need for a father figure. Do you really think he's going to take care of you? He's a horrible person. Stay here with your brother and with Sloane. They're the ones who really care about you."

After being so severely let down by Pip, this statement goes a very small way toward me forgiving her. Not even close to all the way, but a step closer. Even she can see it's not in the fragile girl's interests to be taken away by a homicidal maniac. Charlie's gone beet red, though; it appears he doesn't appreciate her butting in as much as I do.

"I'd take care of what was falling out of my mouth if I were you, sunshine. Irrespective of whatever bullshit you've been filling my daughter's head wiv, she *is* my daughter and I *will* be taking her with me."

"How can she be your daughter, Charlie?" I snap. "You said it yourself—you're going to see the woman who stood beside you for the past thirty years. Lacey and Zeth's mother died in a car accident."

Charlie just shrugs at me. "My Duchess *is* Lacey's mother. The bitch that stole my kids away from me was just some whore one of my boys was screwing. She wanted children, couldn't 'ave any of her own, so she took mine. I couldn't 'ave that."

He couldn't have that? That sounds particularly ominous. And this new piece of information certainly explains a lot—why Lacey went crazy earlier, screaming about going to see the Duchess. He's told her she's her mother, and poor Lace is just about broken enough to believe it. I'm about to ask him how the hell he can be trying to pass off something so blatantly untrue as gospel, but Charlie's had enough. He bends down and shoves his face into mine. "When he gets home, you tell Zeth that I'm very disappointed in 'im. He's been very disrespectful toward me. Most fathers wouldn't tolerate that kind of behavior. Lacey's been a good girl, though, haven't you, sweetheart?" He casts a look over his shoulder at Lace, who beams back at him like he just made her entire year. "She's asked me not to hurt him. Because she's been such a good girl, I'm going to let Zeth come home. His place within this family is still available to him, if he can agree never to question me ever a-fucking-gain." He leans forward, grabs hold of my face with one hand, fingers digging into my cheeks, and he kisses me squarely on the mouth. I purse my lips together, fighting against it, but he presses down even harder, forcing my mouth open. I practically gag when he shoves his tongue into my mouth. I taste blood—he's split one of my lips. Too late, I think of biting his fucking tongue off, but Charlie's already let me go and is standing up.

"You know, back in medieval times in England, it used to be that the lord who presided over an area could fuck any girl he wanted on their wedding night. Or whenever he wanted to really. And that included the cunts their sons were sleeping with. Lucky for you, I have somewhere I need to be, princess, 'cause I'm pretty sure I could fuck you 'til you begged me to stop."

My stomach is rolling; I think I am literally going to throw up. I spit on the floor, trying to rid myself of the taste of him. I'm not surprised when I see the blood in my saliva. "How about you do me a favor? How about you don't even fucking *imagine* touching me. I feel dirty enough already as it is. Zeth's going to kill you, you realize. And if he doesn't, *I will*."

I've never threatened to harm anyone before, but I mean this. I really do. I probably couldn't do it if it came down to it, but right now I want to do him some serious damage.

Charlie gives me a pitying look. "Oh, princess. You think he's gonna kill me and risk hurting his sister so badly? I don't think so."

He points at Lacey, but his point falls a little flat; she's not looking quite so adoringly at him anymore. Her forehead is creased into worried lines. She just watched the bastard try to choke me with his tongue and threaten to fuck me right in front of her. Even I can see his halo has momentarily slipped in her eyes. It doesn't seem to faze Charlie, though. He turns to his thugs.

"Come on. Time we get out of 'ere."

He exits first, followed by the two men who herd Lacey out between their bodies like they're afraid she might bolt. She leans back, her eyes locked on mine over her shoulder, suddenly looking a little anxious. "I'm sorry, Sloane. I'm really sorry."

And then all four of them are gone.

Holy fucking crap.

TWENTY MINUTES LATER, Zeth's shouts are ringing up the stairwell outside the apartment. The door is still hanging off its frame in long, shattered splinters and both Pippa and I, despite some joint-wrenching efforts to resolve the issue, are still tied up like complete morons.

Zeth barrels through the door, alone, chest heaving, and simply looks at us. "What the...?" He appears to be lost for words. He hurries to me first and cuts through the zip tie that's locking my wrists together with the knife I gave Pippa to defend herself with. Fat lot of good it did her. She dropped it as soon as Charlie's boys broke through the door. I would never have expected it from him, but Zeth pulls me into his arms, holding me tightly to his chest. I'm so shocked I can barely breathe. The fear and anxiety from the past hour by no means vanishes, but it definitely wanes a little. I suddenly feel very, very safe. I can hear Zeth's heartbeat slamming in his chest; he's freaking out big time.

"Where's Lacey?" he rumbles.

I've been dreading this bit. Absolutely dreading it. How the hell can I tell him all of this in one go? It's too much. He's going to lose his mind. "She's—gone," I mumble into his T-shirt. "Charlie took her."

Zeth pulls back. hands on the tops of my shoulders, avoiding my wounded arm, which is absolutely killing me. Having my wrists tied behind my back hasn't done much to help the healing process. "He did *what?*" he says.

"He took her with him. We can get her back, though. He's going to the hospital to see the Duchess."

I think this is what it would be like waiting for a nuclear bomb to go off. Zeth's whole body starts to tremble; his arms are locked rigid by his side, and I can tell it's coming any second now. He's going to go supernova.

"Whoa, looks like I missed the party. Am I too late to join in the fun?" a voice asks behind me. The words may be joking, but the tone is far from it. I know the voice and I can't believe, on top of everything else that's going on, that this is happening, too.

I turn around and there he is, like some freaking walking tattooed Hugo Boss advert. I spin back to Zeth. "Really? *Really?* You brought *Rebel?*"

"He came for Cade," Zeth snaps. He still looks like he's about to light up the Seattle skyline, but I think we're at DEFCON 2 instead of 1 now; Rebel's arrival appears to have forced him to get a grip.

My brother-in-law steps over the shattered door, giving Pippa a curious glance. "You seem to have a thing for keeping people tied up in your apartment," he says to Zeth.

"Another minor setback," Zeth replies. "I'm not gonna be able to help you with Cade. I have to go get my sister back."

My stomach lurches. He said it; he used the word. *Sister.* She must have told him. He must have figured it out. But how? I'm too stunned to say anything, and by the look of her open mouth, so is Pippa. Rebel, on the other hand, doesn't have the same problem. "You're the one that's fucked up my game plan with Julio, buddy. You removed my one chess piece from the game. That means it's on you to help me get my boy back."

I have no idea what Rebel's talking about. Zeth scowls at him— he's about three seconds from smashing this place to pieces and Rebel laying it on thick isn't helping. I need to calm him down or there's going to be some serious fireworks. I walk up to Zeth and I place my hands on his chest. I've found that before with patients— even the smallest physical contact with another person can bring their panic or anger down a good three notches. "It's going to be fine. We're going to get both of them back. Don't worry."

He looks down at me and it's like the focus of his eyes sharpens, as though the blinding wrath that overcame him has cleared a little and he's noticing me for the first time. His eyes narrow, and I realize what he's looking at. His right hand comes up to my face, his fingertips touching my split lower lip.

"What happened to your face, Sloane?" And then, whispering, "What the fuck happened to your mouth?"

This is going to be bad. This is going to be really bad. I don't really want to tell him, but he has to know. "Charlie did it."

"Charlie did it how?" Zeth's head tips to one side, his frown growing deeper. "He hit you?"

I'm about to say yes—I feel disgusting enough as it is without telling Zeth what Charlie did—but Pippa beats me to it. "He kissed her. He forced his disgusting tongue into her mouth and I had to watch while he did it, the sick fuck. Now can someone please untie me?"

The whole room goes deadly silent. Zeth just stares at my lip, his body shaking, and I feel even more violated than I already did. Zeth looks horrified. Oh my god, he thinks I'm tainted now. He thinks I'm freaking soiled or something. I suck my bottom lip into my mouth, trying to hide the evidence. He flinches, staggering back three paces. That's when Michael shows up. He's breathless, panting, his suit jacket missing.

"Where did they go?"

"The hospital," Pippa says softly. From the expression on her face, she's realizing what she's done by opening her big mouth just now. Zeth backs away from me another few paces. He looks numb; he reaches into his pocket and tosses a set of keys to Michael.

"The car I stole the other night is still in the basement. Get rid of it. Take Rebel and fetch Medina. Go help him get Cade back."

"What are you—"

"Just do it."

Michael doesn't question him again. Rebel gives Zeth a steely look and follows his cousin out of the room. I feel like a hole has been punched through my chest and Zeth's staring directly through me to the floor on the other side. I take a step forward but he holds up a hand.

"I just—I just need a minute," he says, his voice oddly flat. He puts down the knife he's holding, turns around and walks slowly down the length of the corridor away from me.

"Sorry," Pippa says. "I really didn't mean to cause more problems." I pick up the knife and storm over to her, non-too-gently freeing her from her zip tie. "It's okay, it's not your fault. You only told the truth."

If that's true, then why do you feel like utter shit right now? the Pippa voice inside my head asks. It's just rude that I have to deal with that voice when I also have to deal with the real person looking up at me disapprovingly. "If you're about to give me a lecture on walking away from all of this right now, please just keep it to yourself," I snap.

"Actually, I was going to ask you what the hell you were doing standing there staring at me when you should be with him?" she says.

"What?" There's no way I just heard her right. Absolutely no way.

She sighs, struggling to her feet. "He needs you. I've seen plenty of people shut down like that, and I'm telling you...he really needs you right now. I may not like it, but it's the truth. *Go.*"

16

Sloane

ZETH IS SITTING ON HIS BED, THE BED I SLEPT IN, WITH HIS head in his hands. The moment I see him my panic vanishes. I was nervous; I was worried about coming in here and disturbing him when he said he needed some time, but as soon as I lay eyes on him I know that Pip was right. He is not okay.

Going after Lacey will just have to wait. This isn't something that can just be put aside. This is something that needs to be dealt with now. I walk into the room and sit down beside him on the edge of the bed, leaning forward, elbows resting on knees.

"Is this about—"

"Sloane, I can't."

His voice is quiet, almost a whisper. In the whole time I've known him, Zeth has always had a deep baritone, a rumbling timbre to his voice that's been able to shake me down to the bone, but *this* voice sounds like an admission of defeat. I'm not used to it; he sounds like he's beaten, and now *that's* what's shaking me down to the bone. "You can," I say. "You can tell me what this is, Zeth. You need to. You may still feel like you're doing this all alone, that you are in control of everything, but you're not. I'm a part of this now. I don't know if you've noticed or not but I'm not exactly the sort of person who defers to her man in absolutely everything. I have opinions; I have feelings and I am pretty good at dealing with shitty situations. I'm a member of this team now, and you have to trust me. I've given you my trust time and time again, even perhaps when I shouldn't have. You have to do the same." I surprise myself by how firm I sound. It's true, though. Everything I said is true, and he has to see that.

He turns his head sideways, those dark eyes of his locked onto me. They are filled with anger and doubt, but mostly they are filled with pain. "I'm not the kind of person who can do that, Sloane. I'm not that guy."

"You've already been doing it. You just haven't admitted it to yourself yet. Just because you've never been in this position before doesn't mean you're incapable of making it work. All you have to do is tell me. Tell me why you're freaking out right now. You know I didn't want to kiss Charlie, right?"

He laughs a shaky laugh. "Yeah. You'd have to be out of your mind to wanna kiss Charlie." He inhales and then rubs his hands over his face. "I am struggling to deal with this shit right now because you *didn't* want to. Because he forced you." He turns to look at me again and I can see the well of hurt that exists inside of him. He's breathing down his nose, his eyes so dark and severe, and I can practically feel the hatred pouring off him. It's palpable. This anger has nothing to do with Lacey being taken now; it's about me and what's been done to me. "He made you bleed. I'm gonna kill him, Sloane. I'm. Gonna. Fucking. Kill. Him."

I don't really know what to say to that. I've never been the sort of person to revel in a guy's overprotectiveness, but I'd be lying if I said I wasn't massively relieved right now. He goes back to staring

132

at the ground again, burning holes into the section of polished floorboards between his feet. "I'm not—this isn't easy. But my mother..." He shakes his head. Tries again. "My mother was caught up in some bad stuff. When I was a kid she used to turn tricks to make ends meet. I saw her once, some guy treating her badly, and I was too small to do anything about it at the time. But I'm not small anymore. I can take care of what is mine, Sloane. I'm so sorry I wasn't here. I'm going to get Lacey back, and I'm going to hurt that bastard for what he's done." He stops talking, and the two of us just sit there, stewing over the words he's just said. His mother was a prostitute. I'm sure if Pippa were here right now, she'd be scribbling furiously into her notepad about his need to protect women at risk, that this has to be the reason why he helped me find Alexis. Perhaps even why he prevented a man he knew to be violent toward women from buying me the first time we met.

"I just don't get it. I just don't get why Lacey would go with him," he says softly.

This is going to be the worst part. I take a deep breath, praying that this goes smoothly. I haven't been able to come up with a satisfactory way of telling him any of this, but at the end of the day there's no way to sugarcoat it.

"Zeth, Lacey went with Charlie because he told her she was his daughter." I stop there, let that sink in. Zeth continues staring at the floor, his eyes locked in one place, unblinking. He's holding his breath—I can tell by the rigid angle of his shoulders and the way the muscles in his jaw are jumping. "You said Lacey was your sister just now. How did you know that?"

"My mother," he says. "She's the spitting image of my mother. All that blonde hair. Her smile. The fucking sadness in her eyes. She showed up on my doorstep one day with no explanation or reason and just moved herself right on in. Who else could she be? I don't just let random, broken women insert themselves into my life without purpose. I didn't know for definite, of course. But I did *know*. I just figured she'd tell me her story when she was ready."

I can't believe it. All this time. All this time and he's known all along. It makes perfect sense, really. They've shared such a strong bond; the bond of a brother and sister. He's cared for and protected her for months and months. Of course he's known. I take a deep breath; I'm going to need it to get this next part out. "Well if you know that Lace is your sister, and Charlie is saying he's her father—"

"Don't. Don't say it," he says. "I remember my father. He was a weak piece of shit who never took care of my mother or me. He let drunk and dirty bastards fuck my mother for money and he never lifted a finger to help her. He was the worst kind of man alive, but he wasn't Charlie fucking Holsan."

"Are you sure? I mean, what's your earliest memory? Can you say for definite this guy with your mother wasn't just one of Charlie's men? That's what he's saying, that your mother left with one of his guys and ran away with you."

Zeth does think on this for a moment. And then, "I can't remember anything before the beach. That was my earliest memory, the day my mother got hurt."

I don't want to press him about that. It sounds like a seriously painful memory from the way he chokes over the words. He looks completely destroyed over the fact that what I'm telling him could potentially be the truth.

Charlie Holsan might be his father.

He sits upright, visibly drawing himself together, and then turns to face me. "It doesn't matter who he is. He's a fucking psychopath and there's no way I'm leaving Lace with him for a single day." He seems stronger now, a little more resolved. "I understand if you want to back the hell away from this situation."

"Why? Why would you say that?"

"Because this isn't what you deserve, is it? No one should have to deal with this shit. And I'm a fucking coward. I'm sorry, Sloane. I ran after I heard what you said to that guy on the phone," he says. "I heard you, and it scared the shit out of me because I believed it. I know you love me, and I don't deserve that. I didn't want to stick around and hear you say it to my face because I don't know—I don't know how to even say those words. I don't know what kind of man you think I am. I can never fucking reconcile the fact that when we met I tied you to a bed and screwed you, and now you're here, wanting to be with me like what I did wasn't the shittiest thing on the face of the planet."

My heart feels like it's beating out of my chest. What he's saying is true. I understand how on paper this whole thing is fucked up beyond measure, but that's just how life is sometimes. Fucked up. "I hated you," I whisper. "Afterward, for two weeks, I hated you. I imagined your face, what you would look like, and I imagined what it would feel like to hurt you. For a long time I wanted to cause you pain, but then—then I realized it wasn't you I was angry at. It was me. Because despite the situation and despite not getting the information that I wanted about Alexis, I'd enjoyed being with you." I can't help but stifle an ashamed laugh. "I enjoyed your hands on me, Zeth. I enjoyed you being inside me, and that felt so, so wrong. I was supposed to be devastated over my sister and instead I was replaying our meeting and—and *missing* it."

Zeth just looks at me. He *really* looks at me, as though he's peering into my soul and finally seeing himself reflected right back at him.

"I'm sorry for the way that happened," he tells me, and he means it. "But I am glad it happened. And I'm glad you're here." He reaches up and brushes his fingertips over my swollen lip again. "I'm going to take this away," he says. "I'm not going to let his mouth be the last one that touched yours for long, Sloane. I promise you that. I just need a bit more time."

I nod, knowing that he's telling the truth. So many cards have been laid on the table in the last few minutes; everything feels different now. I feel like...I feel like there's hope. Zeth gets to his feet, holding his hand out to me.

"There's one last thing you should know about the way we met," he tells me. I take his hand, letting him pull me up. He gathers my wrists behind my back, locking them together in one of his strong, powerful hands. The action is barely effective, though. He's gentle, clearly taking my sore arm into consideration.

"What? What is it?" I don't think I can take anymore bad news for one day. The way he's half-heartedly restraining me makes me think he suspects I'm going to hit him. He bends down and whispers his secret into my ear.

"The man who was going to buy you...*was Rebel*."

Zeth

SHE TOOK IT ABOUT AS WELL AS COULD BE EXPECTED. THE whole time we're in the car, heading for the hospital, Sloane is swearing under her breath. "That sick bastard's married to my sister, and he tried to buy *me!* Who *does* that? Lex can't know. She'd never stay with him."

I keep my mouth shut. I have other things on my mind. Like the fact that Sloane told me Lacey was talking to Charlie for days, and it was my fucking fault. She didn't actually say that, but it's true. The cell phone I gave Lace, I should have wiped it. I should have switched out the fucking SIM before I gave it to her. I should have realized, if Charlie bugged the phone I destroyed weeks ago, it was likely he bugged every single one of my phones—burners, disposables, every last one of them. As soon as the fucking thing was switched on, it must have been like a goddamn signal flare going off in the bastard's office. The only reason I can trust the one I have now is because I bought it after I found out about the surveillance. Now I'm heading toward a clusterfuck of a situation with Lacey and the old man, and I have no idea how it's going to play out. I've made a very tense deal with Sloane's friend—she heads inside the hospital and recons the area, tells us whether there's any security we need to avoid in order to get up to the Duchess' room, and in return we let her go. We're not going back to the apartment anyway, and she has no way of contacting us after we part ways, so we lose nothing by freeing her. We won't have to listen to her bitch and moan anymore, so it's actually a bonus.

Newan is sitting in the backseat of Michael's sedan—the Chevy was gone when we hit the garage—pulling sour faces at me. I've finally figured her out. Or at least I think I have. Suffice it to say, it's not so much the fact Sloane picked me over another guy and I'm a bad choice (which I am). I think it has more to do with the fact that Sloane picked me and not *her*.

"You got this?" I ask pointedly into the rearview. "You're going to come back out and let us know what the deal is, and then you can return to your privileged life overlooking the park. Got it?"

"Oh, I've got it all right."

"And you know what'll happen if you call security or you don't come back?"

"Yeah. You firebomb my apartment with me inside it."

I was just gonna say she'll never see Sloane again—her friend will never forgive her if she betrays her twice in one week—but now that she's mentioned it, firebombing—

Sloane slaps my shoulder. "Just please, Pip. Just do this one thing for us, okay?"

I pull up outside St Peter's and Newan gets out. She looks like shit, which I'm sure is making her even madder. She's normally so damn perfectly turned out that her dirty hair and three-days-lived-in clothes are undoubtedly doing nothing for her mood. She pauses by Sloane's side of the car and it looks as though she's going to say something to her. I know what—*this is the last time I'm going to ask, Sloane. Leave this guy. Walk away. Come with me now and you'll never have to deal with any of this nightmarish stuff again.* Sloane can read it in her eyes as well; she gives Pippa a cold look that stops her short. She just nods and then walks across the lot and inside St. Peter's.

Sloane stares out the windshield, hands clenched together in her lap, and I feel like a massive fucking dick. She has to come back here after everything that's happened, to the place she poured her blood, sweat and tears into, but now she's reduced to sneaking in through service entrances like a petty criminal. Even her work colleagues must think she's involved in the death of the woman Charlie picked at random off the street. Fucking Charlie. The man has the touch of disaster to him. Everything he comes into contact with ignites, crashes and goes down in an epic ball of flames. Including me.

"What happens after this?" Sloane asks. "What happens once we have Lacey back and Michael's helped deal with Julio?"

I maybe shouldn't have told her about Rebel earlier; now that I have to try and persuade her to head back to New Mexico with him, convincing her that going anywhere with him is a good idea is going to be fucking impossible. Worth a shot, though. "You'll have to leave," I tell her.

Her head whips around, eyes sharp and spearing straight through me. "What?"

"You'll have to leave. With Rebel. Just for a couple of weeks until this Charlie thing is done."

"Won't it be done with today? If we get Lacey back, what's to keep any of us here?"

She poses a solid question. She must know, though, that letting Charlie live is a bad decision. He's touched in the head; he will never, ever stop searching until he finds us, and I can hardly put an end to him in a fucking hospital. Not without being recorded by a thousand CCTV cameras committing the act. "You know why," I say.

She's prepared for this answer. "If Julio's so scared of Rebel, why isn't Charlie? Can't we just walk away? Let the threat of Rebel protect us?"

"Only sane people can be reasoned with, Sloane. Charlie's out of his mind. There's nothing on earth that'll deter him from what he wants anymore. Too much coke. Too much fucking and drinking and killing. He thinks he's untouchable. And I think—think he's sick."

"Why do you say that?"

I think back to the old man's bedroom, the day when the Duchess stabbed me in the stomach. There was the blister pack of drugs on the nightstand. What were they called again? The brand name of the drug comes back to me, small black letters printed on silver foil. "Degarelix. What's Degarelix used for?"

Sloane's eyebrows shoot up. "Usually prostate cancer. Depends, though."

That makes a whole lot of sense. Prostate cancer. I mull that over for a moment in silence. A minute longer and then Newan's hurrying out of the main doors of St. Peter's, hair flying everywhere in the brisk wind that's tearing through the city. "That was too quick," I say. "She can't have done a proper sweep. Something's up."

Something definitely is up. Newan's a couple of feet out of the doors before they slide open again and a guy dressed in scrubs hurries out.

"Oh no," Sloane hisses. "Oliver."

I have a thing for faces—I remember them very clearly, and this guy has a face I fucking recognize. He was there the day I came to tell Sloane I was leaving to find her sister. He came out of the change rooms hot on Sloane's heels and looking flustered. I didn't like him then, and I sure as shit don't like him now. "What the hell does he want?"

Across the parking lot, this Oliver asshole is grabbing hold of Newan's arm and pointing back at the hospital. Newan's shaking her head, and then the Oliver guy is folding his arms across his chest. Newan's shoulders slump and that's when I know she's going to bring him over to us.

"We have to go." I start the car engine, but Sloane blows out a frustrated breath, placing a hand on my arm.

"Just—just see what he wants."

"Bad idea, angry girl." But I can't say no to the look on her face. It's like my IQ is dropping daily when I'm around this girl; I keep finding myself doing the stupidest shit.

Just as I predicted, Newan leads the guy straight to us. He takes one look at me sitting in the driver's seat of the car and he turns to stone. Pissed-off, rough-hewn stone that wants to come crashing down on me in an unstoppable landslide. *Bring it, motherfucker.*

Sloane buzzes down her window and Newan is already apologizing before my girl can get a word out. "He saw me, okay? It wasn't my fault."

Sloane pinches the bridge of her nose. "What do you want, Olly?"

"You're fucking crazy coming here." He says this to Sloane, but his eyes are still focused on me. Oh, this one hates me already, I can tell. It's rolling off him in a territorial stink that can be smelled a mile away.

"We're just looking for our friend, Ol. She's in trouble. That's the only reason we came."

Newan winces, wrapping her arms around herself against the

cold. "Yeah, Lacey's not here I'm afraid. Seems that woman, the one in the coma, was moved this morning."

"Moved?" Sloane swivels in her seat to face me, panic written all over her face. "They moved her. That means—that means they could be *anywhere.*"

Oliver nods, arms still crossed, veins popping in his forearms. The guy's ripped and he's tensing every muscle in his body, trying to make sure I know it. "She was taken to hospice somewhere. The woman had no insurance or recorded next of kin, and her discharge papers have conveniently gone missing. I saw the guys who wheeled her out of here, though, Sloane, and trust me...they were not health care professionals." *They were scum. They were like the guy you're sitting next to right now, not a motherfucking saint like me.* I want to punch this guy in the face, but his evil looks and bad attitude are the least of my concerns right now.

"So she's gone," I say under my breath. "Lacey's really gone."

"He wouldn't have taken her back to his place?" Sloane asks.

I shake my head, no. "He knows I'd come there looking for her. He has a thousand places across the city he could have taken the Duchess to die. We'll never find either of them unless he comes to us." Fucking typical. The desperation is back again, threefold now. I slam the car into gear, ready to burn out of the place—these two can't help us now.

"Wait!" Oliver slams his palm down on the hood of the car. He's fucking lucky this isn't the Camaro or I'd be out and laying into him before he could blink. "Wait. Sloane, I know you don't wanna hear this but that DEA woman was by here yesterday. She said she wasn't interested in you or *him.* She just wants to know about your sister and the guy she's with. If you tell her what you know, she says she'll clear the slate. For—for *both of you.*" His eyes are on me again; it was hard for him to spit that last part out. Sloane's jaw muscles tighten. She's listening to him. "You could come back to work," he continues. "Nothing will have changed." He pulls a white rectangle of card from the pocket of his scrubs and passes it to her through the window. I see the DEA symbol on there and know it's Lowell's direct line. "Just think about it," Oliver says.

Sloane palms the card into the pocket of her jeans and nods. "No promises."

This doesn't appear to be enough for Oliver. He opens his mouth again, but I've had fucking enough. Lacey's not inside so there's no point us being here. Newan's done her bit and this Oliver guy is just begging me to lay some hurt on him. I gun the engine, spin the steering wheel, and then we're screaming out of the parking lot. Oliver and Newan are tiny, stunned Lego characters who shrink and fade in the rearview as I stretch the blacktop out between us.

"I should have said goodbye," Sloane whispers.

"Oh, I wouldn't worry," I tell her. "Unfortunately, I get the feeling that won't be the last we see of either of those two."

Sloane

WE DON'T GO BACK TO THE APARTMENT. WE DON'T GO BACK
to the warehouse. Once we're on the freeway, Zeth drives like a
model citizen—exactly on the speed limit, indicating when turning,
wearing his seatbelt, checking his blind spot, the works. He makes
sure there's absolutely no reason for highway patrol to pick us up.
We sit in a stony silence. I can't help but play what Oliver told me
on repeat over and over in my head. A clean slate for me *and* for
Zeth. How many times is that going to come around in a lifetime,
especially for Zeth? I mean, I know he's been involved in some
seriously dark crap, but I don't know the true extent of it. I don't
want to know. For them to offer him the whole get-out-of-jail-free
ticket, whatever Alexis has gotten herself involved in must be
pretty serious.

Agent Denise Lowell: the name on the card. The name of the
woman who covertly threatened me and told me she was the one
who shot my sister in the back. It's also the name of the woman

who could change our prospects forever. I could go back to work. That's just as attractive an idea as Zeth being record-free on the national police database. And Rebel hasn't exactly done much to put himself in my good graces right now. Alexis either. I mean, what do I really know? What can I tell the cops? I have a telephone number for Rebel and an address in New Mexico, which is out in the middle of nowhere.

I know Rebel's the head of a motorcycle club, and I know my sister thinks she's in love with this psychopath. Lastly, most importantly, I know Rebel is the evil son of a bitch who put up huge money to screw me.

I suddenly can't take it anymore. I have to know. "Why didn't you tell me sooner? About Rebel? You knew he was trouble, but when we found out about him and Alexis you didn't tell me."

Zeth's voice is back to a low rumble when he answers. "I've heard so many crazy things about Rebel—that he fucks girls and does some seriously grim stuff to them, then leaves them for dead. I've heard a lot of different things about his sexual proclivities that even made me fucking blush. His name is attached to a string of girls who get bought and are then never seen again, Sloane, but the moment I met the guy I knew it was bullshit. He may be fucked up, and he may be into some weird shit, but Rebel doesn't hurt girls. I don't know why he wanted to buy you but it wasn't to fuck you and kill you, I promise you that. Have you seen the way that motherfucker looks at your sister? There's no way she's been in danger from him for a single second."

That's not what I wanted to hear from him. He is a good judge of character. He sees people quite unlike anyone else I've ever met. I was waiting to hear what a terrible monster of a man Rebel is, but instead Zeth has just confirmed that niggling little voice in the back of my head—*he actually seems like a good guy.*

Damn it.

"We're almost there," Zeth tells me. I don't know where *there* is and I don't ask. I just want today to be over. The kid in me figures I can just go to sleep and Michael and Lacey will both be with us and everything will be fine. The cops won't be after us. Charlie and Julio will both have died in some horrific, fluke gas explosion that will also have killed both of their crews. Not a single man left standing. Alexis will be back at college finishing her degree, still too naïve and young to even look twice at a biker and consider him suitable husband material.

Everything would be perfect.

Except, it wouldn't be perfect, because Zeth isn't a white-picket-fence guy. Even in this dreamed-up reality of mine, Zeth is still a brooding, dark creature who I don't entirely understand. Our situation might change but he will always be who he is. Not for the first time, I take a beat to sit back and think about this. Do I want your traditional happily ever after with this man? Would I want to do that to him, even, sending him out every morning to go participate in a blue-collar workforce with a home-made lunch wrapped in a brown paper bag?

The answer is immediate: no. No, I do *not* want that.

That is not the kind of happily ever after Zeth and I will ever share. Our version of a happily ever after...I don't know what that looks like just yet. But I know it would be wrong to try and picture this man beside me in any other way.

"What're you thinking, angry girl?" he rumbles.

I look at him, the cuffs of his tight black T-shirt rolled up a couple of times over those massive arms of his, his ink spiraling over his skin in waves of black and red and green, the always rigid set to his shoulders, and the intense way he's glancing at me every few seconds out of the corner of his eye. I like the way he asks me questions; not the questions themselves, but the way that he asks. Everything Zeth says is said with purpose. He wastes no words. If he tells you something, it's because it's important, and it's the truth. If he asks you a question, it's because he really wants to know the answer, not because he wants to fill the silence, or because he's dreading what you might say.

I realize that's not a bad way to be. "Are you sure you want to know?"

He grunts, as though he knows he might not like the answer, but then says, "Hit me."

"I was just thinking that I'm not afraid of you anymore."

That seems to catch his attention. I get a longer look out of the corner of his eye; he seems so serious, but for some reason I feel like giggling. It's not *I'm-a-stupid-little-girl-giggling-over-a-hot-guy-wow-have-you-seen-those-biceps* laughter. It's the maniacal laughter of someone who knows they're choosing a hard road for themself, filled with potholes and dangerous hairpins that could easily end up sending them toppling over a forty-foot drop, but still choosing it anyway. Still choosing it, knowing it's perilous, and hitting the gas pedal instead of the brakes. I bite my lip and then smile at him. "I'm not afraid of you, and I'm not afraid of what you represent. For me."

"What do I represent for you, Sloane?" he whispers.

Again I ask him the same question. "Are you sure you want to know?"

He gives me one short, curt nod. That mouth of his lifts to one side, though it's not a smile. It's bemusement of some sort; not mockery. It's as though he's just intensely interested in what I have to say.

"You represent a lifetime of worry and potential pain, Zeth. You represent countless sleepless nights while I worry about you, where you are, whether you're okay. If you're hurt. You represent the repeated sheer terror of finding out you *are* actually hurt and the subsequent sheer terror that comes with trying to save you. You represent heartbreak and fear and loss."

Zeth absorbs each word, hands gripped tightly on the steering wheel, eyes no longer even pretending to watch the road. "Sounds like a great relationship," he murmurs. There's a level of resignation that transforms his face as he breathes in, holds the breath for a moment, then breathes out.

"That's what I'm thinking about, Zeth. I'm not afraid of *that* anymore. I'm willing to accept all of that, because I'm also thinking about the other things you represent to me. You represent freedom. You represent forgiveness. You represent loyalty and love," he flinches, "and honesty and protection. You represent strength, not just physically but mentally. When I'm with you I'm not the scared girl I used to be. You challenge me every single day. I don't want to give that up. I don't ever want to give *you* up." I shrug, suddenly feeling very much like I just poured my heart and soul out to him, and he's recording and remembering every second of it in that complex, strange head of his. "So...," I say, closing my eyes, losing my nerve. "That's why I'm not afraid of you anymore."

The car swerves a little, and I crack one eyelid—we're pulling into an extremely dodgy-looking motel: *The All Nite Long Rest Stop. Pendleton's #1 quality accommodation.* It sure as hell doesn't look like quality accommodation. It looks like it was built in the sixties and hasn't had a refurb since. "*This* is where we were headed?"

Zeth parks the car and removes the keys from the ignition. "No."

"Then why are we stopping here?"

"Just wait in the car. Lock the doors," he commands. He gets out, and I think about throwing up in the footwell. I should never have opened my mouth. He's so freaked out by my little speech he had to pull off the freeway for a moment to get the hell away from me. His brows are banked together in one stressed line as he jogs away from the car toward the reception of the motel.

"Fuck." I lean forward, pressing my forehead against the dash. I close my eyes and count, trying to calm myself down. *It's not that bad. It really can't be that bad. He'll take a quick walk, maybe punch a wall or two and then come back right as rain and moody as hell like always.* I must stay there for at least five minutes, telling myself the same things over and over, before there's a tap at my window. I look up and there he is, standing in the rain. When did it start to rain? I have no idea, but he's standing in it and he's pretty much soaking wet. He looks angry.

"What are you doing?" I ask.

He jerks his thumb over his shoulder. "Get out of the car, Sloane."

My fingers feel like they're made out of wood as I open the door and climb out. As though mother nature knows the exact moment my feet hit the parking lot, the rain hardens, lashing down on the asphalt. "Ahhh! What the hell, Zeth?"

He doesn't say a word; he takes hold of my hand and begins to drag me toward the motel, though not to the reception—to the rusted stairway that leads up to the second floor. To the rooms. "So we *are* staying here?"

Zeth doesn't reply, but it seems as though I'm not moving quite as quickly as he would like; he pauses his stride long enough to turn and pick me up at the waist, throwing me over his shoulder.

I scream a wordless cry. The world is suddenly upside down and Zeth Mayfair is running up a set of very creaky, dangerous steps, his strong arms wrapped securely around my legs. We're at the top of the stairs, then we're moving quickly down the long walkway that leads to the rooms. He doesn't put me down. He pulls a key out of his pocket, opens the door he's stopped in front of, rushes inside, slams the door, and *that's* when he puts me down. I land with a rush of air from my lungs as my back hits a very lumpy, springy mattress. "*Uffff!*"

Zeth wipes a hand over his face, ridding himself of the rivers of water that are still running out of his hair. He opens his mouth, flaring his nostrils, and then changes his mind. He starts pacing up and down the twelve-foot-long area between the door to the room and the bathroom at the other end. His hands are balled up into fists, his eyes on fire every time he spins around and glares at me until he gets to the other side of the room and turns his back on me again. I've never seen him this angry. I've never seen him this...I don't know what *this* is but it's a little frightening.

Maybe I spoke too soon. Maybe I should never have said I wasn't afraid of him. I scramble off the bed and find my feet just in time for him to spin and come stalking toward me, chin dipped low into his chest, dark eyes burning into me like brands. He gets halfway to me, his pace quickening, and then stops, shakes his head. He spins, paces back to the far wall by the bathroom, and then launches his fist into the plasterboard, roaring at the top of his lungs. "FUCK! *Fuck,* Sloane."

His hand actually disappears through the plasterboard. White powder and dust flies everywhere when he pulls it out. He faces me, his chest heaving, his mouth open, and I see what he's feeling right there on his face. Total, complete anguish. "Fuck, Sloane." He holds his hands to his head for the briefest moment then everything happens quickly. "Fuck it," he hisses, and then he's rushing toward me.

My heart jumps up into my throat—what the hell is he going to do?—and then his hands are on either side of my face and his chest is crushed up against mine and my back is slammed into the wall and Zeth Mayfair's mouth is on mine. *Zeth Mayfair's mouth. Is. On. Mine.*

My mind goes blank.

It takes a moment to truly register what's happening. He's...he's *kissing* me. A ball of fire launches itself from the pit of my stomach all the way up to my head, stealing the oxygen out of my lungs as it goes. Despite the ferocity with which he launched himself at me, his lips are soft against mine, careful. Unsure. His breathing is erratic and all over the place, but then so is mine. I can't pull enough air into my body to fuel the many reactions taking place right now. I'm frozen solid, standing stock still with my palms pressed against the wall behind me, suddenly not sure what to do. Should I move? Should I kiss him back? I only know the answer to that question— fuck yes!—when he grows more insistent and teases my mouth open. That might not have been enough on it's own, but the choked groan that slips free from his mouth sends a violent, delicious shiver straight through me. He presses against me even harder, as though he can't possibly get close enough. It could just be my imagination, but I almost think I feel his hands shaking as he touches me. He's enjoying this—I can tell from his labored breathing and the lust filled sounds that he's doing a really bad job of keeping at bay—but I also think he's freaking out. Good job, because I am, too.

I've imagined it enough times to have worked out how this whole thing will go—noses aligned perfectly, not too much saliva, just the right amount of pressure—so when our teeth *do* crack together, I'm thrown for a loop. This is *real*. This is ours and this is *happening now*. I need to get my head in the game. Like one of Medusa's frozen statues coming back to life, my hands all of a sudden remember how to work. I wrap my arms around his neck and hold on tight, and he responds in kind, burying his hands into my hair.

I feel small and vulnerable with his great mass pinning me in place, but there's nowhere else in the world I would rather be. The All Nite Long Rest Stop might as well be St Paul's Cathedral right now. It doesn't matter that I'm soaked to the bone and I'm unemployed and I have no idea whether I'm wearing my good underwear. All that matters is Zeth's lips working over mine, his hands in my hair, his hips pressing up against mine.

He makes a choked, breathless sound at the back of his throat, and then he does something that makes my head explode: he slips his tongue into my mouth.

I know the guy is devilishly talented with that tongue. Certain areas of my body have been on the receiving end of its charms many times before, but this is different. This is careful and intense and warm and sweet, and nothing else in my life will ever compare to this moment. He works his tongue over mine, exploring me, tasting me, and I lose it. I claw at his wet T-shirt, desperate to get the thing off. That's obviously not what Zeth has in mind, though. He takes hold of my wrists and lifts them high over my head, securing them with both of his hands. I know he wants me. I can feel his erection digging into my belly, but Zeth breaks off the kiss and looks down at me, panting, and shakes his head. He licks at those full lips of his, as though they're tingling just as much as mine are.

"Not yet," he growls. "I'm not done with you. Fuck, Sloane, your mouth has always been perfect when it's been on my cock, but on my *mouth*..." His eyes look hazy, like he's been drugged. "On my mouth, your lips are sensational."

A small part of me dies inside, in the *very* best way. I am ridiculous, and I am totally in love with this man. I've peaked. This is it, the pinnacle of my entire existence. He leans down and starts the whole thing all over again, except this time there's no teeth cracking or me standing there like a frozen idiot. It's perfect and deep and breathtaking, and feels like it will never end. There has never been another kiss like this one in the entire universe. This is *the* kiss.

The kiss to end all other kisses.

Zeth forgets all about soft and gentle. He owns me in this, just like he owns me in everything else. It's not long before his hands are sliding down my body, exploring over my hips, my butt, my thighs, up and over my breasts.

"You want me, angry girl? You want me inside you?" he pants into my ear. His mouth grazes my jawline, and then travels down toward my neck. I am a shivering mess of nerves; my body can only take so much. I go limp in his arms, which seems to drive him crazy. He grabs hold of me underneath my thighs and hikes me up so my legs wrap instinctively around his waist. He's still kissing me, pressing his lips against my neck, my jaw, my shoulder. I can't help the senseless noises that are coming out of me. I'm one of those clichés you watch on television that completely come undone when their man lays one on them. I am *that* person.

Zeth carries me to the bed and instead of throwing me down on it, this time he sets me down carefully and then stands back, scanning me from head to foot. I think he's going to climb up on top of me but he doesn't. He grabs the single, worn chair from underneath the peeling veneer desk in the corner of the room, spins it so that it's back to front and sits down, arms folded on top of the backrest. "Take your clothes off, Sloane."

There are no nerves anymore. No internal dialogue. There is just me taking my clothes off. I stand up and hitch my shirt over my head, and toss it to him. He catches it, completely straight-faced, and buries his nose into it, making a deep humming sound. It's not seedy, the way it would be if he'd done that to my panties. He's just breathing me in, the same way I would do to him if I had the nerve.

"Pants, Sloane. Take off your pants."

I flick the button on my fly, lower the zip and do as he asks. Somewhere out there, there's a woman who could wrestle out of wet jeans in a sexy fashion, but that woman is not me. I have to stand on the damn things once I've got them around my ankles in order to yank my feet free. Zeth laughs, rests his forehead against his folded arms as though he can't look, and a gutting sensation hits me. He laughed. He looked shy, almost. For that fleeting moment, he was the guy he would have been if all this crazy shit hadn't happened to him. The smile fades from his face as I shimmy out of my bra and panties. He becomes serious again, gripped by a lust I can see right there in his eyes.

Apart from the dressing still wrapped around my injured arm, I'm totally naked, and I'm not even slightly embarrassed. I take three steps forward so I'm standing right in front of him and I place my hand on the back of his neck. He's warm, and for some reason that is so reassuring. He dips his head low, letting me rub my hand softly up the prickly, short hairs that have been shaved at the base of his head.

"This can be different," he says, breathing hot air over the bare skin of my stomach. "But it will never be *that* different. I'm always going to own you, Sloane."

I shiver, feeling...feeling *relief.* "That's what I want. That's what I need."

It's as though he's been holding back and I've suddenly said the magic words that cut the ties restraining him. Zeth rockets to his feet, kicking the chair out of the way. I'm tall for a woman, but I feel so small when he looms over me with that look in his eyes. "Get on the bed. Now."

I walk backward until my legs hit the mattress, and then I lie back down, my rapid breathing lifting my ribcage up and down, up and down.

"Spread your legs for me." I do it. Zeth nods his approval, growling deep in the base of his throat. "Now touch yourself for me."

The first time he asked me to do this for him, I was horrified. Now I don't even hesitate. I slide my right hand down my body, cupping my breast with my left. When I reach my pussy, I slowly rub the tips of my fingers against myself, softly stroking my clit. I'm wet already, of course. That kiss alone would have been enough to prime me. Zeth watches me—his eyes intent and stoic—but I can tell what's going on inside his head. He wants me. He wants to tear into me. To devour me. Instead he refrains, holding himself back.

He waits until I can't help myself anymore and I quicken the pace, working my fingers through the slick folds of my pussy, bringing myself closer and closer to the edge.

He undoes his belt.

"Stop, Sloane. Stop."

I stop.

"Get on your hands and knees."

My heart rate has kicked up a notch at the sight of the leather belt in his hands. He hasn't used a belt on me since the first time we were together, but I want it. He's used his hands to cut off my air supply, but it seems a little more dangerous with the belt. A little more savage. Am I sick for being this excited? I might be, but so what. He would never hurt me; I know that. I trust him. I love him.

I turn over and get up on my hands and knees, and Zeth comes and stands in front of me. He gently, slowly loops the belt over my head and tightens it, and then he does something that surprises me—he hands me the remaining length of leather, so that I'm the one in charge of how tight it becomes. He crouches down so we're face to face; those big brown eyes are soulful and yet demanding. "It's up to you, Sloane. You can do this, or I can. I know how much you can take, but—"

I immediately hand the end of the leather strap back to him. My actions are final. This is how our relationship will be now and forever more. Zeth knows how much I can take, and I trust him with that responsibility. A lazy, sexy smile transforms his face into a dark mask that sends a shot of adrenaline around my body. This is it. He tugs lightly on the end of the strap and my pulse begins to throb at my temples. "Be my good girl and don't fucking move," Zeth says. He lets go of the strap long enough to pull his T-shirt over his head and throw it aside. His shoes, jeans and boxers go next. I'm faced once more with this beautiful, magnificent man who is perfect in his nakedness, and my heart sings because he's mine. His cock is already hard and ready for me; he takes it in his hand and I'm blown away by how hot the sight of him touching himself is. He pumps his fist up and down the length of his erection, breathing sharply as he stares at me. The leather strap goes back into his free hand, then, and I'm straining forward, waiting for him to move.

"Patience, angry girl. You've not been good enough yet."

I whimper, needing him. Needing to taste him. He keeps on pumping himself with his hand, though, just out of reach. The muscles in his thighs are raised and defined, tensed hard, as he works his hand over himself.

"Please, Zeth. Please," I whisper—it's all I can manage. My body feels like tempered steel. I feel strong right now, even though I am not in the position of power. I feel strong because I know I've conquered a considerable amount of fear to allow myself to be here, and that in itself is an accomplishment.

"Please?" Zeth says softly.

I nod. "*Please.*"

"You're very good to ask so nicely, angry girl." Zeth takes a step forward, keeping the tension on the strap taut, but it's still not close enough. I still can't get to him. He slows down his movements, drawing them out and squeezing his hand around his cock hard enough to make himself shiver. I want him. I want him so badly, and I want him now. My arm is throbbing, like a pulsating live wire of electricity, but all I can think is that I need this man. Nothing else is important.

"I'm going to put my dick in your mouth now, Sloane," he says, his voice breathless. "And I want you to be a good girl and suck it."

I nod, curling my hands closed so that they're gripping at the over-starched, crinkly covers. Zeth takes that final step forward and closes the gap between us, and I am finally able to take him into my mouth. Never, ever before in my life did I think I'd be the type of girl to crave this. Giving a guy a blow job always seemed faintly scary—how the hell do you do it right?—but now that I'm literally face to face, or rather face to *cock* with Zeth, I can barely control myself. I'm not thinking about technique or what I'm doing with my tongue. I don't care that I can barely breathe or that the tip of him is grazing the back of my throat, triggering my gag reflex. All I'm thinking about is how absolutely amazing it feels whenever his breathing quickens or he makes a choked gasp, and I know *I* am the one responsible for eliciting those responses.

Zeth grabs hold of a handful of my hair and tugs my head back, and there he is, towering over me, looking me in the eye as I slide his cock in and out of my mouth. The smile that spreads across his face is perhaps the wickedest one he's treated me to yet. A spike of courage courses through me, and I apply a little teeth, though nowhere near as much as last time back at Julio's place. I don't want Zeth to throw me across a room; I want him to come. I want him to come really badly.

At the slight pressure from my teeth, Zeth lets out a tortured hiss. His head kicks back, and I get to watch the muscles in his throat work as he chants something over and over again under his breath.

"Oh fuck. Fucking perfect, Sloane. You're fucking perfect." I'm so hungry for him I don't stop when he gently strokes my hair and tells me he's going to come. "Sloane, you'd better—oh fuck. Ahhh, screw it!"

He gives the belt a firm but controlled tug and breathing becomes next to impossible. A second later, Zeth's coming in my mouth and my head is bursting with black pinprick fireworks. The belt instantly eases, and I swallow the fluid at the back of my throat, not quite sure what to expect. Pippa always said it was disgusting and it was much better to spit it out, but when it's right at the back of your throat, there's not much to taste. The texture's sure not pleasant, but the expression on Zeth's face makes it one hundred percent worth it. Every ounce of tension and pressure has vanished from him, and the blissed-out, heavy-lidded look he turns on me sends a wave of pride through me.

"Shit," he sighs. "You're—that was..." He can't seem to decide on what he wants to say. "Get on your back, angry girl. Time to return the favor."

I'm on my back in a heartbeat. Maybe another girl would feel awkward about receiving head from a guy once he's already come—the situation becomes incredibly one-sided—but not me. Not right now. I want to feel his tongue on me. I want to feel like I'm sliding off the face of the earth.

Zeth climbs up onto the bed and prowls up my body so he's hovering over me on his hands and knees. I always thought guys lost their erections once they'd released but Zeth, once again, appears to be the exception to the rule; he's as hard as ever and coming straight for me. He unties the belt from around my neck, takes hold of my hands, loops the leather around them once, twice, and then secures them to the wrought iron headboard above my head. He's tied me up before, but looser than this. My hands are already burning, my sore arm screaming from the pressure and lack of blood supply by the time he positions himself over my body and stares me straight in the eye. Do I stop him? No, I don't. I can live with the pain—it seems a fair trade for the exquisite bite of pleasure coursing through my body at the same time, muddying both sensations so that I can't differentiate between the two. All I feel is *alive*.

"If you make a single sound, Sloane, I will stop. I will stop and I will leave you here like this. Do you understand me?"

I open my mouth—how the hell am I supposed to not make a

single sound?—but then I see the warning look on his face and I close it right back up again. He's not kidding; he really will leave me here trussed up and naked like a Christmas turkey if I so much as squeak.

"Do you understand?" he asks again. "We can't continue until you let me know that you do."

I nod, because it's the only way of giving him an affirmative answer.

"Good." He leans down and places a kiss directly onto my forehead, right between my eyes. He's almost in a push-up position, holding himself up with his arms, hovering no more than an inch over my body, and the heat rolling off him is enough to make me dizzy.

From my forehead, Zeth kisses my temple, my jaw, my neck. He lowers himself ever so slowly, his weight increasing, increasing, increasing until it feels like I'm drowning in this huge man on top of me, and it feels like the best way to die. His hands are all over me now, all over my breasts, my hips, my thighs. Between my thighs... I gasp, inhaling quickly at the sudden contact of his fingertips against my clit, and he freezes, eyes narrowed at me. "Careful, angry girl," he growls. "That almost counted."

So I can't even breathe loudly? This is going to be seriously hard. It becomes infinitely harder when Zeth descends down my body, leaving a trail of burning kisses over my skin. He reaches the juncture between my legs and that low rumble from the drum of his ribcage sends a wave of electric current fizzling across every square inch of my bare skin.

Then it's not just his fingers on me, it's his tongue as well. The next three minutes are a blur; I'm fighting to keep my vocal chords from destroying me, while Zeth licks and sucks at me, tracing the length of his tongue over my pussy, circling my clit, driving me closer and closer to madness.

I begin to mouth curse words when Zeth inserts one finger, then two inside me as he does his thing with his mouth. That's nothing compared to what happens when he withdraws them and slides his thumb inside me, though, using his fingers to massage my pussy as well as the tip of his tongue to flick over and over on my swollen clit.

I nearly fail his test. I writhe on the bed, biting ferociously hard on my bottom lip, just waiting for the urgent scream hammering against my blocked-off throat to break free. Zeth grabs hold of my hips and pins me in place, continuing his assault. I think I hear that vindictive chuckle of his, but I can't be sure because my head is pounding. Screaming. Swearing.

It builds then, my impending orgasm. It feels as though the lengths of nerves running through my body are expanding their network, tiny filaments of new connections spreading through me like the roots of a tree, and each last one of them is on fire, burning and evaporating, only to have new ones take their place, burning twice as hard.

I am cinder and ash by the time it overtakes me. I want to scream out as my whole self ignites, but there's nothing I can do, so I let my body contort, my back arching to painful degrees as I'm blinded by the tsunami of pleasure that crashes over me.

When I can think coherently again, the sound of Zeth's deep voice is the first thing I register. That and the high-pitched ringing in my ears. I open my eyes—I don't even remember screwing them shut—and he's there, still propped up between my legs, watching me with a steely gaze. "That was perfect," he informs me, and then, to my horror, kisses me between my legs.

I try to scramble away from him, not quite so unashamed as I was ten seconds ago, but he grabs hold of me and pins me again. "Sloane, you're fucking beautiful and amazing and you taste incredible. I want to *live* down here." He kisses me again, and I fight the urge to try and squirm away from him again. He gives me a hard look and then slaps my thigh, hard enough to leave a hand mark. I go still on the bed, still not talking, not sure if I'm allowed to yet. Zeth gives me an approving nod and lifts himself, rocking back onto his heels. I know from the devious look that suddenly forms on his face he's about to do something that might bother me, and he doesn't disappoint. He slowly inserts every single one of the fingers he used to touch my pussy into his mouth and he sucks them clean. He ends on his thumb, his eyelids lowering as he traces my slickness all over his bottom lip. "If I told you that you were allowed to speak now, Sloane, and I asked you if you still want to kiss me, what would your answer be?" he asks.

My throat, all of a sudden, feels scratchy and terribly dry. I answer him, my voice a cracked whisper. "Yes. I would tell you yes."

Zeth's heavy weight is on me in a heartbeat, and his mouth is pressed against mine for the second time since we stepped into this room. I can smell and taste myself all over him, and I don't mind a single bit. I love it, in fact—that he loves being marked with me like this.

There are girls in movies who cry after sex; I've never under-stood that before—they look like freaking psychopaths, it's no wonder the male lead always runs like crazy—but at this moment I honestly do feel like crying. Or laughing hysterically, or something. I'm just so overwhelmed by everything, by the amazing orgasm I'm still aching from, by Zeth actually, *finally* kissing me, that I can't seem to handle it.

Zeth's mouth is careful but demanding now. It's as though he's wanted this one final thing from me for a while and he's only now able to claim it. That's what I feel: well and truly claimed. It's the best feeling in the world.

Zeth huffs heavily out of his nose. His lips stop moving against mine and he just rests his forehead against mine and stares at me.

I nearly jump out of my skin when there's a hammering at the room door. "Time!" a voice yells through the flimsy MDF board.

"What the hell?"

Zeth lifts himself up and sets about untying me, biting back a smile. "One minute, asshole!" he yells.

"What the hell does that mean, *time*?" I scuttle off the bed and start throwing my clothes on. Bra first, T-shirt next. Zeth snags the panties out of my hands, shakes his head at me—*mine*—and they disappear into his back pocket.

"This place charges by the hour," he says.

I put on my wet jeans without the benefit of any underwear, which is extremely uncomfortable, and then there's more banging on the door. No, not banging—*hammering.*

"Sounds like there's a line forming out there for me. You mind waiting in the car?" Zeth quips, raising his eyebrows. He's miraculously somehow dressed, hair pointing in every direction and looking like he totally just fucked my brains out.

"Oh, you're funny?" I say, as though this is a shock, which it kind of is. "Who knew?"

He rubs ruefully at the stubble on his jaw. "Yeah," he tells me. "Who knew?"

18

Michael

MEDINA GRINS LIKE THE FUCKING CHESHIRE CAT WHEN WE
let him out of Zeth's quiet little corner downstairs. Surprising,
really, since he has a gunshot wound to his leg and he looks like
he's on the verge of passing out. We have to practically carry him to
the car. He speaks in Spanish to Rebel the whole way across the
city, as though he thinks somehow I'm uneducated and don't have
the first clue what they're talking about. Rebel drives his Humvee—
we ditched Zeth's stolen Chevy like he asked, and a bike would
have been impractical for this trip—and I sit in the passenger seat.
Rebel's snitch sits in the back, spitting out hard vowels and
cracking his knuckles like he's preparing for a fight.

Medina: *Voy a matar a ese cabrón. (I'm going to kill that bastard.)*

Rebel: *Lo necesitamos vivo, ¿Te acuerdas? (We need him alive,
remember?)*

Medina snorts: *Necesita vivo. Lo necesito para sufrir. Él me dejó
por dos dias sin darme algo de comer. No podia ni siquiera ir al baño.
(You need him alive. I need him to suffer. He left me for two days*

without feeding me. I couldn't even use the bathroom.)

Rebel: *Lo sé. Tu apesta de orines. (I know. You stink of piss.)*

Medina glowers at the back of my cousin's head, eyes narrowed into angry slits. "You may need that motherfucker for a while longer, but let me tell you, when you're done with this little game you're playing, I'm going to fuck him up real good."

Rebel arches an eyebrow, glancing briefly in the rearview at our grumpy car companion. "You think you can take Zeth, be my guest, buddy. If I were placing bets, I sure as fuck wouldn't be putting my money on you, though."

Medina growls under his breath, his knee bouncing up and down. We stop at a low rate drive-thru and get him some food to shut him the hell up, and then we drive for half an hour in silence. I keep my mouth shut, though I am interested in Rebel's afore-mentioned 'little game', and why he apparently needs Zeth. I'll be sure to ask him later. My cousin and I used to be close, but the last couple of years have been a silent void between us. We used to be tighter than brothers. Now I'm the family member who finds out the other guy's married two years after the fact.

People have always had trouble believing Rebel and I are blood relatives given the fact that he's white and, well, I'm obviously not. His Caucasian uncle, my dad, married my African American mother et voila! I am the resulting by-product of this meeting of hearts and minds and...other body parts. I just happen to be a little blacker than white, and that suits me just fine. Rebel's father, my uncle, hated me on sight. I've always thought that was the reason why Rebel and I were so close. There are many misnomers and inaccuracies in circulation about the man sitting beside me, but the one I know to definitely be true is that he hates his father more than any other person on the face of the planet.

"We'll drop you here." Rebel pulls the Humvee over to the side of the road, four motorcycles drawing tight formation at the rear like

Rebel's the damn Pope and in need of protection at all times. He probably *is* in need of protection at all times, but I'm not feeling very generous toward him right now. Sue me. He puts the car into park and twists in his seat, facing Medina. "This is it. You get out of the car, you go to that payphone. You call Julio, find out where he is, tell him you got the jump on Zeth and you want to meet up. Go to him. Once you've found out what they've done with Cade and where we're supposed to meet, you let me know right away. And for fuck's sake, Andreas, do not breathe a word to anyone you've seen me."

Medina's jaw muscles pulse, like he's grinding something small between his front teeth. "I got it, man. And then after this, you and me, we're done. I don't want nothing to do with your bullshit anymore."

Rebel gives him a solitary nod—*whatever*—and then Medina is getting out of the Humvee and hobbling very slowly across the busy road toward a bank of payphones.

"You think he's going to do what you've told him?" I ask.

Rebel grunts. "If he has any sense, he will. There's a bounty on that guy's head down in Colombia. One phone call and there'll be some very interested members of the cartel flying in to pay him a visit."

Since it's just Rebel and me in the car now, I could ask him anything I want about Alexis and this DEA bitch they have hot on their heels, but I don't say a word. I'm not exactly in a chatty mood. Plus I'm waiting on Rebel to kick this thing off; it's on him. He's the one who vanished into thin fucking air.

Rebel doesn't say anything, though. He drives us around, his club guys taking it in turns to peel up ahead and scout out a safe driving path for us. I get a text from Zee letting me know Lacey's not at St. Peter's, Charlie's taken her somewhere else, and that he's moving Sloane to a temporary safe house not too far across the border into

Oregon. He also tells me the DEA are trying to swing some sort of deal with Sloane—a fresh start in exchange for my cousin. I don't even bother to ask about the deal; I know Zeth won't be keen on taking it, so Rebel has nothing to worry about on that front. The place in Oregon, I've been there before. I text him back and tell him I'll meet him there as soon as Julio's dealt with.

"You like working for this guy, Mikey?" Rebel asks—he must know there's only one person I would be communicating with right now, and he sounds a little suspicious.

I close down the message and place the phone back into the inside pocket of my suit jacket. "Yep. You know I do, man. I was happy enough to stay here and work for him six, seven, eight years ago, when you came to me and asked me to move out east. Nothing's changed."

"A lot's changed," Rebel disagrees. "I have a proper operation now. There's a lot I need to tell you. It's time you come work for me."

Rebel's most annoying trait, aside from being arrogant as fuck, is that he likes to tell people what they are going to or not going to do. Doesn't matter what plans you may have made for yourself, Rebel knows better, always has, and you'd better be prepared to do as you're told with him otherwise you'll be finding out the shitty way what it's like to get on the wrong side of him. It's a trait that's been passed down to him by his father. His old man does the exact same thing, but woe betide anyone who might point this out to Rebel. The least said about his father, the better.

I sigh and stare out at the road. No point in arguing with him. I'll just let him take my silence on the matter as an agreement until the time comes when I tell him to fuck off. I may not want to discuss my work arrangements with him right now, but there are a few things I'm curious about. "What the hell were you thinking marrying that girl, anyway?" I ask. I wasn't going to do it; I was going to keep my cool, but some things just need to be said. "You bought her from a pimp, man. What kind of asshole are you these days, because the guy I knew would never have needed to grab himself an over-the-counter wife."

Rebel huffs out a breath, slapping his palm against the steering wheel. "Don't—seriously, Mikey. You *really* don't know what you're talking about. Please don't bring her up again. I would really hate to have to beat your ass for you."

"Try, man. Just try."

Rebel looks over at me, and a grin blossoms on that too-handsome-to-be-a-criminal face of his. Fucker. "You know I can take you," he informs me. The truth is that he can, but I honestly wouldn't mind going a few rounds with him anyway, even if he would end up beating me. I'd get more than a few good shots in, and he deserves every one of them for bailing on me.

"You're mad at me," he says.

"Yes, I'm mad at you."

"Why? You've known where I was this whole time. You could have come to me."

"I didn't want to *come to you,* Jay. I didn't want to work for you back then and I definitely don't wanna work for you now. You have money; I get that. But we are *equals.* You are never going to be my employer. You're my cousin and you *were* my friend, but it appears that as soon as some hot piece of ass comes along, you forget your boy's phone numbers."

Rebel shakes his head some more. He clenches his jaw, runs his hands through his hair, does everything but look at me or talk to me for the next fifteen minutes. The asshole doesn't even deny he ghosted himself out of everyone's lives.

Another fifteen minutes of driving, and driving in silence. This whole waiting on Medina is getting old. The guys on the motorcycles behind us—no cuts, don't want to draw any attention to themselves—are even getting pissy. It's raining, of course, and it can't be much fun sitting out in that, covered in sodden leather.

Eventually Rebel pulls into a gas station and kills the engine. "Wait here," he tells me. He probably needs a piss. Our entourage of bikers draws up beside the Humvee and three of them climb off their rides and follow Rebel not to the bathroom out back, but into the actual station. The only Widow Maker who stays behind is Carnie, a guy I already know pretty well. He came up here with Cade to try and persuade the Doc to go help out with Alexis. They never got the chance to try and convince her, though. Charlie went nuts and attacked that girl at another of Seattle's fine gas stations, which initiated a series of events that have led us here, to me, simmering on low in Rebel's Humvee, and Carnie scratching his ass, soaked to the bone.

The door opens, startling me, and Rebel hops back up into the driver's seat. "That was quick."

He tosses a packet of something silver and shiny at me, starting the engine again. "Didn't need much. Just thought you might appreciate those."

There's a pack of collector cards in my lap—baseball cards. That's what he went into the gas station for. I give him a dry laugh—*ha, ha, very funny motherfucker*—but I still pick them up and run my fingers across the foil wrapper. Matt Shoemaker's on the front, mid-way through a pitch, with a look of concentration on his face I recognize all too well. I was supposed to be Matt Shoemaker. I was supposed to make those pitches.

"Never did come pick up your collection," Rebel says. "Figured you could start a new one."

"That collection's worth thousands of dollars, you bastard. This"—I wave the pack in his face—"is worth seventy-five cents."

"Dollar ninety," he shoots back. "Price has gone up since we were eight."

I let myself laugh. I have to. Rebel laughs, too. This is his way of apologizing. It's a shitty way of doing it, but the effort's there. It's almost a record-breaking effort on his part, in actual fact. An apology is an admission of weakness; that's what his dad says. Rebel clears his throat.

"Listen, things with me and Soph—*Alexis*," he says, correcting himself. "They're way more complicated than they look on the outside. Trust me when I tell you I have not bought myself an over-the-counter wife. Not even close." He laughs, and it's the laugh of a man who might prefer an over-the-counter wife instead of what he actually did get. I know he's joking, though. "I swear I'll explain everything, but all in good time. Right now, I just wanna get Cade back."

As if right on cue, the cell in Rebel's drink holder starts to ring, blaring out a loud, tinny rendition of A Boy Named Sue by Johnny Cash.

"What the fuck?" Doesn't seem like a song choice Rebel would have gone for.

He mutters something about someone driving him crazy and picks up with a brisk, "Tell me."

There's talking on the other end of the line, almost audible though not quite, and then Rebel's hanging up again. Just like that. "What's the deal?" I ask.

"They're at the Downtown Marriott. Julio's planning on slitting my throat open and letting me bleed out." He says it so casually that it almost sounds as though he's talking about going out to grab a bite to eat, not heading toward a meeting he's not supposed to make it through alive.

"So, you have a plan?"

"Sure. Andreas is gonna plunge a knife into that fat fucker's heart before he can lift a finger. We're gonna take Cade and then we're gonna go and get something to eat. Chinese food. I think I could go for some Chinese food."

Now he actually *is* talking about grabbing a bite to eat. He's always been crazy but this is cavalier, even for him. I guess I wouldn't know, though. Maybe this is who he is now, a man completely unfazed by the world.

Rebel sends a text message to Julio—*where are you?*—because we're technically not supposed to have that information yet, and *ding, ding*, two seconds later we have confirmation Andreas has told us the truth. The Downtown Marriott is, indeed, the venue for this showdown.

Fifteen minutes later, Rebel's parking the Humvee and we're heading into the hotel—standard chain hotel. Obscure glass balled objects stacked in beaten copper bowls that are apparently pieces of art, generic, non-offensive contemporary paintings in neutral tones, plush carpets, and polished tiles. We draw attention to ourselves; of course we do. Five guys dressed in torn jeans and covered in tattoos, and a black guy in a pristine dove-gray suit? Yeah, there's no way we're not noticed. We head to the eighth floor, and then Rebel's knocking on the room door, 8205, and this is all happening very quickly.

This is one of those situations you can never really prepare for, though. What would be the point in pausing to take a moment, talk the whole thing through, when the events of the next few minutes are completely out of our control? Someone is going to try and kill Rebel, and since I'm with him the likelihood is that they're going to try and kill me, too. I have a gun; I have a knife. I am forewarned and forearmed. There's nothing else for it.

The door opens and a pair of almost-black eyes are sizing us up. A tall Mexican guy, ripped, covered in ink—I've not seen this guy before but he's clearly no stranger to this type of situation. "Only you, man," he says, stabbing an index finger in Rebel's direction. "Julio said ain't no way you bringing anyone else."

Rebel raises his eyebrows. He passes me a look, then glances at his boys. From his jeans pocket he pulls out a small black clip, opens it, and takes out a toothpick. The toothpick goes into his mouth. "I'm not leaving them out here, friend. So you can tell Julio that. You can also tell him that if I have to turn around and leave this building without my boy, I have some delightful repercussions for him to deal with."

The guy with the gang tats blinks at Rebel, and then he closes the door.

"Well, that went well," Rebel says. He flicks the toothpick over to the other side of his mouth and braces his hands against the doorframe, waiting. When the guy returns, his expression is even harder than before. "You're choice, *ese*, that's what Julio says. Your friend ain't looking so well. He might need to see a doctor. Better you get in here and take him now than wait much longer. You might be carrying him out of here in pieces, otherwise."

This isn't the kind of attitude that my cousin appreciates. Never has been. He nods, glancing at his feet—his boys behind him are fighting back knowing smiles. They see what's coming before the guy at the door does. Rebel reacts quicker than lightning, throwing out a powerful right hook that smashes directly into the guy's throat. He bends at the waist, staggering backward, hands fumbling over his chest as he tries to fight the urge to clasp at his throat and instead reach for the weapon tucked into his waistband. Rebel makes a *tsk*ing sound between his teeth and steps into the hotel room, landing a solid front kick into the guy's stomach just to finish him off. I'm right behind Rebel, and so are the other guys.

We walk into chaos.

A chorus of yelling erupts, a mixture of Spanish and English, and suddenly there are twelve guns pointed at us. Each of those guns is in the hand of an angry gang member, and each of those gang members looks pissed. Julio Perez sits on a sofa amongst all of this with a displeased expression on his face. The fat bastard is wearing sunglasses indoors.

"What the fuck are you thinking?" he asks quietly. The moment he opens his mouth, his men fall silent so he can be heard. "This is very poor etiquette. While I'm here, this hotel room is my home and my men are my guests. You can't just assault them without my permission."

"I don't really hold with the whole *while under my roof* bullshit," Rebel replies, giving Julio a dazzling smile. "You invite me somewhere, Perez, you invite my guys, too. You asked me to come here for a pick-up, so I'm here for the pick-up. Where is he?"

It's true that I don't see Cade anywhere. I don't see Medina anywhere, either. Julio sucks on his teeth, as though he has a sour taste in his mouth. "I thought we might have a conversation first, Rebel. There are some things I'd like to discuss." He gestures to the couch directly opposite from his. "Perhaps you might ask one of your men to remain with you, and the others can wait outside?"

Rebel gives him a look that could freeze an ocean. "I don't think so."

Clearly not the answer Julio wanted. His jowls shake as he tries to marshal himself. "As you wish."

Rebel walks farther into the room, ducking around the men with guns as though he neither sees nor cares about them. He throws himself down on the couch and toys with the toothpick he still holds between his teeth. I sit beside him; his guys position themselves around the room with their own guns out now, openly hostile.

"And what is it that you'd like to talk about?" Rebel enquires.

"Debts," is Julio's response. "A dealer in debts, Rebel. You're a man who collects debts and makes good use of them. I have never been fond of debt. I've never lived beyond my means. I've never borrowed money or drugs. I've never taken anything that wasn't owed to me without a clear knowledge of the consequences. I have been very careful about this all of my life, and yet these past five years I have found myself owing you something. I have to tell you, that does not sit well with me. Not well at all."

Rebel sits and listens to this, twisting the toothpick over and over between his fingertips. "I don't know what to tell you, my friend. We all find ourselves in uncomfortable situations from time to time. I wouldn't lose sleep over it."

"But I *have* lost sleep over it. It's a terrible way to live your life, knowing that one small aspect of it is being controlled by someone else. So when I saw one of your little companions had wandered from the coop, I thought you coming to collect him might be an ideal opportunity for us to discuss this debt that you hold over me."

"I don't see that there's much to discuss, but I'm willing to listen while you state your case," Rebel says.

Julio turns and nods to one of his men, the guy who Rebel throat-punched at the door. He glares malevolently at Rebel as he crosses the room and disappears into a room beyond. I think he's going to fetch Cade, but the man he returns with isn't a Widow Maker at all; it's Andreas Medina.

His hands are tied behind his back, and his mouth is bleeding. He can barely stand properly without the other guy propping him up. It's only been an hour since we let him out of the Humvee and he looks like he's spent the last few days being tuned up. Fair enough, he had a couple of swollen bruises and a hole in the leg from Zeth's attentions, but this...this is something else altogether. Rebel does the eyebrow thing again, looking to Julio.

"Last time I checked, my boy was a little paler than that guy."

This isn't looking good. I know it; Rebel knows it; Julio knows it, too. "Please, Rebel, no more games."

I get the feeling Julio's not exactly happy he doesn't know Rebel's real name. If he did, I'm pretty sure he'd be calling him by his title the same way he does with Zee when he's mad at him—Mr. Mayfair. Rebel's been extraordinarily careful to make sure no one knows who he is, though. Julio could turn over every single rock and stone between here and Washington State and Washington DC and not find a scrap of a clue as to who the man is. Or was, before he walked away from his old life.

"Don't let him do this," Andreas croaks. "You said you'd protect me."

Julio and Rebel both ignore the man. "I don't have any problems with you keeping an eye on me from time to time," Julio grunts. "That's smart business. But when I found out you'd been planting people in my own house, spying on what I was eating for my fucking breakfast, I couldn't have that. I was going to kill him right away, but then I realized that this was an opportunity. A good opportunity to muddy the water a little, if you will."

"You had him feed me incorrect information," Rebel says.

"If you want to put it like that, then yes. I know that he told you I brought you here to slit your throat, for instance. But I didn't bring you here to kill you, Rebel. I brought you here to show you something. First things first, though—" Julio gives the guy holding Medina upright another nod, and the man reacts quickly, pulling a knife out of nowhere. It's an automatic reaction; I reach for my weapon, but I'm already too late—the blade slices across Medina's throat. An arc of bright red arterial blood sprays from the guy's throat, his eyes bulging out of his head. Julio's guy lets go of Medina and he drops to his knees, hands scrabbling at his neck in a futile attempt to close the wound. He dies with a look of horrified surprise on his face. A thick, viscous pool of red spreads slowly out from around his head in an almost perfect circle. People never really realize that that much blood, it has a *smell*. It fills my nostrils, the sharp, bitter tang of metal.

"Was that entirely necessary?" Rebel asks. He sounds bored, but

I know my cousin; he's furious.

"It served a purpose. I'm assuming it caught your attention, and right now I need to know that you're very focused, *my friend.*"

"What do you want?"

"I want your files. All of them. I don't just want what you have on me; I want it all. And I want it in three days time, otherwise—"

"Otherwise?"

Another nod from Julio. This time it's aimed at a guy on the other side of the room, who pulls out a cell phone and tosses it to Rebel. There's a video already loaded on the screen; a big white arrow is blinking at him when he lifts the thing. He hits play.

The screen stays dark for a moment, but the speakers explode with sound—a woman, screaming. "Omg, no, no, no, please stop! Stop! No! HELP! *Please*—"

A pale face appears on the camera and Rebel goes stiff next to me, the tips of his fingers bleached white from his strained grip on the phone. I hadn't recognized the voice—it was too gripped by fear—but I do recognize the face. It's the face of a ghost. A dead girl. A girl I never thought I'd see again. Her name is Laura. She is the reason why Rebel became the man he is today. Her face is thinner, more drawn, devoid of the plumped youthfulness that always made people gravitate toward her like they would gravitate toward the sun. And there's a gloved hand around her throat.

"What the fuck is *this*?" Rebel chokes out.

"I think you know what this is. This is an ultimatum. Your information for this girl. Does that not sound fair?"

Rebel's whole being is vibrating; the bikers at our back are shifting uneasily from foot to foot—this wasn't something we expected. Fighting, killing, running, maybe, but not this. I think Rebel's going to start shooting people, but somehow he manages to crank down his fury. "I want proof of life," he hisses.

Julio appears to consider this reasonable. The owner of the

phone retrieves it, dials in a number and then holds it to the side of Rebel's head. A look of devastation travels over Rebel as he listens. His voice is cold as ice when he speaks. "Lo? Lo, say something."

I don't know what the person on the other end of the line says, but Rebel exhales sharply and tears his head away from the phone, as though the very sound of the person's voice is enough to destroy him. The call is ended and the room remains silent as Julio lets that sink in.

"I'll give you what you want," Rebel says eventually. The other Widow Makers look shocked, but they don't say anything. Julio smiles a sickly smug smile; he struggles to heave himself out of his seat, but fails on the first attempt. Second time lucky, he gets to his feet and paces slowly out of the room. At the door, he turns around, his men shuffling out of the way so that the fat Mexican can have the last word.

"You'll find your friend in the other room. He has a strong force of will. I admire that kind of loyalty. You should reward your pet dog, Rebel. I will see you in three days." He shuffles out of the room, his men following him with guns still drawn, masks of aggravation on their faces, and then we're alone.

Well, not alone. We're left with the still-warm body of Andreas Medina, which is going to be a problem.

"Go check on Cade," Rebel orders. Carnie and one of the other Widow Makers rush into the room Medina appeared out of; their immediate shouts and curses can probably be heard three floors up. Stepping over Medina, I rush into the room and I'm hit with a wall of rust and sweat. Cade is lying on the bed in a pool of his own blood. His face is swollen so badly that I wouldn't recognize him if it weren't for his tattoos. His right arm is bent at an ungodly angle, clearly broken, and a sharp shard of pure white bone protrudes from a wound on his forearm.

"Holy fuck, man," Carnie yells. "They've almost fucking killed him."

Rebel appears in the doorway. He's very pale, but there's a hardness forming in his eyes. He takes one look at Cade and I know that regardless of what he told Julio, there's no way my cousin is giving him what he wants. He's never gonna let him get away with what he's done.

Cade groans, head rolling to one side on the blood-stained pillow, and a bolt of relief shoots through me—at least he's alive.

"Get him up. We'll take him out via the service elevator," Rebel snaps.

"What about Medina?" Carnie asks.

"Leave him."

It takes three of them to lift Cade off the bed, and then a man under each arm to drag him out of the room. Rebel puts a hand on Carnie's shoulder as he passes him.

"Make sure you get him somewhere safe. When you're done, head back to the others. Tell them to get their shit in order."

Carnie grunts, slapping Rebel on the back. "What have you got in mind, boss?"

Rebel's eyes flash when he says, "We're going to war." Carnie leaves, and then it's just the two of us. Rebel puts his hands on my shoulders, eyes burning through me with a righteous fire that I know all too well. That fire won't be quenched until Julio Perez is dead. "So you were saying...you trust this guy, Zeth?" he asks me.

"Implicitly."

"Good. Then take me to him."

19

Zeth

I CAN'T THINK ABOUT LACEY. I FUCKING CAN'T. I KNOW SHE'S safe—Charlie's a fucking psycho but he won't hurt her physically. Not his own daughter. I'm more concerned about the lies he's filling her head with right now. He's told her the Duchess is her mother, which is out and out impossible, and Lacey will have believed him. She needs a mother figure even more than she needs a father figure. And so the girl's going to follow along at Charlie's heels to fawn over this miraculous new mother, only to have that new mother die a few short hours later. That's the most damaging part. Lacey already lost her mother once, but she wasn't old enough to feel the bite of that loss. The Duchess' death will be hard for her; a woman she believes is her blood, so close, only to slip through her fingers again. She won't be able to take it.

I have to find her, but I can't do anything until Michael shows up. Sloane and I traveled the remaining thirty minutes from the motel to the safe house on the shores of the McKay Reservoir, Sloane's face pressed up against the window as we arrived, eyes huge as she took in the mass of water. The reservoir's almost frozen over. That doesn't normally happen until January, but this year's been particularly cold. White frosting coats everything from the blades of grass on the sides of the roads to window panes of the single-story wood cabin I've owned out here for years. It's old, really fucking old, but it has heating and cell phone reception and that's all that matters right now.

We carry our bags inside—feels weird not to have my duffel— and Sloane doesn't complain about the cobwebs or the musty smell in the air. Her cheeks are flushed from the short dash in the cold, and the tip of her nose is red; she looks fucking beautiful. I can't stop staring at that goddamn mouth of hers. I didn't think I could do it; I didn't think I would ever be able to kiss a girl like that. I never even thought I'd want to. The very thought used to make me break out into a cold sweat, but now...

"Feel like lending me a hand here?" Sloane's balling up paper from the stack of five-year-old newspapers—*Crime Boss, Wendelson, Dies at 67! Where did he hide his millions?*—sitting next to the open fireplace. It looks like a family of raccoons has been living in the space behind the grate. I brush off the thick layer of dust that's collected on top of the pile of wood to the other side of the fire and set about tenting a handful of kindling.

"This is very domesticated," Sloane observes. "On the run from two different gang leaders; pursued by the police; making home in a chilly lakeside cabin. *Our* version of domesticated, at least."

I'm shot through with vertigo when she says that. *Our.* I've pushed her buttons and cajoled her relentlessly since the moment we reconnected back at the hospital, if you can call it that. And yet now that she's talking about 'our,' I'm paralyzed by the concept of it. Not because I'm frightened of it. Not because I don't want it. I'm paralyzed because it seems like a fragile idea, the partnership of Zeth Mayfair and Sloane Romera, and I know something shitty's going to happen to fuck it up. Not only that, but it will undoubtedly be my fault.

The fire's roaring by the time Michael gets in touch.

"You arrived, Boss?"

"Half an hour ago. Is Julio dead?" Julio being dead will solve a third of our problems at least.

"No. From the look on Rebel's face, he's shortly going to wish he was, though," Michael replies. I'm given a brief overview of Andreas Medina being killed and the surprise reincarnation of some girl called Laura who everyone's assumed dead for the past five years. I'm not even slightly remorseful Medina's no longer around. Maybe that makes me a bad person—that I don't even experience a flicker of remorse that someone has been murdered—but the truth is I'd be lying if I pretended I hadn't thought about doing it myself. And I don't lie. "We'll be there in a couple of hours," Michael says.

A couple of hours will mean Michael and Rebel are going to be showing up here at one in the morning. "You're still planning on sending me away?" Sloane asks. She's wearing a huge sweater I left here a long time ago, which continually slips off her bare shoulder. Give me the sight of that bare shoulder over a low cut top and pushed-up tits any day of the week.

"Yes."

"For how long?"

"As long as it takes."

Sloane scowls into the fire, knees folded up underneath her chin. "If I go...you have to promise me something," she says.

"I *have* to?" I almost laugh. No one's felt like they can tell me to do anything in an *awfully* long fucking time. It's rather novel. Sloane shoots me a sharp look over her shoulder.

"Let's make a deal. You can control me in the bedroom, Zeth, but out of the bedroom, we're partners. I act under advisement, and so do you. Fair?"

179

This woman, all folded up neatly like origami in front of the fire, has balls. I like it. "Very fair."

"So you need to send me away, but I need—I need for you not to get hurt. Can you please do that for me? At least try?"

I expected her to ask me not to break any laws. Not to kill anyone. But she asks me to consider my own well being instead. I haven't done that in a while. "I can try."

"Good. Thank you." She buries her face into her folded arms, staring at the flames. "When am I supposed to be going with him?"

"Tomorrow."

She nods at this, still not looking at me. "If I'm going tomorrow, then—then I want to sleep with you tonight. Not sex. I want to share a bed with you."

Fuck. I can't do that. I've overcome one pretty big fucking hurdle today, but that one might as well be Mount Kilimanjaro in comparison. "Not gonna happen, Sloane."

"Why not?" She looks hurt. Wounded, like it's the thought of having her next to me that's the reason behind my firm refusal. "We slept together after we had sex at Julio's that time. Was it that awful?"

I get up and start pacing. "Yes. Yes it was fucking awful. I nearly broke your neck when I woke up, remember? That wasn't a one-time thing, Sloane. That's *me*."

She ponders this, watching me pace. I get the feeling she wants me to sit down and be calm, but the idea of sharing a bed with her again and potentially breaking a few of those delicate bones of hers, well, that doesn't exactly leave me feeling easy.

"Why does it happen?" she whispers.

Things have come a long way with Sloane and me over the past few days, but this one last thing—I can't part with it yet. I don't know if I'll ever be able to. I give her enough to let her know I'm not dismissing her, but nothing more. "It's a bad dream, Sloane. A very bad dream, and I'm always going to have it. That's all there is to it."

Before she can try persuading me to explain it to her, I leave the cabin, slamming the door behind me. It's started to snow. Light spills out of the cabin windows, and I feel the cold bite down into my bones a little deeper; it's warm in there. Warm and bright and comforting with Sloane and her *if-only* wishes. I stand on the edge of the lake, and I know this is all a choice. I could choose to turn around and walk back inside, choose the warmth and the light and Sloane's tempting offer of a bed with her in it. I think about taking the steps. Turning around, left foot, right foot, left, right, and then I'd be back in there with her. The mechanics of it are easy, but the reality of it fucking isn't. I've once more chosen the cold, uncomfortable, *solitary* route, because I'm not ready to face that demon yet. The demon that plagues me in my sleep.

An hour later, Sloane opens the cabin door but she doesn't come out. I hear the unmistakable scrape of ceramic on stone; when I turn to investigate, there's a chipped white mug on the doorstep of the cabin and great wafts of steam are rising from it.

Hot chocolate. She must have found the kitchen alright, then. I didn't even know I had hot chocolate. I collect the cup but I don't drink the liquid inside. I just hold it, staring down at it until it goes cold and no more steam rises off the sweet smelling liquid, considering what it means to have someone to care for me. To not want me to get myself hurt. To look out for me.

A pair of headlights appear around twelve thirty, winding down the dirt track toward the cabin—Michael and Rebel, early. A black, mud-splattered Humvee pulls up out front and I can see exactly what Michael was talking about on the phone; Rebel looks pissed. He climbs out of the driver's side and slams the door so hard the echo of the sound barks across the reservoir.

"Didn't need to wait up for us, Dad," he says. "Where's my sister?"

"In-law," I reply. Sloane would shit herself if she heard him calling her that. "She's inside." Michael slaps me on the shoulder; he looks exhausted, the look he gets when he's propped up by too much coffee.

"We need to talk to her. To both of you," he says.

I don't particularly like the way Michael's talking in *we's* now; Rebel's his cousin, I get that, but he's been working for me for years now. More than that—he's been my friend. I can do all of this on my own if I have to, but it's a whole lot easier knowing he has my back.

We head inside; Sloane's already on her feet and looking tentatively pissed off before she even lays eyes on Rebel. I know what's on the horizon before she gets the opportunity to open her mouth.

"There she is," Rebel says. She walks straight up to him and slaps him across the face. His head kicks to the side, and I have to fight the urge to smile. My girl's got grit. I sincerely doubt there are many people in this world who could hit Rebel and get away with it. He nods, running his tongue over his teeth, as though he earned that one.

Sloane looks like she's going in for a second, though. Rebel ducks backward, just narrowly avoiding the flat of her hand again.

"You're a sick fuck, you know that?" she hisses.

"You're sister's told me a couple of times, yeah," he responds. I'm waiting for him to say the wrong thing to her—I will lay his ass out cold—but he doesn't. "Can I ask what I've done to deserve such a warm welcome, or is it just a general greeting that I can expect from here on in?"

"You tried to buy me," Sloane snaps. "You were already with my sister by that point, and you tried to fucking buy me."

I don't know what it is about Sloane getting mad, but her cursing always serves to make my dick really fucking hard. A highly inappropriate reaction for right now, though. I'm actually very interested in what the guy has to say about this. Rebel looks taken aback. His surprise is short lived; he's back on form within seconds, shrugging his shoulders. "Yeah, I was with Soph by then. But I haven't stopped buying girls just because I'm with your sister, Doc."

Michael flinches.

I flinch.

Sloane goes fucking postal. *"Are you—are you fucking kidding me right now?"* She charges, and I have to grab her up before she can reach him. Her arms and legs are everywhere, and she is *far* stronger than she looks. I grunt, trying to get a proper hold on her without doing any damage. I manage to send Rebel my coldest glare while doing this.

"You'd better explain what you mean by that or I'm letting her fucking go, and when she's done I'll be taking a turn," I growl at him.

Rebel holds up his hands. "I buy girls. I buy them before they can disappear down the cracks. I find them a new place to live and a job if I can, and I make sure they don't end up hooked on heroin or dead in a dumpster somewhere. Some of them end up in the fucking dumpster regardless of what I do to help them, but they end up there on their own terms, not because they've been kidnapped or coerced." He gives Sloane a flat look, folding his arms across his chest. "Or *blackmailed.*"

Sloane goes still in my arms, and I can feel her heartbeat thumping like a trapped bird's underneath my hands. "You weren't—you didn't want to—?"

"I knew you were her sister, Sloane. I'm not a fucking pig. Well, maybe sometimes I am but not where that's concerned. I lost my claim on you. I panicked. I came back to Seattle to check on you but you seemed fine. A little frayed around the edges, but you were going to work. You were living. I figured everything worked out for the best, and I did *not* tell Soph."

Everything worked out for the best. That's pretty fucking ironic. *I* bought Sloane. I bought her and I took her virginity because I thought I was protecting her, and it was the shittiest thing I've ever done. She would have been better off if I'd just let Rebel take her.

"Oh," Sloane whispers.

I feel like I'm dying on the inside.

"So please, feel free to slap me as hard as you like, Doc, but maybe we could do it later? I have something I'd like you to deal with first."

I put Sloane down. She gives me a conflicted glance over her shoulder, tucking her hair behind her ears. "What do you want me to deal with?" she whispers.

"Michael tells me you've had some run-ins with a friend of mine? Denise Lowell?"

Sloane hugs her arms around her body, suddenly focused on Rebel. "You could say that."

"She made you a deal, right? She said if you handed over information about me and my crew, you'd get your life back. Clean slates all round?"

"She didn't offer it to me directly, but yes. That's what I was told."

Rebel clenches his jaw, a set look forming on his face as though he's resolving himself toward something. "Good. Then I need you to call her. I need you to call her and tell her you want to make the deal."

20

Sloane

"YOU SURE YOU KNOW WHAT YOU HAVE TO SAY?" MICHAEL'S prepping me like I'm about to go live on air, defending myself against spurious murder charges. I feel dizzy and my palms are sweating like crazy, but I know what I'm supposed to say. I nod, and he hands me over his cell phone. "Remember. Keep it short. The movies are hardly ever realistic, but they *can* track you if you keep the line connected for too long." I nod again—yes, I've got it— and my eyes meet Zeth's. His jaw is set and his eyes are distant, and for once I know exactly what's going on in his head. He's reeling from Rebel's little revelation. Rebel the fucking superhero, not Rebel the rapist. He may not have done the awful things Zeth and everyone else in the underground crime syndicates believed he did, but he still kept my sister away, and I still don't like him.

Everything just got so confusing. I have to sit here and make this call, now, with the three men staring at me, and all I want to do is crawl into a corner and mull over the complexities of my situation from the start.

Rebel clears his throat. "It's the middle of the night, so this will actually work in our favor. She won't be expecting a call from you at all, let alone one this late. You've got the number?"

I hold the card up. "Let's just get this done." Zeth, Michael and Rebel have their arms folded across their chests, frowns on their faces, and their own brand of tense energy pouring off them. And they're all staring at me. Jeez. I twist on my seat so that I don't have to look at their stern expressions. I make the call.

The line rings four times. Five. I get to the seventh ring and a wash of relief overcomes me. She's not going to pick up. She's not going to pick up, which means I'm not going to have to do this.

"Lowell," a hoarse voice says into my ear.

Damn it.

"Detective Lowell," she says again clearing her throat, sounding minutely more awake. "It's you, isn't it? Dr. Romera?" She knows it's me. So much for not expecting me. Maybe I'm way more predictable than Rebel thinks.

"Yes," I say. "Oliver told me what you said to him about the deal. Is it true?"

The line's quiet for a moment while I hold my breath. "I told your colleague that you had a way out of this if you wanted one. I can make sure you're safe. I can make all of your problems disappear, Dr. Romera, but this is a two-way street. You have to give me what I need, too."

"What do you need?" My heart is contracting too painfully in my chest—too much adrenaline assaulting me all at once.

"I need your sister. I need Rebel. I need his whole crew. I need all of it."

Even though Rebel's standing in front of me, nodding at me to say yes, I still feel weird about this. "What's going to happen to Alexis?" I ask.

Lowell's answer is immediate. "If she cooperates, nothing bad will happen to her. I know you might not believe this, Sloane, but I'm actually trying to help your sister."

"That's why you shot her in the back, right?"

Michael makes a *hurry up* motion with his hand. I'm almost out of time. "I did my job, Dr. Romera. I'm counting on the fact that you can be reasonable and see that. And I'm counting on the fact that you want to get back to *your* job. You do want that, don't you?"

"Yes. We need to meet then, and I want this on paper. Our agreement, for me and for Zeth."

Silence. If she refuses to clear Zeth of any and all charges against him, related to whatever it is she's working on and unrelated, too, I am hanging up this phone. But then she says, "Fine. I'll have the paperwork drawn up."

"Have it ready for tomorrow. I'll call you with a meeting place."

"I'm going to need some assurances that—"

I hang up the phone, cutting her off. Michael takes the cell and switches it off, and Rebel slumps down beside me onto the beaten old leather sofa that I've been sitting on.

"That's that, then," he says. "Now we just wait for tomorrow."

ZETH FLITS BACK out of the door once the arrangements for the morning are made—I let him go earlier because he needed the space, but now I go after him because *I* need something. I need to talk. He may not like it, but it's going to happen. He's not standing by the water, stewing, this time; he's almost disappeared from view, headed off on an unseen path, by the time I've pulled on an old, damp-smelling red Parka I've found and hurried out after him.

He turns at the sound of the door, a serious grimace on his face when he sees me. "It's cold, Sloane. It's late. Go back inside."

It *is* cold. It's so cold I can feel the oxygen slipping in and out of my lungs as I jog toward him in the dark. There's no arguing with the fact that it's late, either, but that's not reason enough to put off this conversation. "We need to talk."

Zeth sighs, billows of steam pluming from his mouth in the frigid air. He turns and starts to walk again. "It doesn't really need to be said, does it? I was wrong about Rebel. I was the bad guy. I haven't hidden that from you, Sloane. I've told you from the beginning, that's who I am."

"Yeah," I muse. "You're the big bad wolf. I remember." I don't say it to mock him. I say it because it's true, and I *know* it's true. But it's not the *only* truth. He has a warped view of himself, and we need to iron that out. "You did take advantage of a really crappy situation, I'll admit, but you were trying to protect me. You're not—you're not *evil*, Zeth. You've done some very fucked-up things, but you've done so much since I've met you to help me and protect me, not to mention what you've done repeatedly for Lacey."

His sister's name sticks in my throat. Michael's working on tracking down Charlie and Lace as we speak; until we find out where the hell she is and if she's okay, even speaking her name is hard. Zeth winces, feeling it, too.

"I shouldn't have interfered," he says, stuffing his hands into the pockets of his thick jacket. "I should have stayed the hell away from you. You were better off when you were clueless, getting your work done. You should be dating that fucking Oliver guy right now, sharing inside jokes that no one else gets about surgery and bedpans and shit."

Oliver? He thinks I should be with *Oliver*?

"Oh, come on, Sloane. Don't look at me like that. You can't tell me you don't know that fucking preppy fuck is in love with you. He wants you bad."

"I've—I've thought he's maybe had feelings for me for a while, yes, but that's not what the look's for, Zeth. The look is because you think I'd rather be with him than you."

Zeth makes an exasperated sound deep in the base of his throat. He walks faster, head locked straight ahead, not looking at me. "I'm sure he wouldn't have fucked you in a dark hotel room. I'm sure he wouldn't have screwed up your whole life."

I can't. I can't listen to this anymore. I stop walking, throwing my hands up in the air. "Stop feeling fucking sorry for yourself, Zeth!"

That gets his attention. He freezes, spins around and paces back to me so that his face is in my face. "*What?*"

I jab him in the chest with my index finger to punctuate the words that come out of my mouth. "Stop. Feeling. Sorry. For. Your. Self."

He doesn't like the chest jabbing. He starts walking again. "I'm not feeling sorry for myself, Sloane. I'm feeling *guilty*." He says the word as though the emotion is an unwelcome houseguest who's shown up on his doorstep and refuses to leave.

"Well, you're gonna have to suck it up because I don't need you to feel guilty, Zeth. I'm not angry with you anymore. I'm *in love* with you. And you're just scared because you know you feel the same way, too." The words just race out of my mouth. I regret them as soon as they're said, but it's too late now—they've already escaped me. They've already been heard. Zeth halts in his tracks again—he never gets more than five feet from me. He narrows his eyes.

"You think you've got me all figured out, is that it?" he murmurs. He stalks toward me, and for the first time in days a good dose of real fear swells in the pit of my stomach. His eyes are sharp, intent, and I realize he does look a little wolfish in the pale moonlight. Our surroundings don't help matters, either. The woods that cloak the reservoir; the lightly falling snow; the irony of the fact that the over-sized Parka I'm wearing is bright crimson.

"I haven't figured you out, no. But I know that I'm right about this."

He pauses, close to me again, and I look up at him, trying not to freak out. He looks like he might want to drag me out onto the cracked, icy surface of the reservoir and throw me under. I reach up and carefully, very slowly, place my hand against the rough stubble of his cheek. Zeth's eyes widen a little; he seems surprised by the action. We stare at one another. One, two, three whole seconds, and then it's as though something breaks. I can practically see it happen. The tension releases its grip on his shoulders, and Zeth lowers his head, closing his eyes. My heart begins to beat again when he tilts his face toward me, into my palm.

"I don't know how to feel what you're telling me I feel," he whispers. "I don't know if you're right."

My eyes are pricking like crazy. This huge, strong, colossal entity of a man is crumbling before me and I'm suddenly breathless, terrified by the prospect. I ask him the one question that will change everything for us. It will dictate the rest of our lives, whether we spend them together or apart. I know it instinctively. "Do you want it, Zeth? Do you *want* to love me? Only you can release this unbearable grip you've got around your heart."

He opens his eyes, so dark, so hard and frightening. Even when he's laying his cards on the table, showing his hand, he still has the ability to make me tremble with one look. I think he's going to say no. I believe it with every last fiber of my being, but then he takes a deep breath and says, "Yes. Yes, I want that. I want *you*."

I reach up on my tiptoes and I gently place my lips against his. My other hand finds the center of his chest; I can feel his heartbeat there, faster than normal, like the steady, insistent knocking on a door. "Then all you have to do—is let go," I tell him. "We're going to get Lacey back. We're going to get a fresh shot at this whole thing, Zeth. We're going to make it work, no matter what it costs."

"It's probably going to cost us everything," Zeth tells me, his arms carefully, tentatively wrapping around my waist, drawing me to him.

I nod, because I already know this. I already know it, and I've made my peace with it. "Then that's what it takes."

COLLATERAL

21

Sloane

THERE ARE SO MANY WAYS IN WHICH THE HUMAN BODY reacts to stress. Elevated heart rate. Insomnia. Panic attacks. Trouble swallowing. Chest pains. Dizziness. The list is absolutely endless. I think I experience each and every item on that list as Zeth and I drive across state lines back into Washington.

A smart person would be heading in the other direction. A smart person would be hightailing it straight through the whole damn state to freaking Canada and changing their names, buying a small hardware store in the back of beyond, and hoping to all things holy that no Mexican or English gangsters find their way up there. Not us, though. Oh, no. That would be far too sensible. No, we're on our way to meet with a certain DEA agent—a woman personally responsible for screwing up my residency at St Peter's and also for shooting my sister. I have absolutely no desire to ever see Agent Lowell again, but it doesn't look like I have much choice, seeing as my sister's surprise husband is burning along behind us on the loudest motorcycle ever invented. I swear, there has never been a motorcycle louder than this one. My teeth have been vibrating together for the past sixty miles. The situation's not helped by the four other bikers following a hundred feet behind him, apparently *keeping an eye on things.* We're driving Rebel's Humvee, and Michael's passed out cold on the back seat, oblivious to the throaty roaring of the bikes at our rear.

Zeth's been relatively silent since we set off at dawn, and I haven't felt much like coaxing him into conversation, though now we're drawing closer to our destination I can sense he wants to say something. He reaches over and places his hand on top of my thigh, stilling my jittering knee. I hadn't even realized I'd been bouncing it. "You know what you have to do when we get there, right?" he says.

His hair has grown since he brought Lacey into the ER all those weeks ago. I somehow can't picture him doing such administrative things as visiting a barber to get a trim. He seems too...*alien* for that. Like for some reason, something so very human and necessary shouldn't really affect him.

His aviators shield his deep brown eyes, but I know the kind of look he'll be wearing: Concern. Displeasure. Irritation. He's been switching between those outward displays of emotion ever since Rebel decided I needed to go and meet Agent Lowell on my own. Not Zeth's idea of a smart plan, apparently, but then again, neither is either he or Rebel turning up to the meeting and getting their asses arrested right off the bat.

That's left me solely in charge of negotiations with the Drug Enforcement Agency, and I'm hardly relaxed about the prospect. Hence the bouncing knee. "Yeah, I know what I need to do," I confirm. "Don't back down. Don't give her any information that will lead her to you. Don't stay too long. Make sure I'm not being followed when I leave—"

"They're definitely going to be following you when you leave.

You just have to make sure you lose them before you get on the Metro." Zeth grips hold of the steering wheel so hard his knuckles blanch. He goes back to staring out of the windshield, his jaw clenching and unclenching. "You shouldn't be doing this," he growls under his breath.

He's worried about me. He hasn't said the words, but I know this confusing man more and more each day, and I know he's sweating this decision. And he's sweating it hard—to let me do as Rebel asks so my sister will be safe. I shouldn't be doing this for her anymore. I should have washed my hands of her long ago. But while I doubt I'll be speaking to Alexis any time soon, I still don't want Lowell to get her hands on her. She's my sister. She may not act like it, but that means something to me. Besides, part of Rebel's bargaining system is that he'll also help us find Lacey if we help him with Lowell, and so far we need all the help we can get on that front.

Lacey.

We're still reeling from that one. I just can't wrap my head around it—how she could have gone with Charlie after everything he's put Zeth through. After he tried to run me off the road. After he killed that poor woman in the gas station, for no good reason other than to cause a scene.

Zeth won't even say his sister's name.

I know how he feels.

Despite that, I can't help feeling nauseous. Is Lace okay? Is she freaking out? Is she coping, given it's been forty-eight hours since Charlie took her to see the Duchess, the catatonic woman has no doubt died by now? She must have. Oliver didn't think she had long left at all, and Lacey believed the woman was her birth mother. That will be playing havoc with her head.

"Sloane? Are you listening? Which line are you going to catch?" Zeth's gravel-filled voice interrupts my thoughts, demanding I concentrate.

"The 458. I get off at the university and change over. I meet you guys at Fresco's, and then we get the hell out of there."

Zeth grunts, chewing on his bottom lip. I've never seen him do that before. His shoulder muscles are so tense they're even giving me a headache. "And what are you going to tell her?" he asks. "What are you going to tell Lowell?"

I play the script out in my head, making sure I've got it all memorized. Not hard, really, when Rebel wants me to tell the truth. "I don't know where my sister is. Rebel, on the other hand, is waiting at an undisclosed location for her guarantee she's going to do as we ask, at which point he will hand himself over into her custody. I get the paperwork, including a decree from a county court judge clearing you, Michael and me of any and all charges against us, and then I tell her where he is."

Zeth exhales down his nose, nodding sharply. "Fucking stupid idea," he says under his breath. I think it's a fucking stupid idea, too, but then again we're bang out of options. "Just make sure you get through this, all right?" Zeth tells me under his breath.

I raise an eyebrow at him, feeling slightly victorious. "Why? Are you worried?" I tease him, even though I shouldn't. He gives me a flat look out of the corner of his eye.

"Am I worried?" He laughs softly, and it's not a humorous laugh; it's a pained one. "I'm fucking shitting myself, Sloane. There's no reason why this bitch won't just arrest you and use you as leverage. She's smart. She knows if she has you, she'll have a huge bargaining chip."

"Yes, but it's not like you're stupid. You wouldn't just go charging down there on a rescue mission. You wouldn't just hand yourself over if she did that. It would be pointless, her just arresting me." Silence falls over the car, and my heartbeat thrums in my ears. Zeth clenches his jaw again and a sick sensation washes over me. "Zeth? You wouldn't do that," I say.

He doesn't flinch. "Wouldn't I?"

I swivel around, wrestling against the seatbelt so I can face him. "No, you would *not*. I seriously doubt Lowell's going to pull anything like that. She knows she'll never get Rebel if she does. Either way, if things get messy, you and Michael must go and find Lacey. That's what you do. You do *not* hand yourself over just to free me. I can handle a couple of nights in a cell. She can't realistically keep me any longer than that." Zeth makes a choking sound in the back of his throat; I ball up my hand into a fist and pound it against his arm. "What, you don't think I can handle a few nights in a jail cell? I can. I will if I have to."

Zeth reaches up and removes the aviators so he can look me in the eye. I can see the anger he's battling to tamp down inside himself. "You will never need to spend the night in a cell on my account, Sloane. *Never.* I'll die before I let that happen." He blows out a frustrated breath and goes back to glaring out the window. My stomach churns like it's filled with battery acid. I feel a little stupid. Zeth spent time in prison. He spent countless nights in a cell, probably locked up with a complete psycho, with nothing but time on his hands and no way out. He knows what it means to be shut away from the world, how awful it must be, and here's me making light of it. Making out like I could hack it, when I honestly doubt I could.

"Sorry," I whisper. "I wasn't thinking."

Zeth doesn't say anything for a moment. He drives, eyes forward, tattooed forearms corded with rigid muscle. And then he takes a breath and says something that breaks my heart. "I want to make you happy, Sloane. I want to keep you safe. This life isn't what you deserve. Risking your freedom to find my sister and help Rebel— that isn't something you should ever have to consider doing. So yeah, if Lowell does arrest you, the very first fucking thing I'm gonna do is hand myself over. Rebel, too. I'll hand over anyone she fucking wants in a motherfucking heartbeat. Because there is no way I'm going to allow you to be put in danger or discomfort, to be locked up with hookers and crack addicts, if there's a single thing within my power I can do to prevent it. Not for one minute, Sloane. Not for one fucking *second*."

I don't really know what to say to that. It's madness he would do that, but that's not the reason I'm stunned. I'm stunned because of the passion in his voice. The determination in his eyes. He's never spoken to me like that before. *I want to make you happy, Sloane. I want to keep you safe.*

It doesn't matter that I've told him I love him and he hasn't said it back. This matters. This statement right here is all I need to hear to know I haven't been absolutely crazy in believing in him this whole time. I would never have dreamed those words would come out of his mouth a month and a half ago. I wouldn't have even been able to imagine it. But there's a soft side to Zeth he's finally showing to me, and every time I catch a glimpse of it, I feel myself falling harder.

The aviators have remained on the dash where Zeth placed them. He gives me a glance out of the corner of his eye, and a small, cautious smile forms on his lips. "Tell me you can handle this," he says. "'Cause I need to hear you say it."

"Lowell?" I ask, even though I know that's not what he's referring to. He blinks at me, the beginnings of his smile fading. I reach over and take his right hand from the steering wheel, holding it in my own. It's a brave move—we've not really gotten to stage yet where we're very tactile with one another outside of sex. I'm ready to be, though. I want to be. I don't know how he feels about being touchy feely—until he laces his fingers through mine and holds onto my hand tightly. Relief surges through me. Everything, every small little action, every carefully thought-out word feels like an experiment right now. An experiment that could either be gloriously successful or blow up in my face. "I can handle this," I say, making sure to look him right in the eye. "I can and I will take whatever you throw at me, Zeth. I'm stronger than I look."

He shakes his head slightly, another small, barely there smile pulling at the corner of his mouth. He looks straight at me, like he's looking into me, and then does something that makes my heart sing. He lifts our hands to his mouth and lays a gentle kiss on my wrist. "It doesn't matter what you look like, Sloane. You're the strongest person I know."

ZETH PULLS THE car up outside the entrance to Marlewood Shopping Mall, ignoring the angry beeping from other motorists that have to filter into another lane to get around the Humvee. Michael doesn't even wake up. The man can sleep through anything.

I grab my purse—the one I've somehow managed to retain throughout this madness—and get ready to open the door. Zeth grabs my wrist and grips hold of me tight. "Wait."

I wasn't going to make a big deal out of leaving the car. Saying goodbye, even if only for a few hours, should everything go according to plan, seemed like a bad idea. More tension. More stress to add onto everything else. But I see the indecision in Zeth's eyes. It wavers, and then it's no longer indecision but resolve. He leans across the seat and carefully places his palm against the side of my face.

"Don't do anything stupid," he murmurs. "Don't make me have to come get you, okay?"

I nod, and Zeth closes the final few inches between us. And he kisses me. Kisses. Me. For as long as I live, for as long as we're together, I will never be complacent about receiving a kiss from this man. Ever. I waited so long for the first one that now this and every other time he reaches for me and places his lips against mine will be an action to be treasured. His mouth is hot and demanding. The careful touch of his palm against my cheek quickly evolves as he lets go of my wrist so he can hold my face in both his hands. His breathing comes out ragged and fast, but not because the kiss is turning him on. It's not that kind of kiss. It's because he *means* it.

When he lets me go, I experience the biggest wave of doubt. We shouldn't be doing this. We should honest to goodness be ditching Rebel and heading for the hills. I know Zeth doesn't think we'll be safe until Charlie's out of the way—I refuse to acknowledge the fact he believes the old man needs to be dead—but if we changed our names and bought fake IDs, how hard could it be to run and hide? The reality of it, what running would mean, flashes through my head as I consider it. Not staying in any one place for too long. Working menial jobs. Never finding Lacey. Not being able to put down any roots.

Not being able to be a doctor.

The ship may have already sailed on that one, but the very thought of it still sinks through me like a stone. Fuck. When I look up at Zeth, his forehead pressed against mine, staring intently back at me, I can practically see the same thoughts running through his head. He knows we have no other way out of this. And besides, he's not a man to turn and run from anything.

"You've got to go," he whispers.

As if to cement that fact, there's a sharp rap on the passenger window of the Humvee. Fucking Rebel. He's wearing a grim and distinctly impatient look on his face. I want to castrate the man.

Zeth lets me go, and I climb quickly out of the car. I don't look back. I can't. For some terrifying reason, it feels as though I've just said goodbye to Zeth and won't be seeing him for a very, very long time.

"Awesome way to fly under the radar, blocking a lane of traffic outside the place you're supposed to be attending a covert meeting," Rebel says.

"You want me to do this or what?" I snap back.

"Just saying. Here." He reaches into the pocket of his black jeans and pulls out a thumb drive; he hands it over to me, using both hands to curl my fingers into a fist around the object like it's sacred. "Don't lose that. It's password protected."

"What's the password?"

"Accordia," he says slowly, as though the word holds meaning to him.

My chest squeezes painfully when the Humvee behind Rebel pulls away from the curb and vanishes from sight. I slip the thumb drive into my purse, frowning at Rebel. "Where's your bike? Where's your entourage?" The other Widow Makers are nowhere to be seen.

"Hidden in plain sight. Remember, don't tell her where to find me until you have the paperwork, and don't give the password to the drive until she's held up her end of the deal, either."

"Okay. Fine." I turn and make to head into the mall—I've had enough of talking about this. I just want to get it over with—but Rebel places a strong hand on my shoulder. "Sloane, you have to go see your sister. Please. Once you've got those papers, you need to head to New Mexico. She's waiting for you. And she won't...she won't forgive me for not coming back."

I feel like telling him I could give two shits about Alexis right now, but I get the feeling that won't expedite this situation. He'll only argue the point, and I'm almost late for the meeting. "All right. Shit." I scrub my hands over my face, trying to keep my cool. "I'll go and see her. But it's not on me to fix your relationship bullshit, Rebel. And what the hell kind of name is Rebel anyway?"

The Widow Maker beams at me—not the look you'd expect from a man who's about to willingly turn himself in to the DEA. "One designed to piss off my father," he replies. "Tell Soph I'll be home soon." And then he's turning and jogging off up the street.

I am alone.

I haven't been alone in so long now that the realization comes as a shock. No one watching me. No one guarding me keeping me from harm. And no one preventing me from just walking away. Pins and needles prickle down my arms and backs of my legs. I could just do it. I could walk away. Then the pins and needles turn into a sick, paralyzed feeling. As if that's an option. Seriously, I wouldn't be able to if I tried. The man I'm in love with would always pull me back. I enter the mall with a small part of me screaming inside. I think it's the part that's in charge of my self-preservation instincts.

It takes me a while to find the food court. It's three levels down in the basement, but Zeth told me to take the long way down, using as many escalators as possible, so I could scope out the lay of the land. Commit to memory where all the exits are. Plot out which way to go if I need to make a fast exit. It's almost a waste of time, though. If Agent Lowell wants to take me into custody, it won't be terribly difficult.

It's five past one when I reach the food court—the place allocated as our meeting point. Rebel was at least smart about the location and time of our meeting. The lunch crowds—hordes of people queuing to grab a bite to eat on their breaks—create a wall of bodies, easy to slip through unnoticed. Lowell is already seated at a table in the middle of the food court, eyes downcast, fixed on the lit-up screen of her cell phone. I hurry through the bustling sea of people and quickly sit down on the other side of the table before I can change my mind and bolt.

Agent Lowell doesn't look up from her cell phone. Her fingers move swiftly over the touchscreen, typing quickly. "You're late," she informs me.

"I know."

"That tells me you're unreliable, Dr. Romera. Why would I trust someone who's unreliable?"

I can't help but laugh at that. "You don't trust me. You probably didn't even know for sure if I was going to show up."

A cold, unpleasant smile spreads across Lowell's face. She puts down her cell phone and finally looks up at me. "And supposing you're right? I don't trust you, and you don't trust me. How is this arrangement supposed to proceed?"

I shrug my shoulders, giving her a cold, unpleasant smile of my own. "We rely on the age-old principle of supply and demand, I suppose. You want information I possess. I want something in return. It's very simple, really."

Agent Lowell pouts, stroking a hand over her neatly secured hair. I wonder what this scene looks like to the families and friends and work colleagues seated at the tables around us, quickly inhaling their lunch. Do Agent Lowell and I just look like two girlfriends meeting for lunch? Or can people feel the animosity radiating off us, marring the air like a rotten stink?

"I want both of them," Lowell tells me, her eyes vacant. In fact, she looks a little bored. There are dark circles underneath her eyes, though, and I know her blasé attitude is all pretense. "If I don't get both of them, Rebel *and* your sister, then we don't have a deal."

The arrangement we made on the phone yesterday was for Rebel, but I prepared myself for the eventuality that she would change her mind, move the goalposts, and demand more than we agreed on. I'm ready for it.

"I only have the Widow Maker. If that's not good enough, then you can forget the whole thing." I narrow my eyes at her. "Would you really believe me if I told you where she was, anyway? Would you really believe I'd given up my own sister?"

"Word is you're not so happy with little Alexis these days," Lowell says. She picks at a stale-looking salad sandwich sitting on a plate in front of her, absent-mindedly pulling it apart. "Perhaps you've had enough of protecting her."

I just shake my head. Agent Lowell sighs, pushing the plate bearing the stale sandwich away. "All right. So Rebel for a clean slate. Tell me where he is."

"I need the paperwork first."

Lowell shoots me a disgusted look. The woman is actually quite attractive, but her general disapproval with life has left a few deep lines on her face, making her appear permanently unhappy. "It takes time to get paperwork like that, Dr. Romera. It's also the weekend. I can't just show up at Judge Goldstein's front door and start making demands. It's his daughter's bat mitzvah today. I won't be able to get the sign-off until Monday."

I'm prepared for this excuse, too. "We can rearrange to meet when you're prepared then. I can't guarantee Rebel will still be where he is right now, though. You know these biker types." I flash her a completely insincere smile. "They tend to roam around a lot."

Lowell's mouth twists into a sour grimace. "Since we're here finally having a conversation, how about you and I have a little reality check, huh? There are a few things I'm sure you have no clue about that might change your whole attitude toward these proceedings." She leans down to her side and pulls a manila folder out of her Louis Vuitton purse. In the movies, manila folders are never good news. I doubt this one is going to be any different.

"I don't care what you want to show me, Denise," I snap, placing my hand flat against the envelope so she can't open it. "I'm not interested. All I want is that paperwork, and then our business here is done."

Lowell yanks the envelope out from underneath my hand and opens it anyway. She lays a photograph down on the table in front of me. "This is Ray Peterson," she says, tapping a fingernail against the wide-eyed stare of the dead man gazing out of the image at me. The photo is in color, so it's not hard to miss the pool of blood he's lying in. I brace myself against the tabletop and peer forward so I can get a good look at the picture. Lowell seems momentarily disappointed. Perhaps she expected me to throw up or something. Tactics like that might work on someone who hasn't spend the last two years working in the trauma department of an emergency room, but since I've witnessed more than my fair share of dismembered body parts and internal organs, that should frankly never see the light of day, all Agent Lowell gets out of me is a raised eyebrow. "Your point?"

"My point is that your boyfriend's employer had a falling out with Ray Peterson last August, and then poor Ray here ends up with the back of his head blown out. You're playing this whole thing very cool, Dr. Romera. Is *this* cool with you?" She pulls out another photo, this time an image clearly showing Ray's gaping head wound. I blink at it, then fix Lowell with a dark look.

"I know Charlie Holsan's an asshole. Are you inferring that *Zeth* killed this man?"

"I am."

"And your proof?"

"Zeth was Holsan's enforcer up until a few months ago. Who else would it have been?"

I snort, shoving the images back across the table at her. "Is that the kind of logic that convicts felons, Agent Lowell? Because if it is, I'm seriously worried about the state of the United States justice system."

"It should be," she snaps. "Maybe if it was, then people like Rebel and Zeth wouldn't be free to incite mayhem. People wouldn't be out there kidnapping young girls like Alexis right off the street. Here." She pulls out a wad of photographs—at least twenty—and slaps them down in front of me. "These are all men killed on Charlie Holsan's say-so. If your boy toy didn't murder at least half of them then I shit rainbows, Sloane. And from meeting me, do I really strike you as the sort of congenial person who might be doing something like that?"

My pulse is racing—there are a lot of photographs in front of me right now, all displaying the mangled and very dead bodies of countless men—but I know what she's doing. It's pretty freaking obvious. If she can turn me, make me realize how dangerous the man that I've aligned myself with is, then her job becomes a whole lot easier. Shame for her that none of this is a surprise to me.

I know Zeth has hurt people before.

I know Zeth has killed people.

I know he's done unspeakable things.

I know he thinks he is a monster.

But I also know *him*.

There is no excuse for taking another person's life. I know that. I uphold that, and I firmly believe it. But Zeth didn't kill Charlie's enemies because he wanted to, or felt like it, and definitely not because he *enjoyed* it. He did it because he was hollow. He did it because he's been surrounded by violence from the moment he was born, and he has never known anything else. He did it because Charlie Holsan was the man he looked up to as a child. Charlie Holsan was the role model giving Zeth his cues. He did it because Charlie Holsan ordered him to.

And despite that, despite the brutality of his past and his upbringing, there is still a kindness inside him. He protected me. He fought for me. He found my sister, and he's carried me through so much. He's not hollow anymore. And I know with a certainty he will never take another life again. Not unless he does it to protect *me*.

208

"The man has a mean temper on him," Lowell continues, jabbing at the pictures. "What if it's not some mark next time, huh, Sloane? What if it's your head he's holding a gun to?"

Oh, boy. No fucking way. That's it. I've had enough. I stand so quickly the cheap plastic chair I've been sitting on crashes over. What feels like a hundred people stop eating, drinking, talking, laughing, and stare. "You don't know this man. You clearly don't know this man at all."

Lowell holds up her hands. "I'm sorry. I'm sorry, Sloane. Just sit down, okay? Just sit back down. We're not done here."

"I think you'll find we are."

I'm moving through the crowds, then, shoving and pushing past people, trying to get out. She wasn't going to get the papers from that judge. She never was. She came here to convince me to betray Zeth and nothing more. My blood is boiling in my veins. I have no cell phone on me. Rebel insisted, just in case I was being observed and didn't know the walls had ears, but right now I desperately wish I had one. I want to call Zeth. I want to find him and get the fuck out of here.

I don't turn to see if Lowell's following me, but I know she will be. I know there will be other agents mixed in amongst the crowds observing me, too. That doesn't matter. I charge blindly, my only thought finding a way out of the packed masses. I run up an escalator, shoving past people, determined to get by, and—

I stop.

What the fuck?

As I reach the top of the escalator, I make to push past the man blocking my way, only to find I recognize the person. He's my father.

"Hello, Sloane."

I stumble off the moving walkway, bracing myself against his chest, the palms of my hands laid flat against the brown suede jacket I bought him as a gift last Christmas. He gives me a sad smile, and I know I'm about to have my heart broken.

"If you have a moment," he says softly, brushing a strand of hair that's fallen loose from my ponytail back behind my ear. "I think we ought to have a chat."

22

Zeth

I DON'T KNOW WHAT TO DO. I HAVE NEVER NOT KNOWN what to do. Michael's hardly being helpful in this situation, either. Since we arrived at Fresco's Coffee House, he's done nothing but sit there, fully composed, drinking macchiato after macchiato and reading *The Seattle Times*.

I feel like I'm about to fucking explode.

"Are you going to be vibrating this badly the whole time we're waiting? Should I go sit at another table?" Michael asks.

"Go and sit at another fucking table," I growl. "*I dare you.*"

Michael folds the newspaper in half and places it on the table, fixing a blank look on me. "You want me to make some calls? Find out if anyone knows anything about Charlie?"

"That would be useful." I'm being a massive dick, but I can't help it. I can't even sit still. Michael's right—I'm literally vibrating in my seat, twitching every time the fucking bell on the door jangles and someone-who-is-not-Sloane walks in. Michael pulls out his phone and starts making calls. I stare at the ceiling, my head kicked back, trying to remember how to not fucking lose it.

I have no idea who this person is that I've become, but I'm honestly a little frightened of him. The old me has been wrestling with this new guy, and I have to say, this new fucker's beating the cold, calm, collected version of me hands fucking down.

Some people might consider this progress, I suppose. Right now, I'm not sure what I think. I *know* I'm fucking worried, and that it feels fucking horrible.

"Yeah, yeah, buddy, I understand. No problem. I appreciate that. Thank you." Michael hangs up his call, shrugging his shoulders. His suit's not even wrinkled from sleeping three hours in the back of that monstrosity of car. I feel like shaking him. "Trey and West haven't heard a thing about Charlie all week. They didn't even hear about the showdown at the apartment, so they're either lying or they've had their heads up their asses since Monday. They said they would let me know if they do hear anything, but I'm pretty sure they're not going to."

Fuck. I scowl at Michael's cell phone lying on top of his discarded newspaper as though it's solely responsible for the lack of any worthwhile leads. Thing is, people don't like talking about Charlie. It's bad fucking karma. You say the bastard's name and he appears. Causes havoc wherever he fucking goes. The dark characters Michael's calling on for information know better than to even *think* the name Charlie Holsan, let alone rat on him.

"We just need to be patient, Zee. Charlie's hardly father-of-the-year material. Lacey will cut her losses and run at the first opportunity. She knows how to get hold of you, right?"

"Yeah. Right." The last burner I had before Lace vanished into thin air is still sitting in the pocket of my jeans like a ticking fucking time bomb. No one has the number but Sloane, Lace, Michael and Rebel, but for some reason it just doesn't feel safe. If it weren't for Lacey, I would have ditched the thing days ago.

I take it out and toss it onto the paper next to Michael's. My heart nearly explodes out of my damn chest a second later when a ringtone blares out like a goddamn klaxon. I think it's mine. For one long second I'm filled with dread—Sloane or Lacey. Either way it could be bad news. Terrible news. But it's not mine; it's Michael's.

He picks it up and checks the caller ID. "Rebel." He looks up at me, frowning. He answers the call, talking in hushed tones. "Tell me," he says.

I watch Michael's composure fragment and disintegrate altogether over the next seven seconds. "What do you mean, *she ran?*"

The words are enough on their own to have me lunging across the table and snatching the phone out of Michael's hands. "She ran?" I can feel my heart beat in my fucking temples.

"I had one of the boys watching her. She sat with the DEA bitch for five minutes, looked at some photos, and then bolted. Some old guy apparently stopped her, and then the fucking men in black swept in and grabbed her ass."

"So they arrested her?" I fucking knew this was a bad idea. My hands begin to shake with rage. "If she's in any trouble, I swear to god I'm going to skin you alive, motherfucker."

Rebel grunts down the phone. It's the sort of sound I would make if I were accommodating someone who should know better than to flare up at me. "There were no handcuffs. She hugged the old man. She definitely wasn't arrested, asshole, so you can calm the fuck down."

"Calm the fuck down? Okay, I'll calm the fuck down when you tell me exactly where my girlfriend is."

The word girlfriend trips off my tongue before I even have a chance to second-guess it. No second-guessing is required, though. Sloane *is* my girlfriend. She's even more than that.

"I don't know exactly where she is, obviously. I wouldn't be calling you otherwise. Any idea who the old guy is?"

I fight the urge to smash my damn fist through the wall. "He have gray hair? Skinny? Beginnings of a tan?"

Rebel's voice grows distant as he consults with the guy who must have been on point in the mall's food court. And then, "Yeah, sure. An old guy."

Yeah, sure doesn't exactly fill me with confidence, but it's better than nothing. The old man is Sloane's dad. Has to be. Dr. and Mrs. Romera must have returned early from the trip Sloane sent them on. They were supposed to be well out of the way while this was going down, but now it would seem Sloane's father is right bang in the middle of it all. Didn't see that coming. Shit. "Okay, well...fuck. I suppose I'd better call her mom."

I suppose I'd better call her mom. Ridiculous. Who the fuck am I? Michael aims a look at me that says he's thinking the exact same thing. Rebel chuckles down the phone. "If you want, man. Just whatever you do, don't fucking blow this for me."

"I could give a shit about you, motherfucker," I snap. "You're walking a fine line right now. You're off on some mission to save some girl when you're married to Alexis? You think Sloane isn't one hundred percent pissed about that? Why don't you just—"

I stop dead. Rebel says something on the other end of the line, but I'm not paying attention. My eyes are fixed solely on the newspaper that's still folded in half and sitting on the table between Michael and me.

My mind can't comprehend what it's seeing—a black symbol, a block of solid ink in amongst the scrawl of thousands of words marking the broadsheet. The simple fleur-de-lis might not draw the attention of many people in this city, but a certain demographic react appropriately when they witness it in print. Or tagged on the side of a building. Or tattooed into someone's skin, like it has been tattooed into mine.

Fucking Charlie.

I snatch the paper up and open it out, and sure enough, it's him. Blatant motherfucking bastard.

THE DUCHESS
Beloved partner and mother.
Your loss is too much to bear.
Departed this world Friday morning peacefully in her sleep.
Funeral to be held at St. Finnegan's Catholic Church
Sunday, October 19 at 11 a.m.
Wake to follow at Hunt's Point.
Your attendance is invited and most welcome.

I glance to the top of the page—the obit section. So that's it then; the Duchess is dead. My stomach cramps at this new information. I knew it was coming, but still...the woman did care about me once, and I cared about her in my own way. I toss the paper down, shoving an accusing finger at the fleur-de-lis Charlie uses as his personal family crest. Michael frowns at the paper, sees what I'm pointing at, and his face clouds over.

"Hey? Hey, are you listening? *Zeth!*" My cell phone is shouting at me. Or rather, Rebel's shouting at me out of the speaker.

"*What?*"

"Don't worry about Sloane. I'll find her, okay?"

"Rebel, I wouldn't trust you to find my girl if you were the last fucking man alive." I hang up the phone. I don't want to hear

215

another word come out of his mouth.

I keep forgetting Michael is this asshole's cousin. He curves an eyebrow at me, his mouth lifting in the corners. "Not a fan, huh?"

"Not particularly. Sorry."

"No need to apologize. He's an acquired taste." Michael huffs out a breath, running his hands down the front of his suit jacket. "Okay, so what's the plan? Are you about to go throw yourself on the mercy of this DEA agent or what? Sloane said not to."

I stand, shooting him a filthy look. "It's rude to pretend you're asleep when people are having a private conversation."

"No, it's not. Having a full-blown make-out session when someone's trapped in the back of the same car as you? *That's* rude."

I bite back the urge to growl. We leave Fresco's, but not before Michael returns his macchiato glass to the barista and informs him that his coffee is bad. Really, really fucking bad. The barista looks like he's just shit his pants.

When we're outside, the city is unusually still, as though it's holding its breath, awaiting an approaching storm. In some ways it might as well be. Somewhere out there, Sloane's potentially being interrogated, held against her will. That does *not* sit well with me. If I don't have her back within the next hour, Seattle will be hit by the biggest storm it's ever seen. And that storm will be *me*. Michael hands over the keys to Rebel's Humvee without needing to be asked.

He climbs into the passenger seat, putting on my aviators. "What are we doing?"

"We, my friend, are going to find ourselves some goddamn collateral."

Michael pats the dashboard, grinning. "Sounds like a plan."

"And Michael?"

"Yes?"

"Once Sloane's back where she's supposed to be…I'm gonna need to borrow a suit."

23

Sloane

THE LAST TIME I SAW DAD'S WOOD-PANELED STATION wagon, it was in the rearview mirror of a getaway car. I never thought we'd be able to retrieve it from Julio's compound, and yet here I am, sitting in the front passenger seat, listening to the damn thing's all-too-familiar choking and grinding as we head out of the city.

"So, where do you think we ought to start?" Dad asks, hands firmly at ten and two on the steering wheel.

My chest feels like a heavy weight is pressing down on it, making it hard to breathe. My hands are shaking. I'm so livid I can barely sit still. "Maybe at the beginning? Like how you came to be involved with the DEA, Dad? You've known all along, haven't you? You've known all along that Alexis was alive and you haven't said a goddamn word. That's why you reacted so weirdly when I came to the house to tell you and Mom I'd found her. God!"

"*Sloane.*"

"What, Dad? Don't take the lord's name in vain? What the hell am I supposed to say? You've been lying to us. Lying to us for years." I brace my elbows against my knees, leaning forward, trying to clear my head. Pointless though. I can't fucking believe it. "You haven't even denied it," I whisper. "You haven't even told me it's not true."

His remorse rolls off him in waves that practically pull at me. Like Zeth, Dad's never been one to lie. "I'm sorry, sweetheart. I really am. But it was imperative you didn't know where Alexis was."

"And Mom? Was it imperative she didn't know where her freaking *daughter* was? She thought she was *dead*, Dad!"

"I know, Sloane. I know. But you have to understand, I did what I had to do. It was the way it had to be. It wasn't going to be forever."

I sit up straight so I can look him in the eye—the man I've respected my whole life. The man whose footsteps I've wanted to follow in since I was a little girl. The man who taught me love and justice and honesty. My stomach twists, and I realize something terrible is about to happen. "Oh, no. Dad, pull over."

"What is it?"

"Dad just pull over the damn car!"

He swings the station wagon over to the side of the road, just in time for me to push open the door and part company with the contents of my stomach. I throw up so hard my eyes cloud over with tears. Dad places his hand in the center of my back and rubs up and down, just like he did when I was sick as a kid. The action doesn't make me feel any better. It makes me feel even worse.

I hear a car pull up behind us and the crunch of footsteps on the gravel at the side of the road, then a deep voice saying, "We can't stay here. She can throw up back at the field office."

I don't know the man that voice belongs to, but I already hate him. I swat the tears from my eyes and look up into the face of the tallest guy I've ever seen. His generic SUV is parked right behind us, the passenger door still yawning open. Lowell's at the wheel, staring at me with an impassive, unaffected look. The same one she was wearing when she showed me the bodies of the many men she says Zeth killed. I flip her off, and then I spit on the ground, ridding myself of the foul taste of vomit.

"Tell your boss she can go fuck herself," I inform the giant in front of me. I swing my legs back into the car and then slam the door so violently the whole car rocks.

"You don't know the truth, sweetheart. I think as soon as I explain everything, you'll understand," Dad says softly.

If he thinks that, then he has another thing coming. "I don't care what the truth is now, Dad. It's too late. Both you and Alexis have totally betrayed any trust that might have existed between us. You've destroyed everything. I just...I just don't wanna hear it."

A car horn blares behind us—Lowell bitching about our lack of movement. Dad puts the station wagon into gear and pulls back out onto the road. We're apparently headed to a field office. Somewhere I can be righteously preached at about my recent life choices. I wouldn't have gone anywhere with my father or Agent Lowell given the choice, but it was either this or getting my ass arrested and my assets seized until I complied. I haven't touched my bank account in weeks. It seems that whenever I've needed something it was simply there, provided to me by either Zeth or more often than not by Michael. But at some point I am going to want access to my money, and I am definitely going to want to go back home. But when the hell will that ever happen? The very thought of being able to step back inside the sanctuary I created for myself without towing a whole heap of trouble right after me is laughable.

Besides, my father promised me he'd drop me off wherever I wanted after I'd heard him out, so this seemed like the best option at the time. We drive for another forty minutes passing turnoffs to

Mountlake Terrace, Lynnwood and the Paine Field Airport until we arrive in Everett. I haven't been here since I was a kid—a birthday party for either Alexis or myself, I can't recall now. The place reminds me of screaming children and the smell of hamburgers.

Dad pulls the station wagon into the parking lot behind a liquor store of all places. He kills the engine and removes the keys from the ignition. "Sloane, you have to know that I'm sorry. I didn't withhold anything from you to deceive you, or your mother. I—"

"How about you just show me what you so desperately need to show me and then you can take me back to the people who don't lie to me and abuse my trust, huh, Dad?" It strikes me as very strange that this is actually the truth. Zeth has never asked for my trust and then let me down. He's never hidden anything from me. If I've wanted to know something, if I've found myself in a situation where he has control over me, if a situation's been bad, he hasn't hurt me or betrayed me. He's been honest, and he's kept me safe. Zeth, a man I know to be a criminal, has treated me with more respect than my own father, a man of the church.

Oh, the irony's so bittersweet, I feel like I'm choking on it.

"Just keep an open mind, okay, kiddo?" Dad tells me.

Lowell and her subordinates have pulled up in their hulking great SUVs, and are already out of the vehicles, waiting not so patiently for us to get out, too. I don't answer my father. I get out of the car, shooting an evil look at the woman who seems to be at the heart of this whole fucking mess. Lowell gestures toward a flight of metal stairs that zigzag up the side of the liquor store, wearing a grim smile. "After you," she says. The diamond tread on the steps of the staircase have almost worn clean away in the middle, a slick silver patch of steel in the center of the otherwise rusted metalwork. My footsteps clang out, echoing around the parking lot as I climb up one, two, three flights, and then I can't go any farther.

We've reached the top of the stairs, and in front of me a solid, reinforced steel door covered with dark green chipped paint bars the way. Lowell slips by me and punches a code into the keypad on the wall; the door *shunks* open, and an alarm sounds from within the building, a single-pitched *ernnnn* noise that reminds me of prison gates. The ones I've seen on TV, and hopefully not the one I will soon be calling home.

Lowell hurries into the building, not bothering to check behind her to see if I'm following. I wouldn't have a choice even if I didn't want to; my dad is right behind me, followed by the giant who told us to hurry up on the side of the road before, and two other guys in immaculate suits. Dad smiles sadly at me, and I don't smile back. Inside, the building smells like Pop Tarts. Burnt ones. Someone's obviously charred the hell out of their late breakfast.

A florescent strip light flickers overhead, emitting a high-pitched buzz, as the five of us move in quick, silent efficiency down the corridor. There are rooms off to the left and the right. We pass open doors that give way to empty, bare concrete boxes beyond. No office furniture. No admin workers. Just the occasional smashed-up cardboard box and in one room a broken wooden stool with only three legs instead of the four it obviously started out with.

Lowell proceeds with military precision, turning left and then right as the corridor snakes out in front of us, until we hit another heavy metal security door. Another code goes into another keypad. Another alarm. This time there are people on the other side of the door. Hastily thrown-together work spaces, photo-fit images taped to walls, ringing telephones and curious glances welcome us as we head toward an office with an open door at the far end of the vast room.

Lowell goes inside, as do I. Dad follows behind, but the nameless men peel off to various workstations, dismissed with a perfunctory glare from Lowell.

"Why don't you have a seat?" Lowell nods her head at a chair facing what I assume is her desk. When Dad shimmies around the unnecessarily large desk and sits down on the same side as her, I almost vomit again, right there on the floor. This is fucking crazy.

"Now, since you don't care about my photos just now, I'm hesitant to try and show you any more," Lowell says. "Your father has other ideas, however. He feels you ought to see why it's important for us to find your sister. Are you willing to listen to what we have to say this time? To let us show you what you've gotten yourself into?"

I glance at Dad; he doesn't look away, though I get the impression he wants to. "I'm kind of a captive audience right now," I snap. "Let's just get this over with."

"Good." Lowell opens up a laptop that's sitting on her desk and frowns, concentrating on the screen for a moment. She clicks a couple of times, apparently finds whatever she's looking for, and then spins the thing around so I can see the display. It's footage from a security camera of some description, dark and blurry. It's hard to make much out at first, but it looks like there's snow on the ground. Lowell reaches over and hits the play button, and the still image comes to life. There's no sound. I see a dark figure walking quickly down an abandoned street, alone, and my heart feels like it's swelling in my chest. It's Lexi. I can tell by the huge, sloppily knitted scarf she has wound around her neck—she spent three months trying to finish that thing before winter arrived, and then refused to leave it at home once it was done.

I suddenly know what I'm watching. I know what I'm being shown, and I do not want to see it. I lean forward in my seat, reaching for the laptop, to turn it away, to close the damn thing, to just make it stop, but then Alexis freezes on the screen. She just stops dead in the middle of the sidewalk, her focus fixed on something or someone I can't see. A second later, I do see what she's looking at: a long stream of motorcycles burn down the road—three, five, eight—I don't know how many of them. Half the actual road is cut off on the screen, so it could be thirty for all I know. Alexis stands and watches them pass, the strange sight of so many men on their bikes, ripping through the center of Seattle obviously enough to stop her in her tracks.

"What the hell is this?" I whisper.

Dad just shakes his head. "Keep watching, sweetheart."

The bikers disappear. Alexis remains still a moment longer, dark hair flying about her face, being teased at by a silent wind. She steps up to the side of the curb looks up and down, as though she's going to cross over. However, before she can take another step, a dark figure, a man, runs out of the side street behind her and falls to his knees, reaching out a hand to my sister. He clearly frightens her; she visibly jumps, and skitters backward away from the person.

Alexis pauses, as though trying to decide what to do, and then she rushes forward, bending toward the man on the ground, unwinding that hideous scarf from around her neck.

"She was helping someone?" I ask. I don't take my eyes off the screen, and neither Lowell nor my father respond. I'm supposed to see for myself. I'm scared though. I'm a coward. I don't want to see her get hurt, no matter how badly she's hurt *me*.

The two people on the screen are talking, that much is clear, and it's incredibly frustrating that I don't know what's being said. I squint at the laptop, even though there's no way in hell I'm going to be able to lip read what's coming out of their mouths. The quality of the image is so poor and pixelated that I can't make out their actual facial features. Alexis offers out a hand, but the man on the ground recoils backward. Confusing. He was reaching for her only a second ago, but now he seems scared. He starts scrambling away from her, arms and legs working against the snow on the ground, trying to put some space between them. And then his fear suddenly makes more sense. He's not trying to get away from Alexis. He's trying to get away from the group of men that are approaching her from behind.

I count eight of them.

"Oh my god." I cover my mouth with my hands, half considering covering my eyes, too. Alexis never turns around. She never knows the men are behind her. The tallest of all of them, broad in the shoulders with a pronounced limp, is the first to reach my sister. He clamps a hand over her mouth and physically lifts her off the ground. Her legs kick out desperately, but the guy doesn't put her down. Another one of the men grabs hold of the person still lying in the snow and tries to wrestle him up, but he doesn't succeed. Instead, he takes him by the arm and then drags him back into the same alleyway he appeared from. The other men follow. My sister is carried out of shot and into the darkness by the tall guy with a limp.

And she is gone.

Lowell reaches forward and snaps the laptop closed. "The man you saw in that footage, the one she encountered first? That was Judge Ryan Conahue. His body was found under a pile of trash the morning after this happened. A restaurateur took out his garbage at 5:30 a.m. and got a bit of a fright. Conahue had been stabbed once in the chest, directly in his heart. He'd bled out into the snow."

She produces another file from a drawer in her desk and tosses an image down—a silver-haired man in his late fifties, early sixties, eyes clouded over and staring straight up toward the sky, blue lips slightly parted. There is, indeed, a wound in his chest—the obvious source of the copious amounts of blood that have stained his great coat and turned the dirty snow around him bright red.

"A judge? He was a judge?" I ask.

"Yes, sweetheart. He was presiding over a murder case at the time. A man had been arrested, a very dangerous man, and his companions, the men you just saw in the video, didn't want the judge to find him guilty of the crime. They'd been leaning on Judge Conahue, trying to coerce him into freeing this individual, but he refused."

"So they murdered him." Just when I thought this couldn't get anymore complicated, any more fucked up...

Agent Lowell fiddles with the computer for a second and then turns it back to me. It's already playing. A beaten-up van is careening down the street. It pulls over at the side of the road in front of the alleyway and two men get out. They go to the back of the van and open the rear doors. It's hard to see what's going on in the mouth of the alleyway now, because the bulk of the vehicle is blocking the view, but I can see a scuffle taking place. An arm, a leg. One of the men slips in the snow and lands on his ass, his whole body suddenly in view. I still can't see his face properly, but I have no problem whatsoever seeing his shoulders hitch up and down— he's laughing. *Laughing.*

The rear doors to the van close, and then the man who fell over walks back to the driver's door and climbs in. There's movement at the passenger door but it's so dark I can't see who climbs in there. The van pulls away, and then they're gone. The street is empty.

"Who are they?" I ask. There's a lump in my throat the size of a basketball. I can barely talk around it.

Lowell shifts in her seat, tracing her fingers over the fat file in front of her. "They're a cartel."

"Colombian?"

She shakes her head. "Mexican."

"Not...not *Julio Perez*?"

Lowell looks intrigued, like I'm finally talking her language. "No, not Perez, though he is connected to this group. They're called Los Oscuros. Their leader, Hector Ramirez, started off in drugs but quickly realized guns were more profitable. They were based in

Mexico for years. Some shit went down on US soil and Hector apparently decided he didn't want his business remotely managed anymore. He legally immigrated and set up a carpet cleaning business. He used that as a front for money laundering. Still does."

"And where does my sister fit in?"

"He also sells pussy," Lowell says. My father flinches—I doubt anybody has ever said pussy in front of him before. I definitely doubt they've ever essentially referred to his daughter as pussy. Lowell clearly doesn't give a shit that she's offended my father's delicate sensibilities. "Your sister's a pretty girl, Dr. Sloane. Hector took one look at her and saw dollar signs. He made a deal with Perez. Perez bought her from him, was going to keep her at that little fuck village he's set up for himself out in the desert, but your good friend Rebel somehow managed to get his hands on her. That's where things get tricky. The Widow Makers are at war with Los Oscuros. The cartel found out Alexis was with the bikers and they immediately put a contract out on her life."

My head is officially hurting at this landslide of information, but I do understand what Lowell is telling me. "They wanted her dead because the bikers might be able to convince her to testify that Los Oscuros killed the judge. Right?"

"That's right, sweetheart." Dad leans forward, propping his elbows against the table. "Your sister called me four months after she went missing. I didn't know anything about her disappearance before that, I swear. She told me what had happened and asked me to send her some money so she could get away. She was frightened, but she sounded like she was okay. She told me not to call the police, but—"

"Your father's not an idiot, Sloane," Lowell says. "As soon as he found out Alexis was alive, he did the right thing and contacted the authorities. We've been handling the case ever since."

A bolt of anger fires through me. "And by handling the case, you mean nearly killing my sister?"

"What? She was...Alexis was nearly killed?" The disbelief in my dad's voice makes me scream at him. He thinks he's in possession of all the facts, but in reality he's been kept in the dark. His face has gone as white as chalk.

"Oh yeah, didn't Agent Lowell tell you that? Alexis nearly died because your buddy here shot her?"

The muscles in my dad's face fall slack, all expression completely slipping away. He can't believe the words I'm saying—I can see that plain as day. He turns to Lowell, shaking his head. "Surely that's not true?"

I receive a glare from the woman sitting opposite me, as though me spilling that little secret is highly inconvenient. *Yeah, I'll bet it is, bitch.*

"I only meant to clip Alexis' shoulder when I fired at her. The motorbike she was on swerved and the round ended up hitting her square in the torso."

"You nearly killed her," I snap. *"You nearly fucking killed her."*

"This is all irrelevant now. I didn't kill her. Your sister is alive, and we need to talk to her. Her involvement with the Widow Makers motorcycle club is a mystery to us, but her repeated refusals to leave them leads us to believe she is now working with them. Over the last eighteen months, twelve people have died because of the feud between Rebel's motorcycle club and the cartel. We need the killing to stop, and we *need* your sister. A thirty-minute gap took place between Alexis disappearing down that alleyway and those men shoving her in the back of that van. During that time, she was witness to the murder of one of Seattle's most prominent High Court judges. We need her, Sloane. We need her so she can testify."

Testify.

And there it is. The whole thing makes a whole lot of sense now.

Yes, of course this is why the DEA are so desperate to get their hands on her. They need her to complete their case, and in doing that they want to put Alexis on the stand so she can speak out against a crazy fucking Mexican cartel. And they're wondering why she doesn't want to go with them?

"Great. So you're willing to throw innocent people under the bus to get your own way, right? You're willing to shoot people and rob them of their careers, ruin everything they've worked hard for, ensure they lose everything, just so you can get your guy. Fuck anyone else who might get in the way, right?" I want to get the hell out of here. I want to leave so bad, I feel sick. My father's eyes grow round with surprise.

"It's important that these men pay for what they did, Sloane. It's important that justice—"

"Fuck justice! Fuck the DEA, and fuck *you*, Dad. Lexi asked you not to contact the police, and look at where the hell we are right now. My life is in ruins, and Lexi's recovering from an injury that almost took her life. She could have easily died, okay? And Agent Lowell here couldn't fucking care less."

Lowell slaps her hand on the table, sending a stack of her papers slipping sideways, crashing to the floor. "I care about protecting the people who devote their lives to the law, Dr. Romera. I care about organized crime in this country destroying everything America holds dear."

She sounds like she's given this bullshit patriotic speech a few times before. I roll my eyes. "I'm ready to leave now, if you don't mind."

Lowell slumps back into her chair, letting out an exasperated sigh. "This cartel kills *children*, Dr. Romera. They sell twelve-year-olds as sex slaves. Do you want that on your conscience?"

"My conscience has nothing to do with this."

"It does if you refuse to act. That's a crime of omission right there."

"I haven't broken any laws. I haven't participated in any crime. And now that I'm thinking on it, your threats are empty, aren't they? You have no grounds to seize my assets. You're just clutching at fucking straws."

"Oh, Dr. Romera," Lowell laughs, "that is where you're entirely wrong. Perhaps you ought to read this." She slides another piece of paper toward me, this time writing, not a photograph.

WITNESS REPORT
Grace Miller

My eyes scan over the document, my blood running cold in my veins. It's the blood. The blood I stole from the hospital to give to Zeth. Grace reported me, told them everything. I read, my eyes blurring a little at the words. *Suspicious. Defensive. Missing supplies.*

"I can't believe—"

Lowell snatches back the witness report, swiping it from between my fingers. "You can't believe your friend informed on you? Ms. Miller was being questioned in relation to the crime herself. She obviously felt telling the truth was better than losing her only source of income. Single mothers tend to be quite pragmatic when it comes to looking at the big picture."

Single mother? I didn't even know Gracie had kids. I can't blame her for telling the truth, I guess.

"And as for freezing your assets, we absolutely can do that, Sloane. The RICO Act means anything you own or possess can be ours in two seconds flat if we decide to travel down that road."

"RICO Act?"

"The Racketeer Influenced and Corrupt Organizations Act. It means anything I suspect you may have gained from your involvement with Zeth and Charlie Holsan's little gang, or perhaps from your connection with Rebel and the Widow Makers, can be seized and quarantined indefinitely."

My lungs feel like they're collapsing. From the smug look on the monster's face and the worried look on my father's, I know she's telling the truth. So it's not just my job that I'm losing here. I'm losing *everything.*

"What I suggest we—" Lowell stops talking when there's a sharp rap at the door and another agent, a man I don't know, sticks his head around the door. He looks concerned. "What is it?" Lowell snaps.

"Call just came in. It's him. Mayfair. He said something about a guy called Ernie?"

Lowell's face loses its color. I suspect mine does, too. Zeth? What the hell is he doing? Agent Lowell stands, puts her hands on her hips, paces in one direction and then changes her mind, pacing back the other way. "Fucking asshole. Goddamnit." She looks up at the other agent. "Okay, put him through."

She doesn't even give the line a chance to ring. As soon as the phone erupts into life, she snatches the handset out of its cradle and snarls into the receiver. "You've got some fucking nerve."

My dad just gives me a blank look. I can't hear what Zeth's saying, but from the look on Lowell's face, it's pure gold. She turns an intense shade of purple as she storms back and forth, listening to whatever he's telling her.

"You realize this is just another infraction on your—" Zeth must cut Lowell off, because she halts mid-sentence. Her eyes meet mine, no longer cold but blazing with fury. "Okay. All right. Fine." She slams down the phone and inhales, pulling in a deep, angry breath. "Alan, it seems you'd better take your daughter back into the city. *Now.*"

24

Zeth

THE HUMVEE SMELLS OF PISS. REBEL IS GONNA SHIT BRICKS about the accident that's just taken place, but I'm feeling rather good about things right now. Lowell's Schnauzer—Ernie, according to his bone-shaped nametag—is sitting on the backseat of the car, panting with his tongue lolling out over very white-looking canine teeth. Lowell definitely strikes me as the sort of asshole who would brush her dog's teeth.

"She really believed you'd kill her dog?" Michael laughs. I give him a confused look, and his smile evaporates. "Oh, yeah. Of course. You totally *would* kill her dog, wouldn't you?"

Ernie looks like he's smiling at me when I check him out in the rearview. I'm not a monster. I wouldn't kill a fucking dog just 'cause their owner needs a few lessons in manners. Not unless I really had to.

Michael and I sit in silence, Ernie's panting the only sound filling the car while we wait outside the bus depot for Sloane to arrive. She knows the drill. One of those motherfuckers will drop her off in the city and she'll go to catch the bus, heading straight to that god-awful coffee house we originally arranged to meet at. We're hoping to pick her up before she gets on the bus.

We don't have to wait long. I'm watching out for a black SUV—predictable much?—but instead I'm greeted with the familiar sight of a certain wood-paneled station wagon that pulls up outside the depot. It's Sloane's father's car, the one we abandoned at Julio's place. So I was right; the old guy at the mall was her dad. The car parks, and then...nothing happens. We've positioned ourselves far enough down the road so as not to be seen, but that also means we can't really get a clear view of what's going on. Michael pulls out a set of binoculars and squints through them at the car.

"Is she there?" I ask.

"Yeah."

"What are they doing?"

"The old guy's talking. Sloane's staring at the dashboard. She looks pissed."

I hold my hand out, wanting to lay eyes on her for myself. Michael hands over the binoculars, and then there she is, scowling into space. Pissed doesn't even come close to describing the expression on her face. Murderous. That's closer. Sloane nods, and then she's moving. She climbs out of the car, slamming the door behind her. I toss the binoculars onto the backseat, almost forgetting Ernie's back there. I jump out of the Hummer, not wanting to lose sight of her. That would be fucking typical, wouldn't it? Get the girl released, only to lose her through sheer fucking ineptitude as she tries to catch a bus.

Her dad's still parked outside the depot and is on his cell phone when I slip by his car. He doesn't see me. Besides, with my hood pulled up, face hidden in shadows, I'm the kind of character a man like Dr. Romera would purposefully try not to make eye contact with. I hurry through the depot, heading straight for stand 458. I hang a left, scanning the vacant depot for signs of life, for signs of Sloane. Another left.

And I walk straight into an extended fist.

"Zeth? *What the hell?*" Sloane pulls back her hand, shaking it out. My mouth smarts like a bitch. I touch my fingertips to my bottom lip and the blood I find on them surprises me. She hit me in the fucking face. She hit me and she drew fucking *blood*. I look down at her, and she instantly shrinks back.

"Sorry, I...I thought you were one of Lowell's guys."

I stalk toward her, checking to see if there's anyone around. The place is deserted, which is weird for this time of day but highly fucking convenient. Sloane takes a cautious step back, a look of mild panic on her face. "Zeth, just calm down. It was an accident," she whispers.

I grab her around the waist and lift her so that her feet are off the floor. She freezes for a second—not entirely sure what to do—but then tries to wriggle free from my grasp. I lunge forward with her, slamming her back up against the announcement board that displays the bus departure times, crushing my body against hers. Next comes my mouth. I take hold of her face in both hands and press my lips against hers. I'm not fighting the urge to be rough with her right now. Instead, I'm making myself *be* rough. It feels necessary—my relief at seeing her safe and unharmed is enough to make me dizzy. And I want to devour her in some sick way, to press her into myself so the two of us aren't individual people anymore, but one living, breathing entity, where the threat of separation can never trouble us again. Her skin feels hot underneath my hands. Her heart is slamming in her chest—I can literally feel its pulsing rhythm against my own ribcage. She exhales sharply as I tease her lips apart; I slide my tongue inside her mouth and taste her. She responds, slowly at first, and then something snaps. Her hands are clawing at me, pulling down my hood and fumbling with the zip to my sweater. I want her to take it from me. I want her to take every single last item of clothing from my body and I want to remove hers, too. I want to fuck her until she screams right here and now in the Seattle bus depot.

But we can't.

"Sloane? Sloane, wait. We have to get out of here." I hold her face in my hands again—her breathing is even faster than mine, her eyes completely glazed over. "You should know something, though," I whisper, my lips brushing lightly against hers.

She looks like she's been drugged. "What?"

"You knew you were just being followed, and you turned and defended yourself. Nothing...*nothing* has ever been hotter than that."

A brief attempt at a smile passes over her features. "I'm glad I've impressed you," she says.

I can't believe this woman. What the fuck did I ever do to deserve someone like her? To deserve the look she's giving me right now? It's a mystery I'll never be able to work out. "Sloane, *always* consider me impressed." I lower her slowly so she can find her feet. "Right now, we need to leave before Lowell shows up and castrates me, though."

She gives me a sideways look as I guide her back the way I just came, back toward the Hummer and Michael. "What the hell did you do, Zeth? And who the hell is Ernie?"

I almost want to smile. Fuck it. I let myself have this one. I grin big. "You," I tell her, "are about to find out."

"YOU KIDNAPPED HER *dog?"*

"Technically he *dognapped* him," Michael says. I bundle Sloane into the backseat with Ernie, making sure she doesn't sit in the wet patch he created earlier, and then I climb into the passenger seat. Sloane eyes the Schnauzer dubiously. Ernie eyes her back.

"How the hell did you figure out where she lives in the first place?" Sloane asks.

Michael guns the engine and then we're out of here. "Lowell's based in Cali, actually. I have a guy who finds things out, though. She's staying at a hotel downtown. He hacked her details on their system and told us she'd checked in with an animal."

I watch Ernie lick the back of Sloane's hand, feeling rather fucking proud of myself. "And a DEA agent who can't be separated from her dog while she travels must really fucking love that dog."

"Oh my god, no wonder she went so pale. She's going to string you up for this, baby." Sloane laughs.

Baby.

I've wanted to hit loved-up assholes for using that endearment before. But when Sloane says it... I don't really know what to think. I catch Michael's amused smile, itching at the corners of his mouth, and I don't feel like busting his balls. I just raise my eyebrows at him, a look of shock and amusement of my own. The fucker grins, then, like it's Christmas day and Mom and Dad aren't fighting.

"I suppose we'd better get out of here," he says. The words sound rounder coming out of his mouth, shaped by the texture of his smile.

25

Sloane

WE CHECK INTO A HOTEL, OR AT LEAST I THINK IT'S A HOTEL. The place is called The Regency Rooms, though there's no sign on the outside of the sixteen-story building. No clue as to what kind of star rating the place has. The lobby is yards of endless white marble tile, shot through with whispers of gray. No sofas. No generic artwork. Nothing but the white marble and the reception desk, which, like the rest of the lobby, is the epitome of simplicity. A man sits behind the desk, a dove grey suit and a wall of white teeth greeting us with a conservative smile.

"So good to see you again, Mr. Hanson," he says to Zeth. My stomach clenches at that name—*Hanson.* I know that name. That's the name Eli provided me with back when I had to sell myself for information. It's the name I gave to the receptionist at the Marriot hotel when I was checking in what seems like forever ago. Zeth gives me a cautious glance, and then nods curtly to the impeccably groomed gentleman who is sliding a key card across the smooth, cool stonework toward us. "Will you be staying with us long?" he asks.

"Five nights," Zeth replies. He looks…he looks a little uncomfortable.

"Oh, excellent. You'll be with us for our celebrations on Sunday evening, then. Would you like to reserve a booth?"

Michael coughs, though the cough sounds more like he's choking. The loud bark echoes across the cavernous room like a sharp burst of applause. Zeth turns slowly and gives him a dirty look. I'm not stupid; I can see Michael is trying to disguise a smile as he covers his mouth with a balled up fist.

Zeth scratches at his jaw. "No, that won't be necessary, thank you."

Celebrations? Reserving a booth? Tally those things up with Michael's less-than-subtle reaction to the receptionist's question, and I suddenly have a very vivid picture of what happens at The Regency Rooms. This is the kind of place that hides deviant, provocative secrets in its dark corners. Zeth accepts the key card off the counter and collects our bags—more clothes and toiletries procured by Michael—and then he leads us over to a sleek, minimal elevator. There is no call button, just a black panel mounted into the wall that Zeth touches the key card to. A white star icon appears on the black panel, pulsing ever so slightly.

This place is super fucking surreal. I cast one last look over my shoulder as the single, seamless steel door slides back to give us entry to the elevator, and I catch the receptionist watching us. He gives me a very slow, very deliberate wink. My cheeks burst into flames. I step onto the elevator, unsure whether to mention the man's salacious suggestion to the guys. Because it definitely *was* a suggestion. A single girl headed up to a room in a place like this? With *two* men? I turn around as we wait for the elevator to begin its ascent, Zeth on one side of me and Michael on the other, and a wicked part of me grabs the reins. I make eye contact with the receptionist. And I wink back.

His professional façade crumbles as he sends me an appreciative grin. The doors close, and then it's just the three of us. Michael nudges me in the back and leans forward so his mouth is close to my ear. "Are you misbehaving, Dr. Sloane?"

I can't help it. I laugh. Zeth gives Michael a warning glance. "Better not be fucking hitting on my girl." He cocks an eyebrow at his friend, and his demeanor is all fight, though I can tell he's only joking.

Joking and Zeth Mayfair. I'd never have thought the two would go together, but I've learned of late that the man I call mine is actually a very funny soul. He just hides it really, really well. Michael straightens his tie, glancing up at the display—*twelve, thirteen, fourteen*—and says, "Me? I wouldn't even dream of it."

The elevator car glides to a halt at the sixteenth floor—the top floor, of course—and we find ourselves in an empty corridor. There are only two doors up here. The door on the left is marked *A*; the door on the right, marked *B*. Michael bites back a grin again, and Zeth throws a bag at him. I don't know how I missed it before, but it's a black duffel. My heart starts thumping in my chest at the sight of it. I never thought I'd admit to anything of the sort, but I've missed that bag. I have no idea why Zeth is throwing it at Michael. Or at least I don't until Zeth growls, "Don't say a fucking word. I mean it."

I have a medical degree. I have a science degree, too. I'm a pretty smart person. It's obvious there's something entertaining about being here, in this hallway, standing between these two doors. Michael picks up Zeth's duffel and shoves it into his chest. "I'll see you in a couple of hours, I assume." He doesn't wait for an answer. He pulls a key card out of his own pocket and turns to the door labeled with a B. He opens it up and vanishes inside, leaving Zeth and me with door A.

"Let me guess," I say. "This is normally a *choose-your-own-adventure* moment, huh? Pick the door on the left and get one thing, pick the door on the right for another?"

Zeth shoots me a surprised look. I am loving the slow, glacial melt that's taking place within him. He's a fool if he thinks he's hidden it from me. And the fact he's letting himself go around me more and more these days means I get to witness an entirely new range of emotions on his face. Surprise is a cute one. He looks kind of innocent with those big brown eyes of his growing wider, though the words that come out of his mouth next are far from it.

"You're too smart for your own good, angry girl. Now you know our little secret, you're going to have to be punished."

My toes curl inside my shoes. He's joking again. I think he's joking. He opens the door, slings his duffel inside, along with our two other bags, and then turns to face me in the corridor. He pulls his hood up and begins to pace toward me. "When people come up here, Sloane, one of them always gives the other an option."

Oh, shit.

With his face drawn into shadow in that hood...

With that dark, predatory look in his eyes...

With the way he prowls toward me like he's hungry. So hungry...

My body comes alive.

"They might take the person by the hand," Zeth rumbles, deep in his chest. He takes hold of my hand. "And they might press that person up against the wall." I'm already walking backward, my breath fighting in and out of my lungs in short, heady bursts. My back hits the wall, and Zeth's powerful body leans up against mine, trapping me. "And they might get up nice and close..."

He's about as close as he can get. His mouth is less than an inch from mine. I want...no I *need* him to kiss me. I need it so bad. Zeth licks his lips, and it's not a teasing motion. I can see it in his eyes—he wants to kiss me, too.

"Fuck, Zeth." I mouth the words. I have no breath to spare for sound. Zeth smiles a little. The intense way he's studying me—his eyes traveling from my own to my mouth, to my neck and back again—gives me the impression he's fascinated by what he's seeing. If that's the case, then it makes two of us.

"And that person might say to the other person," he whispers, "pick your poison, angry girl." His tongue flicks out and licks at my top lip, sending a chorus of vibrations humming through my body. My nipples are so hard, they've started to ache. God, this is so messed up. I have to have him.

"What—what might a person's options be?" I'm barely in control anymore. My hands are sweating, desperate to take hold of him. Zeth stares me down for one long second, and then he carefully lowers his mouth, barely touching his full lips to mine.

"Pleasure," he whispers. There's a ball of heat twisting into a burning knot in my stomach. That heats explodes into an inferno, burning up inside me when he takes my lip in between his teeth and tugs, hard. The surprise of the sensation makes me gasp. "Or...*pain*," Zeth tells me.

My head is spinning. From the need in Zeth's eyes, I know this isn't a game. This isn't a theoretic conversation. I am meant to choose now, and I know which option Zeth wants me to pick. For once, there's not a shadow of doubt in my mind. I want what he wants.

"Pain, Zeth. I want the pain."

Zeth growls low in the back of his throat. There's no way he's holding himself back. Adrenalin zips through me as he crashes his body into mine, hands reaching under my thighs and hoisting me off the ground. I wrap myself around him—arms, legs. My heart. I wrap *my heart* around him as I cling on for dear life. He kisses me, his lips finding mine, and I don't need to breathe anymore. His mouth on mine is all I need. His hands holding me tight is all I need.

Just *him*. He is everything.

"Fuck, Sloane, you turn me inside out," he murmurs, his tongue licking at me again, tasting me. I don't know whether his statement is a good or a bad thing, but from the size of his hard-on, I'm guessing good. Hoping. He carries me into the apartment, slamming the door behind him. I don't register a single element of my surroundings. Those brown eyes, searching mine, peering deep into me, are the only thing I see. We move from the main room to another, smaller room—a bedroom—and Zeth throws me down on the bed. Our hands frantically scrabble at each other's clothing. This—our joint desperation, to see, feel, taste, touch each other— makes this different to any other time we've been together. We're coming to this as equals, and for once I feel like Zeth is as out of control as I am.

That doesn't last long of course. He tears himself away from me and rips down his jeans, kicking them off with a dark, seductive look on his face. The excruciatingly beautiful man in front of me, naked as the day he was born, then takes hold of my ankle, lifts my leg, and kisses me on the arch of my foot. "Wait here," he tells me. And then he disappears out the door.

I know where he's going. I know what he's going to come back with. My blood is charging in my veins, lighting me up. He left me in my bra and panties, but I don't want to remove them myself. I want him to take them from me, the same way he takes everything else: roughly. He's not gone long enough for me to regulate my breathing. My chest is still heaving when Zeth reappears in the doorway with his black duffel bag held tightly in one hand.

"Get off the bed. Get on your hands and knees," he commands.

I oblige him, my body prickling with anticipation. I want to suck him. To lick him and bite him and make every inch of him mine. Zeth places the bag on the edge of the bed and rifles inside, completely oblivious to how perfect he is. His body is flawless

242

symmetry, muscles taut and knitted together, shoulders, legs, buttocks, back—every single part of him is expertly put together. As someone who's studied human anatomy for many years, I can safely say that Zeth is the owner of the most perfect body I have ever seen.

When he turns to face me, his cock still rigid and erect, he's holding a length of material in his hand. "Close your eyes," he says.

It's almost unbearable that I have to block out the sight of him, but I still behave. Once my eyes are closed, Zeth brushes the material against my cheek, down the slope of my neck. Across the swell of my cleavage. The fabric is sensuously rough, the threads catching at my skin. I start to shake when Zeth rubs it ever so gently across my lips. I open my mouth, almost begging him to do what I think he's going to do. To feed the length of raw silk between my lips and gag me. He doesn't, though. Instead, he ties it around my eyes, tight enough that I can't see a thing. I sense him moving away from me.

When he comes back, he does exactly as I hoped he would. He removes my underwear, and he is none-too-gentle. He takes hold of my bra straps first, and he slides something cold and hard against my skin. Something sharp. The straps ping loose as he cuts them one at a time. My panties are next. He grabs the material at my left hip and slices it, and then my right, ripping the material from my body.

"Pain is a strange thing, Sloane," he says softly. "People have entirely the wrong idea about it. From birth, children are coddled and panicked over when they hurt themselves, so they grow up believing it's a bad thing. As soon as their nerve endings start sending feedback to the brain, their fear receptors kick in. They freak the fuck out. What do they teach you in medical school about pain?"

"It's a survival technique," I whisper.

Zeth moves closer—I can sense him standing before me. All I need to do is reach up and touch him, but I know I shouldn't. It's not my role. "Right," Zeth says. "But that doesn't mean we should be afraid of it. We should embrace it. Relish it. Know the limits of our pain, and understand what we can tolerate." Something hard presses against my cheek, and my hands, pressing into the carpet, automatically curl into fists. "I know what you can tolerate, Sloane. I've told you that before, and you've trusted me. Do you trust me now?"

"Yes. I trust you."

My lips tingle as he kisses me, then. A soft, light, barely there kiss that causes heat to pool in the bottom of my stomach. "Thank you, Sloane," he whispers. "I'm going to hurt you now, but I promise you're going to like it."

A promise from Zeth means something. If he promises I'm going to enjoy this, I have absolutely nothing to worry about, but that doesn't stop the swell of nerves that rise through me. I can hear him moving around me, pacing, as though he's observing me from all angles, trying to decide where to begin. He doesn't keep me waiting long.

Something pointed traces the curve of my spine, starting at the base of my neck and traveling slowly down until it reaches the curve of my butt. I have no idea what it is. Not cold, so probably not metal. Not sharp, so not the knife.

"You grade pain in hospital, don't you?" Zeth whispers, his voice thick with lust.

"Yes."

"Tell me how it works."

"We...we ask the patient to tell us how much pain they're in on...a scale of one to ten."

"And does that help you?" Zeth trails whatever he's got in his hand across the tops of my shoulders, and I feel more of it against me. Something long and thin, solid and almost warm.

"Yes, it...helps us to grade how much pain relief they need. Tells us the severity of the problem."

The pressure from Zeth's toy vanishes. "We'll use your system today, Sloane. When I ask you, you give me a number."

"Okay." For some reason, I feel a little reassured by this. I probably shouldn't, but I do.

I'm relaxing into the situation a little when a bright sting of pain bites into the flesh of my buttocks. It's the surprise that gets me, more than the pain. I yelp, almost hopping up from my position.

"Stay still, angry girl," Zeth tells me. "Now. One to ten. What was that? Really think about it."

I take a second to do just that. "Three," I say. "It was a three." I can't feel the burn of it anymore, so I can't legitimately grade it higher. Zeth will know I'm lying in order make him go easier on me, and I get the feeling that will have entirely the reverse effect.

"Good girl, Sloane. That was a three." I barely dare breathe as he paces around me. I jump when the cane—it can only be a cane—makes contact with my chest. Zeth strokes the length of wood underneath me, across my breasts, making my nipples throb. "You're so fucking perfect. So fucking beautiful," he tells me. "Breathe, Sloane. You have to remember to breathe."

I inhale, drawing a steady pull of oxygen into my lungs, and that's when the second strike lands. Across my butt again; this time the force is harder. More intense. "*Fuck!*"

Zeth laughs quietly. I can imagine the look in his eyes—the amusement dancing there as he watches me squirm. "Such a foul mouth on you, angry girl. How would you grade that?"

"Six," I say, panting, doing my best to keep still. I want to touch my fingers to the tender area where he caned me—it feels as though there'll be a raised welt there, angry and red to look at if I could see it in a mirror.

"Now, now, that was only a five. Take a deep breath. Fill your lungs, relax your body, and then tell me again. How would you grade that?"

I do take a deep breath. I do relax my body. And he's right. "All right. Five."

Zeth kisses me, pressing his lips against my shoulder. He's standing behind me, but not for long. He moves so he's in front of me. I'm almost ready for it this time when he touches the end of the cane to my skin. Instead of using it to dole out pain, he traces the tip over my stomach and then down, until it rests between my legs. The hard inflexibility of the length of wood slides over my pussy, between the folds of flesh, probing me, searching out the sweet spot. It doesn't take long to find it. Just like with the knife, there's something thrilling about an object that can cause me great pain being used to bring pleasure instead. My whole body hums as Zeth slides the end of the cane repeatedly up and over my pussy, occasionally applying pressure, but mostly just teasing me with it so I can barely keep my arms and legs from shaking. I groan, trying not to let myself rock my hips against it.

I can sense when Zeth figures I've had enough pleasure. Seconds after I realize it's probably coming soon, the cane makes a zipping sound as it rips through the air. A burst of pain explodes in my head as the wood connects with the back of my thighs, just below the curve of my ass cheek.

"*Ahhh! Shhhh...*" I bite back the curse word begging to be screamed out loud, digging my fingers into the pile of the carpet.

"How about that?" Zeth whispers into my ear. His breath on the skin of my neck sends a wave of heat rippling over my skin.

I want to say seven. I want to say seven so bad, but I don't. "Six," I pant.

Zeth makes a grunting sound—the sound of his approval. He runs his fingertips down my cheek, down my neck, over my shoulder and down my back as he walks around me. "Open your legs wider for me, Sloane."

I wince as I place my knees farther apart, doing as he asks. I can't fight the powerful urge to push back against him as Zeth sinks to his knees and presses himself between my legs. He's so hard. So hard, pushing his cock forward so it's rubbing against my clit. He curves himself over me and begins to kiss my back, one vertebra at a time.

"Oh, god. *Fuck*." I want him to slide himself into me. I want to feel him inside me as deep as he can go, filling me, stretching me, owning me, but instead Zeth pulls back and uses the cane again. A seven. This time it's a seven.

"Ahhh! Zeth! *Motherfffff*—" It's getting harder to choke back the cursing. It feels like I'm winded. Like I've fallen on my ass and it's knocked every last bit of oxygen out of me.

"Eight? Or seven?" Zeth asks. I can hear the labored twist in his own voice, like he's short of breath himself.

"Seven. You're enjoying this, aren't you?" I half laugh, my body still quivering.

"Oh, good god, girl. You have *no* idea how much." He leans forward so his cock is pressing urgently against my pussy again, but now he wraps his arm around my body, reaching for my clit. "Are you *not* enjoying it, Sloane? Because it feels to me as though you might be."

He's right. This may be totally outside my comfort zone, but the anticipation of the pain, followed by the reality of it, is driving me crazy. And the burn...the burn is so fucking beautiful. Each time the cane lashes into my skin, I'm practically torn in two trying to escape it, and trying to lean into it at the same time.

"I—I—"

"Say it, Sloane." He leans back and the cane comes again— fireworks detonating through my body. Wave after wave of pain, surging and pulsing through me, riding high on my heartbeat. My throat tightens.

"*Sloane.* Say it."

"Yes. I do. I...I like it."

The cane comes again. This time I can't stop myself from screaming. "What was that, Sloane?" Zeth asks, hissing through his teeth.

"Eight! That was an eight!"

I hear the sound of something clattering across the other side of the room, and then Zeth is slamming himself into me, his cock thrusting deep and hard and fast.

"Fuck, Sloane. Your ass is so red. I want to spank it."

"Please. *Please.*" That's all I can get out. I *want* him to spank it. I want to feel throbbing, stinging, smarting ache charge through me as he slams himself inside me, over and over again.

"Shit." Zeth uses his palm on me. A loud *crack* fills the room as his hand connects, the pain less bright than with the cane but still enough to make me scream.

Every muscle in my body is locked tight and singing with sensation as Zeth fucks me. He fucks me so hard I can literally feel my orgasm building with each and every thrust, the tension hitting me like a punch to the gut. Over, and over, and over, and then...

"I can't—oh, fffffffuck. Zeth, I can't—"

Zeth covers my body with his own, still pounding himself into me. He reaches up my body and takes a hold of my nipple, and he pinches, hard. At the same time, I feel his teeth bite down into the skin of my shoulder, sending a wall of raw energy slamming through me.

I scream. I scream violently as I come, my throat feeling like it's being torn to shreds. I don't scream his name, or ask him to stop. It's just sound, splintering out of me—the purest of releases.

Zeth roars as he comes, too. Up until now he's been holding his own body weight, but he goes boneless as he climaxes, his arms and legs quitting on him. The result is instant and bone crushing. We both go down, him on top of me.

"Fuck. Sorry," he apologizes, gulping in air. He shifts slightly, dragging himself to the side. It clearly costs him energy he doesn't have when he reaches up and unties the blindfold from around my eyes. We're face to face, then, staring at each other, noses only a couple of inches apart. His cheeks are slightly red from exertion, his lips parted. He looks so freaking angelic—dark hair tousled everywhere—that it's almost hard to believe he's the little deviant that just flayed my ass raw. I start laughing first. Zeth joins me a second later. He kisses me roughly, pretending to growl.

"Oh my god, woman. You're not supposed to burst out laughing after something like that," he tells me, mastering his face into a fake stern expression. "That's it. You are in *so* much trouble now."

26

Zeth

WE CLIMB UP ONTO THE BED AND SLOANE PASSES OUT without a word. I don't, though. I lie there staring at the ceiling, fighting the desire to close my own eyes. I'm fucking tired, but I can't let myself go to sleep. I just can't. I've been dreaming about my mother recently, the beach and the boardwalk—but there's nothing to say I won't dream the other dream tonight. Nothing to say I won't freak out and try and strangle my girl to death if I wake up and she's lying beside me. I can't risk that. I lie still a little longer, enjoying the slow draw of her breathing in the darkness, her hand resting lightly on top of my stomach, her head resting on my shoulder, dark hair spilling out behind her onto the plumped up pillows, and I know I have to go.

The problem is I really want to fucking stay.

She barely stirs as I slide out from underneath her. In the kitchen, I make myself a coffee with a healthy shot of Jack instead of milk. I feel like shit. I've never wanted to sleep in the same bed as a woman before. It's a brutal shock to the system, this urge to hold her against me all night, to protect her. Worse, because I'm the one she'd need protecting from. Is this what our life will be like? Having sex and then me ducking out on her every single night, having to creep out of a warm bed so I can go and lock myself away? That doesn't sit well with me. Not fucking well at all.

I finish the coffee, and then I make myself another one, this time without the Jack. As soon as the caffeine kicks in, I throw some clothes on and head over to Michael's room. He answers the door on the third knock. His instant appearance surprises me.

"Whoa. Going somewhere?" He looks like he is. With his black suit and crisp white shirt, it's either that or he's prepped and ready for the Duchess's funeral already. Michael treats me to one of his rare, broad smiles.

"Oh, just planning on seeing a friend."

He's going to go screw someone. In all the time I've known him, Michael has never offered up any information about women—he's been so tight lipped, I've often wondered if he bats for the other team—but I know he goes off to have a little fun of his own every once in a while. I don't think I'd trust him if he didn't.

"Right. Okay, well..." I'm not the kind of man to come between another and his fuck buddy. I begin to back away from the door.

"You okay? You need something?" Michael asks. "Everything's set for the morning."

"Yeah, no. Everything's fine. I just..." I am the most awkward person on the face of the planet. I try to turn and make it back behind door A, but a hand lands on my shoulder, stopping me in my tracks.

"You worried? About sharing the apartment alone? With Sloane?" Michael asks.

A few months ago, I would have laughed at him for making the suggestion. A few months ago, I probably would have punched his arm hard enough to leave a bruise and told him to stop being so fucking ridiculous. But now...I turn and face my friend, fighting for the right words. "I'm not...I don't..." I take a deep breath. "It's not about the apartment. I'm worried about sharing a *bed* with her."

Michael doesn't laugh, which is the only thing that saves him from a fist to the face. He pouts, nodding at me. "So, you're worried about the sleep thing? Because you *want* to share a bed with her?"

God, why is this so hard to admit to another person? "Yes."

Michael carries on nodding, his eyes serious as he thinks this over. "Well," he tells me, "it hardly seems fair that you should have to worry about that your whole life. Does it?" Maybe Michael has foreseen the same future for Sloane and myself that I just did, lying in the dark in that room, hating myself. "I guess the question you ought to ask yourself, boss, is...do you think she's worth facing that particular problem? Is she forever? Because you can only keep one of those elements in your life forever—the girl, or the monster that plagues your dreams. The choice is yours."

The candor of his response makes me a little edgy—we don't talk about this sort of stuff—but I'm at a crossroads here. And what he's saying actually makes sense. It's all well and good being a man about things and showing the world a hard exterior, but sometimes being a man means admitting you need a little help. And...and I think I've reached that point. Even thinking that makes me uneasy, but the girl...Sloane is worth it. She has to be. "Michael, I need a ride."

He doesn't question this. He doesn't say a word. He steps out of his apartment and closes the door behind him, straightening his tie. I already know the answer to the question, but since we're having our own version of a DNM, I have to say I'm interested in what Michael thinks to the question he posed me a moment ago. "Just for argument's sake..." Michael hits the call button for the elevator. We wait in silence a moment, and then I man up and ask the rest of the question. "Do *you* think she's forever?"

Michael stares straight ahead, waiting for the doors to the elevator to open. "Oh, I knew you were her forever as soon as I saw the way she looked at you, Zee." He slides his hands into his pockets, clears his throat. And then he turns and looks me straight in the eye and says, "I'm just really glad you've figured out she's *yours*, man. Because you deserve that. And so does she."

IT'S ALMOST MIDNIGHT by the time Michael drops me off across the city at the entrance to a very familiar park. I didn't give him directions; he just knew where I wanted to go. Well, not *wanted* to go, per se. I definitely don't *want* to be here. But fuck...the woman is the only option I have open to me at this time of night without an appointment.

"Make sure she's safe, man?" I ask, as I climb out of the generic hatchback Michael's procured from "the getting place", as he calls it. He knows which *she* I'm referring to perfectly well.

"'Course. I'll see you later."

"Right." I slam the door closed and slap my palm on top of the car, and Michael burns off down the street. That leaves me standing in front of a building I quite honestly never thought I'd set foot inside of again. Pippa Newan's apartment building is the kind with a night guard and concierge—a smart move if you're a shrink that treats aggressive criminals all day long. However, if you're buzzed into the building and say you're visiting a friend, there's not a great deal anyone can do to keep you out. I pull the Girl Scout trick; I press the first button and drag my finger down the thirty or so call buttons that are lit up on the intercom panel. It only takes a moment for the door to buzz open.

The guard and the concierge don't even question me as I head straight for the elevator. I've often found if you exude confidence and look like you know where you're going, you don't get hassled. I guess in this particular case, it also helps that I look like I could bench their combined body weight. My insides are humming as I ride the elevator up to Newan's floor. I don't know if it's excitement or dread cycling through me, but whatever it is, I feel like I'm gonna throw up. Fucking ridiculous.

When I reach Newan's door, I make myself pause. Is this a great idea? The last time Sloane came here, the bitch turned her over to the DEA. Admittedly, she didn't believe anything bad was going to happen to her friend; she did it because she wanted Sloane to hand *me* over. There's little stopping her from making that phone call again. So no, I suppose it's a seriously terrible fucking idea, but I have to risk it. Sloane is worth it. It feels like there's a lot riding on this. I ball up my fist and thump it hard against the solid wood door.

I wait.

Nothing.

Maybe she isn't home. I'm reaching into my pocket for my lock-picking tools—nothing says *surprise!* like a convicted felon waiting for you in the dark—when there's a soft scraping on the other side of the door. There's a spyhole in the door, but I don't cover it up. I step back so the good doctor can get a good look at who's on her doorstep.

"What the *hell* do you want?" Newan snaps through the door.

I shrug my shoulders. "Your help." That's putting it as plainly as I possibly can. "You offered your services not so long ago. I was hoping that offer still stood."

There's a long pause while Newan takes this in. She laughs. "You kidnapped me and handcuffed me to a toilet."

"You betrayed your friend. You earned that."

More silence. "What makes you think I'd risk letting you inside this apartment? Alone? How do I know you're not here to kill me?"

"If I were here to kill you, I wouldn't have fucking knocked. If you don't want to let me inside your apartment, Dr. Newan, then we can easily talk through the door. I'm fine with that."

A distinct stillness develops. The kind that makes me think Newan's slipped away from the door—maybe to grab her phone? Perhaps Lowell will be here sooner than I'd hoped. "What do you think, Newan?" I ask.

I'm surprised when she answers right away, and louder than before. She hasn't gone anywhere. "Tell me why. Tell me why you want to do this now."

"Because I don't want to hurt her. Because I want to make her happy." These are two of the truest statements that have ever passed my lips. I've never meant anything more. There's a pause, and then the gentle clicking of a lock being turned. The door opens an inch, revealing a suspicious-looking Pippa Newan. She's in her PJs, her hair in a messy knot on top of her head. For all the time she spends making herself look so polished and immaculate, she's far more attractive like this. I can actually see why a guy might check her out. Maybe.

"Stay right there," she tells me.

I take a step back away from the door, leaning back against the opposite wall. I show her my hands—no weapons. She opens the door a little wider and leans against the framework. "You're never going to be able to make this work, Zeth," she informs me.

"And why's that?"

"Because you're a control freak, and participating in therapy means you have to hand over control to another person. Or at least concede that someone else might be better equipped to deal with a situation than you are."

I haven't thought of it like that before, but I suppose she's right. Maybe that's why I was so fucking offended when she tried to bribe me into her session room the first time I came back into Sloane's life. "I can admit you're qualified to help me. Isn't that enough?"

She narrows her eyes at me. Folds her arms across her chest. "Maybe. Wait here." She backs away, not turning her focus from me until she's disappeared into the shadows of her unlit apartment. I do as she says and don't move a muscle. When she returns, I can't keep the smile from my face. She's got a Taser. She holds it up so I can see it clearly. "If we're going to do this, I'm going to have this on me at all times. You understand that I will shoot you and call the cops without a second thought, right?"

"Yes. I understand."

"All right, then. You can come inside."

To be honest, I'm a little surprised she's agreeing to this. If I were in her position, I probably wouldn't have even opened the door. She melts into the shadows again, and I follow her into her apartment, my movements very fucking slow, and very fucking considered. I've never been tagged with a Taser before, but I can't imagine it's any fun. Newan hits a light somewhere inside the apartment, and her cold, sterile little world comes to life under a series of halogen spotlights. She jerks her head toward a massive couch, which has been parked right in front of a vast wall of glass. No sign of a TV. It's as though the sweeping view of the city in the distance, visible through the floor-to-ceiling windows, has negated the requirement for such a thing. I stalk through the apartment, my mouth aching from the effort of keeping myself from smirking as Newan trains the Taser squarely on my chest. I shrug out of my jacket, mainly so she can see I'm just wearing a T-shirt and I'm not packing anything under the leather, and then I slump down onto the couch.

Newan sidles past me and perches on the edge of an arty,

thoroughly uncomfortable-looking armchair. If the chair were a person, it would be a supermodel—far too skinny and far too pretentious. "So what do you want to talk about?" Newan asks.

"Aren't you supposed to tell me?"

She rolls her eyes. I bet this woman was such a spoiled brat in high school. "Zeth, it's midnight. This is hardly your typical session, okay? Let's cut to the chase."

"All right." I fix my eyes on her, wondering how she's going to take this. I haven't told anyone about the darkness that plagues me. Not a single soul on the face of the planet. I've imagined the reaction of others enough times, though. Disgust. Horror. Pity. Pity is the worst. "I have nightmares," I tell her. "And I'm often violent when I wake from them."

"And what happens in these nightmares?" she asks. The change in her is subtle enough, but I see it a mile away—she suddenly becomes a doctor, albeit a highly suspicious, cautious doctor, instead of a woman holding a grudge. The way she asks about my nightmares is so perfunctory, so clipped and clinical, that it's almost easy to tell her. Almost.

"I'm asleep in my bed," I tell her. "I'm young. I don't know how old."

"Before or after your parents were killed?" Newan cuts in. No softly, softly approach with that one. She just comes out with it.

"After," I say.

"Do you know where you are?"

"Yes."

She gives me a look.

"I'm in my bedroom. I'm in my bed at Charlie's place."

"Right. And what happens while you're in bed at Charlie's place?"

"I wake up, and there's a pillow over my face. I can't breathe."

Newan nods, passing the Taser from one hand to the other.

Shouldn't she be writing this shit down or something? "And what do you do?" she asks.

"I freak the fuck out. I kick and scramble and fight myself free. I fall out of the bed, and I hug the wall. I see...I see *him*, then."

"Him?"

"He says he's me, a shadow of me, but I know he can't be. This man is fully grown and smells like bourbon, and I'm small. I'm really small."

"So you talk to him?"

"He talks to me."

"Does he say anything else?"

"He tells me he's going to kill me."

"And how do you react to that?"

I shoot her an unimpressed look. "*Badly.*"

"I'm just trying to get a sense of who this version of you is, Zeth. Sometimes our subconscious embodies our secret fears, making us weak in our dreams, stripping us of our power so we feel incapable of protecting or defending ourselves. This often relates to a sense of insecurity we may not even be aware we're experiencing in our day-to-day lives. And given the life you lead, I wouldn't be surprised if that's what's happening with you."

"That's not what's happening with me," I tell her.

"Oh no? Because you're invincible, I take it? Because you're the big, bad Zeth Mayfair and you don't worry about a fucking thing?"

I laugh at that. She's doing a relatively good job of hiding it, but I feel like pointing it out—*Hey, Doc. Your contempt's showing.* "No. I'm not invincible. And I do worry about things. More and more every fucking day, it seems. I say that's not what's happening with me, because it really isn't. My subconscious doesn't fuck with what happens in my head when I sleep. It's more like a broken video recorder. It plays back the same thing on repeat over and over. *It replays what actually happened.*"

That takes her a second to process. "So this is real? *Was* real?"

"It was."

She gives me the cautious look I assume she reserves for all victims of abuse. "And the man, what...does he actually try to kill you?"

I nod. Seems as though my memories are intent on making themselves known—intent on making their displeasure known. I'm not supposed to share this dark, shitty piece of myself with anyone. I am supposed to hide it away and let it fester inside me. Let it rot me from the inside out. I'm hit with the stale smell of alcohol as I think about what I'm going to share with the woman sitting on the other side of the room. I'm hit with the sour tang of body odor and the taste of my own adolescent fear in my mouth. "He comes for me every time. He comes at me with his fists. His skin is slick with sweat, naked—"

"And does he assault you sexually?"

I told Sloane I was never assaulted sexually, and that is the truth. But it's also true I probably would have been if I hadn't have fought back so hard. "He was...he was always hard. I could feel his cock against me as he wrestled with me. But I never let him get close enough to do anything."

"He never touched you?"

I close my eyes. "No." I was never touched, because I bit, I kicked, I gouged, I fought with every last ounce of strength I had. I fought with the abandon of a person who would rather die than undergo such a humiliation. Young as I was, that was enough. But it didn't stop the beatings.

"How often did this happen?"

"I don't know. Every night. Every night for years."

"But when you dream, it's always the first time it happened that you relive, correct?"

"Yes." I already know why that is: the first time was the worst.

The first time it happened, I was the youngest I was ever going to be at the hands of the monster that crept into my room each night. And later on I expected it. I knew it was coming, and I was waiting. I was used to beatings, even at that age given my uncle's proclivity for alcohol abuse and quick fists. But yeah, the first night was different. That first night, in the dark, when the shadowy, naked figure told me he was going to kill me, I heard the intention in his voice and I knew he meant it. I knew I was going to have to fight for my life.

"These aren't nightmares you suffer from, Zeth," Newan says. "This is your mind begging for help. Your subconscious is pleading with you, demanding that you deal with the trauma you experienced as a child, because a part of you is still fighting that dark figure inside your head. Even though you're an adult now and you're physically strong, every night you're still affected by this blow-by-blow account of what happened to you because you've never felt like you've *stopped* fighting for your life."

Newan's words strike a chord somewhere deep down in the very core of me. The idea of it, though—the idea that I'm still a scrawny little fucker, fighting this same damn fight, after so long—is enough to make me feel sick. "So, what are you saying? I need to man up and face this thing head on? What is there to face? I never knew who the guy was. There were always at least twenty or thirty guys hanging around Charlie's place at night. It could have been any one of them."

Newan shakes her head. "You know exactly who it was. When you're ready, you'll be able to come to that realization on your own. In the meantime, yes, I suppose your rather brief summation's correct. You need to man up. And that means continued therapy. This isn't a simple fix, Zeth. You're pretty fucked up."

I laugh. "That your official diagnosis?"

"I didn't need to talk with you to know you were fucked up. But yes."

"So I have a lifetime of head-shrinking ahead of me? A lifetime of journaling and talking about my feelings? And then I might not try to murder anyone who happens to be in the same room as me while I sleep?" I say anyone, but it's pretty clear who I mean—*Sloane*. Newan tips her head to one side, giving me a curious look.

"You really care about her, huh? I knew you did, but this...this is totally against your archetypal behavior. I never thought you'd be able to get yourself here."

"Don't be too fucking impressed, Newan. I'm still me."

She shrugs. I note with some amusement that the Taser, at some point during the last few minutes, has been abandoned on the arm of her chair. "Okay, then," she says. "In answer to your question, yes. You have a lot of work ahead of you. I can help you, though." She scowls, as though offering her assistance causes her physical pain. "To say I'm conflicted in this matter would be the understatement of the century, but if you're willing to put in the hard yards for Sloane, then I'm the last person likely to talk you out of it. We can see each other twice a week. Get the ball rolling. In the meantime, if your violent outbursts are concerning you, I can give you some medication to help with that."

"Sleeping pills?"

"Anti-psychotics."

I stand up. I'm halfway to the door before Newan realizes she's fucked up. "I don't mean you're a psychopath, Zeth. I just mean that anti-psychotics have shown to help significantly when—"

"Shut the fuck up." I spin around, focusing the full force of my anger on her. "I'm not taking any fucking pills, Newan. Nothing. Not sleeping pills. Not anti-fucking-psychotics. *Nothing*."

"Okay." She holds up her hands—the Taser is once more firmly gripped in her right fist. "Forget the medication. I'll still help you."

"And why the hell would you do that?" I growl.

She looks miserable as she lowers her hands. "Because...despite what you may think, I love my friend, Zeth. And I know I've screwed up, but all I've ever wanted for her is for her to be safe. If I help you, if I make sure you're healthy and handling your baggage, then I know there's no way in hell you'll ever hurt her."

I feel like puking onto her polished fucking tiles. Like no other, this woman has the ability to make me feel like a pile of shit. "Okay, fine. I'll come to you, Newan. But I swear to god, if you try to pull anything with the cops—"

"I won't. I promise. But you have to *try*." I glower at her, fighting the urge to ask what the fuck she thinks I'm doing right now. "Just being here isn't going to cut it, Zeth," she says, as though reading my mind. "You can't keep calling me Newan. You use my surname against me as a weapon—something you did to other inmates when you were in prison? You saw them as your enemies. People to keep at arm's length. You do the same thing to me. If you see me as your enemy, we'll never be able to work together to get you where you so clearly want to be."

A part of me wants to run right now. I want to walk out of that door, slam it and never fucking look back. I can't envision what she's talking about—us working together to fix me. A team. But then I remember the pressure of Sloane's head against my chest, the solid, reassuring weight, and I know I'll do whatever it takes. I want to give her what she wants. Sex is all well and good, but I know her. She craves a level of intimacy from me that I'm terrified to give her right now, because the consequences are just too dire. And more than that, I never thought I'd see the day, but *I* want that level of intimacy, too.

"All right. I'll try."

"Good. I'm glad. I really am. But...you know this is going to be hard, right?"

I open the door, pausing in the doorway. "So far nothing in my life has been easy, *Pippa*. I'd be really fucking surprised if the universe decided to give me a break now."

27

Sloane

I WAKE UP TO THE SMELL OF EGGS. THE OTHER SIDE OF THE bed I find myself in is woefully empty. My heart sinks a little, which is stupid, I know, but sometimes a girl likes to be surprised. In a good way, and not by the barrel of a gun or something equally as horrific. As I'm thinking this, a small yelp breaks the silence of the room and my heart jumps into my throat. I sit upright to find a pair of warm brown eyes staring back at me. Ernie the Schnauzer, stretched out across my feet at the end of the bed. He makes a disgruntled sound—*oww!*—as he licks his chops, clearly unhappy at being disturbed by my waking, and then rests his head on his paws.

"Oh. *You*," I tell him. He glances at me out of the corner of his eye, his long grey whiskers twitching as he gives me a quiet *uffff,* which I'm assuming is only half a woof. He continues to grumble as I jimmy my feet out from underneath him and clamber out of bed. My body is sore in a way that makes me smile secretly to myself. Zeth-sore. I'm a fan of being Zeth-sore.

I didn't see much of the apartment last night. I peek my nose into rooms as I make my way toward the smell of cooking eggs—one, two, three bedrooms, what looks like an office, which seems a little weird, and what I can only describe as a wet room. A miniature pool sits in the center of the last room on the right-hand side before I reach the kitchen, perhaps only ten-foot square, but I can tell by the dark aqua hue to the water that the thing is deep.

"Good morning," a voice says behind me. Michael. I spin around and there he is in an exquisite black suit, complete with black shirt and black tie.

"Good morning," I reply. "Why do you look like you're going to a funeral?"

He cocks an eyebrow at me. "Because we *are* going to a funeral. Zeth didn't tell you?"

"No."

"The Duchess." Michael gives me a sage nod. "Charlie posted an obituary in *The Seattle Times*. He'll be there, which means—"

"Lacey probably will, too."

Again, another nod. "I have a dress ready for you. It's hanging in the kitchen."

Sure enough, when I make my way through to the kitchen, a white garment bag is hooked through a handle of one of the head-height cabinets, and Zeth Mayfair is standing at the cook top, stirring a pot of what can only be eggs. He glances over his shoulder, sees me, and stops what he's doing. I can't help but notice he looks tired. "Did that little shit wake you up?" he asks me.

"Who? Michael?"

"No. *Ernie*." He points behind me—at the rumpled-looking Schnauzer standing right behind me. His fur is all curly and sticking up. Doggy bed head.

"I woke him up, actually," I tell Zeth. "He wasn't too happy about it."

Zeth grunts, masking a small smile. "He could clearly give a shit about being away from Lowell. Poor bastard's probably never gonna forgive us when we give him back."

Ernie cocks his head to one side, his strange little Schnauzer eyebrows seeming to pull together into a comical frown.

"I think you may be right."

Zeth turns back to his half-forgotten task and takes the pan off the heat, serving up spoonfuls of scrambled eggs onto pre-buttered slices of toast. Three plates for the three of us. He hands one to Michael, one to me, and slides cutlery toward us across the kitchen countertop.

I have to say I'm a little shocked when I eat some of the food and it actually tastes like scrambled egg. If anything, I would have expected it to taste faintly carcinogenic—a little burned, or at least way too salty. As it turns out, my man can at least cook the simple things. Michael salutes Zeth with his fork and carries his breakfast out of the kitchen to eat elsewhere.

"You didn't tell me about the funeral," I say between mouthfuls. Zeth leans across the countertop, the bulk of his considerable frame suddenly very much up in my personal space.

"I was a little too pleased to see you were still alive."

"Were you now?"

He nods. "Plus..." an awkward grimace forms on his face, "this whole thing with Lace—"

"I know. She might not want to come back with us."

Cold, sharp steel flashes in Zeth's eyes. "I don't plan on giving her a choice."

Honestly, taking Lacey might be for the best. Removing her from the situation altogether. But all I'm imagining right now is a showdown at a graveside and a handful of very scandalized people who are trying to grieve, and I can't see it ending well. I can't think of anything productive to say, so I keep my mouth shut. Zeth heads off to locate Michael, saying something about a plan of action.

Once I'm done with my breakfast, I find both of them fussing over Ernie in the lounge area. They don't see me for a moment, and watching them scrubbing their hands through the dog's fur, scratching his belly and roughhousing with him, makes me break out into a smile. Neither of these men would have struck me as dog people, and yet the evidence is right there in front of me. They love that freaking dog.

Zeth sees me first. He stands up, wiping his hands on jeans. He clears his throat, pointing at Ernie. "We were just checking him for...intestinal worms."

"Right. How did that go?"

"All good."

I can barely keep a straight face. "That's reassuring. I'm going to get ready now. It looks like we have a long day ahead of us."

ST. FINNEGAN'S CATHOLIC Church is a tall-spired, ancient-looking building on the outskirts of Hunt's Point. The bells are tolling as we arrive, which means the Duchess's casket has already been taken inside. Michael parks the car on the street outside the church—there's plenty of space available—and Michael, Zeth and I head inside. The dress Michael bought for me is respectful yet clings to my figure at the same time, perhaps showing a few too many curves considering the setting. It's not as though I ever met the Duchess, though. And despite the stressful nature of our reason for being here this morning, Zeth's hands strategically brush those curves as he helps me out of the car, a gentle, burning reminder of our little cane game. We make our way up the pathway to the church entrance, and I do my best not to enjoy his touch a little too much.

The interior of St. Finnegan's is typical of any Catholic church. Lots of dark wooden pews, stained-glass windows, gold filigree, and a ten-foot-high depiction of Christ on the cross at the far end of the building in the apse. The smell hits me like a blast from the past. Dusty books, wood, wax, incense, shirt starch—these are the scents of my childhood.

There aren't many people sitting in the pews. Guess that explains the ample parking space outside. The front two rows are taken, perhaps twenty or so backs facing us as we walk down the aisle. My modest heels send echoing footsteps up to the high, vaulted ceiling as we try to sneak into the service unnoticed. No one turns around to see who the latecomers are. The priest at the front of the congregation pauses in his words and gives us a tight, inconvenienced smile as Zeth directs me to one of the empty pews on the left, halfway down the length of the church. He only continues once we're seated.

None of us pay any attention to the service. Of the three of us, I'm perhaps the least subtle as I crane my neck, looking for a flash of familiar blonde curls. I can't see Lacey anywhere. Zeth's knee starts to bounce up and down—he can't see her either.

"Fuck," he says under his breath. Cursing in church? Even though my faith's been absent for quite some time now, I still feel my cheeks reddening. "She's not here." He leans to whisper in Michael's ear. Michael does his own job of scanning the paltry collection of people sitting at the front of the church. He shakes his head. Zeth looks like his blood has started to boil in his veins.

"Fucking *Charlie* isn't here. None of his boys. Not a single one of them," he hisses. That doesn't make any sense.

"But Michael said Charlie posted the obituary? Why wouldn't he come?"

Zeth clenches his jaw, cracking his knuckles one after the other. "Because he knew *we* would."

Someone turns around and shushes us, holding their index finger to their lips—an old woman with her hair coiffed into a urine-yellow beehive. Zeth slips his hand under my arm and gently guides me to my feet. Michael doesn't need any encouragement. He stands and the three of us slip back out the way we came. Less than a minute. We were at the funeral less than a minute, and it appears the whole thing was a massive waste of time. As soon as the church doors close behind us, Zeth pinches the bridge of his nose and swears. Loudly, this time.

"What the fuck is his game? I'm gonna kill him. I'm gonna fucking kill him."

"We shouldn't be hanging around out here," Michael says. "He could have men ready to pick us off one by one or something."

Zeth's sharp eyes flicker from left to right, as though searching out the mystery snipers. "You're right." He takes hold of my hand. "Come on. Let's get out of here."

My pulse is racing when we reach the car. Paranoia has kicked in, big time. There are no suspicious-looking cars idling on the curb. No dodgy men in suits hiding behind the headstones in the church's leafy courtyard. But I can't shake it...I feel like something bad is about to happen. Michael has the keys to the car ready. He's about to open the car door when Zeth drops my hand and grabs him by the arm. "Wait. Wait a second."

Boom, boom, boom—my heart banging like a drum. Zeth stares at the car, eyebrows pulled together. Michael does the same thing. "What is it, boss? You see something?"

Zeth shakes his head. "I don't know. Check the wheel arches."

Michael drops to his knees and begins checking out the underside of the car, while Zeth forcefully prizes the hood of the car open. It's Michael that finds the device. "Fuck, Zee." That's all he says. That's all he has time to say. He jumps to his feet, and then Zeth's grabbing hold of me around the waist and running. I lose my shoes. My ribcage and still-wounded shoulder are gripped with pain. Zeth shouts something, but I don't hear what he says. My jackhammer-ing pulse drowns everything out. And then it comes.

Strangely, it's not the sound of the actual explosion that sticks in my memory; it's the sound of shattering glass. The beautiful stained-glass windows in St. Finnegan's church splintering as the bomb that was hidden in the wheel arch of our car detonates.

Sky.

Concrete.

Sky.

Concrete.

Sky...

I see the concrete coming for me. I feel the weightlessness in my stomach. I feel a multitude of forces, like grabbing hands, pushing and pulling me in eight different directions. I feel the oxygen being sucked from my lungs.

And then I feel nothing.

28

Zeth

"ARE YOU READY, BABY? OH MY GOD, PAUL. WATCH. WATCH."

A high-pitched whistling sound is piercing my eardrum. I have no idea when I've ever felt this bad. My head...my head is *killing me*. It literally feels like my brain is revolting against the rest of my body, intent on causing me so much pain that I simply expire. Fuck. There's a lot of thinking involved in trying to move myself into a sitting position. My shoulders, elbows, wrists—every single joint in my body—feel like they've been dislocated and roughly forced back into place.

I can smell sugar. Something sweet.

"I can't believe it," a woman's voice whispers. It *is* a whisper, soft, the words deeply felt, but the volume of the words is loud. Ear-splittingly loud. I have no idea what the fuck is going on. I risk opening one eye, then the other, and the pain in my head increases. I'm looking at a bright rectangle of white light. Dark shapes move within the light.

"He hasn't even realized. Look," the female voice whispers again.

I squint, trying to clear my vision, and things begin to take proper shape. A cinema screen. I'm staring up at a cinema screen. And on the screen…

"He's such a big boy. I had no idea he was gonna grow so fast."

"Yeah, he's gonna be tall like his dad."

My mother. And my father. Well, the man I remembered as my father, before Charlie ruined my fucking life and announced *he* was actually my dad. My father's arms are wrapped around my mother's waist from behind, his chin resting on her shoulder, and two of them watch as a pudgy little baby holds his dimpled arms above his head and takes staggering, teetering steps down a long pathway.

"He's got your eyes, Paul," another voice says somewhere in the background. "So dark. He's gonna terrorize the ladies with those eyes." My mom turns to the camera—she knows they're being recorded—and pokes her tongue out at the person filming. "Oh, shut up, Dee. I can't bear to hear that. He's never going to grow up. He's just gonna be my little boy forever and ever."

Dee, whoever she is, laughs. "You're going to be the most overprotective mother, aren't you? Your child's not going to bring a woman home until he's already married her for fear you'll hate her on sight."

In the background, the baby tumbles backward, landing on his butt. There are enterprising stalks of grass thrusting their way out of the cracked concrete where he's sitting now, the green blades reaching for the sky. The baby focuses, wrapping a dumpy little fist around a handful, and tries to uproot them.

"No, Zeth. That's not for eating, baby boy." My mother frees herself from my father's embrace and lifts the baby—me—from the ground. She then turns and presents me to the camera, as though I'm a trophy she just can't bear to stop displaying to the world. Even then my eyes were darker than your average chocolate brown. I reach out with dirty, muddied hands and try slapping them against the lens of the camera.

"No, baby. That's Duchess's new camera. You can't break that. Psycho Charlie will get mad."

"Hey, please don't call him that. And don't call me Duchess, either. I hate it."

My mother turns her huge, wide eyes on the camera, looking right down the lens.

"Charles Holsan, you're an arrogant prick and you've been treating my best friend like shit. Now put a ring on her finger and a baby in her belly, or leave her the hell alone." She laughs, her serious expression disintegrating into a broad smile that illuminates her whole face. She looks just like Lacey. Beautiful.

"He's nowhere near as bad as everyone thinks he is. You should get to know him a little better. He really likes you two."

"He doesn't like me. He hates me," my father says. "I can't do anything right for the man."

"He's just never had an accountant before, Paul. Don't worry. It's just his dry English humor. It takes some getting used to. All right, I have to go. You," the woman, Duchess, says to my mom, her manicured fingernails suddenly visible on screen as she points, "need to remember to show your husband some love. He'll start to think you're playing favorites."

Mom smiles at Paul over her shoulder, hugging me tightly to her chest. "Awww, baby. You know I love you, right?" She breaks out into a wicked smile. "But I do love Zeth more. He came from you and me. He's perfection. I will never love anything in the world as much as I love this little boy."

My heart feels like it's doing somersaults in my chest. My eyes are burning like crazy. I try to shunt myself into a more upright position, but my body is so fucking sore. I need to get up. I need to find Sloane and Michael. I grit my teeth, using a combination of what little upper body strength and momentum I have to lift myself.

A voice speaks out into the darkness, almost right on top of me. I nearly shit my pants. "That was always 'er fucking problem, y'know? She always did love you more than anything or anybody else."

Charlie Holsan is sitting to my right, comfortably slouched in an upholstered seat. He turns and gives me a clinical once over. "Not lookin' so hot, my boy. You got a bad 'eadache?"

"Fuck you, asshole."

"Ha! I fuckin' love it. You always did have a fuckin' mouth on you." Charlie goes back to watching the screen, as though I don't even exist. I take a moment to look around. No bodyguards. No Sloane. No Michael. No Lacey. No one. Just him and me in an empty movie theater. It's an old place, traditional. The kind of place with brocaded curtains that draw apart at the beginning of a feature, unveiling the new, fantastical world you're about to immerse yourself in. No drink holders or recline features on the seats. From the elaborately scrolled cornicing on the ceiling and the grand arch over the screen, this place was definitely built back in the twenties.

I wrestle myself to my knees, and then throw myself back into a chair to my left. "Where are the others, Charlie? Where the hell is Sloane? What the fuck are you up to?"

Charlie holds up a hand, pointing one finger in the air. The video reel of my mother and me starts all over again. Her laughter. *Are you ready, baby? Oh my god, Paul. Watch. Watch.* Me taking my bumbling first steps down an uneven pathway.

"I loved your mother from the very moment I set eyes on her. Did you know that?" Charlie says, ignoring my question.

I want to cut out the fucker's tongue just for talking about her. I will not engage in this with him. I will find my friends, and then I will end this miserable bastard's life. "Where. The. Fuck. Are.

They?"

Charlie looks at me again, a small, amused smile on his face. "They're watchin' another movie, I'm afraid. They weren't too keen on this feature. 'Specially not your sister. She's had a rough few days."

"Because you convinced her the Duchess was her mother, when she wasn't, you fuck. And now the woman's dead."

"And now the woman's dead," Charlie agrees, slowly nodding his head. He taps his index finger against his chin, appearing to muse over something. "It was pretty shitty of me to do that, I suppose. But this life is a circular thing, if anything at all. The Duchess wanted kids so fuckin' bad. She couldn't 'ave 'em, though. And your mother stole Lacey away from me before I even 'ad a chance to get a look at her. So I thought it prudent to take Lacey away from 'er in the end. Give her to the Duchess."

"The Duchess is dead. My mother's dead. You can't seek revenge against the dead, Charlie. You sure as fuck can't make up for your failures as a human being by giving a dead woman a fake daughter, either."

"Oh, but that's where you're wrong, Zeth, my boy. I firmly believe in an afterlife, and I firmly believe your mother is watching down on 'er kids. So she can definitely hurt over me fucking with what Lacey believes. And she can definitely 'urt because 'er precious boy knows she was a fucking prostitute. I took everything from 'er. I made it so neither of 'em could work. Not a single person your parents knew would 'elp 'em for fear of what would 'appen if I found out, you see. I made it so there was only one option left open to her, and I made fucking sure it ruined your mother's marriage." He grins. "Exactly 'ow I wanted it. That was before I knew she was pregnant with my kid, of course, but still. All's well that ends well, right?"

I have no idea what kind of shape I'm in—I'm assuming bad,

since I was thrown so far in that blast—but that doesn't matter. If I die trying, I'll make this man pay for the things he's done. The things he's said. But first, I need to know the truth.

"You're not my father, are you?"

Charlie gives me a cold, stony look. He reaches inside the breast pocket of his suit jacket, draws out a small, silver vial, and proceeds to unscrew the cap. I know what's inside it. He tips some fine white powder out onto the back of his hand, holds it to his nose, and inhales sharply. "I did my first line of coke the day the Duchess came 'ome and told me her best friend was knocked up. I was so fucking angry. That was the first time I gave the silly cow a slap, too. A day of firsts all round." He grins at me like he's telling me a funny joke. The drugs do this to him. He acts like he's happy, like the buzz is still enough to lift him, when all it's doing is making him angrier. More sour. More aggressive. More vile.

"The Duchess came bouncing into the room, all hopped up on her good news, babbling about how Celia and Paul were gonna have a baby. Celia and Paul. Celia and Paul. Celia and motherfucking Paul. He wasn't wrong, y'know. I really did 'ate that fucker." Charlie does another bump. This time he doesn't even pretend to smile.

"That was also the first time I'd ever been jealous of another man. I had more money than anyone else I knew. A big fuckin' 'ouse. I 'ad everything I thought I needed, but then along came your fuckin' mother with all that curly blonde 'air and that smile that seemed to light up the world, and I wanted 'er. And I couldn't have 'er because of Paul. Because she didn't fuckin' want *me.* And then you came along, and I saw how fuckin' happy you made her, and I *hated* you. You were *supposed* to be my son. But you weren't. You were the glue that made them stronger." He points an accusing finger at the screen, where my mother is picking me up from the ground, prying plucked grass stalks out of my fat little hands.

It hits me with the weight of a twenty-pound bowling ball to the chest. He's not my father. Charlie really isn't my father. A cold sweat prickles at my skin, my stomach twisting; the relief is just too great. Better my father be a dead man I can barely remember than this piece of work. "So you lied about, Lacey, too?"

Charlie glances sharply out of the corner of his eye, tapping the silver capsule against the top of his leg. "Oh, no, son. Lacey's mine. I put her in your mother one night. I sent your father, prissy Paul, out of town for me. He needed to go collect some money for me, I told 'im. So off 'e goes, and I go pay a visit to your mother. She was always a little wary of me. I'd waited years by this point, though. Years. And I was done waiting for her to be impressed by the shit I bought her or the money I tried to give 'er. I made 'er let me in. And then I made 'er behave herself while I got what I wanted."

Fuck the pain in my body. I rocket out of my seat, launching myself at the man. My fists rejoice in pain as I drive them into Charlie's face, once, twice, and then I'm suddenly being dragged back off him. I lash out; I kick; I holler. I can't get free. O'Shannessey and Sammy are gripping me by the shoulders—must have been lurking there in the dark the whole time. Charlie straightens himself out in his seat, and then spits blood onto the ground. He dabs at his mouth with a handkerchief that O'Shannessey, ever the fucking suck-up, hands to him.

"That was quite rude," Charlie tells me. "To be honest, though, I can see why you're upset about me forcing myself on your mother. But you should know, despite how fiercely she fought me off, I could see in her eyes that she liked it. She always was the sort of woman who pretended to be good, when on the inside she was just begging for it. If I'd met her before she married Paul, she would have been mine. I don't doubt it for a moment."

"You're fucking dreaming." I have another go at jerking myself free, but it seems I'm weaker than I thought. O'Shannessey and Sammy manage to keep ahold of me, though I don't make it easy for them.

"Speaking of dreams..." Charlie says. "How you sleeping these days, Zeth?" Something sick and suddenly frightened curdles in the pit of my stomach. "After you came to live with me, you never could seem to get a good night's sleep."

Fuck. No. I do not want to think about this right now. I do not want to think about *him.* "You'd better kill me now or shut the fuck up, Charlie, otherwise I'm gonna slit your throat for you."

He laughs. "You used to say that when I'd come to you, too. Do you remember? Fuck you, asshole," he says, mimicking the high, reedy voice of a child. "You're not going to kill me. You're not going to touch me. I'll kill you first. I'll slit your fucking throat."

I don't want to remember those words. They don't appear in my night terrors, but they ring fucking true. I said them. I said those words when I was trying to defend myself...*from him.* It makes sense, of course. A deep, obvious kind of sense that I should have realized long before now. The thing is I *have* known. I've known all along, even back then, but I could never admit it to myself. When Charlie came for me and took me from my uncle's place in Las Flores, I thought this strong, powerful man had come to save me. He treated me like a son. I didn't want to believe it was him coming into my room each night, trying to rape me. Kill me.

When it first started happening, I reasoned with myself that the man in the dark didn't really want to hurt me. If he wanted to have sex with me so badly, he had to like me a lot, right? I was too young to realize rape and murder went hand in hand. I thought raping someone was an act of tortured love instead of seeing it for what it is—degradation. Humiliation. An act of hatred so vile and evil that even criminals in prison will beat a rapist to death.

"Don't say another fucking word," I snap.

Charlie raises his eyebrows at me. The video of my mother has stopped playing again. He lifts his hand, gesturing to whoever's in the projection room to start it over from the beginning. "Why don't you want me to talk about it?" he asks me. "Does that mean you won't want me talking about how I killed your best friend and then let you rot in jail for his murder? Does it mean you won't want me talking about how I tried to run your girlfriend off the road? Does that mean you won't want me talking about how I *did* run your mother off the road?"

"*What?*" The night Charlie murdered Murphy, he'd been making trashy suggestions about the Duchess. With Charlie's shitty temper, I've always thought that was the reason why he took a machete to his neck and slashed his throat wide open. But that...that barely registers against his last confession. The official police report on my parents' death was that my father had an embolism that burst. That he drove their car straight into a street sign. But Charlie... *Charlie?*

"Oh, come on. Don't look so surprised. Your whore of a mother ran away with my child. I could hardly let her get away with that. I don't forgive, Zeth. *And I sure as fuck don't forget.*"

29

Sloane

"SLOANE. SLOANE, WAKE UP." SOMEONE'S SHAKING ME.
roughly. It's possibly the worst feeling in the world. I don't feel like
I should be waking up yet. I probably shouldn't wake up for a really
long time. "Sloane, you need to get up. Now!"

The urgency in the person's voice breaks through the fog
clouding my head. It all comes flooding back to me—the church, the
casket, the bomb. The azure blue of the cloudless sky spinning into
the industrial gray of the street below me. The pain and the heat
and the panic. I open my eyes, and Lacey is staring down at me,
concern creasing her face.

"Oh, thank god. You're alive." Her hands are trembling as she
pats them over my torso, fingers gently pulling pieces of my
shredded dress together. I look down my body to find I'm a mess. A
seriously big fucking mess.

"What the hell's going on?" I croak.

"Charlie tried to have you killed. Didn't work, though," Lacey
explains. I try to sit up and fail. Lacey hooks one of my arms over

her shoulder and heaves me upright. The room spins a little, but then slows and stops altogether. Michael's laid out on the floor a couple of feet away. Looks like he's in the recovery position.

"Oh, shit! Is he alright?" I scramble forward on all fours, hands fumbling at his collar, trying to unbutton his shirt so I can check for a pulse. It's there, strong and steady if a little slow.

"His head was bleeding when they brought you here," Lacey says. "It stopped a while ago, though. I didn't know what to do."

She's right—Michael's head is wounded, just above his right temple. The blood's already congealed there, forming the beginnings of a scab. I tease open his eyelids and try to see if his pupils respond, although in the darkness of the room it's hard to tell. I think they do. His body is probably just trying to heal itself, but he still needs medical attention. The first thing I do is scan the room, not for a medical kit or an exit, but for the one person who can make this okay. For the one person who will be able to fix all of this. But he's not here.

"Where's Zeth, Lacey?" She gives me a guilty, torn look. My stomach begins to fizz, like I'm about to throw up. "Lacey, where is your brother?"

"Charlie took him down into the basement."

"The basement? What the hell's in the basement? Where *are* we?" The room is a dark, square box—no windows, no furniture. Nothing. It's entirely empty aside from the three of us. There's only one exit, and that's a steel door with a keypad wired into the wall next to it.

"Used to be an old movie theater," Lacey says, sniffing. "Charlie said he brought my mom here on a date one time. Back when it was still open."

I sit on the cold, hard ground, bridging my knees up and hugging them to my chest. "Lace...god, Lace, Charlie didn't bring your mom here, I promise you."

281

She bites her lip, staring me down. "I know," she says in a small voice. "I know he didn't. But he *said* he did."

"You know the Duchess wasn't your mom?"

She nods. "I never believed him."

"Then—" I can barely speak. A wave of anger builds in my chest, making my throat constrict. "Then why did you speak to him on the phone? Why the hell did you go with him?"

"Because..." She covers her face with her hands. "It sounds stupid now."

"Lacey, tell me!" I'm on the verge of screaming.

"Because I already knew he was my dad. And...and I wanted him to think I believed him when he called me. That's why I said...that's why I said all that awful stuff. I'm sorry, Sloane, really, I didn't mean any of it."

"*What?*" This is absolute madness. She *knew*? First Zeth knew all along that Lacey was his sister, and now she's telling me she knew Charlie was her father? What is wrong with these people? Why the hell do they keep their cards so close to their chests? I want to grab hold of Lacey and shake her. Shake some fucking sense into her. "Why?"

The blonde girl shrugs, pulling at a loose thread on the torn sweater she's wearing. "Because he keeps fucking everything up for Zeth. He tried to hurt you. I wanted to...I wanted to kill him. I *tried* to. That's why I'm in here with you instead of out there with them."

"You tried to kill Charlie?"

"With a screwdriver."

None of this is making any sense. I press my forehead against my knees, trying to breathe through the panic that's gripping hold of me. "He could have killed you, Lace. What were you thinking?"

She doesn't say anything. When I look up, about to scold her some more, I see there are tears streaking down her face.

"I was thinking I wanted you two to be safe. I was thinking about the normal life you guys deserve to share. You can't have that with Charlie still around, and you...you'll never be able to forget it if Zeth kills him. It'll play on you."

I want to deny that, but the words stick in my throat. Honestly, I've done everything in my power not to think about it. I've known for a while that killing Charlie is the only way Zeth sees us having a life together, just like Lacey is saying, but I've put it from my mind. Tried to make myself believe I'm okay with it because Charlie is a bad person. Because Charlie will kill us given half the chance. But I'm not okay with it. I haven't been for a while.

Lacey starts crying.

I shuffle toward her on my butt and wrap an arm around her shoulder. "Zeth would never want you to take on something like that for him. And neither would I. You damn near broke his heart when you walked out with that man."

She turns into me and starts sobbing, her voice muffled in my shoulder. "I know. But...he's done so much for me. Everything. And so have you. And I already killed Greg Mallory. I figured it wouldn't be so bad. I could do it again if I had to."

"Oh, shit, Lace." I hug her to me tight, running my hands up and down her back. This poor girl. I have to admit, I've been angry ever since she walked out of Zeth's apartment with Charlie. She chose to leave us. She chose *him* over her brother and me. That hurt more than words can ever describe, but this hurts more. She did it all, put herself in this awful position, for us. I can't cope with that.

My own tears chase fast and hot down my cheeks. Lacey wraps her arms around my waist, crying even harder. For a brief and fragile moment, we are hopeless and inconsolable. And then I put a stop to it.

"C'mon. Sit up. We need to figure out what we're gonna do." I wipe my face with the back of my hand, and then I wipe away Lacey's tears, too. She blinks up at me, her tiny frame trembling against mine.

"We can't do anything. "

"Of course we can. Being defeatist is the only sure way we're definitely going to lose here," I say. "How many men does Charlie have with him?"

Lacey thinks on this. "They come and go all day. I don't know."

"Okay. Well, I know the kind of man Charlie is. He won't leave us waiting here for long. And when he sends for us, we'll be ready. Right?" I have no idea where this shit is coming from. I know the kind of man Charlie is? We'll be ready for him? Really? That sounds incredibly cliché and entirely unbelievable, but I sound like I mean it. Gives me an air of plausibility. Lace darts a doubtful look my way, but then nods slowly, still chewing on her lip.

"Tell me about the screwdriver," I say.

"I snatched it when they parked the cars in the underground parking lot. They have a garage down there. Some of the guys fix up old cars for Charlie. They were arguing about whether they should go back for you and Zeth, so they didn't notice me slip it into my pocket. It was small." She looks down at her hands. "I should have waited. We were walking up the stairwell to get into the building and I couldn't take it anymore. He just kept sniffing and sniffing, and I knew why. He was off his face. I didn't care, then. I just wanted him to die. I pulled it out of my pocket and I was gonna drive it into his back, but the two assholes behind me grabbed me before I could." She looks up at me, eyes still shining brightly from her tears. "Charlie was *not* happy."

"I can imagine."

"He had this room ready for me. It was full of pink lace and these pretty dolls. The bed was massive. It had one of those things hanging down from the ceiling over it. I don't know what they're called."

A canopy. I had a canopy over my bed when I was a little girl. I felt like a princess, and every night Dad would draw the voile across and lie on top of the covers with me, reading stories out of my Brothers Grimm books until I fell asleep. Poor Lacey never had that. Perhaps in some way, by giving it to her now Charlie was trying to be a father to her. But after your child tries to stab you in the back with a screwdriver, I imagine that changes things. I am right.

"He didn't let me stay in there, though. He said I had to learn some respect and he threw me in here."

"At least he didn't kill you."

"He can't kill me," she says miserably.

"Why not?"

"Because he told me Zeth's not really his. And he has no brothers or sisters. No other living relatives. I'm the only other person alive on the planet that shares his bloodline. And...he's dying, Sloane. He hasn't got long left to live."

CHARLIE HOLSAN'S ON the way out. Thank the universe. I don't think I've ever been so happy to hear a terminal prognosis in all my life. Does that make me a terrible, awful person? I remember Zeth saying he assumed Charlie was sick, and now that it's confirmed it feels like a weight is being lifted from my shoulders. I have no idea why. I'm still locked in a concrete box with no means of escape. I still have no idea where the man I love is, or whether he's even okay. But somehow, just knowing Charlie's not got long left is faintly comforting.

After an hour of holding Lacey in my arms and comforting *her*, Michael begins to stir. His eyelids flicker open, his right hand making involuntary open and closing twitches.

"Michael? Michael, are you okay?" I check his pupil response again, though it's still hard to see how his irises react with so little light. He mumbles something under his breath, eyes not focused on anything in particular, and then it's as though his system reboots right in front of me. He inhales sharply, eyes widening, back bowing, and then Michael is suddenly awake. Properly awake. He looks up at me, two small creases forming between his brows.

"Where's Zee?" These are his first words. No confusion over where we are. No checking himself over to see if he's all right. *Where's Zee?*

"We don't know." I place my fingertips against his neck, checking his pulse. Still slow, but steady. If we were in the hospital, I'd be very concerned about my patient. I'd want to keep him in a couple of days to monitor him. There would be MRIs to check his brain function and internal organs. There would be at least three people, each responsible for making sure a different part of Michael was functioning properly, watching him around the clock.

I would be in the same position. However, since we're not in the hospital, I just have to assess how he's feeling and go from there. Not that I can do anything about it if he does experience compression to his brain, or he is bleeding internally, of course, but still...

"Do you feel nauseous?" I ask.

"No." Michael looks grim with the small amount of light slipping in under the doorway throwing his face into shadows. His whole head looks like that of a skull: eye sockets drowning in darkness, cheeks gaunt and hollowed out. "I feel like murdering somebody," he grinds out.

I had the good sense to be intimidated by Michael when I first met him, but in this moment I can see how he would be truly terrifying if you found yourself on his bad side. "You and I both, buddy. But we're trapped in here."

Michael's face distorts in a rictus of rage. I think he's going to jump up and start beating at the walls, set on smashing them apart with his bare hands, but then Lacey shuffles across the bare concrete floor, twists herself over so that her back's to Michael, and nestles herself into him. His whole demeanor changes in the blink of an eye.

"What you been doing, kid? Huh?" he whispers to her, wrapping his arm protectively around the girl. Lacey doesn't answer. She closes her eyes and falls asleep. I don't sleep. The mere thought of it is laughable. All I can think about is Zeth and whatever the hell Charlie is doing to him. It can't be good. Whatever it is, it can't be good.

Zeth

"YOU WANT SALT? THEY NEVER PUT ENOUGH SALT IN THE fucking food." Charlie slides a saltshaker toward me; I catch it before it can go flying off the end of the polished oak table. The pasta O'Shannessey slapped unceremoniously in front of me, scowling the whole time, is over-salted if anything. I haven't eaten any of it; I can just smell the overload of sodium. After the movie theater, Charlie had me hauled up two flights of stairs to what must once have been the main lobby of the place. The furniture has been ripped out. Nothing but the matted old carpet, worn threadbare in places by the feet of many thousands of people, and the concession stand remain. The place still smells faintly sweet, mixed in with the staleness of dust, age and time.

"Doctors say the radiotherapy's killed my taste buds," Charlie advises me, as he winds some of the pasta around his fork and stuffs it into his mouth. "They're full of shit, though. There are a few things left I can still taste. Garlic. Scotch." He smirks at me. "*Pussy. So long as I can still taste scotch and pussy, I don't give a fuck about everything else.*"

Charlie's mention of radiotherapy confirms my suspicions—he's sick. He's not just sick. He's *dying*. "How long you got left?" I shove the plate away from me, my stomach twisting.

"Told me I had two months," Charlie says, grinning at me. "Five months ago."

"Commiserations."

"Ha!" he thrusts his fork in my direction, splattering sauce onto the tabletop. "You could give two shits if I live or die, my boy. But it's nice that you pretend, right?"

"Oh, I definitely give a shit. When you're dead, Charlie, I'm gonna fucking dance on your grave."

"And what makes you think you aren't gonna be in the ground long before me?"

He has a point there. I just send him a hateful look down the table. If it weren't for the fact that O'Shannessey and Sammy both have guns trained on me, I'd lunge right across the table and drown the motherfucker in his Alfredo Pomdero. I want to see the old man choke.

"Why here, Charlie? Why the hell have you brought us *here*?"

Charlie glances up from his meal, chewing with his mouth open. "The movie theater?" His eyes travel up to the ceiling, as though observing the decaying opulence and seeing something entirely different. "Your mother used to come with the Duchess here every Saturday for a matinee. They thought they lived in the fucking forties, those two. I thought for a little while the Duchess was cheating on me. I 'ad 'er followed just to make sure she was keeping her fucking knees together, and they told me she was coming 'ere to watch Casa-fucking-blanca and old Rita Hayworth movies. Only place in Seattle that used to play that shit at the time. And that silly bitch, she pissed me off one day, so I bought the place and 'ad it closed down. Kitchen still works, though." He winks at me—the wink of an insane bastard. "It's big and it's quiet in here. The building's been 'ere so long, people 'ave forgotten it even exists. It's part of the landscape. People see it without actually seeing it. That makes it the perfect kind of place to lay low when you need to."

Hiding in plain sight. I have no idea where we are geographically —still in Seattle?—but I'm guessing it's somewhere blatantly obvious.

"Aren't you gonna eat your food?" Charlie asks. He's talking to me with the conversational tone of a concerned friend. I choke on the bitter laugh that wants to burst out of me.

"I would rather starve." I'm actually fucking hungry, but the sensation doesn't feel right. My stomach feels like it's pitching uncontrollably, one minute demanding food, the next threatening to expel its meager contents right onto the table. Hot and cold sweats, too. Whatever happened to my body in that blast, it's seriously not happy with me right now, that much is clear. And I have no idea if Sloane's okay, either, which is driving me fucking crazy.

"You should eat," the old man repeats. "You're going to need your strength soon."

That sounds ominous, but guess what? Threats really *are* something I could give two shits about. Physical pain means nothing to me. Finding Sloane, making sure she's okay, and then making this bastard pay, in that order; those are the only things that matter.

"Y'know I wasn't exactly 'eartbroken when I found out you 'adn't died in that explosion. Since I took you from your uncle, I've enjoyed fucking with you. I've gained an immense, bottomless kind of satisfaction from watching you suffer throughout your life. I always thought I'd be there when you died, so I could enjoy watching that, too. The bomb was a little classless, I know, but it felt necessary. You 'aven't been behaving yourself, Zeth. And I couldn't 'ave that. But then, miracle upon miracles, you and your fucking friends survive, and I get my wish after all. I do get to watch you die." He spears some chicken on his fork and shoves it into his mouth. I imagine it sticking in his throat. Imagine his face turning purple as he coughs and splutters and fights for air.

"So with that in mind, I've organized a little entertainment for myself. There are six blokes on their way 'ere, and every single one of 'em 'as a bone to pick with you. I've said they can each go a few rounds with you, see 'ow long they can last. Probably won't be long since you're a berserker and they're fucking stray dogs. I guess that's my fault. When I used to come into your room at night, I created a bit of a monster, didn't I? I created a fighter—a fact that might not have worked in my favor in recent days, but still. Was worth it just to 'ear you fucking cry. And if you're not dead by the time the last man steps into the ring, that's all the better for me. That means I can kill you myself."

I hate that he can talk about what he did to me so flippantly. This man has fucked me over more ways than I can count. He sent me to possibly the worst place on earth and left me there to rot for years. He killed my mother. He stalked the shadows of my bedroom on a near-nightly basis when I was just a snot-nosed shit of a teenager— tried to kill me—and yet he's shown no remorse. Where I'm concerned, it's very fucking clear he's proud of his accomplishments.

"So you have to bring in six guys to wear me down before you'll take a shot at me, old man? Is that it? I seem to remember you being a lot braver when I was a third of the size I am now."

O'Shannessey snickers. Charlie doesn't look at the man, but every muscle in his body stiffens. O'Shannessey realizes he's just fucked up and clears his throat, shifting from one foot to the other. "I'm not a fuckin' idiot, Zeth," Charlie snaps. "I didn't go through weeks of therapy and needles and fucking endless, humiliating exams just so you can smash your fist through my face. You'll have to forgive me if I seem a little...*delicate,* but I want to preserve what life I have left."

The thing is, he doesn't seem delicate at all. He hardly seems like he's aged since the day he showed up at my uncle's place and spirited me away. I clench my hands under the table, feeling wave after wave of adrenalin rattle around my body. Despite being in some pretty serious pain, I'm just waiting for my moment. Waiting for my moment to end this once and for all. And I don't intend on waiting for Charlie's buddies to show up.

I know the kind of men he would have asked here. The kind who have lost family members at Charlie's behest. All it would have taken was a few carefully whispered words in the right ears—*Zeth Mayfair, he's the one that did it*—and I'm sure half of Seattle's underworld is baying for my blood.

Charlie angles his head, but doesn't look at O'Shannessey—the old man hasn't forgotten O'Shannessey's little fuck up just now. I'm betting there will be repercussions at some point. Some point soon. Charlie's never been one to let retribution sit too long. "Go and get the girls," he snaps. To Sammy, he says, "Kill the other one."

Michael is the other one. I'm rising to my feet, ready to start some shit, when I feel the explosion of pain in my chest. My body locks up, and for a moment I can't figure out why. I have no control over any part of me. My hands, arms, legs, none of it works. I tremble and shake, barely able to breathe. I do manage to roll my eyes down to the source of all the pain—two burning hot points in the center of my chest—and I see the probes there, digging into my skin. A Taser. After narrowly avoiding being shot with one at Pippa's, I get shot with one now, here. By Charlie. I never even saw it coming. How ironic.

"Steady, son," he says, smirking. "My aim ain't so good anymore. I could get you in the balls next time."

It feels like the veins underneath my skin are drawing taut, stretching and pulling. The current's still coursing through me, looping over and over in excruciating waves. O'Shannessey and Sammy back out of the lobby, watching me grunt in pain, clearly sorry to be missing out on the fucking show. Assholes. As soon as we're alone, Charlie switches off the Taser, placing the firing mechanism down next to his food. I gasp in a breath of oxygen, really appreciating for the first time how good it feels just to be able to fill your lungs.

"Don't move again," Charlie warns. "This thing isn't exactly police grade, if you get me. I could fry you to death quite easily, and along with my aim, my stomach ain't what it used to be, either. I think the stench of your cooking meat might just be enough to ruin my lunch."

"You hurt any of them, and I'll—"

"You'll sit still and you'll fucking behave! Do not test my patience, *you fuck*," Charlie roars, slamming his palm down against the table. The silverware on either side of my plate of food jumps so high the fork clatters to the floor. "Now shut the fuck up and wait for Lacey and that severely stuck-up cunt to arrive. Open your mouth just once and I swear I'll crank this thing up to its highest fucking setting."

I don't know what the hell I'm supposed to do. Sammy is going to kill Michael, and there's literally nothing I can do to stop it. I'll be incapacitated as soon as I move a muscle, and then what good am I to anyone? I sit in silence, glaring at Charlie down the length of the table, all the while counting the times Michael's eluded being killed. There are at least three occasions I can recall off the top of my head. I'm hoping this will make a fourth.

O'Shannessey returns with Lacey and Sloane only a few minutes later. They're holding on to one another, arms linked, eyes wide. Sloane's covered in blood, her dress shredded from shoulder to hem. She looks like she's in fucking pain. The pull to go to her, to leap out of the chair and snatch her up in my arms, is almost too strong to deny. "You okay?" I ask her, raising my eyebrows.

She nods. "Sore. But, yeah. I'm okay. Michael—"

"Will be okay, too." The confidence in my voice goes against everything I'm feeling right now, but I need her to see everything's going to be all right. I need my sister to see everything's going to be all right, too. Lacey gives me a nervous look, her eyes shining the way they do when she's about to cry.

"I'm sorry, Zeth," she whispers. "I didn't want to leave you. I didn't mean—"

"It's okay." I shake my head. She has to know I'm not mad at her. Confused, sure, but not mad. I should have done a better fucking job of protecting her. "It doesn't matter now, okay?"

Charlie, fucking asshole that he is, continues to twist pasta around his fork. "Why don't you sit down, ladies? You should join us. Lacey, it's customary for the son of the head of a family to sit at his right hand. Since I don't have a son, you're going to have to do."

Neither Sloane nor Lace look inclined to sit with us, but O'Shannessey doesn't give them much of a choice; he nudges them forward with the butt of his drawn gun. Dragging two extra chairs over for them, he sits Sloane to my right, and Lacey on my left. The whole set-up is like some fucked-up family dinner. Lacey stares down at the table, her eyes unblinking. She's tapping her fingers to her thumb, over and over—pinkie, ring, middle, index. Index, middle, ring, pinkie. Not a good sign.

"You need to...you need to take the probes out of him," she says, still staring at the grain of the wood.

Charlie puts his fork down. "What?"

"Take the probes out of him." Her eyes flicker to my chest, barely long enough for her to glance at the small, metal barbs attached to wires that are digging into me. I've always heard the more muscle you have, the more it hurts being shocked with a Taser. I have no idea whether that's true or not, but I *can* confirm it hurts like a motherfucker. My whole body feels like it's still charged. Lacey's fingers work quicker as she grows more anxious—I can see it building in her eyes. Like she's an object of intense curiosity, Charlie studies her every movement with a scowl on his face.

"What the 'ell's wrong with you now?" he snaps.

"You're hurting him. You need to stop hurting him."

"I ain't stoppin', sweetheart. I'm gonna 'urt 'im some more, and you are going to sit there in silence, and you're gonna pay attention. You're gonna 'ave to 'urt people, too, if you're going to make it in this world, Lacey."

A single tear dangles from the tip of one of Lacey's eyelashes. It wobbles, and then falls and hits the table. Still no blinking. She's standing on the precipice of a very high cliff right now and she's about to go over the edge; I've spent enough time with the girl to know her inside out by now, and she is not in a good place. None of us are in a fucking good place, but Lacey isn't equipped to deal with this kind of stress.

"I won't," she whispers. "Just let him go."

The old man snorts, leaning closer to the table. A blind man could see Lacey isn't quite right, that she's mentally struggling to deal with what's happening around her, but not Charlie. No, her own father refuses to see it. He reaches across the table and slaps her across the face, so hard he splits her lip. Lacey cries out, clutching both her palms to her cheek, her eyes spilling over with tears.

Taser or no Taser, I can't let that go by without reacting. I don't even think about the consequences. I jump up and lunge, reaching for the fucker sitting opposite me. I want my hands wrapped around his throat. I want to throttle the fucking life out of him. I want—

White lightning ripples through my body, way stronger, way more intense than the taste I got earlier. Someone screams. My head hits the table, and then I'm falling. Falling to the ground. I can't see through the pain. Can't breathe through it. Can't think through it. All I can do is hear...

Hear the screaming.

30

Sloane

THAT OLD SAYING, THE BIGGER THEY ARE, THE HARDER they fall? That saying is true. Zeth goes down hard. His head impacts with the corner of the table as his body seizes and locks into a rigid stance, and he topples sideways, unable to put a hand out to break his fall. He takes a second knock to the head when it hits the ground.

"*Stopstopstopstopstopstopstop STOP!*" Lacey repeats the word so that it runs into itself, digging her hands into her hair. I slide off my chair, pain singing out loud and clear as my knees hit thin carpet. I grab hold of Zeth's arm, trying to figure out the best way to help him. I can touch him without being shocked, so long as I don't touch him in between where the two probes are biting into his skin. However, I can't touch the actual probes themselves otherwise I'll be hit with the full force of the current, too. Fuck. Fuck! What the hell am I supposed to do?

Hands grab at me from behind, firm and rough, dragging me back. I flail my arms and legs, trying to wrestle free, but I feel like

I'm sinking underwater with a lead weight tied around my ankles. There is nothing I can do to free myself.

"Stop! *STOP!*" Lacey screams.

"Fucking whore." O'Shannessey's face is suddenly in mine, shoved right up close. "You're gonna regret the day you ever stopped us from taking the girl."

I try to twist my way out of his grasp, but O'Shannessey clearly isn't going to let that happen. It's not a move I'm proud of, but I do the only thing I can think of: I bite him on the forearm he's using to try and choke me with. He howls in pain, but even then he doesn't let go.

Zeth's boot heels bounce up and down against the floor with the force of the shock being administered to him. I need to stop it. I have to. Just as I'm about to make one final last-ditch attempt at pulling myself free, I hear a sound that freezes the blood in my veins. A gunshot. I instantly go limp. A pair of polished black Italian leather shoes appears in my line of sight. The room has fallen deadly silent. I hear Charlie's knees creak as he bends down between Zeth and me. The *tick-tick-tick* of the Taser as it does its work. My labored breathing rasping in, out, in, out in quick succession over my teeth.

"Women who get caught up in my world never tend to make it out alive, Dr. Romera. Celia, the Duchess... and so many girls I don't even know the names of that I've sent down to California to be sold by Perez and his Neanderthal flunkies. They all die." He looks at me, then—cold, dead eyes. Not an ounce of humanity within them. "You *all* die. Eventually."

I lash out with my foot, but O'Shannessey gives me a short, sharp jerk—a warning. Behave. "What about Lacey?" I spit. "She's your daughter. You're dragging her into this and you don't even know her. She's not—"

"Perfect. I know. She is *not* perfect."

I wasn't going to say that. It hurts me that Charlie *does* say it, because Lacey is perfect. She's just also very traumatized by the shitty hand life has dealt her. I fire her a quick glance over my shoulder, and the blonde woman is on her knees, arms up by her head, protecting herself. Her eyes are fixed on Zeth; she's silently crying. The table we were sitting at a moment ago is on its side, contents smashed or strewn all over the floor.

"Lacey's broken. That is very, very clear to me now. But I have a little time to fix her before I go, Doc. And then she's gonna be in charge of the little empire I've carved out for myself. Then she will be as black-hearted and strong as her daddy. Ain't that right, Lacey girl?" He stops, looks up at Lace, like he expects her to answer. She rises to her feet, a void expression on her face, and drops down beside her brother.

"Give it to me," she whispers. She holds out her hand. Charlie considers her open palm for a moment, and then shrugs.

"Fine. I don't want him dead just yet anyway." He slaps the Taser into Lacey's hand, and she immediately turns it off. The *tick-tick-tick*ing stops, and so do Zeth's jumping muscles. He exhales softly, like he's been holding his breath that whole time.

"What should I do with her?" O'Shannessey asks, tightening his grip around my neck and chest. Dark spots begin to dance in my vision. I try to prize my fingers underneath his forearm, but the task is impossible. From the corner of my eye, I can see Zeth's arm moving, though the motion is weak. His eyes are open. That's one small blessing. If his eyes are open, then he hasn't lost conscious-ness…which I may or may not be about to do.

"Go find out what's taking Sammy so long. Take her with you." Charlie smiles, and I know what he's going to say next. Panic grasps hold of my heart and squeezes tight. "And…*kill her.*"

I open my mouth to scream as I gather up the last of my energy, trying to wrestle free, but it's not my voice that comes out. Another scream, wild, high-pitched and desperate, rips through the air. Lacey. Everything slows. I see the events of the next four seconds as snapshots, still frames, frozen flashes of memory that will be forever burned into my mind.

Zeth trying to sit up, hand outstretched...

Lacey's arm swinging around...

Lacey's mouth pulled down, eyes spilling over with tears...

Charlie turning. Charlie surprised...

The fork in Lacey's hand driving deep into Charlie's throat...

The old man falling back, landing on his back...

Then, blood. So much blood.

Silence.

Zeth's hoarse voice. "Lace. Lacey, come here."

Charlie collapsing to the ground, hands shakily trying to stem the flow of blood flooding forth around the piece of metal sticking out of his neck.

The room tilting sideways.

Me hitting the ground.

O'Shannessey moving, letting me go.

O'Shannessey hollering, reaching for his boss.

And then not reaching for his boss.

Reaching for his gun.

And then the sound.

And then the shock.

And then more blood.

And then Lacey...

...falling to the ground.

31

Sloane

"NO! OH, GOD, NO! PLEASE, NO. *PLEASE. NO, NO, NO.*" I FEEL like I'm moving under water. I feel like there are hands dragging me down into a deep abyss and if I let myself sink I will never resurface again. Never. I scramble to Lacey's body, my arms and legs not working properly. There's more shouting. Charlie Holsan's hand lifts, grasping hold of thin air as he tries to capture my attention. Anyone's attention. People appear from somewhere. I don't know how many or who they are. I don't care. There's more gunfire. I look down at Lacey's tiny body, the burned hole in the center of her shirt turning red, the blood soaking the material out, out, out like a blooming flower.

Her eyes are still open; they're looking right at me. "Only so many times..." she gasps. Her voice is a wet rattle in her throat—blood seeping into her airways. Her hand flutters, trying to touch her chest. I take hold of it instead, clasping it tight. "So many times a person can be...*fixed*," she whispers. Zeth's beside me then, his face pale as a ghost's. He looks down on his sister and there are tears in his eyes.

"No. Not fucking happening," he says.

Michael then, over Zeth's shoulder with a gun in his hand. O'Shannessey on the floor beside his boss, both men's eyes fixed on the ceiling with the stare of the dead.

None of it computes. None of it registers. None of it makes sense.

"What can you do?" Zeth says, turning to me. "Tell me what you need me to do to help." But I can see the truth in his eyes, even clearer than I can see it in Lacey's—he knows there's nothing to be done. There is no help. I shake my head, a fractured sob bursting free from my lips.

"Zeth." Lacey's other hand finds her brother's. Her eyes are already starting to shutter. I've seen it happen a million times before. A patient's eyes are still open, still technically functioning, but they're not showing the patient what's in front of them anymore. I have no idea what Lacey's pale blue eyes are showing her right now, but she smiles. And it's a beautiful, surprised smile. "*Zeth*. It's…it's going to be okay. Now, everything is going to be… okay."

Zeth shakes his head. I've seen men come apart before. I've seen *Zeth* coming apart these past couple of weeks, showing more and more of himself to me every day, but now…now is an end to every wall he ever built to keep the world out. It comes crashing down on him. And it crushes him. "I'm sorry," he breathes. "I should have done better. I should have done better. I should have done better."

I can see the will of effort on Lacey's face as she struggles to focus, to have just one more cognitive thought. "You did…your best. You gave me…your best. The only one…who ever did. Thank…"

I see the moment when she goes. There's a light inside people, their souls shining brightly through their eyes. I've witnessed that light go out many times before. I recognize the moment for what it is—whatever made Lacey *Lacey* leaving her body—but I just can't believe it.

I don't even believe it when her hand falls limp in mine. It only hits me when Zeth chokes out a single sob. When he lets go of her hand and carefully places it on top of her chest. When he stares down at her lifeless body, a look of utter shock written on his face.

I go to him. I wrap my arms around his shaking, battered and bruised body, and I hold him. He doesn't acknowledge me. He just continues to stare at his sister. On the floor beside us, Lacey's body lies in a pool of her own blood. Her expression is strangely serene, and it hits in a wave of hurt that she was right. Everything really is okay for her now. Everything really is okay.

The poor girl who only ever ate the moons out of her favorite cereal because she hoped it would make her invisible. The poor girl who made herself small to feel safe. The poor girl who only ever wanted peace. Conceived of violence. Lived a life of violence. Poor Lacey, the girl who only ever wanted peace...

She dies in violence, too.

32

Zeth

I. CAN'T. BREATHE.

Sloane

MICHAEL PICKS UP LACEY'S BODY, HIS FACE BLANK AND LOST.
We follow him. Zeth doesn't say a word. He's still completely shut
down, apparently nothing going on in his head. Tears still streak
silently down my face as we make our way out of the rundown
movie theater, leaving Charlie and O'Shannessey's bodies behind
us, along with the dead bodies of two other men I don't recognize.
Michael says they'd come to kill Zeth. I feel no remorse for their
deaths.

We're in a car then. Not one I recognize. It's bright outside. The
sun is shining. I sit in the front with Michael, while Zeth sits in the
back with Lacey, her head in his lap. He doesn't touch her. He stares
out the window, blinking at the world. It doesn't even occur to me
to ask where we're going. The towers and high-rises, the concrete
teeth of the city, grow smaller and smaller in the rearview. Seattle
disappears.

An hour passes and not a single word is spoken. Michael pulls off
the freeway at an obnoxiously big home-and-hardware store, the

kind where you can buy chainsaws in bulk. While he's gone, I reach my hand back through the gap down the side of my seat, and Zeth puts his hand in mine. Michael returns bearing two flat head shovels and a flat look on his face. The shovels go into the trunk. I don't need to ask what they're for.

After that, it's the sky and the freeway and the spreading forest, dark and ominous, that invite us in, deeper and deeper. We don't see another car for twenty minutes as we pull off the freeway again and wind our way down roads that start off as blacktop and end as dirt tracks, choked and bumpy with the roots of so many trees. I don't know how long we sit in the car before I realize we've stopped moving. A long time, I think.

"We have to move," Michael says eventually.

Zeth's fingers twitch, his hand still in mine, but other than that he doesn't move.

"Zee? We can't take her back to—"

"I know." Zeth takes a deep breath and it's as though he comes back to life. Unwillingly, but...*alive.* He opens his door, and then with the greatest care, climbs out and lifts his sister's body from the backseat. It's cold out, but it's not raining. The sun spears down through the tightly packed trees, golden pillars of light that seem to be holding up the sky over our heads. Michael retrieves the shovels from the trunk and heads into the forest first. Zeth clenches his jaw, watching him go for a moment, and then nods, some inner battle waging inside him perhaps, and then he follows. I am last. I watch the muscles in Zeth's back twist and shift as he walks ahead of me, and I want to stop him. To hold him. To comfort him. But I can tell he doesn't need that right now—he needs a moment to figure out what he's feeling. We all do.

I feel like shit. My body's hating the fact that I'm still demanding more of it, when I should be resting in a hospital bed. The blast was just the icing on the cake. I'm still in pain from being shot, from running, from abusing my body a hundred different ways since I met these people. But it's my heart that hurts the most. I don't know how it will ever stop hurting.

Michael stops after a while. The trees have thinned out into a small glade, which overlooks a brook, carving its way through the mountainside. The ribbon of water throws sparks of light from its surface, gold and white and warm.

"Here?" Michael says.

"Here," Zeth agrees.

I wish they'd brought three shovels. The men get to work, digging slowly, clearly hating the job. I sit with Lacey, brushing my fingers through her hair. Her body's started to stiffen. The doctor in me knows it will be well over twenty-four hours before the rigor mortis loosens its grip on her muscles and we'll be able to move her arms and legs again, so I gently settle her so her hands are resting across her chest, her legs out straight. Michael sees what I'm doing and climbs out of the hole.

"She always slept on her side. All curled up," he tells me. "Like this." For such a lethal man, he moves Lace with so much care and love. When he's finished, her body is arranged in the fetal position, hands pillowing her head, knees tucked up into her body. She really does look like she's sleeping. I turn to find Zeth, but I can only see the very top of his head. He's sunk down, sitting in the hole they've half dug, his back to us. I try to stand, to go to him, but Michael takes hold of my hand.

"Don't. Just...give him a moment."

Michael and I sit with Lacey, listening to the birds singing, and for all the world it sounds like they're crying. Michael sits with an arm over Lacey's body, as though he's protecting her.

"You loved her, didn't you?" I ask.

He smiles down at the girl who was only in his life a short while longer than she was in my own, and breathes in deeply. "Didn't you?" he whispers. "How could I not?" And he's right. How could he not?

Eventually Zeth stands up, reclaims his shovel, and begins to dig again. This time he moves more quickly, with a purpose. I stay with Lacey, because it feels wrong to leave her alone now.

When Michael and Zeth are done, the sun is almost setting. The sky looks like it's on fire—like Heaven itself is burning. The men collect Lace, now cold and so very gone, and they carry her between them. The hole they were digging is no longer a hole but a grave.

I am weak. I am a coward. I am hollow and shameless. I cannot watch them lower her in. I walk down to the brook and I cry, hoping the rushing of the water will drown out the sounds of my tears. Michael comes to get me a little while later. The grave is no longer a grave but a patch of freshly turned earth. "You used to go to church, right?" he asks softly. "We don't know what to say. Could you..."

Being asked to say something for Lacey is perhaps even worse than having to watch the dirt cover her pale, delicate skin. But I can't refuse. The three of us stand together, staring down at the ground, and a wave of terror hits me when I realize I can't say the words Michael asked me to say. The words my father would speak:

Death is swallowed up in victory. O death, where is thy victory? O death, where is thy sting? Now the sting of death is sin: and the power of sin is the law. But thanks be to God, who hath given us the victory through our Lord Jesus Christ. Therefore, my beloved brethren, be ye steadfast and unmovable: always abounding in the work of the Lord, knowing that your labor is not in vain in the Lord.

Ashes to ashes...

Dust to dust...

Instead, the words I want to say will be hard to get out, but they are true. True to Lacey. I crouch down beside the freshly turned earth and place my hand palm-down on top of it, as though to lay my hand on the girl's shoulder one last time. "I'm sorry, Lace," I choke out. A deep breath. Another. How will I do this? How? I don't think I can. I'm about to stand up, to shake my head and collapse into tears, but a strong hand lands on my shoulder. Zeth. He drops down into a crouch beside me and wraps his arms around me, pulling me into his side. It's so wrong that he's comforting me right now, but he gives me strength. I *can* do this.

"I'm ashamed," I say, doing my best to pull myself together. "I'm ashamed that you gave your life for mine. In many ways, you were the weakest of us all. You suffered through years of abuse at the hands of people who should have cared for you. Your innocence was taken away, when it should have been protected and cherished. You wanted to give up, but we wouldn't let you, Lacey, because we saw how kind and sweet and loving you were, and we were selfish. You were a light in our lives and we didn't want to lose that light...because our lives are so much darker now without you in them. Because while you should have been the weakest, you were quite often the strongest, too. You saw each and every one of us for who we were and you loved us for it. You saw *everything*." I break off, trapped between laughter and tears, because it's true. She really did. "You saw the world in a way none of us ever have. You saw it as an outsider, looking in, and I'm so sorry, Lace, because you deserved more than that. You deserved to be loved. To have a husband and children of your own. To not feel like you had to be invisible anymore. You weren't invisible to us, Lacey. And even though you're gone, you're still always going to be with us. We won't ever forget you, sister. We won't ever let you go."

The sun has gone down by the time I finish speaking.

Zeth has to carry me back to the car.

34

Zeth

I. CAN'T. THINK.

35

Michael

THE CONCIERGE AT THE REGENCY ROOMS DOESN'T SAY A word about the blood, mud, sweat and tears we're covered in as we move silently through the lobby. He looks up—I see him do it—but the guy doesn't bat an eyelid. He goes back to subtly pretending we're not even there. This is the kind of discretion you pay dearly for. Not that Zee can't afford it. I have no idea why I'm thinking about anything as mundane as money right now. We're all emotionally poor; that's the only thing that matters.

Everything just happened so quickly. This morning we were going to a funeral to try and get Lacey back, and now Charlie is dead, and we just got back from *Lacey's* funeral. Where's the sense in that? I left the apartment this morning thinking, absolutely fucking positively, in fact, that we were gonna be coming back with our girl. So fucking sure of it.

We've all been left utterly bereft by what just took place. And I am really fucking worried about Zee. Not once in all the time I've known him have I seen the man like this. He's just...he's not even there. He hasn't said a word since we put Lace in the ground. His silence is far more scary than his dark moods, where you know he'll tear you a new one if you so much as look at him sideways. There's always fair warning with those. Right now, with this blankness about him, he seems a little unhinged. Like he could go supernova at any second and there will be absolutely no time to run for cover.

Zee and Sloane go back into their apartment without saying a word. I wonder—I hope for the love of god she can help him through this. I hope he will *let* her.

The first thing I see when I open the door to my own apartment is the box of Lucky Charms I picked up last night after I'd dropped Zeth off at the shrink's place. I just stand in the doorway, staring at the smug Irish bastard on the box, too afraid to blink. Too afraid to move a muscle. Charlie dead. Lacey dead. It's all too surreal.

My phone starts ringing. Not the one I had with me this morning. That one blew up in the car. No, this is the spare I left sitting on the kitchen counter. I pick up the box of Lucky Charms and toss it down the waste disposal chute, and then I answer the cell. I don't look at the caller ID. I don't care who it is; I just need the distraction so I don't snap and start trashing the place. "Yeah."

"Where have you been, fucker? I've been calling you all day."

Oh, shit. *Rebel.* "We were kidnapped. We lost Lacey."

"What? Kidnapped? And I already know you lost Lacey. Weren't you going to get her back?"

"No, we *lost her*, lost her. She's *dead*." I can hear my cousin breathing on the other end of the line. Probably can't think of anything to say. I know I can't.

"Was it Charlie?" he eventually asks.

"No. One of his boys shot her after she…Lacey…Lacey stabbed Charlie in the carotid artery *with a fucking fork*."

Rebel stays silent, taking this in. "That's fucking badass," he says softly. This, for Rebel, is an accolade of the highest order. "I'm really sorry, man. I know you cared about her. How's Zeth taking it?"

"Not too well."

"Oh. How *you* taking it?"

"Also not too well."

"Fuck. Well I suppose now's a bad time to tell you that Alexis is in town and she wants to see her sister?"

Bad time doesn't even cover it. I shrug out of my torn suit jacket—it smells of smoke and the iron tang of blood. "I would give it a couple of days, man. Sloane's just as fucked up as we are right now."

Rebel sighs. "Okay, fine. We have our deal with Julio tomorrow. I'm supposed to hand over my files to him. Shit's definitely gonna go down. Can you be there?"

I scrunch up my face, trying to think of a way of politely telling him to go get fucked. Instead I find myself saying, "If Zee or Sloane don't need me, I'm your man."

"Sure? I don't want you if your head's not in the right place." By in the right place, he means in the killing zone. And I am most definitely there. "Don't you worry about my head, Rebel. I'll let you know in the morning if I'm in." I already know I will be, though. I need to punch something. I need to fight. Zee and I are very similar in that beating the crap out of something generally makes us feel better, but this is more than that. This is an unquenchable need that won't be satisfied until I've caused someone severe bodily harm. It doesn't matter that I killed Sammy when he came to try and kill *me*. It doesn't matter that I killed O'Shannessey, plus those other two guys who showed up out of nowhere. I'm still wound with fury. I'm going to have to use my bare hands in order to release it. I'm going to have to rain carnage down onto the heads of those who pose a threat to us, because I can't go through this again. Fuck knows what would happen if Sloane died. It doesn't even bear thinking about.

There would be no way of stopping Zee. He would murder everyone he could get his hands on whether they were involved or not, and he wouldn't care if he got sent down for it. It would be worth it for him. Hell, he would have done the same for Lacey had I not have already killed O'Shannessey before the boss realized what was happening.

I will never, never forget the look on his face when he saw Lacey fall.

I hang up the phone, wondering if Julio Perez is going to die tomorrow, too.

Sloane

I'M SO LOST. I HAVE NO IDEA WHAT I'M SUPPOSED TO DO.
Ever since we arrived back at the apartment, Zeth's been sitting in an armchair, staring out the window that overlooks the city, and I haven't been able to get a word out of him. Not that I've tried to. I know he needs to be alone; I can tell that just by the edge to the atmosphere in the room, but I don't know if I should leave. I could go and sleep in Michael's apartment, but I somehow don't know if that's a good idea either. I think...I think something terrible will happen if I leave him alone.

I decide to stay. I can handle the tension in the room. I can handle it, because I love this man and abandoning him now, even if it's what he thinks he wants, is the wrong thing to do.

I sit on the vast leather couch across the other side of the room, just listening to the silence. How would Pippa deal with this situation? How would my dad? Pip's trained in grief counseling, and my father has an abundant supply of compassion that always serves him well when trying to comfort others. He just always knows the right thing to say.

The answer to my worrying and wondering comes in the most surprising of forms. Ernie. The Schnauzer's claws make soft clicking sounds as he appears from one of the back bedrooms. His huge brown eyes travel over me briefly as he approaches us, but it's not me he heads for. He heads straight for Zeth. The dog pushes his small body between Zeth's legs and then he bumps Zeth's hands with his wet nose.

It doesn't look like Zeth even knows Ernie's there. He just lets the dog rest his head on his leg, which seems to please Ernie immensely. He huffs out a shallow breath and shuffles in closer, so he's as close as he can physically get without actually climbing up into Zeth's lap. After a while, Zeth starts absently stroking the tips of his fingers against Ernie's head, and the dog goes to sleep.

Eventually I fall asleep, too. It's not the physical stress that's exhausted me. It's the crying, like I've cried out my entire energy reserve for a year and now my body is demanding rest. My dreams are quick and dark, and mercifully empty.

In the morning, I wake up in bed, stripped down to my underwear. The sheets are almost black from the filth that's rubbed off my body. I find Zeth in exactly the same position he was in when I passed out on the sofa, Ernie now curled up at his feet. He must have moved at some point though, since I sure as hell didn't put myself to bed, and he also looks like he's had a shower at some point.

"Zeth?"

He's awake. He glances over his shoulder, and I see the briefly unguarded pain in his bleary eyes. "Hey," he whispers. "You should sleep some more." The sun is just rising over the city, though the cloud cover casts a cold light over everything, making it blue and gray and sad.

"Have you slept at all?"

He shakes his head. "I don't need to."

"Zeth, you absolutely need to sleep."

"I *don't* need to sleep. I need to move." He stands quickly, rubbing his hands over his face. I notice despite his irritated tone that he's careful not to disturb Ernie as he steps over him and paces across the room.

"Do you want breakfast?" I ask softly.

Zeth shakes his head. "I'm okay. Really. I just need to..." He never finishes that sentence. He looks down at the floor, eyes seemingly fixed on some irrelevant point on the tile as his brain races. I wrap my arms around my body. Zeth looks up at me and his hard expression fades. He closes the gap between us and folds his arms around my body.

"I'll be back soon." Placing a careful kiss against my forehead, he gives me a tight squeeze and then lets me go. I watch as he collects his leather jacket and a set of keys off the kitchen counter, and then he leaves the apartment. The door clicks quietly closed behind him.

MICHAEL COMES BY an hour later wearing black leather gloves and what looks like running gear. I've never seen him wearing gym stuff, though it's obvious he works out from the sheer size of his arms alone.

"I took him to a fighting gym. We both needed to smash the hell out of something, and that seemed like the safest bet," he tells me. "He wanted to stay. I said I'd go help Rebel with Julio now, but if

315

you want me to stay here with you, then all you need to do is say the word."

I don't want him to stay. To be honest, all I want to do is curl up on the couch and try and work out this whole mess we're in, but I have to be pragmatic. "Am I in danger if I'm here alone?"

Michael shakes his head. "Charlie's gone. None of his boys are stupid enough to bother us now. They have no reason to. There's a power vacuum now. The gangs of Seattle are going to be far more concerned over who'll be filling that vacuum than over Zeth and the rest of us."

That makes perfect sense, even if a part of me is still on edge. "Okay, fine. Then I'll be okay here. I won't go anywhere."

Michael leaves, and then it's just Ernie and me. I spend my morning replaying the moment where Charlie said he wanted O'Shannessey to kill me, and Lacey lunging at him with that fork. I've imagined it from every angle, wondering if I could have helped her, if I could have stopped her before she acted. The conclusion I've come to is, no, I couldn't. She'd said it herself. Lacey had made the decision to kill Charlie long before she accomplished the task. She'd already tried it once before. She would have tried it again, one way or another.

It's almost midday when there's a knock at the apartment door. When I peer through the spyhole, my heart thundering away in my chest—*was Michael wrong? Is it one of Charlie's men?*—I don't have the energy to be surprised or upset or *anything* whatsoever.

The sight of Pippa standing out in the hallway, looking very anxious, is just another straw balanced precariously on the camel's back. I open the door and she rushes in, throwing her arms around me. "Oh, god, Sloane, I am so sorry. Seriously. Zeth texted me; he told me what happened. He said you might need me. Are you okay? Holy...you look like shit, Sloane."

Out of all of this, the one thing that sticks with me is what she said about Zeth. "He *texted* you?"

She looks perplexed for a moment, delicate frown lines forming between her eyebrows. "Yeah. He sent me a very rude message about being a good fucking friend for once. When I asked why, he said...he said because his sister had died, and you needed someone." She looks down at her hands. "I'm so sorry, Sloane. I just can't believe it."

"Of course you can," I tell her, swinging the door closed behind her. "You've been telling me for weeks now that I'm in a dangerous situation. That someone's going to get killed. Well, guess what? You were right." Out of habit, I head straight for the kitchen and put the kettle on to boil. It was always our ritual whenever we visited each other—tea was top priority.

"I'm not here to say I told you so, Sloane. I'm here to be your friend. I know I have a lot to make up for, but...but I really want to try. If you'll let me?"

I place two teabags in two cups, focusing on the rote movements necessary to complete the task. That seems about all I'm capable of doing. I can't even think about all the shit Pippa pulled right now— how badly she betrayed me—because none of that seems important. Only Lacey. Only Zeth. Only my heart breaking into multiple pieces. "Can we talk about this another time?" I ask. "I'm too tired right now."

"Of course."

I finish making the tea and Pip and I sit on the couch in silence. Ernie watches us with his little Schnauzer eyebrows twitching every now and then. "Whose dog is that?" Pippa asks.

"DEA Agent Lowell's."

Pippa just nods her head, as though the fact we have Lowell's dog is completely normal.

"Why did he text you?" I ask.

"Who? Zeth?"

"Yeah. He hates you." I don't sugarcoat it for her. "Why would he text you and send you over here to take care of me? If he knows I'm as fucked up as he is, why the hell isn't he here looking after me himself? Or at least letting me look after him?"

Pippa purses her lips at my first statement, staring at the pale, untouched liquid in the mug she's holding. "You know him better than I do, Sloane. You know what kind of man he is."

I narrow my eyes at her, ready to kick her ass out if she even so much as breathes a bad word about him. She instantly holds one of her hands up—the one not holding onto her mug. "He's been alone in the world for as long as he can remember," she says. "He's never had someone to care for before. And he's never had someone to care for him, either. It's going to take some time for him to come to trust that. Knowing his profile a little better now, I'd probably hazard a guess he's afraid to rely on you for that. Good things have never lasted long in Zeth's life. With Lacey gone now, he probably expects you'll disappear in a puff of smoke, too."

"So you're saying he won't rely on me because he thinks I'm going to die? That's very reassuring. And what do you mean, *knowing his profile a little better* now?"

Pip's already shaking her head before I'm done talking. "Not die. Maybe...just leave him. In his head, you've seen that he couldn't protect his sister. Perhaps he'll expect you to leave him because you don't feel safe. And after the very strange session we had the other night, I *do* have a better understanding of him, Sloane. And, while I'm not entirely sure of him, I do trust him a little more now, too. I know...I know he's doing everything he can to keep you safe. That's all I ever wanted for you."

I've heard that speech before, except this time Pippa's words aren't said with malice or contempt. I hear the ring of truth in them. That's not what I'm concentrating on, though. He went to see Pippa? For a *session*? I had no idea—he never told me he'd done that—but from the look on her face, Pippa doesn't know. I keep my face straight, not wanting to show my surprise.

"So...you don't think I'm crazy for being with him, then?"

"I never said that," Pippa replies. "What I'm saying is, while the situation's rather crazy, I can see why you're in it. Why you won't leave him. And I respect that. I swear, Sloane, I will never breathe another word about you and him again. Never. And I'll do my best to help him overcome all the crap that's happened to him, too. Just please...can we try? Be friends again? One day when you don't have DEA agents breathing down your neck, you're going to need someone to share a coffee date or two with, right? I haven't been to Fresco's in so long."

I'm still angry with Pippa, but I've lost so much over the last few months. Perhaps our relationship will never be what it used to be, but if I don't have to lose her entirely, then maybe that's something I can hold onto. I try out a smile; it feels forced, but it's a start. "We can try," I tell her. "But the moment you start interfering, that's it. We're done."

There's nothing forced about Pip's smile. She grins, and for a moment she looks like she's going to hug me. She doesn't though. She just sips her tea, still smiling at me, eyes crinkled at the corners. "Thank you," she says quietly. "I know I don't deserve this, but I'm going to make it up to you, I swear."

I really hope she can. After everything that's happened over the past few days, a friend would be pretty amazing right now.

36

Zeth

I. CAN'T. EAT.

37

Zeth

MICHAEL TOLD ME WHAT HE SAID TO SLOANE. HE TOLD ME
she was worried about her safety when he left her, and she was
right to be. Just shows she's a smart girl. But Michael was also
right—a power vacuum now exists in Seattle, and nearly every
single gang in the city is going to be battling it out, vying for the
territories that recently came up for grabs. The guys who used to
work for Charlie don't give a shit about Sloane. She's safer right
now than she has been for a weeks.

Me, on the other hand...*I* am not so safe. I may know the truth of
the matter, but Charlie implied I was his son when he paid Julio, the
fat bastard, to leave me alone. At the time I'd taken that news as
irrefutable evidence that the old man *was* my father. Now I know
he only did it because he didn't want someone killing me before he
got the chance. A severe case of *I can hurt, break, kill my toys, but if
anyone else tries to...*

Charlie implying he was my father to Julio was tantamount to
telling every criminal organization on the western seaboard. And if

Charlie's boys believe I was his son, and the heads of countless drug-running, arms-dealing, skin-trading gangs believe the same thing, then there's undoubtedly a price on my head. The only way to let these people know I'm not interested in Charlie's empire is to make a stand. Prove a point. Make it very clear I don't give a shit who takes over from the mad English bastard.

I drive out to Hunt's Point, not thinking about Lacey. Not thinking about Michael and Sloane slowly positioning my sister into a restful pose so that she could be buried. Not thinking about the dirt that I had to scrape out from underneath my nails, the scalding hot water of the shower stripping layers of skin from my back as I tried to wash away the memory of the last twenty-four hours. Because I don't want to. Remember, that is. I want to forget Lacey ever showed up on my doorstep eight months ago, and I want to forget I ever had a living blood relative. I've found blocking her out, banishing her from my head, is the only way I can recall how to breathe without feeling like my rage is going to eat me alive.

I pull up outside Charlie's old place around mid-afternoon. The building looks abandoned, but you can bet your ass there are people watching it. Charlie bought the place in cash thirty years ago before there were such strict money laundering checks when purchasing property. Since no one is going to announce Charlie's dead and no bank has an interest in his sprawling mansion, it won't be long before someone else moves in. Just takes over the place, like the change in ownership doesn't need to be recorded. Possession, famously, is nine-tenths of the law, after all.

There's no one inside the place to buzz open the gates, so I park the crapped-out Volvo I've legitimately borrowed from The Regency Rooms on the street, and I vault over the fence to the side of the property. Brings back memories of when I was a kid, sneaking back in after a night out partying. I'm taller now, so the fence poses no problems whatsoever. I don't have keys to get into the main building, but who the fuck needs keys when you have a pair of size eleven boots and you're in a seriously shitty mood?

Splinters of wood explode everywhere as I kick the door in. Inside, the house is quiet. Deserted. I don't waste any time in carrying out the task I came here for. I find the gasoline in the garage, canisters of it stacked up against the wall so Charlie would never have to lower himself to going to an actual gas station and deal with the unwashed masses. Ironically, I know he visited one recently, since that's where he picked up that poor girl he poisoned.

He always did have a flair for the dramatic.

And right now I'm feeling a little fucking dramatic myself.

I collect two cans, one in either hand; I pop the caps, and then I proceed to walk through the house, sloshing the pungent liquid over the carpets, up the walls, into the beds upstairs. The last room I enter is the one I slept in as a kid. Or rather, the one I was tormented in. Everything looks exactly the same as it did when I hightailed it out of here as an eighteen-year-old. The comics I used to read are still stacked on the shelf, all dog-eared and tatty, which is weird because I took extremely good care of them when I was younger. I know they're falling apart now because Charlie...Charlie would have come in here a lot, I think. He would have sat on the edge of my old bed, thumbing roughly through my comics and the rest of my possessions, reliving the shit he did to me inside these four walls. The shit he tried to do to me.

Even though he was bigger, even though he was stronger, he never won. He was always drunk. High. Something. I never let him win. In hindsight, I think that's probably what pissed him off the most. I pour healthy splashes of gasoline all over the room, drenching the duvet, the carpet, the curtains, everything. I stand there, taking the place in, finally facing what happened here, and suddenly I realize I don't care. I don't fucking care. Charlie's dead. This house will soon be ash. He can't touch me anymore. Once more, he will *never* win.

I head downstairs and do one last thing: I walk through to the back of the house where Charlie's study is located. His safe, a huge fucking thing cemented into the ground, is hidden underneath a Persian rug. I flip it back and I don't hesitate—I enter my mother's date of birth, Christmas day, into the keypad, and the fucking thing clicks open. I feel fucking sick. He said he hated her after she refused him, but he obviously clearly loved her, too. Sick, delusional fuck.

I take every last bundle of cash from Charlie Holsan's safe, stuffing it into carryalls, and then I leave the house. I give myself permission to leave behind the stress and trauma of everything that happened here, too. Outside, I strike a match and toss it, watching to make sure it hits the puddled fuel on the tiles inside the hall.

Flames rise like fingers from the floor, orange and yellow and blue, and then the house is claimed. I turn away, hearing the subtle *whoompf* as the fire spreads, and I do not look back.

LACEY USED TO launder money for me. Back before all this shit went down and Sloane came back into my life, Charlie actually used to pay me pretty fucking well, and Lacey used to clean the money for me. She'd gamble with it—surprisingly good at that—or she'd make large purchases and return them, essentially, just trading my money for someone else's. That didn't necessarily give me a solid paper trail to prove where the money came from, but it was enough for me. And sometimes, when there was just too much to handle at once, the two of us would head out together and bury stashes of money. I've never dealt with a bank. I've never had anything so administrative as a checking account. Cash was always king in Charlie Holsan's world, and I was very much a part of Charlie's world. But now I'm making my own world, and things have got to change.

I need a way to make the stacks of my own money I have hidden behind a brick wall beneath the warehouse legitimate, and I have a very good idea how to do that. There's just one thing I need to do first. I make a brief phone call to Rebel, and then I set things in motion.

I find Agent Lowell in a coffee shop across the road from the address Sloane gave me in Everett. By the looks of her, she's on her fourth cup of coffee for the day. It doesn't make it to her mouth, though. She spits most of it onto the floorboards when she lays eyes on me.

"What the fuck?" she gasps. "You're fucking...you're fucking *crazy*."

I glare at her, wishing I felt differently about hitting women. "I'm fucking tired," I correct her. *I'm also sore, battered and significantly bruised from nearly being blown up and being shocked with a Taser.* "It's time we end this shit once and for all."

"You realize I'm going to arrest you right now, don't you?"

I just raise an eyebrow at her.

"Well, alright then. Do I need to cuff you, or are you gonna walk across the road with me like a civilized human being?"

"There's only one woman on the face of this planet who I'd let fucking cuff me. And *you* are not *her*."

Lowell leads the way out of the coffee shop; I can tell by the way her hand's trembling as we head toward the liquor store on the other side of the road that she's on the back foot and freaking the

325

fuck out. Hopefully that's gonna work in my favor. She guides me up a metal fire escape that runs up the building behind the liquor store, and then she's punching a code into a keypad by a reinforced steel door. We move down a winding corridor, through another access door, and then into a vast, open-plan room, filled with cops. A stunned silence falls over the room. About eighteen pairs of eyes all watch with unveiled surprise as Lowell leads me through their midst and into a cold, sterile interview room. There are three chairs and a table inside and nothing else.

"Sit down," Lowell commands. So I do. "Get comfortable," she advises me, and then leaves me alone in the room. The door locks behind her when she goes.

This may be the most foolish thing I've ever done, but I'm fucking over all of this now. I'm over all of it. I did a lot of thinking last night, Ernie's little head resting on my knee until the sun came up, and I realized this isn't the life I should be living. Not because it wouldn't have been easy for me to slip right into Charlie's shoes and claim Seattle. But because my sister died yesterday. I watched her die, and then I had to bury her. Because the woman I can't live without is inherently good, and deserves someone better than me. Because Sloane deserves *everything,* and I want to give it to her.

Lowell leaves me locked in the interview room for half an hour before she returns—a common, frankly transparent move on her part, designed to make me work up a sweat. The woman is a fucking moron. I'm not going to sweat; I handed myself in, for fuck's sake. She's towing a fucking giant in a suit behind her when she enters the room, her shoulders stiff with her own importance. She undoubtedly made good use of the thirty minutes she left me in here, calling her superiors and telling them the good news—*I did it. I fucking caught the bastard. I know, I know. You can promote me later.*

The giant, I suspect only invited into the interview for decoration and culpability's sake, begins setting up a video recorder, the lens pointed directly at me. They both remain silent until the little red dot is angrily blinking at me.

"Can you please state your full name for the purposes of the video," Lowell says.

"Zeth Mayfair."

"And that's your legal name?"

I tilt my head to one side, shooting her a very bored look. "That is my legal name."

"Okay, then. Zeth Mayfair, you have the right to remain silent. Anything you say can and will be used against you in a court of law. You have the right to an attorney. If you cannot afford an attorney, one will be appointed to you. Do you understand these rights as they have been read to you?"

I lean across the table, staring the bitch down. "Perfectly."

"Good. Then we'll get started. We want to discuss your involvement with a certain individual known to us only as Rebel. Are you aware of this person?"

I sit back, cracking my knuckles. "I am."

"Do you know his exact whereabouts?"

"I do not."

Lowell tilts her head on an angle, pulling a tight smile. "You expect me to believe that?"

"I don't give a fuck what you believe. It's the truth."

"Do you have a contact number for him?"

"Nope." She must think I'm fucking retarded or something. I walked in here without a cell phone. There was no way I was handing Sloane and Michael's contact information over to the bitch on a silver platter.

"All right, Zeth." Lowell takes a deep breath, pressing her fingertips into her forehead. "We'll come back to Rebel. Right now we're going to talk about your involvement in a list of offenses that could put you away for a very long time. Are you going to cooperate?"

"What's given you the impression I'm not going to cooperate, Denise? Didn't I come here of my own free will?"

She pauses, shooting me a dry look. "Have you ever been to Monterello Farm Markets?

"Yeah. Plenty of times. I buy a lot of fruit there. It's organic, y'know?" So, they wanna talk about Frankie Monterello, the last job I did for Charlie. The grocery store doesn't have security cameras inside—more illegal dealings went on inside that place than anywhere else in Seattle—so there's no way they have footage of me heading in there. I was wearing gloves when I shot Frankie— shot him before he shot me—so there won't be any prints. But still, better to say I may have been there at some point than deny it altogether and then have Lowell produce evidence to the contrary.

"Did you know Charlie Holsan had the owner of that place killed?"

I rock back on my chair, pulling a surprised face. "No, I did not know that. How do *you* know that?" I already know how she knows. Rick Lamfetti, the guy I refused to kill for the old man, the guy I sent up to Anaheim, was on Lowell's payroll for god knows how long. He'll have squealed and told her anything she wanted to know just to keep his own ass out of jail. Thing is Rick's dead now, and without his testimony, Lowell's got little more than a statement that can't be backed up.

The agent smirks at me. She knows *I* know she's got nothing on this one. "You killed Frankie Monterello for your boss."

"I have no idea what you're talking about. When was this event supposed to have taken place? I'm sure I'll be able to tell you exactly where I was. Who I was with at the time." I know for a fact the Monterellos never called the cops when Frankie died. No way. If there's one thing I can count on, it's that the Italians will have buried their boss and cleaned up the mess without making a report to the authorities. A family like that doesn't want cops poking around their business. Better to say Frankie moved out of state or something, should anyone ever ask.

"We're not interested in fake alibis, Mr. Mayfair."

"Why would I give you a fake alibi? I'm merely trying to help."

Lowell looks like she's just swallowed a quart of bleach. "Well, I really hope that sentiment holds, Mr. Mayfair. Because you're going to be helping us for a very long time."

38

Sloane

"THE BLAZE STARTED AROUND THREE PM THIS AFTERNOON. Known to be the home of one Charlie Holsan, a man suspected to be involved in a number of illegal operations, the eight-bedroom mansion was valued at two point three million dollars. Mr. Holsan has not yet come forward to speak with authorities or fire marshals about the fire. There is speculation that the sixty-two-year-old could actually be inside the building, though that won't be confirmed until fire fighters have managed to get the blaze under control and officials can investigate. Even that might not be easy. The ferocity and fast-spreading nature of the fire has already significantly weakened the structure of the mansion. It is unlikely much of the interior will be intact by the time the inferno is put out. Stay tuned to Channel Six News Live for ongoing updates."

I turn the television off, a sick feeling twisting in my gut. Zeth did that. I *know* he did. There are plenty of other people out there who had reason to set a fire in Charlie Holsan's former home, but I know in my very bones it was Zeth. Pippa sits on the couch beside me, still staring at the now black TV screen.

"Is it wrong that I'm glad he's dead?" she says softly.

I turn to look at her, surprised. "Really? You're glad he's dead?"

"Of course I am. He did countless unspeakable things to you. And...and to Zeth. He poisoned that woman at the gas station. And he scared the living shit out of me when he broke into that apartment to take Lacey. Not to mention he's the whole reason Lacey is dead."

When she puts it like that, I can see her point. She's just so proper, though. Hearing her admit she's glad someone like Charlie got what he deserved is a little out of character. "I thought you'd rather we trusted in the justice system. Send the bastard to jail, or something."

Pippa shakes her head. "Hell, no. Prison is too good for the likes of him. Better he rots in hell than leeches off the state for the rest of his life. Plus," she says, her voice taking on a hard edge, "he would still have been able to control things from inside. There are always people ready to carry out orders on prisoners' behalves. You and Zeth would still have been in danger."

I don't know if she even realizes she's included Zeth in her concern, but the fact that she has makes me feel like crying. I know we're a long way off yet, but I can almost see a future where Pippa not only supports my relationship with the man she considers solely responsible for ruining my life, but perhaps...perhaps she will even like him. It's a long shot, wishing for something like that, but I have to be an optimist about these things. If I'm not, I'll go crazy.

Michael returns home mid-afternoon with a black eye and a split lip. Pippa rockets off the couch when he stumbles through the door, still in the running gear he was wearing earlier, though now soaked in blood. "Oh my god, is that *your* blood?" she gasps.

Michael lifts one eyebrow at the sight of Pippa at The Regency

Rooms. "Not all of it," he says. And then, to me, "Where's the boss? He back yet?"

I shake my head. "I tried calling him earlier. He didn't answer. I figured...I figured he needed some space."

In truth, it hurt a little that Zeth let his cell phone ring out rather than talk to me, but I know how torn up inside he is right now. He's off dealing with his problems the only way he knows how—by torching buildings and god knows what else. Better not to guess.

"He'll be back before nightfall. He swore he would," Michael says.

"And Julio? What happened with Julio and Rebel?"

Michael casts a cautious eye in Pippa's direction. "Maybe it's better I don't go into details right now. Suffice it to say, Rebel's problems are all solved now. And we don't need to worry about Julio again, either."

He's probably right. Pippa doesn't even know half of the crap Rebel's involved in, and neither do I. Frankly, I don't want to know. So long as Michael's okay, then I'm happy to leave the conversation for another time. From the tone of his voice and the finality of his words, Julio Perez is just as dead as Charlie Holsan and that's all I need to hear.

"There is just one thing, though," Michael tells me, wincing as he sits down on one of the stools at the breakfast bar. "It's your sister." Despite everything that's happened, despite nearly all of this mess being her fault, my heart leaps into my throat.

"What? What is it? Is she okay?"

Michael nods. "She's fine. However, she's here in Seattle. And... she wants to see you."

Lacey instantly comes to mind. I've considered her a sister for so long now; it's been less than twenty-four hours since we buried her, and right now it seems as though the pain of her loss is never going to fade. I've lost a sister, but I still have another one who is very much alive. Should I still be angry with Alexis? Yes. Will I ever be able to forgive her for what she put me through? I don't know. But does that mean I should cut her out of my life forever? My father knew she was alive for a long time, while Mom and I tore ourselves apart worrying about her, and then fearing her dead. But he said I don't know Alexis' side of the story—that she had a reason for what she did. Maybe it's time for me to give her a chance to tell me her side. The very thought makes me angry—like there could ever be a reason good enough—but I guess, from the outside looking in, my own situation might be just as hard for my family and friends to comprehend. I'm sure Pip would attest to that.

"Okay, fine. I'll see her. But...but not yet. I need a little more time." I need my heart to stop hurting. I need my world to stop feeling like it's falling apart. Michael nods silently—the guy looks completely exhausted, like he just ran a marathon while fighting for his life. "Does anything need stitching up?" I ask him. Something always needs stitching up. But Michael just stretches and climbs off his stool, heading for the fridge. He removes three beers, twists the caps off them, and then hands one to me and one to Pippa. I've never seen Pippa drink beer, let alone beer from the bottle, but she accepts it with a small, "Thanks."

"I don't need stitches. I need to get drunk," Michael says. "I need to get absolutely fucked up. And now that we're free of Holsan and Perez, I think we've earned a night off. And...and I want to drink to our girl."

I was going to object to getting completely trashed—the very idea seemed reckless—but as soon as Michael points out we no longer have to worry about mob bosses, as soon as he brings up drinking to Lacey, all doubt flies out the window. I lift my beer bottle, holding it out for him to cheers me.

"To Lacey," I say.

"Lace," Michael adds.

Pip raises her bottle and joins us, and I can't help it—the tears begin to flow again. It'll be a long time until I can think about the girl without falling apart. My sorrow is made even worse when I think of Zeth out there somewhere by himself, feeling ten times worse than I can possibly imagine.

Michael reads my mind. He gently touches his fingertips to my cheek, smiling sadly at me. "He'll be okay. I promise. He'll be okay, because he has you."

39

Zeth

SEVEN HOURS. LOWELL AND HER SILENT GIANT KEEP ME locked up for a further seven hours. She questions me endlessly about Monterello, and then asks the same questions over again three different ways. She tries and fails to make me slip up, to say something that contradicts my previous answers, and I just keep on giving her the same answers.

She questions me about my past with Charlie. She questions me about the death of her colleague back at the hospital—the one Charlie shot, not me. She questions me about an explosion outside St. Finnegan's Church yesterday morning. She questions me about the death of one Andreas Medina, whose body was found face down on the floor of a suite in the downtown Marriott. She questions me about anything and everything that might be used to bring charges against me.

And the delightful truth is that she has nothing she can pin on me. Absolutely fucking nothing. It's fairly obvious what she's trying to do. Lowell knows she's got shit, but she's hoping I'm a complete moron. She's hoping to put the fear of god into me with talk of these heinous crimes, so that when she gets around to asking me what she really wants to know I'll be ready and willing to comply with her in order to save my own ass. She's just started in on her fourth round of questions about Medina—*when did you see him last? What was said between you and the victim?*—when I finally lose patience with the bullshit.

I lean across the table, bridging my fingers together and glaring at the evil bitch. "You want Rebel. Why don't we cut the shit here, Denise? Why don't you ask me what you really want to know so you can go home to your microwave meal dinner and I can get the fuck out of here?"

Lowell goes rigid, as though I've ruined her game and she's pissed about it. "All right, Zeth. You're seriously fucking optimistic if you think you're getting out of here after we're done talking, but okay. For argument's sake, let's talk about Rebel. Do you know where he is?"

"No. I already told you I don't."

Fire lights up in Lowell's eyes. I can imagine her telling the giant to turn off the camera so she can go find herself a phone book—the bent police officer's best friend—but she doesn't. She manages to rein in her fury long enough to ask me another question. "What can you tell me about him, then?"

"Why do you want him so bad?"

"I think you're confusing the dynamics of our relationship, Mr. Mayfair. You don't get to ask me questions."

"I do if you want specific information."

She huffs, tapping her index finger nail against the scratched surface of the table between us. "Fine. Rebel buys girls. He buys them and then they disappear. No trace. We know he's heavily involved in human trafficking. We know he's murdering those women. We just don't know where, and we don't know how. Given your recent involvement in trying to find Dr. Romera's sister, I'd have thought perhaps you might just give a shit about these women."

So she's heard the same rumors I heard about Rebel. Believes the same things I believed before I met the guy. I know the truth now, though; Rebel aided and funded the relocation of broken women who were being sold as sex workers. He didn't murder them; he helped them.

"Tell me again, what does DEA stand for, Agent Lowell?"

"Are you being fucking smart?" Lowell spits.

"No, not at all. I'm just wondering why the Drug Enforcement Agency...that is what it stands for, right? Why the Drug Enforcement Agency are involved so heavily in a case that doesn't involve drugs, as far as I can see."

"You don't need to worry about the paperwork, Zeth. All you need to worry about is assisting me in my inquiries, and that way maybe, *maybe,* I'll cut you a deal so you won't have to spend quite as long back in fucking Chino, getting served on a nightly—"

"Do *not* threaten me." Lowell instantly falls silent. Maybe it's the look of cold rage on my face, or maybe it's the clear warning in my voice, but either way the bitch shuts her mouth. It's the smartest thing she's ever fucking done. "I tell you what's going to happen. You're going to organize the clean slate you were supposed to have arranged for my girl when she went to meet you in that mall. And then you're gonna get it signed. You're going to bring it back here, and you're going to put it in my hand, and then I will tell you everything you need to know about Rebel."

"You really think you're in a position to be making demands—"

"And if you don't do this," I say, lowering my voice, "you will have to release me in forty-eight hours due to the fact you have no evidence to bring charges against me. And when I get out, Agent Lowell, I will be a *very irritated man.*"

"Oh, are you threatening *me* now?" Lowell asks. Her face has gone white, but there are two small red splotches burning angrily in the center of her cheeks.

"Wouldn't dream of it. Just talking about my feelings. My counselor back in Chino said it was a good idea to share them every once in a while." She should never have brought up sending me back to that fucking prison. The very mention of that place is enough to darken my mood to fucking pitch-black degrees.

Lowell knows, despite my denial, I most definitely was fucking threatening her. She must be able to see the threat clear as day in my eyes. "Tell me what you'll give me and I'll consider your offer," she says.

"I'll tell you where the girls have gone. I'll tell you who kidnapped them in the first place. I'll tell you where the Widow Makers' clubhouse is."

"You must think we're idiots. We already know where their clubhouse is, Zeth."

"I'll tell you when they're going to be there. And I will also tell you where you can find the body of Charlie Holsan."

That has her attention. "Holsan's dead?"

"So I hear. Can't confirm that, of course. Just what I've heard on the grapevine." I can see she's interested; I know I've got her. Now for one last little thing to sweeten the deal. "While we're at it, I'll give you the locations of every single one of Holsan's cutting shops. You could actually seize some drugs while you're there. Might make that paperwork you told me not to worry about a little easier to file, right?" I know as well as she does those missing girls aren't within her jurisdiction. The Feds should be all over that case. I imagine they would be if they knew about it, which means Lowell's kept it from them. This is personal for her.

She smiles that sour smile of hers, nodding, eyes fixed on the table. "You give me that and I'll see what I can do."

"Paperwork first, Denise, and then we'll talk. And in the meantime, how about you get me some food and a nice cup of tea? I'm a little hungry, y'know?"

Five long seconds pass while Lowell glares at me with the intensity of a burning sun. She can't say no. She wants to—nothing would bring her more pleasure than to toss my ass in prison and throw away the key—but with the shitty hand she's been holding since the moment we walked into this room, she knows she has no other option but to comply. She rises to her feet, mumbling under her breath. The video camera gets switched off.

"I'll get you your paperwork, Mayfair, but I swear, if you don't give us everything we need, I'll make sure you never see the light of day again."

"Fair."

"And Ernie...Ernie had better be okay, you motherfucker."

"Oh, I forgot about Ernie." I smile, feeling a perverse sense of pleasure in what I'm about to say. "We'll be keeping Ernie, Denise."

I HAVE THREE folded pieces of paper in my back pocket, burning through my jeans, when I walk up the steps to The Regency Rooms. I feel light. Really fucking light, like I could float away if I'm not careful. The only thing anchoring me to the sidewalk is the persistent memory of Lacey. I see it every single time I close my fucking eyes. The briefest of moments when she spoke to me before she died. "You gave me your best. You're the only one who ever did."

It kills me that my best wasn't anywhere near enough to keep her safe. To keep her alive. I find the idea physically sickening. I got so caught up in my own shit with Charlie, Sloane and her sister, that taking care of Lacey took a backseat. Of all the people in the world to drop the ball with, Lace should have been the last. She was unstable. She was a complete fucking mess, really. I should have had a weather eye fixed on her every goddamn second of the day. I feel like I failed her.

Surprisingly, that's not the part that makes me the saddest, though. I'm the most raw, simply because I miss her. I miss her already. My sister has only been gone from this earth for a short space of time, but the length of time doesn't seem relevant right now. Perhaps it's the knowledge she won't be coming back, not *ever*, that makes the ache in my chest so unbearable.

I sat there all night staring out the window while Sloane slept, and I fought my very nature. I wanted to smash everything. I wanted to burn everything to the ground, not just Charlie's place. I wanted to go on a rampage and beat people, kill people with my bare hands. But then I came to a number of realizations. The first was that there was no one left to beat. No one left to kill. Nothing left to burn. The second was that my complete and utter fucking failure as a brother meant I was never going to fail the important people in my life again. That especially went for Sloane. The third realization that hit me, as the sun was rising over Seattle and Ernie was snoring gently in a soft gray heap at my feet, was that I'd fucked up Sloane's life. I'm not crazy. I was already well aware that I'd fucked up her life, but I realized it was on me to fix it. So that's what today has been about—fixing things, for me and for Sloane. Because though I definitely don't fucking deserve it, my sister always wanted me to be happy, too.

Three pieces of paper burning a hole in my back pocket. One burned-down mansion. Hopefully a tentative bridge built between

Sloane and her ever-so-fucking-annoying friend. I only have two more things to cross off my list. Two items that are currently in the works. I made a brief stop off on the way back to the hotel to resolve one of them, so really it's only one.

The concierge of The Regency Rooms is a woman this time. She gives me an inviting smile as I head for the elevator, and I find that I'm smiling back, though not how I might have done before Sloane. Now I am polite, but I am also taken. I will never be smiling at another woman the way she just smiled at me.

Inside the elevator, the cell phone I left in my ride when I went to see Lowell chimes.

212-776-4540, Rcv'd 7:59 p.m:
You told her what I told you to tell her?

Me:
Yes. She'll be coming for you next week. You got everything planned out?
Sent 7:59 p.m.

212-776-4540, Rcv'd 8:00 p.m.
I'll be ready. Catch you on the flip side, brother-in-law.

During the brief conversation I had with Rebel earlier, the president of the Widow Makers told me to give Lowell the thumb drive he'd given to Sloane. Once I'd handed that over to the Agent, along with the password—Accordia—Lowell then had access to a group of files containing the personal details, locations and addresses of all the women Rebel had relocated. Lowell seemed almost disappointed that none of the women were dead.

Along with that information, Rebel also told me to give her the date he would be back in New Mexico. By the eighth of December, in ten days time, the Widow Makers will be back at their clubhouse, ready and waiting. I don't know what his plan is. Technically Lowell can't investigate him for the girls, who are all still alive, but she can come after them for Alexis. They're crazy, but I understand why they want to face her. The same reason I had to face her today: so he and Alexis can get on with their lives. For there to be an end to this madness.

When I step off the elevator, the first sound I hear is that of breaking glass. I charge straight for the apartment I share with Sloane. Was I wrong? Maybe one of Charlie's boys held a grudge. Maybe one of them found out where she was and decided to finish what the old man started. My pulse is hammering all over my body by the time I manage to get the door open.

Pippa is lying on the floor on her back, laughing hysterically. I come to a halt, one fist raised, struggling to understand what I'm actually seeing. Pippa on the floor? Pippa on the floor, *laughing?* She sees me, her eyes sluggish as she tries to focus on me, and lets out a shriek. "*Zeth!* Zeth's back!"

I hear a strangled sound somewhere farther into the apartment—the bathroom, maybe? Sloane's head peeks out in the hallway. "There you are!" She comes running and throws herself at me. Her arms wrap around my neck, her legs around my hips. She kisses me, and she tastes like beer. It takes me a moment to kiss her back. Not because I don't want to be kissing her, but because I'm savoring the moment. Her lips on mine, her body pressed up against me. I was glad when she gave me some space yesterday—I needed it desperately—but right now having Sloane this close feels imperative.

I fix my arms around her back, fiercely holding onto her the same way she's holding onto me. She stops kissing me then, and rests her forehead against mine.

"You're drunk," I tell her, in case she hasn't realized.

"I know. You were gone."

"I know. I'm sorry. It was worth it, though, I promise."

"Michael's sick. He drank himself sick," Sloane whispers. She looks adorable like this, wide-eyed and more than a little drunk.

"Looks like you all did, huh?" She nods, and I have an overwhelming urge to carry her out of this apartment and away. I have no idea where, just *away*. Somewhere I can keep her to myself. Instead, I carry her to the bedroom and place her in the bed, fully dressed. "Take a nap. I'll be back soon," I tell her. She doesn't need much convincing; her eyes are already dropping closed by the time I've covered her over with the blankets.

There's broken glass all over the tiles in the bathroom—that was the smashing sound I heard out in the hallway. Michael's slumped over the toilet, head resting on his forearm, completely out cold. "Fuck's sake." I just look at him for a moment, and I consider leaving his ass there. But I know why he's like this right now. He was as close to Lace as I was. I can't blame him. If I let a single drop of alcohol past my lips, I would be way, way worse than he is. I'd be catatonic. I'd be broken. I'd be dead. I couldn't let that happen this time.

I grab hold of his wrist and lift him, hauling him up so I can lift him under his shoulder. It's a short, awkward shuffle to the shower, guiding him so we avoid the pool of beer and shards of glass all over the tiles. My boy can't stand up in the shower, so I stand in there with him, holding him up, and I crank the cold tap.

The frigid water sprays down on the both of us, and Michael nearly jumps out of his skin. Suddenly wide awake with the shock of the cold, he grabs hold of my shirt with both fists and yells.

"Fuck! *Fuck, fuck, fuck.* What the hell, man?" I just hold him up, making sure he stays under the flow of the icy water. Anger flares in his eyes; he tries to push me away, but I hold onto him tight. "What the hell, Zeth?" he shouts.

343

"Just deal with it."

"Get the fuck off me," he roars.

"No."

He hits me. It's a good job he's blind fucking drunk, or I'd feel compelled to return the favor. His blow is barely felt, anyway. I'm too numb from the cold, and to be honest, I kind of need it. I feel dangerously numb in general. He raises his fist and lashes out again, though this time there's no intention to hurt. It's a matter of seconds before he's collapsing into my arms and he's crying.

He cries silently, his body shaking with the power of it, and I let him. I love him for this. I love him because he loved Lacey. I stare at the grout in between the tiles, trying not to join him. I cried for Lace yesterday, though. I cried for the first time since my uncle decided it would be okay to raise his fist to me twenty-eight years ago.

"I'm sorry, man. I'm sorry." Michael says this over and over again, as though he somehow thinks what happened to Lace was his fault. I don't say anything, because I know he won't remember. When he calms down and begins to take some of his weight on his own legs, I turn off the water and guide him out of the shower, careful around the glass again, and then into one of the unoccupied bedrooms. I give him a towel and his privacy, and go to check on the third component of this little free-for-all. Pippa's fallen asleep in exactly the same position she was in when I rushed into the apartment, flat out on her back, arms and legs star-fished out.

A very large part of me wants to actually leave her there—be fucking uncomfortable to wake up on a cold, hard floor in the morning, which would serve the woman right—but she came here when I asked her to. And she didn't call the cops when I went to her apartment. I suppose some people would call that progress.

I put her to bed in the third and final bedroom, and then I make sure Michael's not choking on his own vomit. Fucking idiots. I have a quick, hot shower, and then I find myself standing in the hallway outside Sloane's room. With all the spare beds now occupied, I should go and sleep on the couch. If not the couch, then in one of the rooms in Michael's apartment.

The thing is...I don't want to.

I really don't fucking want to.

I let my hand hover over the door handle, weighing my options. I could sleep in a bed with Sloane and everything might be okay. I could sleep in a bed with Sloane and I could wake up and think she's Charlie, and try and kill her. The risk just seems like it's too much. Fuck. I pull my hand away, turn and head down the hallway, hating myself more and more with each step.

Charlie's fucking dead. He's fucking dead, and he should not still be able to fucking dictate my life. He should not get to ruin the one good thing I have going for me. It's crazy. It's absolutely fucking crazy that I'm still letting him.

I make a decision there and then that I won't anymore.

I stop. I turn around. I head back to Sloane's room before I can change my mind. No hovering outside the door this time. I go straight in, and Sloane is curled into a ball in the middle of the bed. Her breathing is slow and even, the sounds of someone deep in sleep.

I can do this. I can sleep in a bed with her and not hurt her. I lose my towel, and climb into the bed, completely naked. As though she senses my presence, Sloane wriggles into me so her back is pressed against my chest. This is entirely alien to me. I don't really know what I'm *supposed* to do, so I do what I *want* to do—I wrap myself around her and I draw her in tight. This is so different to the time Sloane and I passed out on the same bed at Julio's. This time I'm actually holding her, and I'm *meant* to be here. I fall asleep for the very first time with a woman in my arms. It feels like heaven.

40

Sloane

I FEEL LIKE I'M BEING COOKED. I FEEL LIKE MY BODY IS MADE out of lead. The world's still dark when I wake up, and there's a strong possibility I'm suffocating. For a moment it's as though I'm paralyzed and I can't move. Panic surges through me, setting my heart racing. But then I realize I'm not paralyzed; I'm merely being pinned to the mattress by a very heavy, sleeping man.

Zeth is in bed with me. Zeth's in bed with me, and he's fast asleep.

He did it. He got into bed with me, after all this time, of his own volition. I carefully turn over so I'm facing him, my nose pressing up against his collarbone, and I take a cautious breath in.

He smells incredible—a mixture of shower gel and something manly and distinct, something that doesn't smell like anything else on this planet. It's just Zeth's smell, and I love it. My head's pounding—I'll have the hangover from hell by the time the sun comes up, but right now I'm at that in-between stage where I can still feel the alcohol powering around my body, but I'm stone-cold sober.

Zeth's arms tighten around me. At first I think it's a subconscious action carried out in sleep, but then I feel the press of his lips against my forehead and I know he's awake.

"Sorry," I whisper. "I didn't mean to wake you."

"S'okay," he tells me, his voice thick with sleep. "Come here." He places a hand on my hip and inches me closer somehow, even though we are already skin on skin.

"You...okay?" I ask carefully. I don't want to make a big deal out of him being here. But it is a big deal. It means a lot to me, and this, how he's being with me, is definitely a big deal, too.

"I'm okay," he whispers. There's so much feeling behind those words. I know Zeth's not just talking about the fact he's here in this bed with me. He's talking about Lacey. It's going to take a long, long time for any of us to get over her death, but for right now Zeth's letting me know he's holding his shit together. That might not necessarily be a good thing. It might be better for him to break for a little while, but I can't be the person to tell him that. He'll break or he won't break, and either way I'll be here to help him. He moves slowly, sleepily, bringing his fingers up to touch my cheek. The action is soft. Gentle. Unexpected.

"Sloane...we're *free*," he whispers.

"Are we? Julio—"

"Julio's been dealt with."

"Michael said that. But how?"

"I don't know the details yet. But Rebel said he was long gone."

"As in dead?"

I can just about make out the outline of Zeth's faint smile in the darkness. "I really don't know. But long gone is good enough for me right now." He continues to trace his fingers over my face, the pads of each fingertip tenderly exploring the lines of my nose, my cheekbones, my chin. "And you don't need to worry about Lowell anymore, either. I took care of it," he says.

"Took care of it? Like took care of *her?*"

"No." Zeth chuckles quietly, the sound a low rumble in his chest. "I promise you, Sloane, there'll be no more *taking care* of anyone. Not ever again. I made a deal with Lowell. I exchanged information in return for those get-out-of-jail-free cards she teased us with."

I pull back so I can look him square in the eyes. Is he being serious? Though it's tough to see much in the dark, I can make out the intense look in his eyes. The tight pull of his lips. He is. He's being one hundred percent serious. "Oh my god. What happened?"

Zeth tells me about turning himself in to Lowell. About the seven hours of incessant questioning while Lowell tried to trip him up. About handing over information Rebel *wanted* Lowell to have in exchange for three sheets of A4 paper—one for me, one for Zeth, one for Michael—each clearing us of any criminal charges that may or may not have been brought against us.

"And so...that's it. No more Charlie. No more Julio. No more Lowell."

No more Lacey. I don't say that, though. Instead, I ask, "No more nightmares?"

Zeth sighs, burying his nose into my neck. "I don't know. Maybe."

"But none just now?"

"None just now," he confirms.

"So...you want to go back to sleep?" I don't want to go back to sleep. I want to do something else, and I think Zeth might just be on board. Even though I'm fully dressed, it hasn't escaped me that he's naked. And I can feel him growing harder, his erection digging into my stomach as he holds me close.

Zeth doesn't say anything in response. He just looks down at me, those dark eyes considering me in a way I'm not entirely used to. I'm used to the dangerous spark in his eyes. It's still there, but...I feel like the divide that was keeping us apart is now gone. It makes me catch my breath.

Zeth leans down and kisses me, and his mouth is gentle and soft. A low, bass sound rumbles in the back of his throat. His lips feel incredible on mine—demanding and slow, yet firm. He works his hands into my hair, and then brings them down to carefully cup my face. Everything about the moment is different. He's not normally like this. Normally, I feel like I'm being swept along in an unstoppable tide, being pulled under and rolled by a force much greater than myself. Being with him has always reminded me of the only time I tried to surf when I was on vacation in California as a teenager. The instructor gave me some valuable advice that worked remarkably well: *If you're pulled under a wave, don't fight it. You'll never win. The ocean's a hell of a lot stronger than you. It's wild. All you have to do is hold your breath. Relax. Go with the wave, and eventually you'll rise to the surface.*

Zeth has always felt like that wave to me, wild and unstoppable, and that's part of what's thrilled me about being with him. But right now, it feels like we're an equal force and we cancel each other out. As much as I love the freedom of letting go, of letting someone else have control over me, this is the most connected I've ever felt with him, and nothing can compete with that. Nothing in the world.

His hands work their way down to my neck, where his fingers trace the lines of my throat, across my collarbone, making me shiver. Slowly, carefully, Zeth reaches down and gathers my shirt, lifting it over my head. My pants and underwear go next, Zeth's hands moving confidently and carefully, until I'm as naked as he is.

"Close your eyes," he whispers. He's told me to do that so many times before, but this time I'm not even remotely fazed by what he'll do once I've shut out the world. I close my eyes, and Zeth rains kisses down onto my forehead, my eyelids, my temples, my cheeks, and down my neck. By the time he reaches my breasts, my head is spinning.

He rolls me onto my back, rolling with me so he's hovering over me, and the kisses keep coming. With a demanding nudge from his knees, Zeth pushes my legs apart so he can settle himself between them. His cock is rigid and warm, so hard against me. His hands travel over me; he takes his time, mapping me out, kissing and licking and gently biting me all over, paying homage to my body.

I can't keep quiet. I gasp each time I feel his teeth on me. Each time the heat of his tongue licks at me. Each time his fingers graze my sensitive skin.

"You wet for me, Sloane?" Zeth growls into the skin of my stomach. "If I go down on you, are you already going to be wet for me?"

A tremor ripples through me, making me shake. "Yes." Because I am. There's no way I'm not. I want him so badly, and he knows it. In the past, this might have been where Zeth would have tied my wrists to the bed, or told me I couldn't move, but now he says nothing. I don't doubt the next time we're together, his black bag will be back in full effect, but I need this right now. And so does he. He travels lower, dipping his head in between my legs, and I suck in a sharp gasp at the pressure of his tongue on my clit.

With hot, wet, deliciously slow, sweeping strokes, he works his tongue over me, sucking on my clit and licking at my pussy. I don't fight myself, or him. I bury my fingers into his hair, grabbing two decent handfuls and pulling tightly. Zeth hisses, pausing a moment to look up at me. Our eyes lock down the length of my body and I can feel the tension and heat pouring off him. There's a warning half hidden in his eyes, but it's an amused one. I pull a little harder, and he smiles, mouth open, eyelids heavy.

"You pushing my buttons, angry girl?"

"Uhuh." I feel winded by the way he's looking at me—I feel the color rising in my cheeks from the blatant need I see on his face. He doesn't dip back down right away; he stares at me, eyes fixed on my face, and he slowly slides his fingers inside me. Not one, but two at once. He scissors them open, and the tense, pulling sensation deep inside me lights me up.

"Fuck, Zeth. Oh my god."

"You want me to keep going?" I nod, not trusting myself to speak. Zeth pushes his tongue between the slick folds of my pussy, taking his time as I shiver and buck beneath him. He's relentless with his fingers, sliding them in and out of me with torturously slow movements that have me on the verge of tears. I lose control at some point, unashamed of the choked, needy sounds that come out of my mouth.

I begin to think Zeth is intent on making me suffer, that he will drag out my pleasure forever until I can't take it anymore, but just as I'm about to start begging he stops what he's doing. He moves up my body with a predatory, dark look on his face, eyes searching me all over, hungry and desperate. Is he going to fuck me now? I think he will, but then he climbs off me and lies down on the bed beside me.

"Sloane...I'm yours," he whispers. I feel like I'm choking on my own tongue. I can't have heard him right, surely? Zeth Mayfair doesn't submit to anybody. But the truth of his words are right there in his eyes, all over his face, written in the lines of his powerful, possessive body. He is mine. He is giving himself to me. And I know he's not just talking about this very moment, the shared secrets of our bodies moving together in the half light as Seattle slowly comes to life. He's talking about all of him. He's talking about always. He is mine, and I am his, and suddenly it feels like everything is snapping into place.

I climb on top of him, positioning myself over his straining cock, and I sink myself down onto him. I need to feel him inside me more than anything else I've ever needed. It seems like the final part of a silent promise we're making to each other, and to join our bodies together is the most sacred part of that promise. Zeth's hands find my hips. He takes hold of me, and doesn't let me go. With eyes locked, we move against each other in powerful, potent strokes, the two of us no longer separate, but *more.*

"Fuck, Sloane. Hold on." Zeth sits up, and then his arms are around me, holding me so tight I think I'm going to pass out. I shift so I can wrap my legs around him, and then he's kissing me, stealing my breath from me. His hands take ahold of *my* hair now; he pulls my head back to gain access to my neck, his teeth biting into my skin.

"Ahhh! Oh, shit, Zeth, I'm gonna—" I don't need to finish that sentence. Zeth lifts me straight up, spins me over, still inside me, and throws me back down on the bed, landing heavily on top of me. He's shaking, his whole body vibrating—he's about to come, too.

The fire of the moment burned my hangover away long ago, though my head is still swimming and dizzy. Dizzy from him. From lack of oxygen, and from the intensity of the want stabbing through my body every time Zeth pulls out of me. The loss of him feels too great to bear. He drives himself back into me each time, as though he feels that loss too, and is dead set on remedying it.

"Come for me, Sloane," he growls. "Come hard for me. Scream for me."

I do. I scream so loud I'm pretty sure the people five floors down hear, and I don't care. In the perfect moment where I come, Zeth comes too, roaring with me, clinging onto me like he's afraid I might drift away. Trapped under his shaking, sweat-covered body, there's no chance of that, though. I am exactly where I am supposed to be, and so is he.

Zeth lifts himself onto his elbows, but he doesn't pull out of me. He rests his forehead against mine and stares at me, breathing heavily, fighting to regain himself. We don't say anything. We don't need to. I tell him everything he needs to know with my eyes, and he does the same. And then we fall asleep.

41

Zeth

I WAKE UP, AND I DON'T TRY TO KILL MY GIRLFRIEND. AS beginnings to a day might go, this is an epically fucking brilliant one. I get out of bed and head to the kitchen to find Pippa Newan doubled over the kitchen sink, throwing her guts up.

"Good morning, Pippa," I tell her. Pippa from now on. Not Newan.

She shoots me a filthy look. "Got any drugs in this place?"

"If there are, they're not legal," I inform her. "Besides, you're the one with the script pad. *Prescribe yourself something.*" I slap her on the back, doing my best to hide my evil smile when she groans.

I stand out in the hallway for thirty minutes, making a number of phone calls. There's still that one loose end I'm working on tidying up, but by the time I'm done on the phone, everything is set in place. I have plans for Sloane today. Big plans. I feel positively fucking devious when I head back into the apartment, almost itching with excitement. Been a long time since I've felt like this. In fact, I can't ever remember feeling exactly quite like this.

Michael and Sloane are up. The three of them, Sloane, Michael and Pippa, are slumped on the couch in the lounge, looking mighty sorry for themselves. Sloane looks the least sorry—I'm pretty sure I fucked the hangover right out of her this morning—but she's clearly still a little green around the gills. Ernie is spread out across all three of their laps, docked tail quickly flicking back and forth like a demented windshield wiper.

"You should have me put down," Michael groans. "I feel worse than death. What happened last night?"

He doesn't remember me coming in and holding him up in the shower, or he doesn't *want* to remember. Either way, I don't say anything about it. "You were all disgracefully drunk. I put you all to bed like fucking three-year-olds."

"Any three-year-old put to bed by you would be mentally traumatized," Pippa says, pressing her fingertips into her eye sockets. I point at Michael, enjoying the look of panic on his face.

"On your feet. I have a job for you this morning." Michael looks like he's about to puke again, but he doesn't. He lifts Ernie's backend up so he can rise shakily to his feet, and takes a deep breath.

"What? How are you planning on torturing me now?"

I write down what I need him to find for me on a Post-It Note, which I hand over, and Michael's eyebrows rocket up to his hairline. Or where his hairline would be if he didn't have a buzz cut. "You're kidding me, right?"

I shake my head. "Better get moving, I need all that by the end of the day."

Michael shoots Sloane a dubious look and then leaves, grumbling under his breath.

She gives me a confused look. "What was that about?"

"You need to get in the shower. We're leaving in twenty minutes," I tell her. "And despite how lovely it is to see you, Pippa, it's time you went home. My girl and I have things to attend to."

Pippa glowers at me. Good to see some things haven't changed, but it's nice to see she can bear to be in the same room as me for more than two minutes without trying to warn Sloane off me, too.

Once Pippa's disappeared and Sloane's showered and changed, I drive her across the city, listening to her softly humming in the car. She begins to get antsy as we approach the warehouse. "Where... where are we going, Zeth?"

"Exactly where you think we're going."

"Oh."

Since we're no longer being stalked by crazy gang bosses, it's definitely safe for us to come back here. I can understand her hesitancy, though. Things have been easier at The Regency Rooms. They're a blank slate. And, well, Lacey never stayed there with us. All of her things are at the warehouse, scattered all over the place—a fact I used to give her shit for all the time.

I haven't been back here since well before she died. If I could get out of being here now, I fucking would, but I need to face it. I need to begin processing what life's gonna be like without my sister in it. When we arrive at the warehouse, we head inside in silence.

The place feels like it's haunted, though not by Lacey. It feels haunted by the people we were a couple of weeks ago—angry, lost, and unhappy. To some degree, we're still all of those things, but now things just feel different. Now, I don't want to be any of those things.

We walk past the many reminders of my sister, Sloane's hand in mine, and I guide her to the access door past my bedroom. Down we go, down the stairs into the basement, and I collect the sledge-hammer I left resting against the wall months and months ago, the last time I came down here.

"Here." I hold it out to Sloane. She eyes it cautiously, folding her arms across her chest.

"What do you want me to do with that?"

"I want you to smash it into that wall behind you."

"What?"

"Smash it into the wall. Tear it down." She just looks at me like I'm mad.

"Are you going to bury me behind there or something?" she asks. Once upon a time, she might have asked me that question in all seriousness. Thankfully, she's joking now.

"Just do it, angry girl."

Sloane reaches out and accepts the handle of the sledgehammer. She's way stronger than I give her credit for, though this shouldn't come as a surprise to me anymore. I know exactly just how fucking strong she is. With one last mildly concerned look at me, Sloane hikes the sledgehammer onto her shoulder and then swings.

The thin layer of plaster cracks and explodes in a shower of dust and debris, and there it is—a huge hole in the wall. "Oh my god. I just did that," Sloane says, excitement creeping into her voice. "Here," she holds the hammer back out to me. "You try."

"No." I take a deep breath. "You do it."

She frowns at me, then. "Why?"

"Because if I start hitting things, Sloane, I'll never stop. And right now, I'm trying really hard..." That's the truth of the matter. I've been calm. I've somehow managed to maintain this delicate, fragile calm, but I have no idea how. I am still consumed by a rage I'm too worried to even think about—the very depth of it scares me. If I give in to that rage for even a second, I will sink into it and I don't know how long it'll take me to climb back out again. And I need to be here, right now. For Sloane. For me, too.

She nods, understanding like I knew she would. It takes her seven more clean swipes at the wall to create a hole big enough for me to reach inside and pull out the bags I left behind there.

"Duffel bags? Tell me you didn't make me smash down a wall so you could retrieve some sex toys?"

I smile, testing the weight of the duffels, one in either hand. "No. Not sex toys. Open it." I hold one out to her.

She scoots down and unzips the bag slowly, as though there might be a bomb inside. Her eyes grow wide when she sees the stacks of money.

"What the hell is all this?"

"This is eight years' worth of pay from my last job. My boss was an asshole, in case you were wondering why I quit." I've never needed much to live; I was always very careful with what I spent. Eight years' worth of pay from Charlie is a shit ton of cash.

"That...that's just obscene. That's an *obscene* amount of money, Zeth."

"Yes, it is. And right now we have to hurry. We're gonna be late."

No matter how hard she questions me—girl could give fucking Lowell a run for her money—I don't tell her where we're going after that. I throw the bags of cash into the trunk of the car I still have on loan from The Regency Rooms, and then I drive Sloane over to the western part of the city, in the direction of the hotel. That's not where we're heading, though. When we reach our destination, I come to a halt, wondering what the hell she's going to say when she realizes what I've done.

She takes one look out of the window and then spins on me. "A fighting gym? You've brought me to a fighting gym?"

I take the keys out of the ignition and press the teeth into the palm of my hand. Maybe this was a stupid idea. "Yeah. Not just any fighting gym. *My* fighting gym." I glance at her out of the corner of my eye—*does she think I'm fucking crazy?*—to find that she's not looking at me at all. She's looking back up at the building, squinting at it like the two-story structure is getting harder and harder to see. Perhaps she just can't imagine it—me owning a legitimate business. Doing something aboveboard, making it work.

I stare at the car key in my hand. I should put it back into the ignition. Drive away. I'm about to, but then Sloane's hand rests on my arm, and she looks like she's on the verge of tears. "So we're not going to leave Seattle?"

"What? Fuck no. I'm not running from my home, Sloane." It hadn't even crossed my mind that she'd expect us to leave. Not now. "There's no reason for us to go. We're staying right here. And if anyone's stupid enough to wanna come fuck with me, they'll know exactly where I am." I point at the building outside: the cracked, crumbling brickwork in desperate need of repointing, the faded wooden board, complete with peeling green paint that reads *O'Shannessey's Irish Boxing Club For Boys*.

Sloane touches the window with her fingertips, checking the place out again, eyes fixed on the sign. "O'Shannessey's? As in the same O'Shannessey that..."

I pull a tight smile. "Not for him, no. For his dad. Father O'Shannessey had two sons. One of them was my best friend, Murphy. Charlie killed him to hurt me, slit his throat right in front of me. The O'Shannessey you had the pleasure of meeting was his brother. He watched as Charlie killed Murphy, and he did nothing to stop it. He let it happen, and then he stuck with Charlie all these years since." I shrug my shoulders—no matter how many times I've tried to reconcile that in my head, especially while I was sitting in prison with nothing better to think about, I've never been able to understand. "Father O'Shannessey's too old to run this place now. Michael brought me here yesterday morning to burn off some steam, and it just made sense. I knew I needed to buy it."

My certainty yesterday, the deep *knowing* I'd experienced, seems to have fled me now, though. Fuck. This was a stupid idea. How the hell did I think running a boxing gym would be a smart move? I have one skillset, and one skillset only. Hurting people is all I'm good for. I curl my fist around the key, feeling the bite of pain and clinging onto it for dear life.

"I think...I think it's a wonderful idea, Zeth. I think it's perfect. I can help you run the place."

I let go of the key, risking another glance at her. Her expression has changed, as if it was only taking her a moment to refocus her vision of the place, but now she's seeing it more clearly. Not O'Shannessey's Irish Boxing Club for Boys anymore, but something else entirely.

"What will you call it?" she asks.

"Blood 'N' Roses Fighting Gym," I tell her.

She laughs. "Blood 'N' Roses? Why Blood 'N' Roses? Seems a little contradictory, don't you think?"

"Maybe. I don't know. It just seemed appropriate. It's the life I've been given so far. Not perfect. *Far* from perfect. It's been bloody and hard, with plenty of sharp edges, but..." I look at her, listening to me so intently, and I feel like a total dick.

"What? *Tell me*," she says, laughing quietly.

"But it's had its beautiful moments, too." *You. It's had* you *in it, and you make the rest of that shit worth it.* I shrug. "Fighting's a lot like that. It's hard. Pushes you to the limits of what you're capable of, but then it makes you stronger and clears your head, too. Gives you strength for when you need it later. Fuck it. I'm probably not making much sense."

"You're making perfect sense." Sloane climbs out of her seat and into my lap, wrapping her arms around my neck. "I get it. And I think it's perfect, too. The gym's a perfect idea, and so is the name. It's going to be a roaring success. And you can teach me how to beat up anyone who wants to give *me* shit. Deal?"

I'm about to kiss her, but that stops me dead in my tracks. I cup her face in both of my hands and I make sure she believes me when I tell her, "No one's going to be giving you any shit from here on out, Sloane. *No one.* I will kill anyone that tries. You're going to have a normal life from now on. Well, as normal as it can get with me as a boyfriend. But you don't have a choice in *that* matter, I'm afraid."

She smiles, and that smile lights up my whole fucking world. "I don't want a choice, Zeth. I just want you."

We get out of the car, and I collect one of the bags of money from the trunk. We go inside together, and I get to introduce my girl to Father O'Shannessey.

And then O'Shannessey's Irish Boxing Club for Boys becomes the Blood 'N' Roses Fighting Gym.

42

Sloane

WE SPEND THREE HOURS AT THE GYM, WHILE AN EXCITED
Father O'Shannessey shows us around and regales us with stories
of the countless boxing legends that have trained with him over the
decades. I'm a little confused as to why Zeth calls O'Shannessey
Father all the time—he definitely doesn't look, act, or dress like
he's been running any churches lately—but that's only until the old
man with the shock of silver hair winks at me and says, "I left the
priesthood when I met me boys' mother. I would have defied any
warm-blooded man to stay celibate with that woman sitting in his
pews. That was over forty years ago now, but these ingrates still
insist on calling me Father."

I've no idea if Father O'Shannessey knows his only remaining
living son is now, in fact, dead, but I don't breathe a word of it. Zeth
catches my eye and I get the feeling that the news is better left
unsaid. At least by me, anyway, which I'm grateful for.

I let the men talk, and I walk around, imagining how to improve
the place, what we can do to freshen it up—an awful lot—and how

to draw in a younger crowd. I'm sure Zeth has plenty of ideas of his own, but I can see it myself—the potential the place has. It's exciting, picturing how everything will work out here, yet I still feel like my stomach's in knots as I familiarize myself with the place. I know why, too. I can't think about that, though. Zeth will be good at this, and so will I. It will be our life together. I cast a quick glance over my shoulder, and the two men are watching me, neither saying a word anymore. Zeth gives me a cautious smile, still leonine and confident, but a little secretive, too, and I know everything has worked out the way it was meant to.

AT FIVE, ZETH drives me back to The Regency Rooms and tells me to wait in our apartment. I make a fuss over Ernie, feeling like crap for leaving him so long, and make myself a cup of tea. Zeth returns shortly after with a backpack slung over his shoulder and two garment bags in his hand.

"Here, you'd better put this on. We're going to be late."

"Again?" I eye the garment bag he's holding out for me. The last time I wore something that came out of a garment bag, we all nearly got blown up. My body still aches every time I move in evidence of that fact. I'm black and blue down one side of my body from where I hit the ground so hard. "Late for what?"

"Less questions. More action. Do I need to dress you myself, Sloane?" He takes a step forward and the challenge is clear in his eyes. From what I can tell, I sincerely doubt he wants to dress me; I get the feeling he's more interested in *un*dressing me.

"That depends on whether we are actually nearly late for

something, or if you think we have time to kill," I say.

Zeth makes a growling noise at the back of his throat. "Fine. Then get moving."

I take the dress from him—I'm assuming it's a dress—and I head for the bedroom. When I unzip the bag, I see it *is* a dress. A beautiful one, made from Irish-green silk with a huge split up the front. There are matching silk covered heels, too, and a lovely art deco hair comb to match. I get dressed, feeling incredibly seductive as the material whispers over my skin. I haven't felt like that in a very long time.

At the thought of seduction, I suddenly remember what the concierge told us when we first arrived here: that there were *celebrations* happening soon. The kinds of celebrations Zeth used to attend before he came back into my life. The concierge had even asked if we wanted to book a booth. My heart is suddenly galloping in my chest. Is he...is he planning on taking me to some sex party? I remember the last one all too well.

I stride out of the bedroom and into the lounge, getting ready to lay into him, but then I catch sight of the man, and I lose any and all ability to speak coherently. In a beautiful black suit, white shirt and black tie, Zeth is magnificent. The small cuts and scrapes on his hands and face only seem to add a savage edge to his beauty. He's fastening his cuff links, smirking at me as he makes eye contact.

"Everything to your liking?" he asks.

Am I to your liking? He knows damn well he is, the arrogant bastard. I scowl at him. "Are you planning on taking me downstairs to some freaky sex club, Zeth?"

He looks genuinely surprised. I watch the moment when realization dawns on him. "Oh, you think..." He laughs. Actually has the audacity to laugh. "No, angry girl. No more sex clubs for you. Or for me. That is, unless..."

I throw a couch cushion at him, but he sidesteps out of the way, still adjusting his cufflinks. I shake my head, going to him and holding out my hands. He places his in mine, and I carefully thread the silver button through his cuff.

"There." When I look up, Zeth's grinning at me.

"What?"

"You're disappointed, aren't you?"

"That you're not taking me to a sex club? No!" I can feel myself blushing, though. I can hear how ridiculous my denial sounds. Zeth's grin vanishes in a heartbeat. He leans down to me, so that his lips brush my ear when he says, "I can tolerate people watching, Sloane. I can tolerate you wanting to watch others. But we have new ground rules now. No one's ever allowed to touch you again. And I will never touch anyone else, nor allow anyone to touch me, either. So...all you have to do is say the word."

A cold, anxious shiver runs down the length of my body, but I'm not anxious because I think *he* wants that. He's telling me that because he thinks *I* might want it. And...I'm anxious because of how the prospect of it makes me feel.

"I don't want that," I say breathlessly.

Zeth nods, though I can see the flicker of dark amusement in his eyes. "Come on, angry girl. We have a ride waiting for us down-stairs."

Our ride is Michael, of course. And our car is a sleek, black limo. Neither of them caves and tells me where we're going as we glide silently through the city. I still haven't guessed, not even when we pull up outside yet another church.

Zeth helps me out of the car, a small smile playing over the corners of his mouth. He looks so entertained by my confusion.

"What are we doing here?" I can hear music inside—the sound of violins and cellos, and the music of many voices all talking at once. Tea light candles light the path up to the church entrance, and small fairy lights have been wrapped around the branches of the trees in the courtyard. It's stunning.

Zeth looks slightly bashful as he reaches into his pocket and produces a square of dirty, battered card. There's blood splattered on the back of it, and the corner is torn, but I instantly realize what it is: the invitation to Suresh's wedding. He told me...Zeth told me weeks ago he would take me. I'd forgotten all about it. So much has happened in between now and then. So much to change and shape us. Zeth unfolds the invitation and holds it out to me.

"I thought they were getting married in a hotel. In the morning?" I whisper.

"The bride's very Christian parents were delayed," Zeth explains. "They pushed back the time and changed the location on account how scandalous not getting married in a church was, apparently."

I look back up at the church, struggling to cope with the sheer rightness of the moment. "I can't believe it."

"I was hoping you'd still want me to be your date?" Zeth says softly.

My eyes are stinging. I can't believe, in amongst all the fighting, running, violence and pain, he remembered *this*. "I would love for you to be my date."

I can't believe this man. I can't believe how much I love him. I can't believe how lost I would be without him in my life. I would definitely have been safer these past few months, but in retrospect, it seems as though Zeth was right. This has all been blood and roses—pain and heartache, but also bittersweet and beautiful, too. There are plenty of things I'd change, losing Lacey being one of them, but I'd still have him. I'd still have this, and this is perfect.

"Want to go inside?" he asks.

I nod, yes. "I definitely want to go inside."

The ceremony is wonderful. The inside of the church is decked out in a million tiny white flowers, decorating the pews and the aisle. Rebecca, Suresh's bride, is radiant in a sea of white lace and silk, the same tiny white flowers tied into her hair. I'm surrounded by faces I know from the hospital—Oliver's sitting at the front of the church with a date, a slim blonde woman with a knockout smile. He notices us halfway through the ceremony and gives me a hesitant smile. Once the vows are over, the whole church full of people walk down the street, not caring about the cold or the wind that ruins their hair. Zeth links his arm through mine and we walk with the rest of the crowd, surrounded by laughter and smiling faces.

"Sloane! Oh my god, Sloane." A hand lands on my shoulder. The next thing I know, I'm being pulled into a rough hug. Suresh, beaming from ear to ear, squeezes me tightly, then holds me at arm's length so he can look at me. "I'm so glad you're here," he tells me. "Now everything's perfect." He plants a wet kiss on my forehead, and Rebecca, suddenly at his side, laughs brightly.

"Yes, so glad you came," she tells me, kissing my cheek.

"Thank you. You look beautiful."

"And I see you used your plus one," Suresh says. "You must be the guy Sloane's fucking." He holds out his hand to Zeth. All the blood rushes from my face. I cover my mouth with my hands, remembering what Suresh had said back in the hospital canteen the day he reminded me about his wedding—that I couldn't just bring a friend. It had to be someone I was fucking. When I peek at Zeth, he's shaking Suresh's hand, not even remotely fazed.

"Yep. I'm *that* guy," he says. "Zeth. Pleasure to meet you."

"You too, man. Zeth? Cool name." He slaps Zeth on the arm, and then the bride and groom move on through the crowd, smiling and hugging more people as they go.

The sea of milling people eventually reaches a small boutique hotel three blocks away. Not time for speeches or food yet, a string quartet begins to play as soon as the wedding guests arrive. Zeth holds his hand out to me, and the night gets even weirder.

"You want to dance with me?" I ask.

"Yes." Zeth takes hold of me and pulls me into him, breathing me in. "I want nothing more right now." He holds me, and we dance, and in this small moment, the nightmare we've just been through doesn't matter anymore. Nothing does. It's well after midnight, after the food and the speeches and lot more dancing when Zeth tells me we need to leave.

"What? We have to go? Why?"

"Because." He kisses me lightly, his mouth lingering on mine. "The clock's already struck twelve. That's how most fairytales go, right? The beautiful young woman has to leave before the end of the ball?"

"No," I say, laughing, shaking my head. "Not this one. Not this time. And this time the princess gets her Prince Charming, too, right? You said it yourself. One night only."

He smiles. "I'll give you more than one night, Sloane, I promise. Or at least I'm gonna work on it. But right now we do have to leave because you have to be up early in the morning."

"I do?"

He just nods, fighting back the beginnings of a smile. We slip silently out of the wedding party, and my heart feels heavy in my chest. It would have been nice to stay and eat, to laugh and dance more, but I'm intrigued by his cryptic clue.

In the back of the car, Zeth hands me a black backpack. "Here." It's the backpack he had over his shoulder when he came back from Michael's place earlier. I look at him, trying to figure out what's inside even as I open the zip.

My heart stops beating when I see what's inside.

Scrubs.

Blue scrubs.

"What...what's this?" I can barely breathe.

"That's what you normally wear to work, right?" Zeth bites back a grin as I pull the scrubs out, my mouth hanging open.

"But...*how*? How did you...? Oh god, you didn't threaten anyone, did you?"

"No. Money talks, Dr. Romera. Though threats were gonna be next if that chief of medicine woman didn't give me what I fucking wanted."

"You *bribed* Chief Allison?"

He tuts. "I gave her something *she* wanted."

"Which was?"

"A new MRI machine."

"Zeth! MRI machines cost millions of dollars! There was a lot of cash in those bags, but there wasn't a million dollars."

"There wasn't, no. But Charlie had a fair chunk of cash sitting in his safe, and he didn't exactly need it anymore. And I sure as hell didn't want any more of his money."

God. I try to imagine the chief's face when Zeth handed over that amount of money in cash. She'd have had to accept it as an anonymous donation. The paperwork on something like that would be a nightmare. I suddenly feel like throwing up.

"So I'm going back to work? I'm really going back? Tomorrow morning?"

Zeth checks his watch, as though my shift is about to start any moment now. "Nine am sharp. Which means, Sloane, we have just enough time to go home and *spend some time together* before you need to sleep." His hands are already sliding up the silk of my dress, and I can barely believe this is happening. He fixed this for me. Doctors don't just get to steal medical supplies and involve themselves in shootouts inside hospitals and then expect to go back to work. He made all of that disappear.

By the time Michael pulls up outside The Regency Rooms, I'm severely sexually frustrated and my hair is all over the place, and I am even more in love with this crazy, sexy man. Michael goes to park the limo, leaving Zeth and me to ride up to our floor in the elevator.

"What are you going to do all day without me if I'm back at work? You're gonna miss me, aren't you?" I tease.

Zeth presses me up against the side of the elevator, hands working quickly as he slides his fingers underneath the lace of my panties. I gasp as he slips two of them inside me, a devious smile on his face.

"Don't you worry about me, Dr. Romera. I have plenty of things to keep *me* busy."

"Don't go looking for trouble," I whisper.

He gives me that wicked smirk of his. I knew from the very beginning that smirk was going to be the ruin of me. "Always," he says. "But you know how it is, Sloane. Trouble does seem to have a way of finding me."

EPILOGUE

Sloane

THE HEAT OF NEW MEXICO IS SOMETHING I'VE READ ABOUT but never really experienced first hand. I leave the car parked on the side of the road as I was told to, and I set off down a long stretch of dust track that stretches out into the distance. No trees. No shade. Only the road and the sun overhead, and my already parched mouth.

According to Rebel, the walk is only a short one, but I get the feeling the bastard may have been lying. He seems to do that a lot if he thinks it means he will get his own way. It strikes me suddenly that I'm actually wrong. Rebel doesn't lie to get his own way. He lies to me to get *Lexi's* way. It would appear my sister has her man well and truly under her thumb.

Some people might say the same about Zeth and me, though. Zeth, the man who never lies, has lied for me. He will do anything he can to help me or keep me safe. The past few months have shown me that.

It's been a month since I went back to work at St. Peters. A whole month since Charlie and Lacey died. A month since Zeth bought out O'Shannessey's Irish Boxing Club for Boys and turned it into something else—something of his own. The transition from gang enforcer to business owner seems to have been an easy one for my man. It helps, I think, that his new business involves hitting people all day long, except now they're paying him for the pleasure.

I never got to see Lexi when she was in Seattle. After Lacey, the world just seemed too full and complicated. I couldn't handle facing her. Not just yet. But now, after a month of work and continual days and nights of being doted on by Zeth, I woke up three days ago and decided it was time. So I got in the car and I drove. I left Zeth, Michael and Ernie behind, and I set out on my own, for the first time not worrying about cartels or English mob bosses who might be out to kill me, and I felt like I could breathe.

I took my time in getting here, following the directions Rebel sent me, but now that I'm here, staring down the barrel of the long road toward the life my sister chose for herself, I'm gripped by an uncertainty. I know Alexis has no clue I'm on my way. Rebel wanted to keep it quiet—in case I changed my mind and never showed, no doubt—and now I'm glad of it. Her ignorance of my arrival means I get to decide if this is what I really want. Do I want my sister back? Do I want to hear her side of the story? A story that seems as complicated and dangerous as my own. The answer to that question is a paradox. Yes, I do want to hear what kept her from letting her family know she was alive. Yes, I want to know why, for two years, she's been living with a biker gang that is apparently still involved in underground crime. And, yes, I want to know why she fell in love with and married a man like Rebel.

However, on the other hand, I don't want to know. I've been so mad at her for so long that knowing her story feels frightening. It might mean I will have to let go of all the frustration and feelings of betrayal, and I honestly don't know how that will leave me. Sad?

Hollow? A little lost, perhaps?

Because if all this isn't Lexi's fault, then it's nothing more than terrible, terrible luck and a shitty hand life dealt out, and that's outside my control. I don't like things being outside my control.

I stare down the dirt road, gripping hold of the shoulder straps of my backpack, wondering which option is better: living a life in which my sister abandoned and betrayed me, or one where awful, terrible things happen, and there is nothing I can do about them.

I'm being a coward.

I begin to walk.

Rebel's idea of a short journey is laughable. I'm sweating and completely out of water by the time I see a building on the horizon. I get that worrying sensation at the back of my mind, like the low complex of buildings aren't even really there. The hazy, wavy heat lines coming off the desert floor give the impression they could easily be a mirage.

But as I keep walking, I see they are, in fact, very real. The odd glancing ray of brilliant light of sunshine reflecting from chrome eventually tells me I'm in the right place. The dark brown, grey and black blocks on the horizon become different buildings, and eventually a high fence comes into view as well, topped off with razor wire.

The place looks like a prison.

Is this where Alexis has been living all this time? In some weird compound out in the middle of fucking nowhere, surrounded by desert hills and burnt, red rock? This is a far cry from the rain and wind and civility of Seattle. No Starbucks. No fast food chains. No restaurants or cafes. No nothing.

I have about eight blisters on my feet by the time I see a lone figure approaching from the other end of the road. I know it's a guy from the loping gait and the swing of his shoulders, though I can't tell who it is until I'm much closer.

Cade. It's Cade Preston.

What I'd taken as a swaggering pace a couple of moments ago is actually a pronounced limp, as he makes his way toward me. I never saw Cade after Julio took him, but Michael painted a very vivid picture of the injuries he'd sustained. Zeth had been to visit the guy, them being friends and all, and said he was pretty messed up. That was weeks and weeks ago now, though. If he is still struggling to get around, then he must have been really bad. Really, really bad.

"What's up, Doc?" he says in greeting as soon as he's within earshot. He's grinning at me with that broad smile of his, a light dancing in his eyes, though I can see the pain that's also residing there.

"Should you really be walking on that?" I ask, jerking my chin toward the leg he is favoring.

"Use it or lose it, right?"

"No," I laugh. "Not always. Sometimes using it is the worst thing you can do. Didn't they take you to see someone?"

Cade shrugs, brushing off my concern. "Yeah. And it's much better now than it was, that's for sure."

Me being me, I've brought my medical kit with me. "I'll take a look at it for you later." Cade just nods, as though there's no sense in arguing with this at all. And he's right. There really is no point. "Did they send you out to welcome me?" I ask.

"Something like that. Carnie spotted someone approaching and was all for getting his sniper rifle out. Thought I'd better come out and see what's what for myself before I let him go gung ho, though."

"Well thanks for that. Being shot is very low on my to-do list today." Being shot the one time is enough to last me a lifetime. My arm still burns at the memory of the biting pain that slammed through me all those weeks ago. I was lucky. Very lucky. My own wounds could have been so much worse.

"She's not expecting you," Cade tells me, ruefully rubbing at the back of his neck. "She's gonna freak out. After you didn't see her in Seattle, well..." He trails off, letting me imagine how she took my refusal to meet with her. Maybe she was angry. Maybe she was upset. At the end of the day, I hadn't been able to face it, though. I wasn't ready back then. If I'd have seen her at that point, when I was raw and overcome with everything that had happened, I might have been able to listen to her. I might have been able to forgive her. But I don't know whether I would have been able to accept her as my sister again. She would always have been my blood, but the bond we'd always shared—we were so close before she disappeared—that might not have been something I would have been able to open up to again. And that was the whole point.

I wanted my sister back. I *want* Alexis back. Nerves thrill through me as I admit that to myself. "You don't think she's going to be pissed I'm here, do you?" I ask Cade.

He shoots me an amused glance out of the corner of his eye. "Oh, Doc, you have no idea how stupid that question is."

I don't know if I should be offended, worried or reassured by that response. Cade doesn't seem to feel inclined to expand any further on his comment, so we walk very slowly together back toward the compound. I can see as we get closer there are countless motorcycles propped one after the other in a long row around the inside perimeter of the fence. So many people. I don't know what I was expecting, but a horde of bikers wasn't it.

"You call this inconspicuous?" I say as I exhale.

"No. I don't call it that." Cade smiles at me—a warm, friendly smile. "I call it home. I call it safe. I call it necessary."

Safe. Necessary. Those concepts aren't unfamiliar to me. Up until very recently, I was being shunted from pillar to post because it was *necessary*. Because I wasn't *safe*. When things grew markedly safer and it wasn't so important that we hid in the shadows all the time, we never really made it back to Zeth's warehouse, though. We tried sleeping there one night and it just felt too weird. Too *alone*, even with Zeth, myself and Michael to fill the place with sound. We'd moved straight back to The Regency Rooms, and now that place feels like some strange semblance of home, in its own odd way.

I catch sight of Rebel as we arrive in front of a huge, ten-foot-high chain link gate—the only way in or out of the compound as far as I can see. My brother-in-law is leaning against a metal post, apparently waiting on us, chewing a toothpick over and over in his front teeth. "Well, hello," he says, giving me a tight smile. There's no quick, sharp wit to him today. Only a tense, almost anxious look I find strangely worrying. This isn't a side of him I've seen before. I'm used to the annoying, over-confident version of him that drives me crazy. This quiet, reserved Rebel is new and unexpected.

He pushes off from the metal post and opens the gate in front of us. "I can't say I'm not a little shocked, Dr. Romera. I thought I was gonna have to kidnap *you* to get you here."

"You think Zeth would have let you?" I quirk an eyebrow at him, noting the flash of something that passes over his face when I mention Zee. Not irritation. Not anger. A hard emotion to place. I don't know him well enough to decipher what it means.

"Probably not, I'm sure. I wouldn't really be stupid enough to try and take something from your man, Sloane. I like my body the way it is. *Intact.*"

He slaps Cade on the back, and then the other man hobbles off, giving me a brief wave as he heads into the closest building, where loud rock music is blaring out into the courtyard.

"I'll come see that leg before I go," I call after him.

"He's got eighteen pins in there. He can barely ride anymore," Rebel informs me.

"What? He should be in physical therapy, surely?"

"Oh, don't you worry your pretty little head, Doc. Cade's receiving PT alright." There's a smirk to Rebel's voice that I might not be able to see with his back to me, but I can hear it all too well. There's obviously a story behind that comment, but I'm sure as hell not going to ask what it is. "Soph's in the bar. I'll show you where that is and then I'll leave you two to it."

I don't question why the hell my sister's in a bar already and it's only eleven a.m. I'm learning not to question a lot of things. Rebel leads me across a broad patio toward a low-lying building with cracked plaster, painted a very pale sunshine yellow unlike the industrial grays and blacks of the other buildings.

"Is that your clubhouse?" I ask.

Rebel looks over his shoulder, face drawn into a look of horror. "What about this building screams Widow Makers HQ to you?"

"The charming décor, obviously," I grumble.

"Our clubhouse is downtown. We run an ink shop out of there, too. Gotta keep things looking legit for the tax man, right?"

"So what do they think this place is then?"

"Running bets are on religious cult or free-sex community."

"Oh." Not much I can say to that, really. Rebel gives me a grin that's only half as wicked as normal. He opens the door to the bar and stands back so I can enter. "Good luck," he whispers. And then the door is slamming behind me.

Motherfucker. So much for letting Lexi know I'm here. Guess that's all on me. My eyes struggle to focus in the sudden dimness of the room. It smells of sticky, syrupy liquor and fried food. The kinds of smells you'd associate with any normal bar. Except there's a chemical bite to the air in here as well. Something unfamiliar yet recognizable at the same time. It hits me at the same time my eyes manage to adjust to the darkness. Paint. It smells like wet paint.

"Sloane?"

I spin around startled by the voice behind me. And there she is, my sister, dressed in what can only be an oversized man's dress shirt, though where she got that is anybody's guess. Seems as though it'd be hard to find a guy around these parts who frequently wears anything but a black T-shirt and a leather cut. Alexis shakes her head slowly, as though she can't actually believe her own eyes.

"Did he tell you I was dying again?" she whispers.

"No. He didn't. I just...I thought..."

Alexis walks toward me, her eyes locked on me like she thinks I'll vanish if she even blinks. "You came to see me," she says simply.

"Yes."

"Oh." She puts something down—a paint palette. The object looks odd in her hand. I'm used to seeing her with a textbook pinned under one arm and a cell phone in her other, but a paint palette? Yeah, I'm having trouble making sense of the image. The shirt she's wearing is actually covered in paint—small splashes and long laces of color that stain the white fabric from collar to cuff. "Um," she says, and the two of us just look at each other. "Is every-thing okay with Mom and Dad?"

"Maybe you should go visit them. I'm sure Mom would love to see you. It's been a long fucking time since she laid eyes on you, y'know?" Since running into Dad with Agent Lowell, I've spoken to him twice on the phone—once to let him know I was back at work, and a second time when he called me to let me know he'd told Mom. Told her the truth. Since I knew Alexis was alive and things with the DEA had come to a head, he figured it was okay for Mom to finally hear the truth—that her daughter hadn't been in a horrific car crash and forgotten who she was. That instead she found herself involved in a dangerous court case that had swept her as far from her family and her old life as she could get.

"I just don't know...what to say to them." She paces around me, a look of anxiety pulling on her features. She's different now. The last time I was with her, I didn't take the time to look at her properly. I was too busy exploding at the news that she was married. Now that I'm seeing her in this environment, the subtle differences and the changes in her are plain to see. Even though she's stunned by my sudden arrival and clearly on edge, she carries herself with a confidence she never really possessed before.

I'd always thought she was still a baby before she vanished into thin air. The truth is that she was an adult even then, but now she seems older. More woman than girl.

"I can understand that. But...you should still make the trip. It won't matter what you say to them. They'll just be happy to see you alive."

Alexis walks across the bar, eyeing me carefully out of the corner of her eye. She goes to stand in front of a canvas that's been erected in front of a window, where the tables and chairs of the bar have all been pushed back to make room. "Aren't you going to give me hell?" she asks. She picks up a paintbrush and slowly draws it over the material in front of her, though I can tell she's not really paying attention to what she's doing.

"No, I'm not." I surprise myself when I say this. The whole journey here, I've gone over everything I want to say to her. How badly I want to tell her she hurt me. How badly I worried. How sick and twisted my head got when I used to lie in bed at night and imagine what was being done to her. And lastly, I thought about how I would tell her all about what I gave away in order to get her back.

But now we're here and Alexis is standing in front of me, I don't want to make her feel bad. I just want to understand, and I want to move on. Desperately. I want to shelve the toxic anger eating away at me, and I want to stop feeling so betrayed.

Alexis places the tip of her paintbrush handle into her mouth and turns to face me, drawing in a deep breath. "I can understand how you feel. And I'm really sorry for keeping things from you. You deserved better than that. You know..." She sighs, apparently struggling with her words. "I always loved you, Sloane. I *do* love you. I didn't *want* what happened to me, and once I found myself in a situation I couldn't get out of, I didn't want you to be dragged in or harmed in any way, either. I did what I thought necessary to keep you safe. And I know it backfired. I know you ended up in danger anyway, and I know you nearly lost everything because of me. You'll never know how sorry I am for that."

"You should have trusted me," I whisper.

"I did trust you. I *did*. I just didn't trust other people to keep their word. That's what it all came down to in the end. It was very, *very* complicated. I couldn't explain that to you or Mom and Dad back then."

"Well, how about now? Why not explain it to me now? I just drove all the way here, little sister. I have nothing better to do, and I'd love to hear this story, I really would." I try to keep the bite out of my voice, but it's hard to do. Alexis slowly nods her head. She places her brush down on the lip of the easel, and comes toward me.

"Alright," she says. "I'll start at the beginning, then."

ALEXIS TELLS ME the story of a young woman going to her parents' house, only to find herself kidnapped and sold twice over. She tells me a story of a girl who falls in love with a boy, even though she knows she shouldn't. She tells me a story of insane DEA agents and Mexican cartel members, intent on finding and destroying her. And I begin to understand.

I don't like it, but it starts to make sense.

By the time Alexis is done with her story, I don't hate my sister anymore. I'm not mad at her. I'm still angry, though. After holding onto that emotion for such a long time, letting it consume me from the inside out, there's no such thing as just letting go. It's still with me, though I have no real focus for it anymore. I'm just angry. At the situation Alexis found herself in. At the situation I found myself in. At all of it.

Alexis tells me she loves me, and I find it easier than I thought I would to tell her the same. We're hugging when Rebel comes to find his wife.

"God, I thought you'd be killing each other by now," he says, leaning in the doorway. He is arrogant and cocky, and does multiple things in a day to make me want to smack him, but I understand him a little better now. And I'm glad my sister has him. "The boys will be here soon, Soph," he tells my sister. "Better get your canvas packed up before it get trashed and someone shoves their boot through it." I watch as he helps her pack up her paintbrushes and pots and between the two of them they carry her art equipment out of the bar. I'm handed a small wooden box filled with tiny paint-encrusted tins, cloths and jars of different fluids. I catch sight of Alexis' canvas, carried carefully by the frame in Rebel's hand, as we leave the bar, and the painting it bears makes the breath in my throat catch. It's me. A young, smiling, happy version of me, from before all of this madness.

Alexis gives me a shy smile when she sees my expression. "Sorry, it's not very good," she whispers, biting on her lower lip.

I just shake my head. "It is, Lexi. It *really* is."

Rebel's shoulders hitch up and down as he laughs quietly. "I can't get used to hearing that," he says. Turning to my sister, he plants a firm kiss on the top of her head. "*Lexi*. It'll never be your name."

A part of me wants to kick him in the back of the leg for that. The possessive part that still thinks Alexis belongs to me and my parents, and not him. But I don't because I can see the truth. She really isn't Alexis anymore.

She is Sophia, and she *does* belong to Rebel. All I need to do to confirm that is to look at her and see the love pouring out of her. Alexis was the sister I lost. The woman in front of me is a different person. She is Sophia. And she is still my sister—a new sister who I will love just as much as I loved the old one.

I LOOK AT Cade's leg—so much metal inside, it will take serious work to ever function properly again—and then I get on the road. Staying the night would be the smart move, but I just...I *can't*. I need to go home. I need to see Zeth.

It takes me just a day and a half to arrive back in Seattle—half the time it took me to get my ass out to see Sophia. Without the apprehension of facing something unpleasant holding me back, I break countless speed limits in my haste.

When I burn back into the city, my man is exactly where I expect him to be. The gym is still empty and will be for some time yet. There's so much work to do, refitting the place from top to bottom. Every time Zeth comes close to finishing the place off, he suddenly finds another reason to push back the opening date. The floors need replacing. A wall needs to be knocked down. A cage needs to be installed. The repairs and construction would go a hell of a lot quicker if he had more than himself and Michael working on the project, but I get the feeling time isn't a factor here. The gym will be opened when Zeth's good and ready and not a moment before.

He's stripped to the waist when I enter the building, even though it's just as freezing inside as it is outside. He has sweat pouring down his back, though—the lump hammer he swings repeatedly at a dividing wall between one side of the gym and another—I swear he only just put up that wall—reminds me of doing the very same thing myself. Only that time it was in his basement, and there was money involved. An awful lot of money.

"You're early," Zeth grunts out. How he's heard my light-footed entrance over the steady swing and crash of his hammer is beyond me. He just knows…

"I did what I set out to do, and then I came home." I place both my hands palm-down on his back, wanting to feel the twist and stretch of all that muscle as it works. Zeth tenses at the touch, stopping what he's doing. He's smiling when he turns around.

"You missed me, right?"

"Maybe."

He snakes his arms around my waist, crushing me to him. Some girls might shrink away from all that sweat, but not me. I revel in it. I lean into him and I breathe him in. He returns the favor, and for a moment we just stand there, wrapped around one another.

"You've ruined my plans," Zeth whispers lightly into my ear.

"And what plans might those be?"

"You'll just have to wait and see, won't you?"

"Tell me."

He shakes his head, pulling back to grin down at me. "Oh. There she is. My angry girl. Been a while," he laughs. I'm getting used to this now—having a boyfriend who laughs sometimes. It's the most delicious feeling.

"No more surprises, Zeth," I grumble, though I can't even pretend to be pissed for long.

He is immoveable, as ever. "I'm not telling. How about I show you instead?"

"Now? I thought I was early?"

Zeth shrugs. "Fuck it." He pulls on his T-shirt—more muscles moving and shifting, sending warm spirals of want through my body—and then he's taking me by the hand and guiding us to the Camaro he has parked two streets away. The Camaro. I never thought he'd get it back, and yet somehow he did. He just came home with it one day and I didn't ask questions.

I have plenty of questions as Zeth drives us out of the city, though. Once we've left Seattle's limits, he pulls over onto the side of the road and pulls a length of silk out of the glove box. It's the same length of silk he used to blindfold me when he introduced me to the cane.

"Oh?" I ask.

"Uhuh." He reaches across and ties the strip of material around my head, and I let him.

"Am I going to need to grade my pain in a moment?" My breath catches in my throat.

Zeth's laugh is a deep rumble in his chest. "Wait and see."

We drive for no more than ten minutes, the road swinging from left to right as we head down what can only be mountainside roads, before Zeth pulls the car over again and kills the engine. I know better than to remove the blindfold without being told it's okay, so I sit there, my blood buzzing through my veins in anticipation, while Zeth gets out of the car and comes to open my door.

"Careful. Watch your step," he whispers into my ear, his mouth dangerously close to my skin. With my hand in his, we walk about twenty paces before he stops us and carefully unties my blindfold. His face is the first thing I see, and he's excited. I can see the light of it in his eyes. I don't avert my gaze to see where he's brought me— I'm far too fascinated by the look he's wearing. He cups my face in his hands and he kisses me, carefully placing his lips against mine—a feather-light touch.

"So," he says. His smile fades a little, replaced by...nerves? Is he nervous? "We can't stay at The Regency Rooms forever. And I know how you feel about the warehouse. So...I thought..." He steps to the side, and I see it:

My house.

My beautiful house that I spent so long making my own. Except now it looks a little different. The window frames have all been repainted. I have a new front door that looks positively impregnable, and there are security lights every few feet, dark now but promising to light up the entire hillside as soon as the sun goes down.

"What's this?"

"I figured...I figured you should move back up here. And...so should I."

I turn away from the house, fixing my gaze on Zeth. "You moved yourself into my house while I was gone?"

"Don't pretend like you're not ecstatically happy about it, angry girl," he says, pulling me to him. He buries his face into my neck and nips me with his teeth, and I can't help but laugh.

"Oh, I'm happy about it. All right, all right, I'm happy about it!" I can barely breathe with how tight he's holding me. He quits biting me and leans up to brush the tip of his nose against my ear. "On a scale of one to ten, Sloane?"

I close my eyes and let my body go limp against him. "Ten," I tell him. "Definitely a ten."

Zeth doesn't say anything, but his smile broadens. Then, for the first time, I see a little Lacey in him. They were always polar opposites, but in the space of a heartbeat—there one second, gone the next—I see the faintest flash of his sister in his smile. "I'm going to carry you inside now and I'm going to fuck you in our bed, Sloane. But first..."

"First?" I feel like I'm on the verge of passing out.

"First...I heard you say something once, Sloane. Something you didn't mean for me to hear."

The world suddenly whips back into focus with the force of a snapped elastic band. Oh god. Why the hell is he bringing that up? My stomach feels like it's about to fall through the floor. "Uhh, yeah. Well, that's not impor—"

"It is important. I need...I *want* you to say it again." Heat blossoms in my cheeks, no doubt turning them bright crimson. I try to back away, but Zeth won't let me. His hands tighten on my hips, and he brings his mouth down so it's almost touching mine. "I want to hear you say it, Sloane. I want you to tell *me*."

Some people might say they hear nothing but the sound of their heartbeat hammering in their own ears at a moment like this, but not me. I hear so much more. I hear the promise in Zeth's voice. I hear the skip in *his* heartbeat. I hear the stir of the mountain and the slow hum of the city in the distance—the place where Zeth and I met and our lives became forever entwined—while he waits for me to speak. And then I hear myself saying the words he wants to hear, and they sound perfect and so right.

"I love you, Zeth. *I love you.*"

He closes his eyes and nods, as though suddenly overcome with relief. When he opens his eyes again, staring straight into me, into my heart, into my soul, he says something I never thought he would. His words are so quiet, so softly imparted, as though they're the darkest of secrets, that I can barely make them out.

"And I love *you*, angry girl. I really do."

I don't get a chance to react. Zeth Mayfair, the man I've been terrified of and lost without and a million different things in between...he does as he promised he would. He picks me up, and he carries me inside the house that will now be our home, and he fucks me until his name is echoing off our bedroom walls.

SO IT'S OVER!

SOME OF YOU MIGHT HAVE A FEW QUESTIONS, AND I CAN pre-empt a couple of them for you right now. If, for some weird reason, your copy of Collateral has opened at this point, please go no further! There are spoilers ahead...

Q. **What happened with Julio and Rebel? This is the end of the series and we never got to read the outcome of those characters' storylines.**

A. This is in actual fact the end of Zeth & Sloane's story, but it's not the official end of the series. *Rebel* falls under the Blood & Roses series banner, and will be out at the end of the year (2014).

I couldn't show you guys what happens when Michael goes off to help Rebel with his Julio problem, because that would ruin elements of the other book. But don't worry! All will be explained soon.

Q. **Is this the last we will ever see of Zeth & Sloane?**

A. The characters which I've loved writing so desperately are not gone and lost forever. I feel that way when I finish a series—I feel like I've lost friends in the characters I can no longer read new adventures about. While that feels particularly awful and gut wrenching, in some ways I do hope this is how you feel about Zeth & Sloane, too, because that means I am doing my job properly.

And no, this is not the last you will see of them. They will appear in other books I write in the future. I have already received a ton of emails from readers asking for a whole book for these guys next year, and depending on my workload, the timing and whether or not you as the reader want a catch-up story, I may just crumble and write another book.

Q. **Will any of the other characters besides Rebel be getting a storyline of their own?**

A. Yes. Michael will 100% be getting a story of his own next year. I'm so thrilled you guys have loved reading about him as much as I have enjoyed writing about him.

There is also the potential for Cade to get his own story as well, though I will wait and see whether people are still interested in reading about his adventures when the time comes.

Q. **Why did you kill Lacey????**

A. I'm so sorry if I've caused any heartache over Lacey's exit from the series, but it felt like the only honest thing I could do for her. The only kind thing. Lacey's deeply rooted psychological problems weren't something I felt comfortable sweeping under the rug. She was abused and she killed in self-defence, and it didn't seem right to me to wave a magic wand and fix her in a later book.

I know a lot of you wanted to read a story where Lacey and Michael, or even Lacey and Cade got together and had a happily ever after of their own, but that felt dishonest to me.

This was the peace I could give to Lacey, and I don't regret giving it to her.

Q. **Are you working on any other projects right now, besides Rebel?**

A. Yes, I am. If you're wondering why there's a bit of a gap between the release of Collateral and Rebel going live, it's because I have a super top secret project I am working on for my agent. Hopefully I'll be able to tell you more about this project in time, but please know I am working my booty off, and will have more deviant, sexy, broken men ready for your reading pleasure soon.

ACKNOWLEDGEMENTS

THIS SERIES HAS BEEN SUCH AN UNDERTAKING, AND HAS involved so many wonderful people that I always panicked that I was going to forget to thank someone. That is still a real concern of mine, but I'll hopefully fit everybody in, whether that's by name or by tip of hat.

Firstly, I have to thank my girls, Jessica Roscoe, CJ Duggan and Lilliana Anderson. Without these girls I would never have started this series. What started out as an experiment became a passion, and if they hadn't pushed me, Zeth and Sloane would never have come into existence. Thank you from the bottom of my heart, ladies, for all the talking down from ledges, the encouragement, inspiration, love and support. No one has ever had a support network like you guys. I consider myself truly lucky to have met you all. I know we'll be plotting and planning together for many years to come.

Next, my personal assistants, Nessa Leret and Manda Lee. I don't really know how I managed before I had you two helping me behind the scenes. I would never have been able to put these books out so quickly if it hadn't have been for your efficiency and your stellar organizational skills. Thank you!

Caisey Quinn, thank you for thinking it was crazy I didn't have representation yet! I would never have pursued an agent if it weren't for you, and now I can say I have one of the best in the business (thanks, too, to Amy Tannenbaum for actually signing me!)

My Deviant Divas, you are literally the highlight of my day, every day. The first thing I do each morning is head over to my street team page and see what madness has been going on while I've been sleeping. You've helped me endlessly ever since Deviant came out, reading ARCs, providing feedback, occasionally beta reading, and mostly just providing me with moral support and endless pictures of Tom Hardy in various states of undress (you will never know how much that particular one has meant to me! hahaha!) I love you, Divas!

Marion Archer, Sarah Benelli, Anita Saunders, Prema Editing, Fiona Wilson, to you ladies, I say a huge, massive, colossal thank you for editing, beta reading and proofing my work. Without you guys, my work would be full of typos and weird English-isms no American would ever understand. My sincerest thank you. You all help me put my best foot forward.

Max Henry, you have the patience of the saint and a keen artistic eye. My paperbacks would look terrible if I didn't have you to work your magic. I am so in love with the way these books turned out, and that's down to you. My heartfelt thanks for your fast and beautiful work.

To my kick-ass husband. There's so much I owe to you, husband mine. You are the whole reason I get to write every morning. Without you, I'd be lost. Without you, I'd be working retail and daydreaming of a world in which I got to be a writer. Thank you for helping to make my dreams come true and supporting me every step of the way. I love you.

Lastly, perhaps my biggest thank you goes to you, my reader. Without you, I'd be writing for a very small crowd of one. I really do have to pinch myself every time I realize there are people out there—actual, real life people!—who enjoy and look forward to my next book. That brings me such indescribable joy. You have put me in a position where I get to make up all of these crazy characters and stories for a living, and that is such a precious gift. I will always cherish that gift. I'll keep writing in the hope that you'll keep reading.

Thank you, thank you, thank you.

All my love,

Callie

ABOUT THE AUTHOR

CALLIE HART IS A BAGEL EATING, COFFEE DRINKING, romance addict. She can recite lines from the Notebook by heart. She lives on a ridiculously high floor in a way-too expensive building with her fiancé and their pet goldfish, Neptune.

If you want to know all of Callie's news, and announcements the second they go live, head over to **http://eepurl.com/IzhzL**.

You'll get immediate updates on releases, exclusive sneak peeks, including trailers, teasers and excerpts. Your information will never be shared, and you can unsubscribe at any time.

CALLIE WANTS TO HEAR FROM YOU!

To visit Callie's **website**, head to
http://calliehart.com

Find Callie on her **Facebook Page** , at
http://www.facebook.com/calliehartauthor

or her **Facebook Profile**
http://www.facebook.com/callie.hart.777

Blog
http://calliehart.blogspot.com.au

Twitter
http://www.twitter.com/_callie_hart

Goodreads
http://www.goodreads.com/author/show/7771953.Callie_Hart

To sign up for her **newsletter**, head over to
http://eepurl.com/IzhzL.

TELL ME YOUR FAVORITE BIT!

Don't forget! If you purchased this and loved it, then please do stop
over to Amazon or iBooks and let me know which were your
favorite parts! Reading reviews is the highlight of any author's day.

Made in the USA
Coppell, TX
25 March 2021